WORST VALENTINE'S DAY EVER

A LONELY HEARTS ROMANCE ANTHOLOGY

KILBY BLADES   L.G. O'CONNOR   EVA MOORE

R.L. MERRILL   MARIE BOOTH   ERIN ST. CHARLES

PRESLAYSA WILLIAMS   CERI GRENELLE

AVERIL DAYE   DEB LEE   DAPHNE MASQUE

For permission requests and other inquiries, the publisher can be reached at: info@luxepress.net.

ISBN: 978-0-9991532-9-1

Cover Design By: Elizabeth Mackey Graphic Design

Editing By: PlotBunny Editing

PART 1
THE STORIES

"PERFECT ODDS" BY L.G. O'CONNOR

LUCKY IN LOVE, INC. BOOK #0.5

"HE'S A FAMOUS SURGEON. GOOD FAMILY..." Olivia Yu's mother chattered on in rapid Mandarin, making another vain attempt at taking control of Olivia's pathetic love life.

On today of all days, Olivia had even less patience for her mother's guerilla dating tactics. She held her cell phone away from her ear, half listening, and shouldered open the glass door into her corner office at Lucky in Love, Inc.

Olivia cut off her mother's diatribe. "Sorry, Mom. I have another call. It's business. I'll call you later." She disconnected without a shred of guilt.

Her gaze zoomed in on the heart-shaped box of chocolates with a frosted red-and-black bow sitting on her keyboard.

Eyes narrowed at the chocolates, she approached the large bank of high-definition screens behind her desk that flashed a multitude of Vegas and offshore odds, spanning horse racing to sports games to a whole sector of niche betting, including theirs.

Her lips twitched up at the corners when she spotted the unconventional black velvet skull and cross bone pattern covering the shiny red box like some gothic love parody.

She snickered softly and dropped her backpack on the floor next to her desk.

Sebastian cleared his throat behind her.

Olivia hid the remnants of a smile and cast a glance over her shoulder at the guy with a blond ponytail and golden stubble covering his angular jaw. Arms crossed nonchalantly over his chest, he leaned against the jamb, wearing ragged jeans, a black Nine Inch Nails hoodie, and a shit-eating grin.

"'Morning, Bach..." Olivia smirked.

Business partner and best friend, he'd earned his nickname from an uncanny resemblance to 80s rock icon, Sebastian Bach. As good of a way as any to make the most of having the same first name as that British kid who saved Fantasia in *The Neverending Story,* or the lead singer of Skid Row. Too bad the guy standing in front of her didn't believe in Luck Dragons and couldn't sing worth shit.

But what he lacked in whimsy and vocal cords, he made up for in brains and eye candy, though she'd never confess to that last part. A healthy dose of ego came with all that pretty. And if it inflated any larger, he'd levitate like a balloon and slam head-first into their fifteen-foot ceiling.

Picking up the chocolates, she waved the box and said with more than a little sarcasm, "You shouldn't have," then tossed the gift on her desk. It landed with a *thunk* and slid to a halt halfway across the sleek Lucite surface. He knew how much she hated Valentine's Day and the loss it represented.

Five years had passed since Marcus's death, and every year since then she and Bach did this dance. Olivia wanted to suffer in silence and let the day pass, and Bach wouldn't let her. Every year he took great pains to flaunt convention. Last year he'd chosen black roses with red, hand painted spiders.

The holiday's irony wasn't lost on her. For them, every day was Valentine's Day in a business that made a crap ton of money betting on love. But the actual day, that represented something else entirely.

Sebastian strolled over and dropped his lean, muscled frame into one of her leather guest chairs. "Happy V-Day, Livvie."

He knew better than to utter the actual V-word in her presence. Still, she couldn't figure out whether it was the look in his eye, the bad-boy smirk, or the British accent that made that statement sound like he was referring to a venereal disease rather than a holiday.

He pointed to the discarded box, his blue eyes sparkling with amusement. "Come on! Open the damn thing. Those chocolates cost me a bloody fortune. I had special molds made and everything. Twelve different poison bottles."

Olivia raised a brow and refused to break.

He rolled his eyes and relented with a hangdog look. "They're your favorite. Dark chocolate with different liqueurs."

Damn him for resorting to chocolate. He knew her too well.

Olivia smiled, ripped open the wrapping, and removed the lid. Twelve finely crafted confections sat encased in purple tufted satin. She offered the first to Bach.

He waggled his eyebrows and selected the one in the center. A bulbous container marked "Hemlock" in gothic script. She snatched the one that read, "Belladonna," and bit into it. Her mouth filled with raspberry liquid and she let out a throaty moan.

A dimple dented Bach's cheek when he smirked. "Did you just orgasm?"

"I might've," she teased and gave him a wink. "Next time, bring coffee. We've got work to do."

He chuckled. "Ingrate."

Olivia blew him a kiss. "It's nothing but love for you, baby." Then she logged into the system. "Let me pull the latest entries..."

Trepidation and excitement filled her veins as she downloaded the potential matches for their next love intervention and Lucky in Love play for the bookies in Vegas.

They needed to win big to make up for an unexpected hiccup during their last intervention that had decimated their liquid cash reserves and ruined their perfect winning streak.

Sebastian slouched in the chair and cracked his knuckles. "How many submissions did we get?"

She pursed her lips and glanced at the file's row count. "Over three hundred." A healthy crop of heartfelt contest entries, stories of close friends or family members who deserved a second chance with the 'one who got away.' All for the cost of the ad and a $1,000 prize for the selected entry. *Thank you, Facebook.*

He let out a low whistle and plucked a bottle of "Arsenic" from the satin-lined box. "Nice. Spin them through the *algo* and see what pops out."

"On it," Olivia said, and fed the file through an algorithm they'd developed to validate the entries and scrape the web to build comprehensive profiles on each potential couple, including every data point and social profile in digital existence to predict compatibility and receptivity, before winnowing down the options and identifying couples most likely to succeed...or not.

Either way, they were guaranteed a percentage of the *vig*—a cut of the charges for taking the bets—from the bookmakers. But the real money and the risk came from betting on the right outcome.

God, she loved this business model.

She and Bach had come a long way since that night in business school when they'd cooked up the idea for Lucky In Love, Inc., and their *One Who Got Away* game. All because Bach posed the question, "What are the odds she'll pick that bloke?" from his end of their ratty sofa where he sat playing online poker, while she indulged in a mindless night of television with her guilty pleasure, *The Bachelorette.*

His question triggered an all-nighter spent dissecting the elements of love and concluding that successful love matches boiled down to receptivity, attraction, compatibility, and opportunity. They believed that if they could engineer the opportunity and predict the rest, then they could manufacture love. Better yet, they could monetize the outcome.

All they needed was live data, a few proprietary algorithms, and a few really good bookmakers.

Fast forward three years, Lucky in Love, Inc. had a net worth close to $100 million. More than enough value to satisfy and entertain a pair of twenty-six-year-old Wharton MBA dropouts.

It had taken Olivia showing her traditional Chinese parents her bank balance after LIL's first year in business for them to forgive her for ditching out on a Master's degree program from one of the country's top universities. Too bad that hadn't stopped her mother from calling eight times a day and trying to fix her up with pedigreed Asian men. Nothing like a non-stop litany of "I want a grandson before you turn into old maid" in Mandarin to make your day.

Her computer screen lit with ten high-probability matches from the three hundred plus submissions.

Olivia slapped Sebastian's hand as he reached for another chocolate and snatched the box from his grasp. "Hey! Pay attention and stop poaching my poison."

His lips dropped into that pouty thing he did when he made fun of her. "Sorry, lamb chop."

Insufferable wretch. Despite them both being vegan, he still enjoyed needling her with meat endearments.

"Wow, really?" she deadpanned. The profiles printed and she slid them across the desk. "Here you go, turnip, your turn to pick. Make it good." They traded off, and she had selected the last pair.

He scoffed and scanned the dossiers on the ten couples while she checked her email.

Twenty minutes later, a wicked smile twisted his lips, and he tapped the paper with a fingertip. "This one."

Olivia read their names aloud. "Tanya and Tate. *Aww.* They sound cute." Their story had been submitted by Tate's mother. Olivia sat back in her chair and started to read their dossier.

Tanya Gates, a flight attendant, and Tate Manning, a firefighter, had met in high school and were now both in their early thirties. Olivia's gaze scanned their history and snagged on a connection to 9/11.

She swallowed hard and glared at Bach. Damn him, he'd picked them on purpose. He wanted her to invest. To care more than usual. To confront her demons. Blah, blah. God, she hated him sometimes.

Unblinking, Bach sat, fingers tented and silent, waiting for her to finish. She pressed on and checked the probability charts. "Wow, their scores are through the roof for compatibility and receptivity," she said, still irked at him but pleased with the numbers.

Bach gave a noncommittal nod.

Her gaze drifted to the inciting incident supplied by the algorithm that would create the opportunity to reunite Tanya and Tate. She shot Bach another hard look. "A faulty toaster? Really?" If artificial intelligence ever took over the world, they were all screwed.

Bach's shit-eating grin returned as he leaned back in the chair, the front two legs hovering off the floor. "All it takes is one match. The guy's a fireman, Livvie. Sometimes a spark isn't enough, you need a *flaaame.*"

She chewed her lip to choke back an inappropriate laugh at his crazy eyes and fingers wiggling like an out-of-control brush fire. "You're a sick fuck sometimes, Bach. Goes to show that video games *do* rot your brain." He wrote the damn algo.

Bach righted the chair and gave a smug smile. "That's why you fancy me."

She glowered at him.

He blew out an exasperated breath. "Oh, come on! Lighten up."

Her glower didn't waver. "This is beyond risky. If we do this, no one gets hurt, and I mean *no one*."

He rolled his eyes. "No one will get hurt, I promise."

"How do you know that?"

This time, Bach wore the hard look. "Leave that to me. I wouldn't have made it an option if we couldn't control it."

She relented with a heavy sigh. "All right, but this scenario is going to cost us on the back-end to fund a rebuild. It better pay off. Big." What the algorithm suggested went beyond what they typically engineered, and she didn't love it. They'd be playing with fire. Literally.

"If we do this right, Spiro and the lot will set high enough odds to cover it with just our cut of the vig. The offshore bets will be gravy. Set us right after last time. What could go wrong?" Unperturbed, he stretched his long limbs like a languorous cat and laced his fingers behind his head. His hoodie rose to expose smooth, taut abs above his low-slung jeans.

She forced her eyes away from his exposed skin and frowned. "*Really?* What could go wrong?" Did he seriously just ask her that?

Try as they might to engineer Fate—that wily bitch—on rare occasions she rebelled and threw them an X factor, an unexpected variable so ludicrous their algorithms couldn't account for it.

He let out a breath and unlaced his fingers from behind his head. The hoodie dropped back into place. "No algorithm in the world could've predicted the guy's dog would get bitten by a rabid fox and ruin the couple's evening. The chances of something like that happening again are like one in a bajillion," he said, punctuating his point with a dismissive hand wave and an overly dramatic stare heavenward.

She sulked, wanting to believe him. "That's a bogus statistic."

He huffed a laugh. "Maybe. Just let it go."

Easier said than done. The rabid fox incident had happened during her play and landed them in their short-term financial crisis.

Clearly done with that topic, he wagged his eyebrows. "What do you say we can take some time off when this is done. A little R&R in the Florida Keys?"

Olivia hid her surprise behind an expressionless glance, though the thought of escaping frigid New York City in mid-February for hot weather sounded enticing. "Us? *Together?*"

His face fell into a defensive scowl, and he shrugged. "Yeah, why not? We can rent a house on the beach."

That would be a first. She couldn't deny something unexpected fluttered in the pit of her stomach. She shook her head to clear it and mumbled, "OK. Maybe." Then she remembered his slovenly ways and gave him the stink eye. "If we do, I'm not picking up your underwear off the floor."

He laughed and flashed more dimple. "I dare you to stop yourself. You're the most OCD person I know who doesn't have OCD."

She stuck out her tongue. "Ha, ha. And no parading around naked." He'd been shameless when they were suite-mates in grad school. Probably because he had nothing to be ashamed of. She'd never quite gotten over that flash of full, uncut frontal.

His smile went from smug to amused. "Only if you ask nicely."

She blew out a breath and circled back to their earlier topic before a full blush crested on her cheeks. "I'm worried about this play."

He rocked forward and propped his elbows on her desk. All kidding gone, his stare turned earnest and his voice soothing, "This will pay off, Liv, and no one will get hurt. I promise."

Olivia avoided his gaze and scanned the report in front of her. "Famous last words," she mumbled and reluctantly stood down. "Fine. I guess giving someone the worst Valentine's Day of their life is a small price to pay for finding true love. Get the team ready to deploy." They had fifteen hours—until midnight—starting now, to set up the scenario and have it play out with the unsuspecting couple.

Olivia ran the data through a second algorithm, one that turned their targets into avatars to conceal their true identities and added additional attributes and dramatic elements to make the game interesting, as well as to mask the true probability of success. These were the results they provided to the bookmakers.

The original algorithm was theirs and theirs alone. They used that one with its unfiltered probabilities to break the rules and place their offshore bets.

Spiro would kill them, literally, if he ever found out. And if he didn't, a parade of mob-connected bookies behind him would.

But that was the key to their business model. Love had a price, and that was their secret. Lucky in Love, not Las Vegas, was always the house.

———

"YO, MANNING! 'S'UP?" Gunner said as he entered the Maplewood, New Jersey fire station, and offered Tate a fist bump. Gunner's platoon started to roll in, adding to the flurry of activity in the firehouse as they prepared to take over when Tate's team came off their 24-hour shift.

"It's been quiet, too quiet. Know what I mean?" Tate said, hoping he wasn't cursing them with a last minute call. He couldn't wait to reacquaint himself with his pillow and enjoy the next 72 hours off-the-clock. He had rooms to paint, a spare bathroom to renovate, and a damn squirrel to trap.

The little guy had made some recent late night visits inside the rafters over his bedroom, and Tate had yet to find out how the squirrel had gotten inside. He suspected the telltale oak tree that fanned over his home like an umbrella played a part in the little guy's escapades.

Gunner nodded with a crooked smile and glanced at his watch. "Still an hour until eight. Never know what can happen." He winked as he walked by, heading toward the chatter in the upstairs kitchen.

Tate moved deeper into the garage and tucked himself inbetween two fire engines, hoping for a few minutes of privacy to make a call.

He hated Valentine's Day almost as much as he hated his ex-wife. It had been three years to the day since she'd pissed on their marriage. Nothing says, "I love you," quite like, "I'm leaving you for my personal trainer and taking half your net worth." In his mind, her betrayal would be forever linked to this holiday.

But there was one person who adored it, and for her, he'd make the effort, regardless of his personal feelings. She answered on the second ring.

"Tate, honey! Happy Valentine's Day."

"Happy Valentine's Day, Mom," he said, a smile touching his lips.

"Thank you for the beautiful flowers, sweetheart. That was so thoughtful," she said, sounding as delighted as she did every year when his bouquet of red tulips arrived.

A tradition his father had started and that Tate had picked up when he was seventeen, after his father's death in 2001 on 9/11. Widowed at forty, his mom had never remarried. Now fifty-eight, she had a high-powered career as a financial services executive and was well able to take care of herself. But as her only child, Tate felt a responsibility to look after her—something his greedy ex-wife had always resented, no matter how nice his mom had been to her.

"I'll pick you up at noon on Sunday," he said.

"You sure you won't come to church with me?" she coaxed.

Tension invaded his jaw, but he managed a polite reply, "Not this time." Unlike his mother, his faith had died with his father in the collapse of the World Trade Center.

"Got to run."

"Before you go, honey, did you catch that squirrel yet?" Her question contained both curiosity and concern, as much for him as for the squirrel. She was a staunch believer in the 'catch and release' method, even for bugs.

He sighed and rubbed his temple. "It's on my agenda for tomorrow." He hoped there were no early morning skirmishes over his bedroom before then. He needed some sleep. Who knew the damn things could make so much noise?

His mother laughed softly. "It could very well be a *she*. Mating season started this month."

Oh, joy. At least someone was getting tail back at the house. He gave a mirthless laugh. "Noted. See you Sunday."

As Tate headed to the stairs, an alarm tone pierced the air and his personal radio crackled at his side with a call from dispatch. So much for a quiet night.

The good-natured ribbing in the kitchen above him abruptly stopped. Chairs scraped across the floor followed by the thunder of heavy footfalls as Tate's team rushed downstairs to gear up for their last call.

Tate joined them, and in less than a minute, the garage bays emptied. A fire truck and two engines peeled out with sirens wailing on their way across Maplewood to put out a residential fire.

———

"WHAT THE...?" Tanya Gates muttered. Her stomach clenched at the sight of all the emergency vehicles with spinning red and blue lights that filled her new condo complex's parking lot.

"Uh...Is that where you live?" asked the hipster Uber driver with more than a little trepidation as he pulled up in front of the temporary wooden blockades marked "Maplewood Police Department."

Tonya gulped, speechless, as her eyes tracked the high-pressure water arcing from the fire hose to the flames coming through the second-floor windows of her townhouse unit.

"This can't be happening," Tanya muttered. Tears welled in her eyes and blurred her vision.

Here she thought her day couldn't get any worse between working a turbulent flight from San Francisco that placed her in the unfortunate path of an infant's projectile vomit and discovering a flat tire on her car in the Newark Airport employee parking lot.

Those things had been unpleasant, but this...this was unspeakable.

Too shocked to think straight, Tanya mindlessly grabbed her handbag and the small suitcase on the floor beside her.

The driver turned and gave her a concerned glance. "You going to be okay? Want me to take you somewhere else?"

She stared at the fire, transfixed, and whispered, "No." Then she exited the car into the brisk, smoky night air and slowly walked toward the mayhem, suitcase rolling behind her.

Several firefighters worked the blaze from a ladder truck, while others worked hoses and various duties near the other large red vehicles.

As Tanya drew closer, mouth agape, she noticed her townhouse was the only one burning. A testament to fireproofed walls, she guessed.

A portly police officer with kind eyes stopped her as she wandered closer to a fire engine and the emergency personnel gathered there. A plume of smoke-filled air that smelled like a chemical campfire blew in her direction, making her eyes water from more than tears.

"Miss, you need to stay back," he said gently, blocking her way.

"That's my home," she whispered as she watched water douse the flames.

He pointed at his squad car. "Come sit for a minute. Let me get your information."

She stared at him blankly. This couldn't be happening. Didn't he understand that her sanctuary was collapsing before her eyes? Sit? She didn't want to sit.

He squeezed her shoulder through the wool coat she wore and gave her a gentle shake. "The paperwork will help you with the insurance company." He tipped his head. "Come..."

The officer's words passed over her, like water over rock.

She stood rooted, unyielding, her gaze trained on the smoke billowing from her home, and her knees weakened when the tragic realization hit her. Her photographs. The suitcase handle slipped from her fingers and her throat tightened.

"No!" She wrestled free from the officer and ran blindly, lungs heaving, toward one of the fire engines pumping water.

"Miss!" the police officer yelled behind her.

Ignoring him, Tanya kept running full tilt until she reached the closest firefighter. He turned as she skidded to a halt.

One glance into his handsome face and time collapsed in on itself. The shock of recognition buckled her knees. Even with the ginger beard and the passing years, she would recognize the man standing in front of her anywhere, with his red hair and piercing blue eyes. If he smiled, there would be a dimple denting his left cheek.

He stood before her like an angel answering a whispered prayer. More tears slipped down her cheeks. If there was one person in the world who would understand, it would be him.

"Pictures...of my dad...in the bedroom," she choked out, expending her last shallow breath before her eyes rolled back in her head and the ground rose to meet her.

———

TATE FROZE IN PLACE, staring in disbelief, as he caught the gaze of the tall, willowy woman in front of him. He blinked and took in her delicate features and the long, elegant neck swathed in a silk scarf with a familiar airline logo.

He'd seen that unusual combination of wide-spread hazel-green eyes and warm cocoa skin on only one person in his life. On a girl he once loved. Someone he'd lost touch with a long, long time ago.

His heart thundered and blood rushed through his ears as recognition sparked on her face. "Pictures...of my dad...in the bedroom."

Her words hit him like a gut punch. "Tanya?" he whispered as she collapsed in a dead faint. Like his father, hers had been one of the 2,606 souls who perished in the World Trade Center on 9/11. The shared experience had galvanized their friendship.

He lunged and caught her under the arms before she hit the pavement, then swept her into his arms. "I need an EMT!"

She felt small and weightless in his arms as he ran toward the ambulance with her cradled to his chest. An EMT met him halfway.

"Check her for shock." Tate carried her to an awaiting stretcher and reluctantly laid her down. But not before he took a long look at her to memorize every detail. "Take good care of her... she's a friend. I'll be back."

Then he jogged toward the fire truck and the Battalion chief. "I'm going back in," he said, slipping his mask over his face.

His captain glared. "Like hell you are, Manning! Wait until they finish knocking down the fire," he said, but Tate was already moving.

Tate knew it was stupid and reckless—that he should wait for the secondary sweep—but he understood like no one else what she'd lost. If those photos weren't protected by a door, they'd be as good as gone...if they weren't already.

The guys from the engine company were still fighting the blaze upstairs as he entered the charred first floor.

The point of origin had been an appliance in the kitchen.

A toaster.

There didn't seem to be any evidence of arson or accelerants, but he'd leave that to the investigators. Either way, the situation was almost under control. If he was lucky, the open flames would be out by the time he hit the second floor.

Tate took the stairs two at a time and caught up with the hoses in the smoke-filled hallway. Any visible flames had been extinguished when he reached the master bedroom.

"Hey, what are you doing up here?" One of the guys asked over the intercom.

"Trying to save something important," he said, and entered the bedroom. He did a visual sweep of the soot-stained walls and charred furniture. Smoke obscured his visibility, but he could make out the dresser and he searched there first.

A few framed photographs were among the remains. Soot covered the cracked but intact glass. He couldn't see the pictures inside but snatched them up anyway. He examined the other surfaces, then headed toward the closet. He checked the door first to eliminate unwanted surprises. There were none waiting in the large walk-in space.

The contents inside were smoke-damaged but untouched by fire.

He shined the beam of his flashlight methodically around the closet, along the shelves over the hanging clothes, and then underneath until he spotted two brightly decorated photo boxes. He grabbed them both, adding them to the photographs from the dresser. One last sweep over the plastic tubs in the corner turned up nothing relevant. Satisfied, he left the way he came in.

The guys assigned to the secondary search and overhaul headed inside as he exited the front door. He slipped off his face mask and proceeded toward the ambulance.

He still couldn't believe it was Tanya. How long had it been, anyway? Eighteen years since he'd met her at Montclair Academy, their private high school, during grief counseling for kids who had lost parents on 9/11? Seventeen years since she'd left for L.A. to try her hand at a singing career, and he had headed to Notre Dame on a football scholarship?

He hadn't wanted to lose her. They'd promised to stay in touch, visit, not stop...loving each other. Promises kids couldn't hope to keep with time and distance working against them.

Emotions stirred things inside him he hadn't felt in longer than he cared to admit. She had been the one person who'd understood him down to his soul, and no one since then had ever come close.

And here she was, living less than a mile from his house. How had that happened? *When* had that happened?

Tate rounded the back of the ambulance. Tanya looked up from where she sat on the stretcher, looking shaken but all right.

"She's fine," the EMT said, winked, and stepped away, giving them some privacy.

His gaze locked with Tanya's and he drew in a nervous

breath. The boxes suddenly felt awkward in his hands. She was even more beautiful now than when they were teenagers.

He cleared his throat and said the first thing he thought of. "This is all I could find."

Her brows furrowed and her hazel gaze slid to the boxes with the charred frames balanced on top. She bit her quivering lip, nodded, and held out her hands.

He had a million questions racing through his mind, least of which was, *"Why did you break our promise?"*

———

EVERY WORD TANYA wanted to say to Tate lodged inside her throat. The boxes and soot-covered photo frames shook in her hands.

Tate had recovered her pictures. Most of them, anyway. Her favorite was missing. A photo of her and her dad when she was fifteen at the Paper Mill Playhouse after her professional musical debut as Cosette in *Les Misérables*. Landing the part as a mixed race lead in a mostly white production had been a coup back then.

She loved that picture of the two of them sharing her proud moment, their heads touching with bright, matching smiles. Euphoria filled her eyes, the same shade of hazel-green as her father. She kept the photograph next to her bed, close enough to look at every night before she went to sleep.

Even with its loss, gratitude welled up inside her. Everything in her home was replaceable, except for what Tate had recovered.

He stood before her, looking unsure of what to do with his hands, a tentative and assessing look creasing his brow.

Still not trusting her eyes, she swallowed hard and managed to rasp, "Tate? Is it really you?"

A look of relief washed over him. He nodded and dropped to

one knee so they were at eye level. A small smile lifted the side of his mouth, a dimple denting his ginger-bearded cheek. "Yeah, it's me."

He lifted the boxes from her hands and placed them carefully on the ground then he removed his gloves and dropped them onto the pavement alongside the boxes.

Slowly, he took her hands in his. "Is there someone you'd like for me to call...?" He hesitated and cleared his throat. "A husband, maybe? Or your mom?"

She shook her head, avoiding his gaze and thinking only briefly of the engagement she'd broken off six months before. "I live alone. My mom's in Arizona now." The thought of calling her mom before tomorrow was out of the question. She'd never get through a conversation without shattering into a million pieces. No. Not tonight.

"Hey..." He squeezed her hands, surrounding and warming them with strong fingers and rough palms, the palms of a man who worked with his hands. She found that comforting somehow. "Tanya? Look at me."

She met his earnest blue gaze. The intensity sent a flutter rippling through her middle.

"Do you need a place to stay tonight?"

She bit her lip and a tear slid down her cheek. She nodded and dipped her chin. Any plans to slip into flannel pajamas and enjoy a night in her new home, binge-watching Netflix, was a distant memory.

Dropping a hand, he brushed the tear away with his thumb sending a shiver over her skin, and said softly, "You'll stay with me then."

Her head jerked up. "What?" They hadn't seen each other in years and he was offering her a place to stay? "I-I can't let you do that," she stammered.

"Yes, you can," he said, his jaw set in a determined line. "I have a guest room. It's not a problem. Really."

She'd heard through a friend that he'd gotten married to his college sweetheart. He could have a whole brood of children by now. "I don't want to impose on you and your...family."

He laughed softly. "Divorced. No family to impose on." Relief and veiled excitement sparked inside her.

He fished a key ring out of a pocket on his turnouts and removed one of the keys. Pressing it into her palm, he closed her fingers around it. "Take it. I live five minutes from here. 25 Highland Place. You shouldn't drive. Want me to get you an Uber?"

No need to mention her stranded car and the flat tire. She nodded, at a loss for anything else to say. The key felt warm in her closed fist. "Thank you," she whispered.

A pretty, petite Asian woman in her mid-twenties with pink-tipped hair, wearing black jeans, combat boots, and an expensive fur-trimmed parka walked up. "Sorry to bother you," she said, and extended a gloved hand. "Hi, I'm Liv."

Tanya tentatively shook it, surprised at the woman's firm grip, while Tate rose to his feet.

Liv pointed around the corner to another set of townhouse units, "We're neighbors. I just moved in. I'm so sorry about your home...I didn't mean to eavesdrop, but I'd be happy to give you a ride over to Highland. I'm running into town to pick up a pizza. It's no bother." She flushed and put a hand to her mouth. "I hope that doesn't sound weird...I just want to help."

Something about the tiny woman's self-deprecating demeanor disarmed Tanya and immediately set her at ease. It was nice to finally meet someone in her complex, even under dismal circumstances.

Picking up the boxes with the frames resting on top, Tanya smiled softly and rose from the stretcher where she'd been sitting next to the ambulance. "Thanks. I'd appreciate that."

Tanya had never seen Liv before. Not surprising. Tanya had only moved in three months before and had barely been home since she'd closed on the sale. She'd yet to meet any of her neighbors beyond friendly waves in the parking lot.

Tate eyed Liv with caution. "What unit did you say you lived in?"

Liv smiled broadly. "46G," she said, and pointed to the silver vehicle on the other side of the police barrier, "That's my Range Rover." She winked at Tate. "You can take down my plate if you're worried."

Tate eyed her warily and nodded with a tight smile, seemingly satisfied, then turned to Tanya. "I'm rolling off shift. I'll pick up something for us to eat on my way home from the station. In the meantime, my house is your house. Make yourself at home. I mean it."

His warm, protective gaze ran over her again, as if to make sure she was stable on her feet. "Towels are in the closet next to the upstairs bathroom if you want to take a shower. I'll be there in an hour or so."

Warmth spread through her like a comforting blanket. "Thank you, Tate."

He eyed her purse. "Can I see your cell phone?"

"I'll hold those," Liv volunteered cheerily. Tanya transferred her precious cargo to Liv, retrieved the cell from her purse, and handed it to Tate.

He keyed in some numbers and handed it back. "I programmed myself into your contacts. Just text if you need anything." He started to go then turned back like he had forgotten something. "It's really good to see you again, T-Girl," he said softly, her long ago nickname rolling off his tongue and sending her back in time. Then he continued his jog over to the nearest fire truck.

Tanya drew in a deep breath as she watched his tall form and retreating back. It all felt so surreal.

She'd always expected to see Tate on the field playing for the NFL. How had he ended up a firefighter? Then again, it made sense. He had wanted to make a difference after his father died, and they both had the utmost respect for all of the emergency workers who'd sacrificed their safety, and some ultimately their lives, to work the 9/11 pile looking for survivors and remains. Her father had worked for Cantor Fitzgerald, and his for Marsh & McLennan. In the end, neither of their families had much to bury.

Exhaustion hit her along with hunger pangs. She hoped she could wait until Tate came with food. She would need the strength. It would be a long night ahead, starting with a call to her insurance company.

A parting glance at her smoldering home left her feeling queasy.

She smiled weakly at Liv and took back her photos. "I have to pick up my suitcase before we go," she said, and glanced across the parking lot next to the police car where she had abandoned it earlier.

It was gone.

———

LIV PULLED up outside a brightly lit two-story Victorian home that looked like it had slipped off the pages of *Architectural Digest*.

Tanya's lips fell open, and she double-checked the address. Definitely number twenty-five.

Did he live here *alone?* This was no bachelor pad. The Victorian was stately and elegant, sided in tan clapboard with white trim, gray fish scale shingles hung on the peaks over the windows, while dentil molding and architectural fretwork accented the house in all the right places. Low boxwood shrubs surrounded a wraparound porch and a tall, majestic oak tree overhung the house, completing the picture of suburban bliss.

Tanya grabbed the passenger door handle.

"Good luck with everything," Liv said, and gave a sly wink. "Especially with that hunky firefighter."

Tanya blushed. "He's an old friend from high school..." She inwardly cringed, thinking about what had happened at the end. All her fault. Every bit of it. "My track record with men is pretty bad. I still owe this one an apology."

Liv gave her shoulder a little nudge and smiled wide. "Get woke, woman! Did you see the way he looked at you? My money's on forgiveness." She winked. "Don't let me down."

Tanya's cheeks heated, and she couldn't hold back a grin. "Thanks for the ride. It was really nice to meet you," she said, her words heartfelt.

As for Tate, she hoped Liv was right, but she'd been around the block enough times to know that life was never that simple. Tate had offered her a place to stay. That was all.

Clutching her precious cargo to her chest, Tanya approached the house and sighed.

She caught the stench of burning embers clinging to her clothes. A shower ranked highest on her priority list, even over food...until she remembered that all her things were inside the stolen suitcase.

Her shoulders slumped. All she had right now were the clothes on her back and the memories cradled in her arms. It reminded her of a time when she'd lived with less.

She thought of those lean years in L.A. after she'd broken out with her hit single, *I'll Carry You with Me*. After she'd overextended herself financially only to find out the contract she'd signed with the record label had lined everyone's pockets but hers. After she'd ran through her inheritance to break the contract, paid off her debts, and cut new demos to move her career forward. But that never quite happened. She toured with some bands but never saw another record deal. Ten years of her life were spent trying to keep the promise to her father before she walked away, disillusioned, and became a flight attendant.

Sadly, the only time she sang now was in the shower.

Tanya climbed the wide front steps. She juggled the boxes in her hands and slipped the key Tate had given her into the lock. It opened with a soft click, and she walked into comfortably warm air. R&B music played over a built-in sound system, the effect simultaneously unsettling and welcoming.

Her cell dinged with a new text. She laid her stuff on a small table inside the door that had a small tray containing a pair of earbuds and some loose change and dug for her phone.

Looks like you arrived safely. Turned on lights and music with app on my phone. Didn't want you to freak out and think someone was in the house

Relief cascaded through her in a giant wave. Her shoulders relaxed and she laughed softly before typing a reply.

Thanks for letting me know. I'd wondered.

He responded. *What do you like on your pizza? I'm stopping at Arturo's*

Her stomach answered with an eager gurgle at the thought of one of their wood-fired creations. *Anything but peppers!*

You got it! See you soon.

Something warm fluttered again in her chest. Choking back discomfort with the intimacy of her next request, she typed, *Mind if I borrow something to wear? My suitcase seems to have disappeared.*

Three dots appeared.

LOL, help yourself. Will call my buddy, he's a cop in Maplewood. Will see what I can find out about the suitcase.

Tanya smiled despite herself. *Thanks!*

Tucking her cell phone back inside her purse, Tanya could have sworn she caught a flash of gray out of the corner of her eye as it dashed around a corner and disappeared into the room on the left.

Tanya's mood brightened. A cat? Tate hadn't mentioned a cat. She loved animals but traveled too much to have a pet. She felt bad for startling the poor thing.

She kicked off her heels next to the entry table, padded across the shiny hardwood floor, and wandered after the animal into what turned out to be a richly appointed living room with modern art, inset lighting, and an Oriental rug to warm the space.

Tanya's brow rose, impressed. Then again, Tate had fine taste even back in high school. Wasn't he the one who helped her pick a new duvet set and repaint her bedroom in an effort to cheer her up when they'd first met?

Masculine and functional, the room had a massive flat screen television that hung over the fireplace mantel with a plush dove gray sectional arranged for perfect viewing. In front of it, a large square coffee table made from a highly polished slab of burled wood on an iron stand. On top sat a basket of remote controls, a bowl of mixed nuts, a nutcracker, and randomly scattered coasters with navy blue Giants logos.

Picking up one of the coasters, she wondered again why Tate didn't go pro after college, and then chastised herself.

Maybe you'd know if you hadn't abandoned him all those years ago.

She sighed, shoved back the regret, and wove her way through the dining room, where tarps and paint cans were piled neatly in a corner. It was a work-in-progress compared to the living room.

Still no sign of Tate's feline companion, she stepped into his renovated kitchen and gasped. Painted in pearl gray with white maple cabinets and a matching island, the kitchen was a chef's delight with richly grained granite covering every surface, a Viking professional stove, and a Subzero refrigerator. All complemented by the gray-stained wooded floors. A chill traversed her spine with the first uplifting thought she'd had since discovering the fire: This is how she would rebuild her kitchen.

A chiming doorbell interrupted her reverie. Tanya walked swiftly down the hallway and pulled open the tall door expecting to see Tate.

Instead, a large package sat on the front porch with a big red bow and an envelope with her name.

Brows furrowed, she cautiously approached the brightly wrapped box, plucked the small card from where it was taped, and opened it.

> No one's Valentine's Day should ever suck
> this much.
> Liv & Your neighbors at The Commons

─────

"ARE you out of your effing mind?!" Bach's exasperated voice boomed through the Bluetooth multi-media speaker in the rented Range Rover. Parked around the block from Tate's house, Olivia slumped lower in the seat and tried not to feel like a stalker.

Bach had blown a gasket when he'd found out she'd gone to Jersey, entered the play, and made contact with their targets.

Olivia ground her teeth, lowered the speaker volume, and hovered her finger over the disconnect button on the steering wheel, seriously contemplating hanging up on him.

"Liv, you're breaking every rule in the book! What the hell's the matter with you?"

"Don't get preachy," she finally snapped. What was one more

broken rule? Their offshore bets would do more to land them in hot water than her inserting herself into a play. "I was worried! We burnt someone's house down. Shoot me! I wanted to make sure she was all right." That was one of the reasons, anyway.

It had been a while since Bach had gone ape shit on her for something she'd done on a play. He'd get over it, he always did. But Bach's tight tone told her it might take a while this time.

An unintelligible growl preceded his next words. "That's what we pay deployment and execution teams for, Liv! I can't believe you told her your *name*. And you left her a bleedin' package? Are you insane? What's so difficult to understand about 'no involvement with the targets'?"

Olivia pictured Bach's flushed face as he sat on his plush leather couch in front of a bank of monitors covering the betting pools and the live odds for every bookmaker taking some of the action. As the scenario unfolded between the couple, the execution team processed their observations and uploaded fresh data into the algorithms, which potentially changed the probability of success and the bookmakers' odds.

Of course, the team had spotted her. She hadn't been trying to hide. But they knew better than to record it or report it to anyone but Bach.

She and Bach had only two rules: stay out of the plays and don't get caught laying their own offshore bets.

Lucky in Love had already banked the first payout for Tanya and Tate reconnecting at the fire scene, upping their corporate coffers over a million dollars, but that paled in comparison to how much they had riding on the final outcome—a kiss before midnight.

Today of all days, she wanted Tanya and Tate's happiness as much as she needed that juicy payout. Hence, her flagrant disregard for one of their rules.

"That's the second time you've questioned my sanity in one

phone call," Liv said to the lunatic who'd programmed a fire scenario into their algorithm. A sexy, lovable lunatic, but still a freaking lunatic. They were getting nowhere. She should've never answered the phone. Just wait until she told him what she'd snatched from Tanya's apartment before the team had even arrived. Then he'd really question her mental health.

"And you still haven't answered me!" he snarled.

Heat traveled along her neck. "And I don't plan to!"

Bach's frustration was palpable. "We're not the only ones with eyes on this. What do you think Spiro will do if he catches wind of this?"

Something she didn't want to think about. Okay, fine. He had a point. Regardless, she pouted and changed the subject. "Why did you call anyway?"

He released a breath. "For the love of Pete, don't change the bloody subject!"

She dug her heels in, her tone turning frosty. "Why'd you call?"

He swore again and sighed. "I wanted to make sure you were...all right."

Crap, here it comes. "Why wouldn't I be all right?" she asked, swallowing hard, not wanting to discuss it. The second reason why she sat there on her ass running surveillance when it wasn't her job. Plain and simple, she needed a constructive distraction.

His voice softened. "You know why."

She played dumb. "I do?"

He blew out a defeated breath. "Come on, Liv. I called because...I was worried about you."

Five years later and it still gnawed at the center of her chest. The mugging, Marcus collapsing in a pool of blood and dying in her arms on Valentine's Day.

"I'm fine, really," she lied, then waded into Bach's personal shark-infested waters. She wasn't the only one with steamer trunk-sized baggage. "What about you? How are you?"

He met her question with silence.

"Bach?"

Nothing but a deep exhale. "Stop deflecting. This isn't about me," he said finally. "Leave Jersey and come back to the city... Come to my flat." His voice held a familiar ache, the one it got when he tried to take care of her. From anyone else, it would feel too close to pity, but not from him. Not tonight.

Despite all the innuendo they traded, they'd never come close to crossing the line. Besides, her being a hot mess since Marcus died and Bach's unending parade of women to avoid his pain, on paper, they weren't well suited. Regardless, he'd always been there for her. No matter what. And she for him.

In reality, her feelings for Bach were complicated. Not to mention her strict 'don't shit where you eat' policy. Like it or not, their livelihood depended on it. And in truth, even dead, Marcus still occupied a big part of her heart. But more and more lately, Bach's pull on her grew.

"I can't," she whispered. "Thanks. I'll call you later." She hit the "end call" button on the steering wheel before he could reply.

She may not be getting a happy ever after tonight, but she damn well wanted to give one to Tanya and Tate.

She checked the GPS tracking app on her phone. Tate's car was still parked at the firehouse. Screw it, she'd circle back and monitor this scenario from a visual distance. What else did she have to do?

Her phone rang. She checked the caller ID. Her mother. *Oh, hell, no.* She sent it to voicemail.

Bach called back. She let it ring. He called again.

Again.

Again.

She parked two houses down from Tate's, far enough away

from the surveillance van, and killed the lights. Circumventing Bluetooth, she answered on Bach's fifth attempt.

"What?!" she whisper-hissed into the phone.

"About fucking time! Since you've inserted yourself into the surveillance, did you think to tap into the camera feeds lately?" he ground out, thoroughly pissed off.

What was the point of that? Tanya was alone. Rather than answer, she sniped, "We have people for that, as you recently reminded me. Why?" Couldn't he just let her stalk in peace and play Candy Crush until Tate arrived?

"You're not going to bloody believe it," he gritted.

"What?" she asked, her annoyance turning to apprehension.

"We have an X factor," he said.

The hairs prickled on the back of her neck. Was he serious? God, this couldn't be happening.

She counted to five and calmly asked, "Can we adjust the bets?" The payouts would grow in inverse proportion to the likelihood of success. A massive payout for anyone who beat the odds and bet the kiss would happen, but a huge loss for the same bets if it didn't.

"Too late, we're locked. We need that damnable kiss by midnight or we'll be living on gluten-free noodles for the foreseeable future." His voice held an edge of panic.

Shitballs. She checked her watch. Three hours until midnight. Plenty of time to eliminate a threat. Taking a deep, cleansing breath, she rubbed her forehead and asked, "What is it? Please don't tell me it's another rabid fox."

"Close. There's a bloody goddamn squirrel in the house."

She almost laughed. "Really? Is it rabid?"

"Doesn't look like it, no. Must have gotten in since we set up the cameras."

"What are we going to do?"

"I can't believe I'm actually saying this," he said, and growled with frustration. "The team needs your help."

Her brow furrowed. "My help? Why do they need *my* help? Do I look like I know anything about freaking pest control?"

He blew out a breath and seemed to regain his patience along with his cool. "Please, Liv. Just go meet Jeff. He'll fill you in."

Pressing her eyes shut, she sighed and hoped she wouldn't be sorry. "Fine. I'll call you later...And Bach? I have a feeling you're going to owe me big time for this one."

He snorted a laugh, "At this rate, I may have to pay you in trade."

"Swine." She hung up and did her best to ignore the warm tingles filling her nether region at the thought of a trade payment from Bach.

———

"YOU WANT ME TO *WHAT?*" Olivia sat in the surveillance van across from Jeff and Tim, their execution team, and stared at them, incredulous. To quote Bach, had they lost their effing minds?

Jeff held up his hands in an attempt to reason with her. "The trellis on the back of the house is a no-go for us, but it could easily support your weight. It's attached to a lower roof, a clear path to the second-floor windows."

Her gaze bounced between the two men—one with a cast on his left leg and the other who tipped the scales well over three hundred pounds—and she scowled.

"Given that inane logic...sure, why the hell not?" she said, her voice dripping with sarcasm, and threw up her hands. "You seriously expect me to scale the side of the house on a rose trellis, crawl in through a second floor window, bag a frightened squirrel, and escape—with the squirrel!—unnoticed?"

They nodded in unison and had the audacity to crack enthu-siastic smiles.

"*Bèn dàn,*" she muttered. The Mandarin equivalent of idiot. "Are you both crazy? Do I look like I specialize in breaking and entering? That's what we pay you for!" She glared, wiping the stupid grins off their faces. "How do you expect me to catch this thing? With my bare hands?"

Jeff held up a finger, then rummaged in one of the storage lockers and pulled out a small dart gun with a cassette of multi-sized cartridges. He loaded the smallest cartridge into the chamber and offered her the dart gun with a self-satisfied look.

"We added this to the toolkit after the fox disaster. Just nip the little guy with one of these. Takes about ten seconds to knock him out, then scoop him into the burlap sack. Should be easy."

"Ha! Easy for a professional," she grumbled and pointed to the monitors lining the van's interior. Tanya was upstairs in the guest room next to where the squirrel had temporarily holed up in a closet. "She's too close. How are you going to distract her?"

Tim opened the costume trunk and pulled out a policeman's uniform, a utility belt with everything including a sidearm, and a radio. "Leave that to me."

They were good, she'd begrudgingly give them that.

She rolled her head back to stare at the van's roof for a second, then took a deep breath and snatched the dart gun. "I can't believe I'm doing this," she muttered.

———

OLIVIA'S HEART pounded as she jimmied open the unlocked second-floor window, and gingerly stepped into the sparsely decorated guest room.

"Sweet Jesus, I'm in," she muttered. The night vision goggles were badass but the headgear made her feel like a coal miner.

Their furry four-legged friend could be anywhere among the butt load of unpacked boxes, folded tarps and paint cans that surrounded the bed and small dresser. It looked more like a storage room than guest accommodations.

She lowered the window and crept farther inside. Not wanting to fry her retinas, she avoided glancing through the goggles at the slim, blinding shaft of light that filtered in through the slightly open bedroom door.

"Where is it?" Olivia whispered.

"Still in the closet," Jeff said through her earpiece.

In the bathroom on the other side of the wall, she heard the rustle of makeup and Tanya singing along to a Sade tune that played on the sound system. Tanya's pitch-perfect voice sent a shiver down Olivia's spine. That girl could sing.

You better do right by her, Tate, Olivia thought. Not to mention, make this squirrel hunt worth it.

"You there?" Jeff asked, pulling her back.

"Yup." Olivia shucked off the backpack, unzipped it, and removed the dart gun. The downstairs doorbell rang.

Officer Tim, right on time to return Tanya's stolen suitcase, the one Liv pilfered to ensure Tanya wore the eye-popping present she'd left on the porch. They needed that kiss.

Tanya's footsteps receded then echoed down the wooden staircase.

A scratching sound came from inside the closet.

"He's in there," she whispered.

"Whatever you do, don't spook the little guy. They can shred the place in no time fast."

Olivia rolled her eyes. Like she didn't know that?

As Tanya exchanged a few words with Tim downstairs, Olivia crept to the closet and peered inside.

The squirrel froze with a peanut clasped in its tiny paws.

Just as Olivia aimed the dart gun, the squirrel let out a

squeak, dropped the nut, and leaped out of the closet. In a fluffy blur of tail, the squirrel dashed out the open bedroom door and into the hallway.

Mandarin curses flew from Olivia's mouth that damned not only the rodent's mother but its entire bloodline.

"Abort! I repeat, abort!" Jeff hissed through the earpiece.

———

WINE BOTTLE TUCKED under his arm, Tate balanced the hot pizza box and dug for the spare key hidden inside the potted shrub at the base of the front steps.

His pulse quickened at the thought of seeing Tanya. "I must be out of my damn mind," he muttered. Inviting her here had seemed like a good idea in the moment, but he hadn't really thought it through.

But she needed him, right? That's what mattered.

Old bullshit could wait. Yet once the shock had worn off, it's all he thought about since he'd stepped into the shower at the firehouse. How she'd let him down then disappeared from his life without a trace... until tonight's fire.

He keyed open the lock and walked in. Over the R&B music, her favorite, he heard her engrossed in conversation on the phone upstairs.

Not wanting to disturb her, Tate headed down the hall to the kitchen. He didn't envy her the hassle of dealing with the insurance company or sifting through what remained of her burned and smoke-damaged possessions.

Footsteps descended the front stairs as he placed the wine on the granite-topped island and rested the pizza box on the stove.

"Hey," a familiar sultry voice said from behind him, sending an unexpected shiver over his skin straight down to his groin.

Damn. Seventeen years later, the sound of her voice still unwound him.

He took a steadying breath and pivoted. "I hope you like mushroom and meatball on ..." The words died in his throat. He blinked, once, twice. "Holy... You look... Amazing."

His appreciative gaze soaked in every detail—the heels; the slinky green sheath dress that matched her eyes and clung to her curves; all that smooth cocoa skin. She wore no makeup other than gloss on her full lips, which would've been enough to make her traffic-stopping gorgeous even if she'd worn a potato sack. Her spiral locks fell loose, taken down from an earlier bun, and touched her bare shoulders.

Holy. Wow. She looked like Naomi Campbell in her super-model heyday. That, coupled with her incredible talent had been the impetus behind her moving to L.A. after high school to pursue a music career.

As he stood there gaping like an idiot, he remembered the missing suitcase. His brow creased, "Wait a second, you couldn't have found that in my closet."

She glanced down at her outfit, and her lips twitched up into an amused smile. "I didn't. It was a gift from Liv and my neighbors at The Commons. They left it in a box on your porch. I'm shocked that it all fit."

Thank you, Liv. Rebooting his brain with a mental bitch slap, he pulled out a corkscrew, swallowed hard, and reached for the wine. "Resourceful bunch. Much better than a pair of my sweatpants." He chuckled, but the thought of her in his clothes had the same effect on his blood flow as the dress.

He held up the wine bottle. "Drink?" God knew he needed one if only to inebriate the jackrabbit doing a River Dance in his stomach, and to rid the air of nervous tension.

She nodded, her shoulders relaxing. "Thanks for calling your friend. A police officer dropped off my suitcase."

His brows flicked up. Why hadn't his buddy let him know? "Really? That's great," he said, not thinking too hard on it. With a light pop, the cork slipped free of the bottle. He brushed his gaze over her again. "For what it's worth, that's a great dress."

Her smile smoothed the worry lines on her face, and for the first time all night, he saw his T-Girl poking through. "Thanks."

"I heard you on the phone. Insurance company?" he asked.

She nodded, pulled out one of the stools from under the island and sat. "I have an appointment with the adjuster tomorrow morning at ten." Then her lips curved up into a soft smile and she met his gaze. "Thank you, Tate...for everything."

Warmth filled his chest and he cleared his throat. "Did I get all of the pictures?"

Her smile faltered a fraction. "Most."

He frowned. "What did I miss?"

She gave a shrug like it didn't matter, but after all these years he could still read her tells—the quick glance away, the quirk at the left side of her mouth. "The one on my bedside table."

His frown deepened and he shook his head. "I checked every surface, T. There weren't any pictures next to your bed. I promise." Losing his own father had been tough, but they'd never been as close as Tanya and her dad. "Does your Mom have a copy—"

She reached over, squeezed his forearm, and said softly, "It's all right. I'm so grateful for what you found." The touch of her fingers unlocked a familiar yearning for more.

He covered her hand in his, gave her a gentle squeeze, and slipped free of her grasp. He needed space between them, to get away from her gravitational pull before he did something stupid.

"Hungry?" he asked, feigning nonchalance, and moved across the kitchen to retrieve two wine glasses, plates, and some napkins. He pointed to the pizza. "One slice or two?"

She gave a little laugh, dispelling the tension. "Two. I'm starving."

That made one of them. He still couldn't believe she was here. In his mind, she'd always been the one who had gotten away. And he still didn't know why...what he'd done for her to disappear on him like that. A question that's haunted him for seventeen long years. If nothing else, he needed the answer.

He doled out the wood-fired pizza, sat beside her, and poured them each a glass of Chianti. He held up his glass, "Toast?"

Her eyes lit up and she touched her glass to his.

Hoping he wasn't being too presumptuous, Tate said, "To new beginnings and getting to know each other again."

"I'd like that," she said, giving a tilt of her head and taking a sip.

The wine hit his tongue in an explosion of flavor. He downed half the glass before thinking better of it, and let his frayed nerves slowly settle.

They ate in companionable silence. He refilled their glasses and plates. The tension of unanswered questions rippled silently between them as he worked up his courage.

When he looked at her, he still saw the girl who held him in her arms and sang to him softly during those dark days filled with survivor sadness. The same girl he held when she broke down, unable to keep the tears from falling. Out of the sadness came solace and a soul-deep friendship that turned into more. Insepara-ble, they spent almost a year together. He gave her his body and his heart, and when he left for Notre Dame, part of him stayed with her.

More than anyone, he understood the root of her passionate drive to pursue a singing career, the one thing beside him that held her together when they were teens. Yet, in his desperation, he had tried to hold on to her.

He started slow, and asked quietly, "Where've you been all these years, T? Why didn't you keep our promise?"

———

WHERE TO BEGIN? Tanya thought, letting out a soft sigh and pushing her empty plate aside. She stared into Tate's expressive blue eyes. Old pain and hurt stirred behind them and cut her to the core.

She couldn't believe she sat here in the kitchen of the boy, now man, who she'd left that day and who had owned her heart from the moment she met him in their grief group at seventeen. Staring into his eyes, she realized her soul had never stopped yearning for him. He deserved an answer.

The last time he'd seen her was the day he'd left for Notre Dame, and she'd left with her mother on their cross-country road trip to L.A. to pursue her dream.

Her throat tightened. She'd sacrificed her promise to him to keep another. She'd promised him that she'd give their long-distance relationship a chance.

At the time, she had no idea what it would take to keep the first promise she'd made...The one she'd made to her father—to pursue her dreams of a music career. She'd naively thought she could keep both.

What she hadn't counted on was how quickly the lifestyle she found in L.A. would devour her days and nights. Her calls to Tate grew less frequent, her letters shorter.

It all came to a head that first fall, Tate's freshman year at Notre Dame. She'd promised to visit him for the biggest football game of the season and stay the weekend. Part of their plan to stay together while they both pursued their dreams.

Her eyes welled, and she opened her mouth to speak, but no words came.

He reached for her hand and wrapped it in warmth. His brow furrowed, his gaze penetrating, "I waited at the bus station for hours. You never showed up or returned my calls... I got the note a few days later. What did I do?"

The thought of Tate waiting and worrying...

Her tears spilled over, and she wiped them away with one hand as she squeezed his hand in her other. "You didn't do anything wrong," she whispered, "It was me."

He brushed his thumb across the back of her hand. "Tell me," he said softly.

She pressed on, ashamed at how she had handled things. "I had an audition a couple of days before I was supposed to see you. A producer for one of the record labels who represented a few big named R&B bands heard my demo of 'I'll Carry You with Me.' One of the bands had an unexpected opening for a backup singer. The producer said, if I got it, I'd have the opportunity for a solo spot to crowd test the song."

He nodded, his gaze coaxing but unwavering.

She paused and slipped her hand from his before she continued. It didn't feel right to be touching him as she relived this. She stared at her lap and let the scene play out in her head. "They hired me on the spot. But they didn't tell me until I got there that I would need to join their tour the next day, and that I would be gone for six months."

She paused, remembering the awful scene that night with her mother and her manager as she tried to persuade them to ask the producer to delay her start by a few days. Her insides had ripped apart over the decision as she'd clutched the bus ticket Tate had sent her. Not wanting to choose between seeing him and the potential opportunity of a lifetime.

Tanya sighed. "My mom and I had a big fight. She said I had to choose...that if I passed up the opportunity, I'd resent you."

"Baby, I know you think you love that boy, but you can't fool yourself into thinking you can have Tate and this dream you're chasing. You need to focus on your music. Don't give up your

dream for foolish promises you can't keep. Make your daddy proud."

Tate swallowed. "I would've understood. You didn't have to cut me out of your life." Anger tinged his hurt.

Her voice quivered and she shook her head. "She was right. In my heart, I knew if I couldn't choose you then I had to let you go. Not because I didn't love you, but because I couldn't put you first," she sniffed and wiped away a tear. "I didn't know how to tell you. Any of it. Then it was too late, so I sent the note..." How often she'd thought of that note over the years. Every cowardly word of it.

> Forgive me, Tate. I'm so sorry for what I've done
>   and for what I'm about to do. It's not because
>   I don't love you, it's because I do.
> There are places I need to go that you can't
>   follow.
> I'm giving you back your freedom and taking
>   mine.
> Not forever, but for now.
> This isn't goodbye.
> I promise.
> I love you, Tanya

"My life went crazy after that. When I got back from the tour, I signed a record deal for 'I'll Carry You with Me,'" she said, giving him a sad smile. "But the song wasn't just about my dad anymore it was about you, too." She placed a hand to her heart. "You've always been here, Tate. Even when I couldn't be with you, I've carried you with me."

Tears flowed freely down her cheeks. There so many times she thought of Tate and what they could've had. So. Many. Times. When it all went wrong with the record company, she thought of giving up the dream and coming home. And she almost had...

A smile ghosted over his lips. "I remember when the song came out. I was so proud." Then a pained expression crossed Tate's face. "You said you'd come back, T."

She brushed her fingers down the soft wool sweater covering his arm. "I did..."

The muscles in his arm tensed under her touch. "What do you mean? I never saw you again."

The tears came faster than she could brush them away. "Christmas break your senior year of college. You were home for the holidays with your mom." When they'd still lived in Montclair.

Tate frowned deeply and shook his head, his blue eyes burning. "What are you saying...?" he whispered.

She gave him a watery smile. "I was in New York City, on a 10-city tour with an R&B band. I worked up my courage and dropped by one night. I prayed that you'd talk to me. But you weren't home. You were out for the night with your girlfriend." She remembered her feelings of utter desolation along with her guilt over how she'd let him down.

Tate's jaw twitched and his eyes misted. "I didn't know."

Tanya laid her hand on his. "That's because I asked your mom not to say anything. After what I'd done, I didn't have a right to disrupt your life. I was too late...That girl, she was the one you married?"

He nodded once and swept a hand over his face. "God, T. Why didn't you tell me? Why didn't you trust me?" he asked with a hint of frustration.

"I'm so sorry. I never wanted to hurt you."

He passed a thumb over her cheek to wipe away the tears, and said, "I would've given anything to be with you." He looked as bereft as she felt.

His words cracked her wide open. "You had dreams, too, and I couldn't let you give them up." Had he been home that night and unencumbered, maybe things would've been different.

He stepped off his stool and pulled her into his strong arms, her head resting against his chest. His heart beat strong under his sweater. "But you were always meant to be part of those dreams," he whispered into her hair. "It's not too late. Give us another chance?"

Her heart stuttered in her chest. The tragedy of the fire faded into the background, along with obstacles that kept them apart for all these years. This moment felt so much bigger. More important. Magical.

He reached down and tipped her head back so that she stared up into his eyes. Eyes filled with heat and longing.

She touched his cheek, his beard soft under her fingertips. Her gaze lingered on his full lips, and she nodded. Yes, she wanted that too.

But first, she needed to know. "What about you? Your football scholarship? The NFL?"

He shrugged and ran one of her curls through his fingers, his touch sending a shiver over her skin. "Bum knee from an injury during my senior year, so I came home after graduation. Opened a construction business and made a fortune during the housing bubble. Got divorced and lost half of that fortune. Then I transitioned from voluntary to paid firefighting, and I still do construction on the side."

His fingers moved from her hair to her cheek, his body pressed flush to hers. "I've missed you," he said, lowering his mouth.

Her heart soared as he came in for a kiss.

Tate's lips halted on their descent at a loud crash in the living room.

She laughed softly. "Your cat has impeccable timing."

He pulled back and his brow knit in confusion. "What cat? I don't have a cat." Then his eyes widened and he bolted for the living room, "Oh, shit!"

She followed on his heel. As they rounded the corner, he snapped on the light.

Sitting in the middle of the coffee table was a toppled nut bowl, scattered nuts, and a fluffy-tailed gray squirrel holding a peanut.

They all screamed at once.

Tate grabbed the blanket on the back of the couch, unfolded it, and held it out like a matador.

The squirrel dropped the nutshell as Tate tossed the blanket. In a panicked dash, the squirrel leaped from the table to the back of the sofa in time to avoid the falling blanket, then onto the floor. Tiny nails scrabbled on the hardwood around the corner into the front hall.

Oh my God, she needed to get her eyes checked. How had she mistaken a squirrel for a cat?

Tate swore and leaped over the back of the sectional with the blanket in hand. "You okay?"

Her heart pumping, she nodded and slipped off her heels.

"We need to trap that little bastard, and get him out of the house before he destroys the place," Tate said, his jaw set in a determined line.

"I'll try not to scare him this time," she promised and dashed in stocking feet behind Tate.

Something crashed to the floor above them. He opened the front door as they passed, letting in a chilly gust of air. "We'll flush him out if we can't catch him," he said.

She followed behind Tate as he took the stairs two at a time and met him at the top.

He pointed to the right. "You go that way, I'll go this way. If you find him, call me and trap him in whatever room you find him in. OK?"

She nodded and headed into the open guest room where she'd left her things. Everything looked undisturbed, so she checked the bathroom where she'd taken her shower. Nothing. The closet door stood slightly ajar. She opened it the rest of the way and turned on the light. A pile of nutshells sat in the corner, and above it, a hole chewed through the ceiling from the attic above. Well, that explained how the squirrel got into the house.

A blur of gray fluff flew by the bedroom doorway with Tate on its tail.

She followed them and ground to a halt behind Tate where he'd cornered the petrified animal in an unfinished bedroom.

A mature female voice boomed from downstairs. "Tate, honey! Are you home?"

"Christ on a bike," Tate muttered. Holding the blanket in front of him like he was about to block a pass, he turned to her. "T, it's my mom. I have no idea what she's doing here this late, but can you tell her I'll be down in a minute?"

The squirrel chittered in a distressed wail, clambered up the wall, and launched itself onto the ceiling fan.

"Please don't hurt the little guy," Tanya said.

He craned his neck and shot her a reassuring half smile. "Don't worry, T. I won't."

She closed the door and hurried downstairs.

"Mrs. Manning!"

Claire Manning stood inside the door with a man her age at her side. They were both dressed for a night out on the town. A look of surprise on his mother's face shifted to delight. "Tanya, is that you?"

Tanya hadn't realized how much she'd missed Tate's mother. This Valentine's Day held the best and the worst experiences she could ever imagine.

Tanya rushed into the woman's arms and hugged her. "It's so good to see you again." Then she eyed the large wire contraption resting on the floor at Claire's feet. "What's that?"

"A trap. Tate told me he's having a squirrel issue. I'd planned to leave this on the porch."

The stress of the day had finally caught up with her. Unable to stop her giggles, Tanya broke into laughter. Trying to catch her breath and speak at the same time, she held her stomach, "He has it cornered upstairs in the bedroom."

His mother's eyebrows rose. "Is that why the front door was open?"

Tanya nodded and wiped away her mirthful tears. She was really doing a number on her mascara today. "I'm sorry, it's been a stressful day." Tanya stared at the man and held out her hand, "I'm Tanya."

He shook it and smiled warmly. "Mike."

His mother grabbed the wire trap and started at a fast clip toward the kitchen. "Time for introductions later, we need to bait this thing."

Tanya headed to the living room for a handful of nuts while his mother slathered a bunch of crackers with peanut butter and they headed to where Tate had bunkered down with the squirrel.

The creature dangled upside down from the ceiling fan, clutching on for dear life when Tanya and Tate's mother slipped inside with the trap. Tate had the window wide open and stood nearby with the blanket. Mike had been reluctantly relegated to the living room to wait it out.

"Hey, Mom. What are you doing here?" Tate asked, then caught sight of the trap. "Sweet."

Claire propped open the cage door and arranged the squirrel bait inside. "Mike and I were on the way home from our date—"

Blanket still in hand, Tate's head snapped around. "Mike? Mike who?"

She laughed softly and blushed. "Mike Garibaldi...he owns the hardware store downtown. We're dating."

Tate's brows popped up followed by a look that could only be described as hurt. "You are? When were you going to tell me?"

"At brunch, on Sunday," she said, then cleared her throat and winked at Tanya. "I'm not the only one who's been holding out, am I? Why don't we leave our little friend here, and take our chat downstairs." Tate's mother smiled at Tanya. "I think we all have some catching up to do."

Inching out of the room, they closed the squirrel inside with the baited trap and joined Mike downstairs. Tate greeted him with familiar warmth. Turned out, Tate was also a frequent customer at Mike's store.

Tate lit a fire and they gathered on the dove gray sectional. Wine in hand, they settled in and traded stories.

Tanya went first. She filled them in on her years in L.A., her hit single and ensuing lawsuit, her career change to become a flight attendant, and buying her home in Maplewood without realizing Tate and his mother lived only a few miles away.

Claire went next and regaled them with how she'd visited Mike's hardware store for years and how their long-standing flirtation had recently turned into a relationship.

Finally, Tate shared his story about the purchase of his home, the on-going renovations, and his immense pleasure at hosting his first official house guest.

Two hours later, Claire and Mike left with one extra passenger stuffed to the gills with peanut butter and mixed nuts. They planned to release the well-fed squirrel in Mike's backyard across town.

But before they left, Claire caught Tanya alone in the kitchen.

With misty eyes, she pulled Tanya in for a hug. "I'm so sorry about the fire, sweetheart. But you being here is like a blessing."

When she'd released her, she brushed away a tear. "I've never forgiven myself for not telling Tate you came to see him that night."

Tanya released a heavy sigh. "I'm sorry I put you in that position."

Tate's mother smiled and squeezed Tanya's arm. "For Tate, you were the one who got away. Be gentle with his heart. He's a good man."

Tanya's throat tightened. "I know," she whispered. "I promise to do right by him this time."

"That's all I ask, honey."

After seeing them all off, Tanya and Tate returned to the sofa and snuggled in front of the fire.

A quick glance at the cable box revealed the time at almost midnight. This truly had been Tanya's best and worst Valentine's Day ever.

Tate pulled her close and brushed back a lock of her hair. "Where were we?" he asked, eyes sparkling and wearing a crooked smile. He traced her lip with a finger.

She shivered under his touch. "Am I forgiven just a little?"

"Only if you promise to make it up to me," he teased, then clasped her hand in his and brought it to his lips for a kiss.

Had it only been a few hours since her world tilted on its axis and she'd found Tate again? Whatever this was, whatever this could be, she wanted to give it the chance it always deserved.

It had taken her ten years of chasing her dream to figure out that it wasn't the music career her father wanted her to have as much as what it had represented...happiness.

"I promise that and more," she said. Bridging the gap between them, she cradled his head in her hands and kissed him in a dance of lips and tongue until everything receded and all that remained was she and the boy who'd pulled her from grief and stolen her heart at seventeen.

———

OLIVIA MADE it to Bach's Upper West Side apartment building by 2 a.m. and slipped inside behind a couple too absorbed in a quiet conversation to notice her.

After the squirrel debacle and confirming their win, Olivia visited the fire scene. She slipped the beautiful photograph of Tanya and her father into the top drawer of the charred nightstand next to Tanya's bed.

Like Tate and Tanya, Olivia had lost someone on 9/11. Her grandmother, a kitchen worker at Windows on the World, died in the collapse of the north tower when Olivia was eight years old. One of the most treasured possessions Olivia owned was a picture of her sitting on her grandmother's lap when she was five. When Olivia had seen the surveillance footage inside Tanya's townhouse, she knew what she had to do. She had to save that photograph.

She nodded at the doorman manning the security desk. He eyed her with recognition as she passed, tipped his head and smiled. Hanging back, Olivia waited for the elevator doors to close in front of the canoodling couple and caught the next one.

She remembered nights like that in another life when she'd been with Marcus, and she wondered if she would always feel like an outsider looking in. But if that were true, why was she on her way to the 17th floor? She and Bach could easily tally their winnings tomorrow, but the truth was that she needed him—and only him—tonight.

The win hadn't been enough. Even with the threat of their nut-loving little friend, they'd beaten the odds and won. She'd watched Tate and Tanya kiss less than five minutes before the stroke of midnight, but the rush she felt had fled by the time she'd driven through the Lincoln Tunnel, leaving her aching for comfort that only one person could provide. Screw how much this could complicate things.

She pressed Bach's buzzer. The door cracked open less than a minute later, and a sleepy-eyed Sebastian greeted her wearing only pajama bottoms, his bare, chiseled chest on full display. "Liv?"

"Hi," she whispered, at a loss for anything else to say. But no words were necessary.

A lazy smile slipped onto his lips and his blue eyes shimmered with a naked softness. He met her gaze with an array of emotions that sucked her breath away. Relief mixed with yearning and desire. The two things he'd never acted on or said out loud. Feelings she knew well and denied just as fiercely.

He reached for her hand and tugged her inside. She entered the darkness and he led her to his bedroom. Stripping down to her underwear, she crawled into his bed after him. He wrapped his arms around her and spooned her tight to his body like he had so many other nights. Tonight was different; she felt it deep in her soul. Tucked beneath the blankets, she let his warmth permeate her skin.

"How many times did your mum call today?" he asked quietly, his breath warming her hair.

She would've found the answer comical if the calls hadn't pissed her off so much. "Thirteen."

"Did she ask about Marcus even once?" His voice was an aching whisper.

Olivia's throat tightened. The cork popped on her bottled emotions, and they spilled over like wasted champagne. A sob broke free. "No..."

Of course, not. Marcus hadn't been a wealthy doctor from a good Chinese family. He'd been a British musician with a kind heart who'd loved her unconditionally—a thoroughly unacceptable choice by her parents' standards. If he had lived long enough to put the ring on her finger they'd found in his pocket the night he died, her parents would've disowned her.

"He was my brother, Liv. I miss him, too..." Bach said gently, stroking her hair as she shook and her wails hit a crescendo.

Minutes passed. He held her tight, his chin tucked alongside her neck. After what felt like an eternity, she swallowed hard, completely wrung out of tears, and breathed his name. "Sebastian?"

"Yeah?"

"It's time we let him go," she sniffled.

"I know." His voice a gentle caress.

Looking back, she realized Sebastian had been leading her to this moment for a long time. She was finally ready to embrace it. That didn't mean leaving Marcus's memory behind, it meant living her life alongside it.

She pushed the pall of sadness off her shoulders with a final desperate shove. "Let's go to Florida," she said, and wiped the remaining tears from her cheeks.

His arm tightened around her. The corded muscles making her feel safe and cared for. He laid a gentle kiss on the back of her head, and whispered, "I'd like that..."

"Promise me something?" she asked, squirming out of his grasp to pull a few tissues from the box he kept on this side of the bed just for her. He'd seen her at her worst more than once, but she'd never been self-conscious about blowing her nose in front of him until now.

"All right..."

She spooned back into his warmth and gave him a half-hearted elbow. "Update the algorithm. No more effing squirrels."

Chuckling softly, he moved her hair aside and kissed the delicate skin at the base of her neck. "I promise that and a whole lot more...if you'll let me."

The touch of his lips sent a shiver far and wide, awakening

long dormant bits of her anatomy. She smiled in the dark, and whispered, "I'll consider it."

He gave her another squeeze. "That's all I ask. Sleep now, Livvie. Tomorrow's a new day." He found her hand and threaded his fingers through hers. "We'll face it together, all right?"

For once, the thought gave her a thrill. Her body relaxed against him, the only place she wanted to be. Content, she drifted off to sleep, and for the first time in five years, she looked forward to what tomorrow might bring.

"LOVE YA, BABY" BY MARIE BOOTH

A GATES SERIES STORY

I GRITTED MY TEETH, holding back a growl. My boss was tall, good looking, generous and patient, but he was late and I had a situation only he could deal with. His San Francisco breakfast meeting should have ended by nine-thirty, giving him plenty of time to get back to the club.

Male voices in the hallway gave me a bit of hope. Finally appearing, Damien smiled a greeting as he entered. "Good morning, Rachel." He continued in the direction of his office. "I'm expecting a call at noon from the architect."

"Good morning, *Mr. Granger*."

My irritated tone and formal address stopped him in his tracks. "Is it going to be one of *those* days, Ms. Abercrombie?"

"You can count on it. My coffee's not done because Victor is set on making it again today. He left a note on my desk." I read it aloud: "*I'll be up early to make the coffee. I have a special blend I want to try.*"

We glanced at the wall clock. Eleven a.m.

Damien shrugged. "As long as it isn't that island blend. The office smelled from coconut for weeks."

"It's eleven."

"I know, but he works late every night."

I slumped. "It's this movie project he's working on. An entire film score. He doesn't like to disturb Sloane, so he comes to the club if he thinks he'll be working through the night."

My boss treated me to a wry smile. "She has him wrapped around her apron ties."

Pot-kettle. Damien could talk about Victor giving in to Sloane but Damien adored his Cassie. Both men treated their wives like goddesses, which was as it should be.

"Could you speak to Victor about starting the coffee earlier? Maybe actually setting the timer?" Ever since he'd learned to use the office coffee pot, he'd been experimenting. Sometimes to our horror. I could still smell the spicy taco blend.

"Can't you..." Damien stretched out his hands in a pleading gesture.

"He's *your* partner."

"We inherited our positions from our fathers."

"C'mon." I laughed. "Would that have made a difference?"

He smiled and shook his head. "If I'd had a choice I would have picked Vic as partner. However, I believe it may be time to reevaluate other members of the staff." With one brow arched, his gaze pinned mine.

"Did you practice that look in the mirror, boss? 'Cause it needs work."

"I've discovered storefront windows are most gratifying. The window dressers run in terror."

Most people found Damien Granger intimidating, mostly due to the deliciously deep toned British accent, his large physical presence, and his keen intelligence. Having grown up in a rough area of Boston, I'd gotten over the whole alpha-boss thing in about ten minutes. The elderly lady who'd owned the neighborhood deli would have beaten Damien in a stare down without breaking a sweat.

Damien turned to leave, but I was having none of that. "There's more. Victor drools on his desk when he sleeps. If you don't want this particular pregnant woman to toss her cookies all over the expensive oriental carpet, someone else will have to clean it."

"Try to aim for the trash can."

I continued to glare. "Still waiting for my coffee."

"Pregnant women aren't supposed to drink coffee."

"I have orders not to make my *decaf* until your lazy partner brews his special blend."

"Purchase another pot for the office. I believe the club budget will sustain the expense."

"Ha, ha." Damien Granger had enough money to buy a small country. Not only was he half owner of The Gate Club and City Block Realty, but he also ran a fine art acquisitions business for high-end art collectors. None of that included the money and property he'd inherited or the successful investments he'd made along the way.

"Why not get one of those pod contraptions?"

My hands shot up, palms facing forward. "Please. I have my standards."

"Knowing Marley as I do, I believe your standards could be called into question." Damien, Victor, their friend Blake, and Marley attended private school together.

"Marley is no longer a concern." I hadn't seen him in six months and all my efforts to get information had fallen flat.

"No word from the Mindful Wanderer?"

"I'd rather not talk about him." I handed Damien a stack of messages. "Have fun with the mayor. She's as pissed as a snake in a pit full of elephants."

"Thank you, Rachel. Your way with words always astounds me."

I let my Boston accent out of its cage. "Ya might wanna think about droppin' the snooty accent. Weren't cha born here in Frisco?"

"I spent half my life in England." He leaned closer. "And Cassandra enjoys it." He winked.

I held up my hand. "TMI. Go clean up your partner's drool so I can make my coffee."

"I'm here, I'm here." Victor stumbled into my office, which also served as the all-day break room for the three of us. His longish dark hair hung in his face, somehow still looking styled and rock star appropriate. "Why don't you drink tea?" he grumbled, scratching his stubble.

"I do drink tea. Herbal tea. Just not in the morning."

Victor yawned. He was very pretty. And tall, although not as broad across the shoulders as his best buddy. And he had a smile that could wet a dozen pairs of panties a minute. Just a guess.

"Herbal tea is not actually tea. It's tisane," Damien offered up.

"If it says tea on the box, it's tea," I argued.

"I suppose you think soy milk comes from the udder of the soy, a rare creature found ambling about the Pyrenees?"

"I don't know how Cassie puts up with your arrogant ass."

His grin was brilliant. "Neither do I, Ms. Abercrombie. Neither do I." He grabbed up a stack of paper towels.

"What are you doing?"

"I believe I'm on drool duty, correct?"

He'd finally gotten me to smile, a game we'd played ever since Marley left for his stint in The World Organization for Peace and Tranquility, or TWOPT, a group similar to the Peace Corps. Kinda. "Well, get to it. Don't want the saliva eating through his blotter. He loves spicy food."

"Jeez. I slept on the couch. Is it gonna be one of those days?" He waved the coffee scoop in the air and the grounds sprayed onto the carpet.

"You can count on it," Damien answered for me, shaking his head in Victor's direction.

"Crap. Now I lost count." Victor dumped the coffee back in the container and put the scoop on the counter. "You've become a freakin' tyrant, Rach." He curled his fingers into claws, made a funny face, then pulled the hand-held vacuum out of the cabinet and cleaned up his mess.

"You try being eight months pregnant!" I shouted over the noise.

"An impossibility, I'm afraid." The two men smiled at each other.

"Oh, shut up. At least I don't have dangly bits to deal with."

Damien sighed, pretending to be hurt by my comment. "Our dangly bits should not be discussed in a workplace environment."

"Just wait until Cassie and Sloan are pregnant. I'm gonna give them all kinds of tips for ways to torture you."

They weren't laughing now. Victor got busy making coffee.

"Perhaps a raise..." Damien began.

I laughed. "How about adding free day care to the club?"

"You're one of ten female employees. Most of the others are past child bearing age."

"I'll speak to Sloane about it." Victor's wife was planning another protest to force the club owners—these two—to accept female members. Damien and Victor had been dragging their heels. "After all, she has Victor wrapped around her apron strings, right?"

"What? Did you tell her that?" Victor scowled at his friend.

"Pay no attention to the pregnant secretary."

"You and Cassie are coming with Chinese tonight, right?" This had become a regular Thursday event since Marley left.

"Would we ever miss an evening with you, the future hellion, and food from Wat Foy?"

"I could eat a spring roll or two right now." I'd been running late and had only managed a health bar.

"Coffee's going. Wait, did you skip breakfast again? I'll run to the cafe and get you a couple of bananas or a yogurt." Victor turned toward the hallway.

My heart did a little flip. I had the best bosses in the world. Their wives had even thrown me a baby shower. "You bought me a case of yogurt from the big box store last week. I'm fine. Really. And thanks for letting me continue to work. Sitting around at home drives me nuts."

I'd left out the word, *alone*.

When Marley had proposed and left on his adventure, my bosses and their wives had stepped in to help. Thursday was Chinese food night with Cassie and Damien. On Saturdays, Victor and Sloane arrived with a delicious meal from Sloane's restaurant, even when they were going out together later that night. I was always invited to Sloane's parents' house for the Mangia Monday feast where the entire Gabrielli-Hanley clan, along with the Grangers, got together to eat the best home cooked Italian food west of the Rockies.

These food-eating orgies with friends were the highlights of my week. Not what I'd envisioned for my life before my move from Boston three years ago to the apartment in Mill Valley, but the succubus I carried around was grateful, and so was I.

"Strawberry or blueberry?" Victor had his head in the fridge, giving me a very nice view of the rest of him.

I wasn't dead. Just missing my man. "One of each, please."

As usual, my thoughts were drawn to a nameless village on the Amazon River. Marley and I had been together for more than two years, yet he'd given me one week's notice after I'd accepted his proposal, explaining that he'd never had a chance to give something back to the world. To make a difference. To save a life. To teach a life-altering skill.

Marley was a successful grant writer who worked with not-for-profits. He was handy at fixing things around the apartment, but how often did they need curtains hung in the Amazon jungle?

But Marley had a beautiful soul, a yin to my yang. From our first meeting at the club, we'd fit together like hot chocolate fudge and vanilla ice cream. I even understood why he'd wanted to go. He'd grown up wealthy, and unlike the rest of his family, believed he had a duty to the world that needed to be addressed before he could settle down. He'd signed on for two stretches of twelve weeks each in South America, all the while spouting on and on about how he adored me and wanted to marry and spend his life with me and no one else.

He'd sworn to keep in touch, but the only correspondence I'd received was on ragged scraps of paper stuffed inside dirty envelopes.

Marley didn't know that I was pregnant. I'd suspected before he left, but I couldn't ruin his dreams by sounding all needy and shit. Truth was, I'd been afraid. Afraid he'd still have gone, and that would have hurt so much worse.

Damien pushed my tissue box closer. "Without you here, we'd be wading through drool, knocking over stacks of papers to get into our offices, and losing track of our most important clients." He waved around the messages I'd given him. "You have a job as long as you want it."

"We'll never accept your resignation, so don't even think about it." Victor presented me with a spoon, the two containers of yogurt on a plate and a mug of decaf next to it. "I made your coffee first. I'm usually half asleep when I write those stupid notes. Ignore them. You have all of us on speed dial, right?" Victor asked for the tenth time that week.

I wiped my eyes and nodded.

"If he's anything like you, that tiny hellion is going to be something special," Damien said.

"It's a girl." Victor grunted in derision. "Sloane is positive."

"Cassie swears she's carrying a boy."

"Care to place some money on that?"

"Get out of my office!" I shook my spoon in the air and they scooted.

———

"EXCUSE ME."

Something was jabbing me repeatedly in the shoulder. "Wha... What?"

"You were snoring, Mr. Winchester. Passengers have complained."

I blinked and turned toward the flight attendant, a guy who really rocked the uniform. I could never pull that off. "Sorry. I haven't slept this well in six months."

"You were working abroad?"

"That was the original idea." I shrugged.

"Can I get you anything?"

"Coffee?"

"Of course."

I checked my watch. I'd had a three hour layover in Miami and was four hours into my flight to Oakland. I stood and stretched, then settled into my seat again. In two hours, Rachel would be back in my arms. That is, if she heard my message. She hadn't answered her cell when I'd called. Her voicemail had kicked in.

Rachel here. If you're too lazy to leave a message, take a hike and don't bother calling back.

I'd laughed, the sound of her voice a balm to my beat up spirit. I'd left a message and called right back, but still no answer.

In Oakland, I waited around at the airport for half an hour, but it was late and the U.S. Embassy had booked me a room for two nights. I decided to let her sleep and try again tomorrow. I tossed and turned in the enormous hotel bed. I was too used to sleeping on a blanket on a wooden floor.

TWOPT had assigned us a back country village named Casalando and our guide had delivered us exactly as planned. The villagers had greeted us with smiles, looking healthier than I'd imagined. The supplies had arrived on schedule, and we'd begun to build out a communal house, which would also serve as an activity center for the villagers.

When the house was almost finished, Orlando Cortez and his rebel crew had barged in shouting threats and waving guns in the air. They'd forced my group of carpenters to finish the building, surprising everyone by speaking in perfect English. My father had trained me to build from the first day I could hold a wrench, but that wasn't the main reason the organization had sent us here. As well as providing medical care and decent housing, we'd arrived with two yoga instructors, two massage specialists, a meditation guru and a fitness trainer, TWOPT being of the mindset that villagers everywhere would benefit from the improvement of the spirit as well as the body.

By the time the three ready-to-assemble hot tubs had arrived, our group had figured out TWOPT was a world class scam. They were providing free labor to the highest bidder. Orlando and his crew had used previous TWOPT members to build a small town and now we were there to turn it into a private resort.

They forced us to fashion our own jail, a house with two rooms, four holes they'd called windows, and several buckets, some empty, some filled with water. In the morning they'd bring us a pot of rice and beans and two tortillas each while they barbecued meat in a nearby pit. After our meal, we'd head off to our various jobs and villagers would arrive to deal with the buckets. At night they'd leave a basket with bananas and mangos, sometimes including a bit of their leftover meat.

Our guards enjoyed regaling us with made up horror stories of what they would do to a TWOPT volunteer who didn't cooperate. We realized early on we were lucky to have blankets, food, water and shelter from the heavy rains. We cooperated.

When our twenty-four weeks were up, TWOPT jeeps arrived to transport us to the airport. The Americans among us insisted on being taken to the U.S. Embassy, promising the driver he'd be paid well.

He was detained for questioning.

I forced the memories away and allowed the large hotel bed to finally work its magic around dawn. Unfortunately, I slept through the entire day, waking up at six in the evening. I tried to call Rachel again, but still no luck, so I showered, dressed in what the embassy had given me, grabbed my duffel bag and headed for our apartment. Rachel should be home from the Gate Club by now, but if not, I'd worn my apartment key on a chain around my neck the whole time I'd been gone.

It would be so great to be home.

———

"YEAH, I'M FINE." Mom called me from Boston every day now. Driving me up the fucking wall.

Anxious maternal chatter.

"I do too exercise. I take a walk every day. The doctor told me my weight is normal." Or in the ballpark. Maybe the bleachers.

Disparaging maternal chatter.

"That's a really old Instagram picture." At least a week or two. "Yeah, I know you only gained twenty pounds when you were pregnant with me and you ran on the beach. But you're five foot one. If you'd gained forty-nine point seven pounds you would have tipped over and had to wait until the tide came in to right yourself. I'm close to six feet tall."

Worried maternal chatter.

"Mom, really? The Marin County criminals are not targeting me because I can't run fast. The criminals in this area steal packages off porches then try on the designer clothes in front of their gilt framed mirrors. I hope the guy who took my silk thongs is enjoying how they make his ass look."

Maternal chatter I tuned out.

"Mmm-hmm. Uh-huh. Mmm-hmm. Uh huh. I am too listening."

The doorbell dinged, the most wonderful sound in the world. My stomach had been growling for twenty minutes.

"No, Mom. Don't. Oooh, hiii, Daaad."

Concerned paternal chatter.

"No, I don't need money. I have a great job. I don't need a husband. No, I haven't heard from the man who will not be named. I gotta go. The succubus is hungry. Love you both too."

I ended the call and struggled to my feet as the doorbell rang a second time, my mouth already watering. I was gonna suck down those pot stickers like a porn star with a time limit. I unlocked the four locks Dad had insisted I install and flung open the door.

The sexiest, sleekest, most lick worthy man in the universe stared at the much larger version of me with his mouth hanging open. "Is it a gluten problem?"

It took me a few seconds for my mind to boot up. "Abso-fucking brilliant greeting, Marley." My knees wobbled. I rested a hand on the door frame.

"Baby, I didn't mean..."

I held up a hand to shush him. "I am not your baby."

"Didn't you get my calls?"

"No." I'd deleted a whole bunch of calls from unknown numbers.

"You don't look happy to see me." I continued to stare, trying to keep it neutral. This was not the time or place to go demonic. "I know you're pissed off. Let me explain."

My cheeks burned. I fisted my free hand. "Come back in another six months."

"You can't mean that."

I'd hurt him with that comment and the hurt had bounced right back to hurt me. The woman who'd fallen in love with Marley wanted to throw her arms around him. Kiss him hard, Chain him to the bed. But he'd behaved like a douche and had to leave. Showing up like this without any warning made me feel vulnerable, and I'd worked extra hard during the last six months to stay strong.

"Will you let me in so we can talk?"

"No. I'm expecting my Chinese food any minute and...and... and the delivery guy's the jealous type."

"The jealous type?"

"We're lovers. His skin smells like fried wontons. Mmmm."

"What's his name?"

Marley wasn't budging. "Ambrose."

His lips twitched. "Ambrose?"

"Just go. Now. Come back never." I tried to close the door but he'd wedged his boot over the threshold.

"Why didn't you answer your phone?"

"Unknown numbers are always telemarketers."

"I left messages. You didn't listen to them?"

"No! Go away." My untrimmed nails bit into my palms. I was gonna rip him a new one if he didn't leave.

But if he turned away, I'd fall apart.

"Give me a chance."

Those fucking eyes.

A door down the hall started to open. "Get inside. Mrs. Norton in 5B has her nose up everyone's ass. She'll post a video on Facebook and my rep as a respectable member of society will be trashed."

I tugged him into the entranceway as he grinned and dropped his bag. "When were you ever a respectable member of society?"

I hesitated. "When I was eight, I joined the Girl Scouts."

"How long did that last?"

"Couple months. I used the glue and glitter to make their hair all pretty." I turned away and my billowy top shifted to the side, clinging to my belly.

"You're pregnant." The door clicked shut and he froze, staring at my silhouette. "Very pregnant."

I waited and watched, hoping he'd flinch and leave, proving my anger had been justified.

Praying he'd smile and hold me close so I'd know saying yes hadn't been the biggest mistake of my life.

The transition was slow but told me everything.

Shock.

Wonder.

Joy.

My lip trembled and my eyes burned, but I stayed strong. "What clued you in, other than me looking like I swallowed a dinosaur egg? My triple D boobs? My elephantine ankles? My pink and blue fuzzy teddy bear slippers?" He reached out but I shuffled away. "Don't touch me. Who knows what dreaded disease you picked up on the banks of the Amazon. And stop staring at me." I wrapped my arms around my enormous body, suddenly shy.

"I can't. You're beautiful. More beautiful than ever. I've missed you so much, baby."

He was the beautiful one. Always had been. I'd missed him too. Ached for him. Cried for him.

I pushed those thoughts away and sat my fat ass on one of the kitchen chairs, yearning for a time lord to show up and take me back seven months when I could have told him I didn't want him to leave. That I needed him with me. That we were going to be parents and turn into real adults, at least in public.

"How pregnant are you?" He knelt at my feet, placing his hands on my knees.

My body tingled in a really good way. "Eight months down. Ambrose and I are very happy."

His lips twitched. "We were together eight months ago."

"I was cheating on you. Now you can leave and not feel guilty." I folded my arms and rested them between my boobs and my belly. A shelf designed for that purpose. Mother Nature knows her shit.

But his happiness covered every inch of his face, from glittering eyes to lips curled up and showing teeth. He rested his hand on my gigantic belly, as gentle as feathers, as comforting as a fuzzy blanket. "She's mine. Ours."

The tenderness in his voice almost ripped me apart. To hold onto my sanity, I needed him gone. "First of all, the succubus could be a he. Second of all, this baby is mine to raise. You left and never sent me one proper letter or text or email. What guy screws a woman for two years, three months and nine days, tells her he loves her more than life, then takes off and doesn't contact said woman?"

"I sent you notes. I couldn't manage more. Didn't you get them?"

"They were written in Greek. Who speaks Greek? I took Spanish!"

"I couldn't take a chance someone might find and read them.

I thought Damien could translate for you. He's a language geek like I am. Do you have them or did you..."

"I have them."

He lifted my hand and kissed my palm. My wrist. My knuckles. "I'll read them to you."

I should snatch my hand away. Like right now. "You might make up a bunch of stupid mushy stuff."

He nibbled my thumb, then kissed it. "Show them to Damien. I'm telling the truth."

Those puppy dog eyes were crumbling my resolve. "Why did you leave me? We'd started to plan a wedding, then suddenly saving the world was more important to you than our life together."

"I was a fucking idiot."

"You could have come home."

"Our group was held prisoner by guerrillas. We were threatened with death if we tried to leave or contact anyone."

I rolled my eyes. "Did King Kong show up too?"

"Guerillas," He cocked a gun. "Not gorillas." He scratched his sides like a monkey.

"Oh. So how did you get the notes out?"

"One of the yoga teachers escaped on the day the supply guy arrived with the hot tubs." His brow wrinkled. "They are unbelievably flexible. I think she dislocated a shoulder or something to get through that hole. She convinced the supply guy to take our letters whenever he could.

"Was she pretty *and* flexible?"

He put his arms around my nonexistent waist and leaned his head against my breasts. "There's no one but you. You know that."

"How did you escape?" I threaded my fingers through his hair and he sighed as I combed it out. It was on the long side, thick and wavy, a brown that shined with red in the sunshine. He'd grown a scruffy beard that matched.

"The rebels disappeared one day before TWOPT showed up to take us back. When we talked to the drivers about the rebels, they pretended ignorance."

Marley nuzzled my breasts and rubbed my belly. My body was all, *Oh yeah,'bout time*, but I nudged him away. "What the fuck are you doing?"

"I learned all about massage while I was held captive." He kneaded my inner thigh. I held in the moan. "Every day we were threatened with death. It helped us cope, but it wasn't sexual."

"Rubbing your nose over my nipples isn't sexual?"

He laughed. "That was just me saying hi to the girls. Missed them too. Triple D?" Before I could push him away he grasped my shoulders and kissed my cheek. "This is the best day of my life." Cheek two was next. "I'm home with you." He brushed his lips over mine, then smiled against my mouth as he whispered. "I'm gonna be a Dad."

This closeness with Marley was something I'd yearned for since the day he left, but... I pushed on his chest and he sat back, still on the floor, his hands massaging one of my calves. Heaven.

"A new adventure will come along and you'll take off."

"I'll never leave you again. I'll sleep on the couch or the floor or the stoop, but I'm not going anywhere."

The downstairs doorbell buzzed. Damien and Cassie Granger waved at the security camera. Marley buzzed them up before I had time to waddle over.

How was I going to get rid of him so I could go all pathetic and cry hysterically in Cassie's arms and have her tell me he's scum and I shouldn't let him anywhere near me or the baby? I deserved at least one night of drama before I totally caved and let him get reacquainted with more than just the girls.

I hadn't had a decent orgasm in forever.

But he had to pay.

I gasped. "I completely forgot. It's threesome Thursday. You should leave before things get hot and heavy."

"Damien is your boss and Cassie is a good friend."

"Things have changed. Better go. Like right now."

"You expect me to believe you have sex with the Grangers?"

Why was he laughing? "I'm a watcher. A...a lurker. A...a..."

"Voyeur?"

"Yeah. That."

"Rach, if you were into ménage, you wouldn't be watching."

"Oh?" I glanced down at my ridiculous body. He was never going to want me in this condition. We were strangers now. How could I strip in front of him?

"I dreamed about fu..."

I slapped my hand over his mouth. "Shush! G-rated around junior."

"You dropped the f-bomb."

"Children never listen to their mothers." A well-documented fact.

"C'mere."

I made a half assed attempt at pulling away, but he smelled so good, and his laugh brought back all the best memories. His lips pressed against mine, and oh, god...his kiss. Marley's mouth was heat and sweetness and salty bursts of happiness. I wanted to rub up against him, only I couldn't give in. He deserved his punishment. He'd left me and I had every right to make his existence a horrible nightmare.

"Our Valentine's Day three-year anniversary is tomorrow. I have a surprise planned." His sweet breath warmed my ear.

I nuzzled his neck. "Invite someone else. I'm not going."

"I can't invite someone else to the anniversary of our first meeting." He kissed my ear, my throat, my shoulder. I allowed it.

"We're not married. It's not a real anniversary. Your fault by the way."

"Do you remember how we met?"

The doorbell rang. Who the fuck was ringing the... Oh, yeah.

"If you don't leave, I'm going to scream and Damien will beat the crap out of you."

"He won't. We're old friends and I know what he used to do for a living."

"You'd blackmail your old friend?"

Marley shrugged. "If he tried to beat the crap outta me."

"Men. Open the door. I'm starving."

He did. Cassie and Damien's expressions turned sour.

"Marley?" Cassie rushed past him and gave me a hug. "Are you okay?"

Two sniffs and a couple of blinks. "I'm fine."

Damien glared at Marley, moving into the room with long strides. Marley took a step back. "Where have you been?"

"Trying my best to get home." Marley answered.

Damien placed the large bag of Chinese food on the table "You fucked up big time. Rachel's been worried about you."

"Language."

"Sorry, Rachel."

Cassie pulled down plates and started opening food containers. "I got a double order of pot stickers so you'll have some for tomorrow, sweetie." She turned to Marley. "You should be horsewhipped." She glanced at her husband. "Punch him in the nose or something."

Damien had just taken off his nice leather jacket. "Give me a chance, hun." He hung it on the hook by the door, then grabbed Marley's collar and pulled him closer. "You deserve it."

Marley didn't look all that scared. "I do."

Damien let him go. "As much as I care for Rachel, I don't

believe a broken nose would help the situation. Maybe you should explain."

"Mmph." Cassie touched my shoulder. "Come and eat. The two ridiculous men are going to *talk*." She rolled her eyes. "I bet Sloane's brothers would know how to handle this."

"We're not going to bother Sloane or her family tonight, are we, dear heart?" Damien suggested.

"It would only take a second to make the call. Joey might be at the club beating someone up this very minute." Cassie said, pacing.

"He's the club boxing coach. He isn't my personal hit man."

This was sweet and all but... "I can handle Marley myself." I didn't want him bloodied by anyone but me. Marley stepped closer but I couldn't let Cassie and Damien think we were okay again. Cause we weren't. Not at all. Not even a smidgeon.

His mouth had tasted so sweet.

"Where are the notes? The ones I sent you?" Marley asked.

I opened the kitchen junk drawer and handed them over. Every time I'd pulled them out to throw them away, I saw his handwriting and stuffed them back into the drawer. "Here."

"Shall I read them to you, or..."

I snatched them out of his hand and thrust them at Damien. "What are these?" Damien asked, taking them.

"The only letters I was able to send because my life was in jeopardy," Marley explained.

"I heard TWOPT had a peaceful relationship with the locals." Damien said.

"TWOPT is a scam organization. I found out the hard way."

"These are written in Greek." Damien skimmed through the first one. "Ancient Greek. Nicely done. It's like riding a bike, yes?"

"It is. I was surprised how quickly the three genders came back."

"And right to left is no joke," Damien added.

"These notes are written right to left?" I asked.

"It's Ancient Greek," they said in unison. Like duh.

"Leave this to me." Cassie approached the two *bros* with a kitchen knife. "Your balls are going into the sweet and sour soup if one of you doesn't start reading."

"And I'm hungry enough to eat one." I murmured. "Maybe two."

"Oh, I'm sorry. Sit down, sweetie." Cassie gestured toward my chair. "Let the boys chatter on while we start."

Marley shifted his stance as if he could protect his family jewels from a duo of ferocious females. In his dreams.

Damien ignored us and turned back to Marley. "Why this language?" he asked.

"I couldn't send anything the rebels could read. A few of them had studied abroad."

I ignored the idiots and bit into a pot sticker, moaning with happiness. I finished two, then asked Cassie, "Is Wat Foy married?"

"The head chef's name is Harold." Cassie said after swallowing a wonton. "He giggles a lot."

"Is Harold married?" I asked. Lifetime access to yummy Chinese food sounded pretty good right now.

"The guerillas referred to themselves as rebels fighting for their freedom. They were actually fighting for a way to get rich and lord it over the less privileged," Marley explained to Damien.

"Read the damn letters!" Cassie called out.

"Yes, dear, but later..."

"Anything. Just read the letters. *Please.*"

Damien's sexy grin was the kind he only reserved for his wife. I cleared my throat and he glanced down and read.

Do not be afraid. I am a prisoner but have not been hurt. I imagine you every day and wish I could smother and kiss you.

You meant embrace, correct?" Marley nodded.

Please do not respond to the authorities. The lives of every pris-oner is at stake. I will write again.

"Not bad, although the tense at the end..."

"You really wrote that?" I'd risen and drifted closer.

"Yes. And all the others." He pointed toward the pile.

"I almost threw them in the recycle crate."

His eyes glittered with warmth as his gaze met mine. "You were all I thought about." This time when he opened his arms I stepped into them. His rib bones poked me.

I slid my hand over his abs. "You've lost weight. What did they feed you?"

"Mostly fruit, beans and rice but the diet kept us alive. TWOPT is in for some serious legal battles. The guerillas pay them for free labor."

Cassie tugged on Damien's arm and he kissed her on the cheek before following her to the table. "The food will be cold if we don't sit down to eat."

Marley took the chair next to mine. He told his story as we ate the delicious food, even better now that Marley was here looking after me. He poured my tea, pushed the containers closer so I wouldn't have to reach for them, even encouraged me to eat some vegetables.

"Our daughter needs the vitamins."

"It's a boy." Cassie sounded so certain.

Damien scowled. "You should know that Rachel is doing fine, no thanks to you. We've been looking out for her."

"Thank you, but I can take it from here." He turned to me. "You shouldn't be going into the office this close to giving birth."

"No, no, no, no. You don't get to boss me around just 'cause you're the baby daddy."

"You should be resting more." He glanced at my belly. "Um... How much have you... I mean..."

Cassie was furiously shaking her head. Damien winced and concentrated on spearing a prawn from his Kung Pao Shrimp. They knew the rocky ground Marley was treading. They also knew what a hormone-ridden Rachel was capable of.

I straightened in my chair. "According to my doctor, I'm within the normal parameters of weight gain." Kinda.

"Should we...maybe... get a second opinion?"

I stood, dumped one of the food containers in his lap, unlocked the four locks, opened the front door, then dragged Marley's surprisingly heavy bag into the hallway. Did he bring back a fucking crocodile?

"Hey!" He'd jumped up, using his napkin to wipe the food off his jeans.

"You can leave now," I grunted. "My baby is not being raised by a sizeist. I've lived through that with my mom."

He came toward me, a little wary. "I'm sorry, baby. I'm only thinking about your health. And...um...just wondering."

"What?"

"Did you know? Before I left?" He hefted his bag and brought it back inside.

Cassie straightened in her chair. "Wait. I thought Rachel told..."

I frantically motioned to Cassie, repeatedly using the universal zip-it gesture.

"You didn't tell him you were pregnant before he left?" Damien asked.

"He would have gone anyway," I blurted out.

"How could you think that? How could you think I'd leave you to go through all of this alone?"

"I was never alone. I had Victor and Sloane and Damien and Cassie."

I glanced at my boss for support. Unfortunately, Cassie had snatched up their jackets and was dragging him to the door.

"Marley loves you sweetie. Give him a chance." The door closed behind them.

Huh. Those traitors. Our argument had probably killed their appetites. Maybe they'd come back if I apologized.

But Marley had peeled off his jeans. "That was over the top."

It was. "I'm sorry. I'm kinda sensitive about my weight. Mom is constantly harping on it. But I can't help that the parasite is eating like a shark. Are you okay?"

"Fine, except I smell like shrimp." He took my hand. "Come and eat."

He led me to a different chair, moved my plate over, then dished out food for himself. We ate in silence for a few minutes. It was nice, this peaceful quiet between us. We'd always had that.

Shit. I still loved him. He still loved me. But I'd grown up tough. Never letting anyone get the best of me. If I forgave him. If I gave in and let him stay and hold me and kiss me and... Well, if I did that, would he hurt me again? When he saw my body, would he flinch and look away? It wasn't like he'd seen it change in stages.

"I can hear you thinking."

"What?"

"Are you finished eating?" I nodded. "I'll get you more tea."

He cleaned everything up while I sipped my tea. I dreaded what might come next. I ached for what might come next.

"Let's shower."

"Together?"

"We used to do it all the time."

"Yeah, but I wasn't a brontosaurus back then."

"The most beautiful brontosaurus in the universe." He kissed my cheek and took in a deep breath, his nose in my hair. "My memories of you were what got me through the night."

"We might not fit in the shower." I couldn't look at him.

"I want to be with you, however you're comfortable. Say no,

and I won't touch you. Tell me what feels good, what you want, what you need. I'm here for you, Rach."

"Will you give me a... a massage after the shower? My back hurts sometimes."

"A very gentle one."

"Okay."

———

WE TOOK our time undressing each other, and she was more beautiful than I'd remembered in my lonely dreams on that hard floor. The softness and scent of her skin, her pink nipples and full lips calling to my mouth. I was painfully hard, but I was here for Rachel. I washed quickly, then took my time washing her, making sure to bring her only pleasure as I did. To take away her apprehension and replace it with her usual confidence.

I kissed her and she yanked on my hair. "Touch me... Please..."

I knelt as the water pelted my back, her belly heavy with life, her pussy shining with need for me. I lifted her leg and placed in on my shoulder, then brought her hands to my shoulders so she could stay steady.

"You okay?"

"God, yes. Don't stop." I rubbed my cheek against her sex. "Yes, there. Oooh, that beard is never getting shaved off."

I laughed against her skin, enjoying each sweet whimper and breathy gasp I brought with my tongue and my lips. I held her legs to keep her steady and drew it out as much as I thought she could bear.

"Marley... Mar... yes... I'm... Oooooh..."

I sucked on her sex, easing her down until I heard the best sound on earth: Rachel Abercrombie's giggles, my cue to kiss her.

She rested against the wall and I lowered her leg, rising to kiss her hard, nipping at her lip, ravaging her mouth. She gave back as good as she got, what I'd always adored about my love. She was a fighter. Someone who'd tell me off in no uncertain terms when I'd fucked up, who'd argue a point until we were either growling at each other or rolling around on the floor, our bodies entangled in passion.

She poked me in the chest. "Have you been practicing?"

"I didn't have an Ambrose."

She laughed as I helped her out of the shower and we dried off, her gaze aimed at my erection. I wrapped a towel around my waist, then made a quick call as she used the bathroom.

"Who were you talking to?"

"My sister. My family needs to know I'm back."

"I'm sure they'll be shooting off fireworks any minute."

"More likely they'll be pouring martinis."

"How is Sarah? She's the only one from your family who kept in touch."

"I'm not surprised. She says she's doing fine. Has another one on the way."

"That makes three."

"Yes. She gave me some advice." I lost the towel and pumped my cock. "Did you miss him?"

"Mister Man? Maybe." She giggled. "Don't tell me you asked your sister."

"Who else would I ask? I guess I could have looked for a You Tube video."

"What if I don't want it?"

"You silly ass. I would never force you. I'll be happy just holding you. But maybe we could try."

"You and your puppy dog eyes."

"You still love me?"

"What do you think?" She pulled me toward the bed. "The succubus is quiet tonight."

I kissed her belly and whispered. "Daddy's here. I'll take good care of Mommy. You rest."

We kissed deeply, exploring our bodies with hands and lips, and tongues, whispering words of love I thought I might never hear again. I urged her into a spoon position and massaged her back as well as some more sensitive areas. When she was ready, I slipped inside her sweet body from behind with a comfortable ease. She gasped, her sex tightening, her slick heat almost pulling me over. After a few deep breaths I regained control and moved in a gentle rhythm, making it last, until finally we peaked in release and slept, skin to skin.

I dreamed of Valentine's Day, of how we met and how our lives had quickly fit together the same perfect way our bodies did. Tomorrow would be a new beginning.

———

I KISSED his hairy cheek and left him sleeping. It was early yet, but I was determined to get to work before he woke. I didn't want an argument after such a perfect night and I was sure he'd make an appearance at some point. If they knew what was good for them, Damien and Victor would back me up.

I sighed as I got into the back seat of my usual ride share. My body still floated and buzzed and tingled with the memory of each touch and kiss and gentle word. My regular driver grinned at me.

"You're looking happy, Ms. Abercrombie."

"I had a good night, Samson."

"I'm glad. My Kendra says it's important to rest in the last stages."

"I slept better than I have in months."

"Glad to hear it."

Samson switched on News radio 55.5, because I liked to keep up with the local news during the twenty minute drive.

"And that's it for sports. Something just hit my desk. We have an alert out for dangerous wind conditions in the Bay Area for late this morning, beginning at around eleven. The storm is driving toward San Francisco at around ten miles per hour and is in the San Jose area as we speak. You can expect downed power lines, trees, and cell towers, so charge up your devices while you can and stay indoors."

"Rain is also expected, along with possible lightning strikes. This is definitely a day to stay in with your loved ones."

"The last big wind storm was in '95. I'll never forget the mess it left. Do you want me to turn around and bring you home? I'm sure your boss will understand."

"I'm feeling great today. Victor and Damien are in, so if there's a problem, I'm sure they can get me home safe and sound. But thanks, Samson."

The Gate Club was on the western side of Marin County, right near the water. Damien, being who he was, had redesigned the club to withstand the apocalypse, so I was safer there than in my apartment building. The club would still be standing at the end of days.

I thought of Marley probably still sleeping. If the weather was bad he could watch TV or something. Damien or Victor would get me home this evening.

The day seemed a perfect one, with a bright blue sky and a beautiful view. As we drove through the wide club gate I peered up at my favorite tree, an enormous California Black Oak. The club itself loomed ahead, a stately building designed by Victor's great-great-grandfather and renovated to some extent by the partner owners in each following generation. A lot of the original brick and stone work had survived earthquakes, hurricanes, floods and fires. The grounds were spectacular as well, with a golf course, eight tennis courts, two full basketball courts, an archery range, and more recently, an outdoor pool.

To me, the Gate Club added a sense of history to the constantly-changing San Francisco area. I loved working here.

Samson opened the car door and helped me out. "Here you are, Rachel. You take care, and Happy Valentine's Day!"

My jaw dropped as Samson drove away. It was Valentine's Day and Marley had planned something special for us to do. I'd call him and apologize. Ask him to pick me up. It wasn't too late. I trudged inside, trying to make my feet move faster without over-balancing and ending up sprawled on the ground.

Miracle of miracles. Victor already had the coffee going. "I heard about Marley's arrival. Should I punch him?"

"No."

"Are you okay?"

"Yes." My grin told the tale.

"Ah. Well, okay then. I'm happy for you, Rachel. He always seemed a decent guy. I suppose he had a reason for not getting in touch?"

"Yes. A good one. In fact, I have to call him. I didn't realize it was Valentine's Day."

"Sloane and I were going to take the boat out but the forecast sucks. What are you two doing?"

"Marley made plans but didn't tell me what they were."

"You should have stayed home."

"I should have."

Victor frowned. "Are you feeling okay? Because you're looking a little pale and you never agree with me."

I was feeling a little queasy. But then I hadn't eaten. "I'm fine. Really. I just feel guilty about not remembering it was Valentine's Day."

Damien's door opened. "I thought I heard your voice. Why are you here? You should be snuggled up with Marley on Valentine's Day. Is everything all right between you?" Damien downed the dregs in his mug then glanced at the pot.

"I'm calling him now." He'd picked up a temporary phone at the airport and given me the number. "No answer." I left a message and decided to try again in a few. He might be in the shower.

Damien filled his cup and took a sip. "Are you trying another new blend?"

"We finished the good stuff. I made decaf for Rach."

"I'm drinking decaf?" Damien shifted his gaze in my direction. "I thought I suggested you order another pot."

"Yeah. Yesterday. Only I kinda had other things on my mind."

Victor had poured me a mug and left it on my desk. I took a sip. Perfection.

"You're my favorite boss."

"Hear that?" He smirked at Damien.

"It's the hormones."

"Order a coffee pot with a timer," I said, as Damien walked back into his office.

The alert sign flashed on my phone. "Shit. I hope it isn't a kidnapped kid."

Victor checked. "Nah, it's the weather. Storm's getting closer. Moving fast. You can see the dark clouds." He moved toward the window in his office.

Clouds skimmed across the sky, looking ominous. "It was clear when I got here fifteen minutes ago." I walked closer.

An open patio umbrella flew past the window.

Victor stepped between me and the window, but I pulled away to look. Dirt and leaves whipped around tornado-style. Broken branches and other debris flew across the driveway, some of it crashing into the main building. Another umbrella moved along the ground, this one dragging a table behind it.

"Wind's picking up." Victor was trying to make light of it but his tone had lowered.

I tried my phone, but I had no service. "I can't make a call." I was surprised by how shaky I sounded.

Damien was back. "I'm sure it's a temporary situation. If it's a cell tower, they'll have it up and running in an hour or so."

The long handled net the pool boy used to clean the pool crashed into the window but didn't do any damage. I jumped back, almost losing my balance. Victor caught me in time. My lower belly tightened, only this time I was pretty sure it wasn't indigestion.

Victor led me to his desk and I sat. "We'll secure the windows and close the curtains." They were a heavy brocade which should offer some protection if the glass shattered. "Please call security."

"Boss, we got problems." Steven, the club's head security guard carried a man into the room. His head was bleeding and he looked to be unconscious.

I took a closer look. "That's... That's... That's..."

Damien scooped Marley up and laid him on the couch in Victor's enormous office. Victor ran to get the first aid kit and Steven wet a rag with cold water. I snatched it out of his hand and, after a lot of huffing, knelt beside Marley.

"Baby, wake up. You're okay. Please, wake up. Call a doctor!"

"Phones are out. Internet too," Steven said, scowling.

"What?"

"Electric will be next."

"Enough." Damien shut Steven up, but the damage was done.

"No, no, no, no. Marley needs a doctor."

Another twinge, this one stronger.

Damien took charge, rising to his feet and speaking with authority. We have an emergency procedure manual and we will follow it to the letter. If the electric goes out, our emergency generator will kick in. Steven check the sign-in sheet to find out if we have any doctors, nurses, or EMTs in the building. Also make sure our emergency staff has their handsets."

"Handsets are already set, boss. This guy was hit with an umbrella. The blue striped one."

"I think we saw it fly by." Victor said, returning with the kit.

I cleaned the wound and bandaged it, but Marley didn't wake up. "He's breathing steadily and his color is good." I'd done a lot of babysitting.

"We'll have someone keep an eye on him. Who's available?"

"How about the pool boy? Victor's nephew, Chad," Steven suggested.

"Perfect. We can't use him for anything else today," Damien said.

Chad Gabrielli was summoned to the office. He wore cut-off shorts and the club logo tee shirt, and usually looked bored or irritated by having to work at all. Today his eyes were wide as he rubbed his arms and shifted from foot to foot, his dark hair electric outlet wild.

"Damien... I mean, Mr. Granger. I had the shed open, was trying to put some of the chair cushions away, and...and the pool net went flying off. I didn't have a chance to catch it. I got as m-much locked away as I c-could. B-barely made it back."

The poor kid's teeth were chattering. "Someone get him a jacket."

Victor grabbed his favorite leather jacket off the hook by the door and tossed it to the sixteen year old. Chad's eyes glazed over as he slid it on. Victor was our resident superstar, and most of the member's kids and grandkids were huge fans. He'd written some of my favorite songs.

"Was anyone on the archery range, the golf course or the courts?" Damien asked Chad.

"Not that I saw, sir."

"We got everyone off the grounds when the forecast sent out a warning," Steven said.

"Good work, Steven."

"How many members are in the building?"

"I'd say around forty. Most of them are milling around near the door."

"We can't let them leave in this weather. Rachel, can you help organize things? You can do it right here from Victor's desk so you won't be far from Marley."

"Okay." I swallowed down my fear and the growing discomfort I was not going to mention. "Okay, sure."

"You know how to work the console?"

"I know what to say." I leaned into the microphone as my voice was broadcast throughout the building and over the grounds. "Attention, all members. This is Rachel Abercrombie. For your safety and the safety of all concerned, please stay away from windows and doors and make yourselves comfortable in one of the following rooms: The spa lounge, the interior dining room, the gym, the locker room, the dance studio, or the auditorium. We will be checking on you shortly and will be bringing around refreshments and anything else you may need.

"The Gate Club is secure and safe, so as long as you stay in the rooms I've mentioned and away from windows, you will be fine. Please do not attempt to get to your car or leave the property. The flying debris might strike you down. If anyone has been injured or is feeling ill, please see one of the security staff and they'll see that you get help. Every one of them is equipped with a walkie talkie. Unfortunately, phone and internet services are down. However, you can trust that Damien and Victor have everything under control. Thank you. Signing off."

When I turned the dial on the control panel, I was met with a room full of grinning men. "You are a treasure, Ms. Abercrombie. Thank you. Please turn it to channel three." Damien leaned over and spoke into the microphone. "This is Damien Granger. There will be an emergency staff meeting in the staff lounge in ten minutes beginning with Group A and continuing ten minutes later with Group B. If you're not at the meeting, I ask that you help our members to one of the designated rooms in a calm and professional manner. The storm is forecast to last only a few hours. Please do your best to convince them not to take their lives into their own hands by leaving the building. Thank you."

I covered Marley with a blanket I found folded over the couch, then sat beside him. Damien placed a hand on my shoulder and squeezed. "You're exempt from the meeting. I'll get you something to eat and perhaps some tea? The gas stove should still work.

"Herbal. Tisane."

He laughed. "Of course."

"You can take Chad with you to the meeting."

"He'll be back in fifteen minutes."

"No rush."

When they left, I got up and closed the office door, rubbing my belly as I walked. The pain was worse now, the contractions coming closer together as if the ozone in the air and the howling wind were making baby anxious to see what all the fuss was about.

Lifting Marley's hand, I kissed his palm. "You have to wake up, daddy. Junior's on his way."

I would try to stay quiet and not say anything until Damien and Victor had everything settled at the club. Then, all bets were off.

I winced when the next contraction hit. It lasted a little longer than the last one. I rose and paced for a few minutes, then leaned over and kissed Marley's cheek. "If you don't wake up in time to see our baby born, I'm going to..."

Oh, shit!

I stumbled to the console and clicked it on, not realizing I was talking to the entire building. "One of our members had better be a fucking doctor, because my water just broke."

Two minutes later, Victor burst into the room, wild-eyed and dragging a man behind him. I'd seen him once or twice but didn't know his name.

"Don't cry, Rach. I brought help." Victor looked as scared as I felt.

I wiped at my cheeks, just as the lights went out.

————

THE SOUND of Rachel crying and yelling at someone cleared my hazy mind and brought me back to consciousness. I rose and attempted to swing my legs over to the side so I could stand, only to be stabbed between the eyes by a very sharp dagger.

"Wait, Marley. I'll help," Chad said. He offered his hand.

"Who's hurting her?"

"Your kid. She's in labor. They took her down to the spa."

"She's that loud?"

"They thought she'd be more comfortable on one of those spa couches. Plus, there's lots of towels and water and shit."

The elevator doors opened at the spa entrance.

"Doooon't touuuuch meeeee theeeeere you pervert!"

"I need to examine you," came a stranger's voice.

"You are not going anywhere near my lady parts. Who the hell are you anyway? Where's *my* doctor?"

"Carlo's an EMT. The storm..."

"Fuck the storm." She panted. "He has a mobster name. No mobster is..." Oh god. Ow, ow, ow, oooooow.

"Breathe, Rach."

"Shut up, Victor!" She'd actually growled that time.

"Rachel?"

"Maaarleeey! You did this to meee."

I stumbled closer. Chad got me a stool. I sat and took her hand in mine. "Sweetheart. When? How?"

Damien laughed. "I think we know how."

"Don't you dare laugh at me!" She tugged on my hand and I leaned closer. "They won't give me drugs. Or booooze," she wailed. "I quit!"

Carlo shook his head. "We don't have the approved drugs at hand and I suspect you're too far along. When did the contractions start?"

"About an hour ago."

"Lots of women have babies without drugs," Victor chimed in.

"You're strong," Damien added.

Rachel was pale, her hair drenched in sweat and stuck to her face, but her expression would have made a Viking shield maiden hesitate. "Walk away now or I'll use your balls to demonstrate the importance of pain killers."

Victor and Damien stepped back, a little lost. None of us knew how to help. "Rach... I..." My voice shook. She had to be okay.

Another contraction hit her hard. The men in the room held their breath, and if they were anything like me, thanked the gods they weren't female.

"I'm having my baby surrounded by men who don't have a fucking clue!" She sobbed. "I want my mom!"

"You do?" She and her mom didn't have the best relationship.

"Ditch that comment. I want druuugs!"

"Think about the beautiful baby who can't wait to meet you." I washed her brow with cool water, kissed her cheek, her palm. She seemed to calm.

Another security guard ran in. "I smashed some ice. Saw it on TV. Chips are good for her to suck on."

"Thank you." Carlo pressed on Rach's belly while I fed her ice. "Baby's in the right position. Everything seems good," Carlo said.

"Is your head okay?" Rachel reached toward me, tears streaming down her cheeks.

"I'm fine." My pain was nothing compared to what she was going through. I looked to Carlo. "What can we do?"

"Sit behind her and support her back, hold her hand, rub her belly. Your job is the most important. I need to check..." He gestured toward the obvious place.

"Rachel." I crawled behind her, drawing her back between my legs.

"Don't even. Oh!"

"Breathe baby. Deep breaths in. Blow out. One. Two. Three. Four. Five."

She followed my lead until the contraction calmed. "I hate you." Her voice was too weak.

"I hate me too. Lean into me. I'm here. I'll never leave again. I love you."

"It's coming so fast now."

Carlo turned to our group. "Does she like music?"

"Yeah. She does. I'll grab my guitar." Victor raced toward the stairs.

I handed Chad the cool cloth. "You can help too. Keep her cool and comfortable."

"Sure. This shit is crazy."

"No fucking cursing...around Junior!" Rachel croaked out.

"Oh, okay." He slumped, whispering, "I'm never having kids."

Two security guards entered. "All is secure Mr. Granger." They whispered. "Can we ask her a question?"

"What?"

"We have a pool going. What do you think? Can you tell? It's a boy, right?"

"Take them out." Carlo said.

Damien ushered them through the door. "She's in a delicate state." Damien leaned closer and lowered his voice. "Cassie's sure it's a boy."

"You are so...so dead to me, boss," Rachel grumbled, panting again.

"Let me check you," Carlo pleaded.

"He's an EMT. He's delivered dozens of healthy babies, Right?" I looked to him for support.

"Um..."

"UM?" Rachel dug her nails into my thighs and rose up as much as she could. I'd probably have scars.

"To be honest, I just started last week."

"What exactly have you done?"

"Resuscitated a couple of elderly people. Splinted a few broken bones. Treated a burn."

"No babies," I said, resigned.

"Not yet, but I've taken the training."

Victor laughed. "I could write a song about this."

Rachel twisted her head in Victor's direction. "Start strumming, Music Man!"

"Okay, okay. What tune do you want?"

"My favorite. Play my favorite or I'll shove your picks where the sun don't shine."

Victor played one of his biggest hits, a mellow song about love and loss and forgiveness.

"What is that crap?"

"Your favorite."

"Not anymore. It's not helping. Play a different favorite."

He played a few chords. "Not that stupid one."

Carlo scooted closer, but Rach started to sob. "He's not my

doctor. My doctor is a forty eight year old woman with three kids of her own. She knows what's happening to me. Tell me the fuck what's happening to me!"

"Your cervix is opening so the baby can fit through. The child is in the perfect position. You're doing great."

"I know that shit. Oh god, Marley!" The pain seemed worse this time. "I want to push. I have to..."

"No pushing unless you let me examine you."

"Will you geld Marley when my baby is born?"

Damien and Victor laughed.

She narrowed her eyes. "Them too."

"Sure. Marley, hold her steady. Damien, Victor, keep her legs open wide. I'm going in."

Victor slid off the guitar strap. "First baby born at the club. We're making history!" He pumped a fist in the air, before taking his assigned position.

"Can you...just stab him with that...that pair of scissors?"

"You're fully dilated. Great job. Go ahead and push at the next contraction."

"Like I have a choice."

Rachel screamed and grunted and groaned. I had to keep from crying out myself, she was holding my hand so tightly. "The baby's coming, honey. Just a few more minutes."

"Why isn't it out?"

"Doesn't usually happen in one push," Carlo said, busy doing whatever he was doing down there.

"Two pushes or I'm quitting."

He smiled. "You can't stop the process."

"I was supposed to have another few weeks. Oh noooo."

"Push now."

She screamed. Victor screamed. Damien looked horrified. Steven grinned. Chad covered his ears. But a moment later, Carlo was holding a gooey, red skinned, squirming baby. He used banana clamps on the cord, rubbed its tiny back until it choked out a cry, dried it thoroughly, then wrapped it in a fresh towel and placed it on Rachel's belly.

"Meet your son."

"My son?" Rachel whispered, still breathing hard.

"Our son." I kissed Rachel's cheek, then the forehead of our tiny miracle. "He's beautiful."

Rachel twisted her mouth into a scowl. "He looks like an old version of you. Puppy dog eyes and all."

Victor had edged closer. "Are you sure it's a boy, because Sloane was positive it was a girl."

Rachel lifted the towel, her eyebrows rising. "Definitely a boy."

"Cassie was right." Damien smirked.

"Lucky guess." Victor grunted.

She frowned. "Uh... Doc... Something's wrong." Rachel howled and Carlo gestured to Steven.

"Take the baby, please, Steven. You're not finished, Ms. Abercrombie. There's another one on the way. Everyone back in position."

Victor and Damien were stunned into silence. A rare occurrence, at least for Victor.

"Now!" Carlo's tone was not to be denied. Everyone shuffled back.

———

WHEN MY LATEST CONTRACTION CALMED, I glanced around. Steven had placed our son in a bin lined with cozy spa towels. At least Succubus One and Two and I had made it to the club. I might have been giving birth in Samson's Lyft stuck somewhere in the middle of the storm. Or worse yet, in the apartment with only Marley to help.

I banged my fists on Marley's muscular thighs. He probably didn't even feel it. "How could my nice doctor not know there was another succubus?"

"It happens." The EMT shrugged.

Stupid answer. "It doesn't just happen, Santino."

"I have twins in my family," Marley added. I twisted my head to look at him. He lost the grin fast.

"You're just telling me this?"

"We hadn't spoken about children."

"All this time I thought I was super fat. My mom..."

"Don't listen to her. Ow."

I was crushing his hand. Tough shit. "I have to push, I have to push. I have to puuuuush!"

"Do it!" Carlo had an intensity to his gaze I hadn't noticed before.

Damien and Victor joined in. "Push, push, push, push."

"Bikini wax appointments!"

They shut up.

With a final bust of energy, I pushed baby two into Carlo's waiting arms. The tiny thing cried right away. "A girl."

"I knew it!" Victor punched Damien in the shoulder.

"The boy was first." Damien said.

"So what?"

"Marley, your first... job as a father is to ...to kill my bosses. Doc, If there's another baby, send it back. I'm done."

"Just the second placenta." Which looked like nothing I wanted in my body ever again. Uch.

Carlo had rested our tiny daughter on my chest. I could tell right off, she'd look a lot like me when she grew up. Plus, she was much noisier than the boy, already giving me attitude.

I passed her to Marley. "Here ya go, Daddy. Might as well get used to holding them."

Damien and Victor rolled over a couple of stools. "Twins are a lot to take care of." They sat. "I suppose you'll be out for a long time."

"Maybe years." Victor's words caught in his throat.

They'd pulled out their pleading faces. Victor was better at it than Damien. Damien's still looked like a snooty rich guy.

My slow smile had them leaning away. Who's got the power now, bitches? I motioned to Marley to wipe the sweat off my face. "I'll take two months."

Victor smiled. "We can manage two months."

"That's not long enough!" Marley complained, sliding out from behind me and adjusting the spa chair so it supported my back.

"It's gonna be fine, honey, because when I come back, there's going to be a door cut into the wall leading from my office to the empty office next door. Inside will be the best nursery ever built just for our babies and an amazing nanny will be there to help out. I will have free child care for as long as I work here. Correct, gentlemen?"

"That used to be my office," Damien said.

"Do you use it? Ever?" Victor asked. "We've been using our Dads' old offices."

Damien sighed. "I agree."

"Yes, from me! What a relief."

"Oh, you think I'm done?"

They shook their heads in unison, resigned.

"A limo will pick us up and drive us home. Offer the job to Samson first." I didn't want him to lose out on his regular client. He had a large family.

"Yes, to all your demands." Damien said.

"Good. Now come here so you can meet our babies."

"Exceptionally cute."

"Yeah, adorable."

Wrinkled newborns weren't really their thing, "Thank you both. I can't ever..."

"Shush. You're family."

Victor slapped Marley on the back. "Damien and I have a proposition. We're starting a charity foundation in Damien's Dad's name and we need someone to run it. The Mission Restoration Project will be just one of the organizations we'll be sponsoring. I don't suppose you'd like to submit your resume?"

My sweetie looked gob smacked. "Uh, sure. Thanks."

"You can have Victor's old office." Damien said.

"What? Wait a minute."

"Fair is fair." I said, laughing at Victor's expression. "I suggest we meet at a later date to discuss my raise, Marley's salary, and the hiring of my assistant."

"Your assistant?" Damien repeated.

"I'm going to have to nurse my babies once in a while." I glanced down. "In fact, I should probably..."

"Everyone out!" Damien shuffled Victor, Chad and Steven out the door, then picked up his handset. "Attention. This is Damien Granger. We are pleased to announce the birth of Succubus One and Two. A healthy boy and a healthy girl. The boy was born first."

Cheering sounded in the hall outside our door. Had everyone been lurking there, worried about me? Tears filled my eyes as Carlo handed me my hungry son. "Maybe I'll name him Carlo."

"Don't. I had to live with people *making me an offer I couldn't refuse* my whole life."

"I'm sorry about..."

"You did great. I still want you in the hospital as soon as possible so they can examine you and the kids."

"Okay, Doc. You did great too."

"I'm going to clean up, but I'll stick around until an ambulance can get here."

"Thanks."

The little guy latched on without a hitch, and before long all kinds of peaceful hormones were flowing through my body. Marley picked up our daughter, humming a sweet song to calm her as I watched my little man suckle. I felt like the luckiest person on the planet. Yeah, walking didn't exactly sound like something I'd want to do right away, and I think I could sleep for a month straight, but shit, I'd popped out twins, then negotiated the best deal any secretary could ask for with two powerful, wealthy business owners.

Mom can talk about my birth all she wants. I win hands down.

Marley kissed me, sweet and delicious. "Love ya, baby. You did good."

"You too, Daddy."

"Happy Valentine's Day."

"LOVE IT OR LEAVE IT" BY
EVA MOORE

LAUREN SYKES GRINNED as she reposted another viral
Valentine's Day video. The latest popular challenge revolved
around stunt proposals, and her feed was blowing up. Her
hashtag #LoveItOrLeaveIt had an avid following. She loved
her job.

Well, she'd much rather be creating the content for The
Windy Wendy, the online lifestyle magazine she worked for, but
she'd settle for collating it and spreading the joy for now. That's
how she'd grown their social media following into the six figures
over the last year. Her hard work was about to be rewarded with
her first feature. This was her big break and would open the door
to more writing opportunities. She was on her way. *Look out,
world! Here I come.*

Her phone chimed with the special tone for her boss, and she
picked it up immediately.

Wendy: Come see me. Now.

Oh shit. What now? When the editor-in-chief, Wendy
Nichols, wanted to see you instead of just texting, something big
was up. Since it was nearly five on a Tuesday, she packed up her

laptop and grabbed her coat, before hustling to find Wendy. Two days a week the small staff all met up at the free range office for meetings and collaboration. The rest of the time they worked wherever they could get WiFi. The day pass was cheaper than renting permanent offices and kept the group flexible, but it was limited to eight hours and hers were almost up. It also meant that she had to wander a bit to find where her boss was set up for the day. She found Wendy making tea in the gourmet communal kitchen.

"Hi, Wendy. What's up?"

"How's everything going for the Valentine's Day story?"

When her boyfriend, Devin Ballaster, scion of the Cogman-Ballaster pharmaceuticals empire, had invited her to a charity ball to fight heart disease, she'd seen her chance. She'd pitched the inside story to her editor as her first chance to write a featured story for the magazine. Her plan was to Instagram story her entire night and then do a full feature write up for the next morning's upload.

"It's going great. I've got a more detailed outline of the evening if you want to see it."

"No. But I think I have something that you should see."

That didn't sound good. Lauren looked at the phone Wendy turned toward her and saw her boyfriend Devin with his arm around Monica Delancey, the lithe blonde actress that she recognized from the latest Marvel movie. "Real Life Avenger Fights Heart Disease," read the headline. God damn it.

"You didn't know."

"No. I didn't know." That bastard. Her mind was reeling, but she clamped down on her urge to curse in a bid for professionalism. "But don't worry. I'll still get you your article."

Somehow. How the hell was she going to pull this off? She'd figure it out.

"Lauren, if you can't…"

"I can make this work. Trust me."

Before her boss could take away her shot, Lauren turned and hustled out the door. Before it closed, she had her phone tucked against her ear as she juggled bags.

"What the fuck, Devin?"

"Hey, you saw the picture. I was gonna call you."

"Actually my boss saw the picture and wanted to know why the guy I thought was my boyfriend is taking someone else to the Valentine's Day ball."

"Oh, come on. I couldn't pass on a chance to bring a movie star."

"I told you about the article. What am I supposed to do now?"

"Come take pictures and post about us. It'll be fun."

Lauren's jaw dropped. Was he really that clueless? How had she missed this?

"You bastard. You can fuck right off."

"Lauren, don't be like that..."

"Don't be like what, Devin? You know what? Don't answer that. I hope you enjoyed stabbing me in the back. You won't get the opportunity again."

"Lauren..."

Click. Who did he think he was to just toss her aside? Well, good riddance. She was better off without him. Except that her story was screwed. She was going to lose her opportunity, and who knew when Wendy would give her another chance.

Her anxiety was spiraling, and her mental chatter wasn't helping. She needed her friends, and she needed them now. She walked to catch the Blue Line at North Avenue while texting her best friends, Alexis and Cash, on her way home to Wicker Park.

Lauren: Tonight. Mother Hubbard's?
Alexis: What happened?

Lauren: Long story. Broke up with Devin. Job drama. Need you guys.

Cash: At work till 1 o. Meet you there?

Lauren: I'm buying.

She had five hours to kill. Yoga was only going to get her so far. She added take-out Thai to the list and a pedicure. A solo bottle of wine was damn tempting, but if she was going to Mother Hubbard, she'd better hold off. No one needed Black-out Betty to show up.

All she really needed were her friends to show up, and she knew they would. They always did.

———

IT WAS 10:30 by the time Cassius Hendricks rolled into Mother Hubbard's, exhausted and feet throbbing. The eight-top birthday party had decided to linger long past the check drop and the not-so-casual resetting of adjacent tables.

So instead of getting to run home, shower, and change, Cash was strolling into Mother's on industry night, sweaty and smelling like the salmon special, still sporting his white button-down, black pants, and thick soled black gym shoes. At least he'd remembered to take off the stupid black bowtie before he'd left. Thankfully, in a room full of people who worked in hospitality and showed up for the cheap mid-week drinks, few would judge. Mother Hubbard's was one of the few bars open till 4 that kept the kitchen running so everyone could eat after their gigs closed. It was also the unofficial hub of an underground network of service industry professionals.

All he wanted to do was go home, find his humanity again under a hot shower for about an hour or so, and work on his latest essay submission. But he'd told Lauren he'd be here, so here he was.

Cash nodded to the bouncer who let him in with a wave and scanned the rowdy pub for her trademark auburn ponytail. He found her cozied up with Alexis at the end of the bar, tucked up on the green vinyl barstools, coats draped over a third, presumably for him. Lauren rested her head on Alexis' shoulder and was leaning into some serious head patting.

Oh Lord, how long had they been here?

Wading through the crowd of people enjoying drunken flirtations and some aggressive drowning of sorrows, Cash dropped onto the open stool.

"Hello, ladies. Did I miss the airing of grievances? I got a couple more rejection letters to throw on the pile."

"Cash! You're here." Lauren shot him a watery smile.

"She's almost done with the wallowing portion of the breakup." Alexis smiled tolerantly and sipped her red wine.

"Then I'm in time for the bitter mocking! Excellent. That's my favorite." Cash waved to Mickey, the bartender nearest, for a gin and tonic.

"I thought righteous anger was your favorite," Alexis teased.

"I have many favorites. Why should I limit myself?" He raised his glass in mock toast. "To Douchecanoe Devin, the Brocialite Ball-Ass-ter Bastard. Sure he's got plenty of Mommy's money to throw around, but he's clearly compensating." Cash wiggled his eyebrows and crooked his pinky finger at Lauren, trying to tease a smile to her plush rosy lips. "I really thought you'd have learned that lesson from Flaccid Phil sophomore year, but sometimes we need to make a mistake more than once."

"You're one to talk," Alexis muttered into her wine glass. Cash shot her a glare and kept razzing Lauren's ex.

"I've never met someone so self-centered. I'll be he slept with his phone so he'd never miss an alert. Did he Instagram while you guys made out?"

Lauren choked on her lemon drop with a laugh, and Cash

guessed he'd gotten close. He really hadn't liked this guy. She was better off without him.

"Where are we on Lauren's drunk-o-meter?" he asked Alexis.

The drunk-o-meter was a scale they'd developed in college. They each had their own benchmarks, but Lauren's was particularly reliable. Each drink moved her one rung higher on the ladder. She was usually content to hover between Buzzed Brittany (just loose enough for sexy dancing) and Tipsy Tina (still fun to dance with but slightly more balance challenged). Only once had she gone full Puking Patti and Black-out Betty. Luckily, he'd showed up late for that party and had gotten her home safely.

"I'd say she's working her way up to Love You Lucy. No sign of Evil Emily yet. She's had two lemon drops since we got here."

"I didn't have anything before, because I knew I was coming out with you two. I can always count on you guys. I love you so much." Tears welled up in Lauren's blue eyes, and Cash grinned.

"We love you too, Lucy," he teased.

"No, for real. Every fuck-up, every break-up, you guys have my back, and I just want you to know I appreciate it." She dropped her head on Cash's shoulder this time, and he resisted the urge to press a kiss to her hair. He fell back on his humor, trying to joke her out of her mood. He had a well-established role as the jokester of their trio, and he wouldn't let her down despite feeling a bit bruised himself.

"About that... If you could see your way to fewer breakups, my liver would thank you."

Lauren punched Cash in the arm, but she grinned while she did it, and his heart buzzed in his chest. Her smiles didn't used to make his anatomy do odd things, but lately that had changed and he didn't know how to handle it. So far ignoring his impulses was working, but how long could he keep that up? And what would happen if he slipped up?

"Give her a break. You've got to date a lot of losers before you find the winner. Who knows? He could be right in front of you. He could be in this very bar tonight!" Alexis teased and gestured wildly. Cash glared at her through his G&T glass.

Thanks to his own drunken ramblings one night, Alexis knew that he'd started having "more-than-friends" feelings for Lauren. That same night, Alexis had let it slip that she had a thing for the girl who worked at the Exchange with her. Now that Lex had come out and had been dating that girl Bree for nearly a year, her secret had lost its power. His had not.

For as long as he'd known Lauren, he'd liked her. Their little trio had formed during a freshman year critique group, had solidified over movie marathons at the campus theater, and had survived the transition to adulting and countless terrible karaoke nights.

They were inseparable. Lauren had dated guys pretty consistently throughout college, and it had never bothered him. They came and went, and their trio remained unfazed. But in the last year, he'd come to the troubling realization that he *like* liked her. And in a much more grown-up way than the third grade distinction implied. He had fallen for his best friend and was terrified.

Alexis was the calm voice of reason for the group, he was the joker, but Lauren was the dreamer, the optimist. When he'd drummed up the courage to share some of his writing during that critique class, she'd encouraged him to keep going. When he toyed with dropping his English degree to pursue business, she'd smacked him upside the head and told him not to waste his talent. He knew how rare it was to find that one person who believed in his dreams as much as he did, if not more so. He wasn't going to mess that up by kissing her. Even though he really wanted to kiss her.

"I'm taking a break from men. Clearly, I need some perspective if I was ready to move in with Devin. Why did I think that was a good idea? The fact that I'm more upset about my job than breaking up is a sign." She paused to take a sip of the fresh lemon drop Mickey had just set in front of her. "No more men. I'm going to focus on saving my career."

"Whoa, back up. You said, job drama. Why does your career need saving? I thought you were happy running the social media for the magazine, even though Wendy doesn't understand half of what you do." Cash toyed with the lime in his drink, trying to piece together the rest of the story that hadn't been in her texts.

"She really doesn't. I mean I took her from five hundred local followers to six figures worldwide on Insta alone! I am damn good at my job, but you know I want to write, too. Well, Wendy finally gave me a chance. I was supposed to photo document my Valentine's Date for the IG account, kind of a deep POV millennial take on love in the big city, and then do a full feature article to run on the fifteenth."

"That's great, babe!" Alexis raised her wine glass in a toast. Lauren raised her fresh lemon drop in response, spilling half of it out the side of the martini glass.

"Easy there, Sloppy Sarah." Cash muttered as he ineffectually wiped down the bar in front of her with a tiny square napkin before she could put her elbow in it.

"Crecks hun," Lauren slurred. "It *was* great. Fancy dinner, stroll through Millennium Park, The Healthy Hearts fundraiser ball at the Peninsula. I mapped it all out, made all the reservations, got it all approved."

"So? You can still go. All you have to do is post convincing pictures. Hell, half of Insta is photoshopped anyhow." Cash wanted to run a hand down her back to console her. But her shirt bared top half of her torso, and he was afraid that touching her skin, even innocently, would unlock a new level of hellish awareness he'd have to pretend to ignore. God, repressing all these feelings was exhausting.

"I made all the reservations in his name and sent him all the details. That bastard cancelled them all. I'm sure the table is gone, and he's going to use the tickets to the ball on *her*." Tears threatened again.

"I repeat, *that bastard*." Cash muttered.

"All men are bastards. You should switch teams. We'd love to have you," Alexis teased.

"Hey, easy there. The non-bastard man at the table thinks you shouldn't do anything hasty." Cash scanned the darkened sports bar, mulling over details of a plan coming together in his mind. The decor at Hubbard's wasn't winning any awards. Dark floors, slightly sticky green and white checkered vinyl tablecloths, and big screen TVs vying with beer signs for wall space, it was a classic Chicago dive bar. No one came for the ambiance. They came for the big games, the cheap booze, and the people. Narrowing his eyes on his target, he nodded to Alexis.

"I've got an idea. See if you can't get her up to Evil Emily while I'm gone. She's gonna need her courage." He turned to the bartender. "Hey, Mickey, can I get another G&T and a Macallan neat?"

The beauty of industry night at Mother Hubbard's wasn't just the discounted drinks. This was the place to make connections within the hospitality community and get shit done.

Need to take your girl out somewhere special for her birthday that you forgot about? Tap a hostess for help. Want to park downtown for Lolla? Make friends with a valet. Interested in the hot new bar? Odds were good that bartender was buying his drinks at Hubbard's. And Cash intended to tap that network tonight.

"Whuzzat you're planning?" Lauren asked, eyes watery and consonants shaky.

"Trust me," he teased.

"Always," she whispered soulfully, and he wished like hell he had the right to lean in and kiss her worries away.

With the fresh drinks in his hand, he made his way back to the pool tables where his quarry was racking a fresh game.

"Hey, D! What's up?" he greeted the tall skinny man currently chalking his pool cue who drank Scotch like water.

"Hey, Cash. You want in on a game? I'm taking quarters."

"Nah, I've got a Macallan with your name on it and a favor to ask."

"No, I can't get you an hourly rate. It's the motherfuckin' Peninsula, dude."

"Funny. Is there any way you could sneak me and a friend into the charity ball on V Day?"

"She a friend or *a friend*?" Dwayne took the whisky from Cash and winked.

This was it. She was single and in need of a hero. This was his moment to shine. "Depends on your answer to the question."

Dwayne took a sip and rolled it around his mouth, before breaking into a grin.

"Anything to get a brother laid."

"Knew I could count on you. I'll text you tomorrow."

He made his way back to his two best friends in the world, determined to change that status quo once and for all. If he wasn't too chicken-shit to go after what he wanted... *Dear God, don't let me blow this.*

"How we doing? Is she feeling brave yet? Because I've got a plan."

CASH KEPT HALF an eye on the door while he served his tables full of couples in various stages of love. He had the full gamut from newly dating and still awkward with it to married 50 years and content. It was Valentine's Day, the second busiest night of the year in the restaurant business, and he stood to quadruple his tips tonight. He only had to work the early seating, each table was a two-top and everything was prix fixe, so it was relatively easy to keep his attention split between his diners and the door. She was coming, and he couldn't wait.

As he reached down to clear a soup bowl, he glanced up at the door. There she was. He was damn lucky that the lobster bisque was irresistible, because the bowl was empty when his fingers went limp. He bobbled it before catching it. Stunning in a dark cranberry lace sheath, every curve he shouldn't notice highlighted, her skin seemed to glow through the dress. She took his breath away. How she could look at him and not see all of the needs that battered him?

But she hadn't. And honestly why would she? What did he have to attract her? An apartment he split with three smelly dudes? A dead-end job waiting tables while he waited for someone to want his writing? Piles of student debt? Yeah, it was no wonder she'd never looked in his direction.

Some days he thought about running away, leaving the city and all of its struggles behind, moving to the middle of nowhere to pursue his writing in peace. And then there were days like today, when he took one look at her and realized, even if they never became more than friends, there was nowhere in the world he'd rather be. He'd miss her smile, and her goofy laugh, and the way she always encouraged him to chase his dreams if he left. Hell, without her encouraging him, he knew those dreams would quickly wither and fade. And that wasn't a world he wanted to live in. He had to find his courage.

He handed the dirty dishes off to a back-waiter, and strode towards the hostess stand. This was his chance. She needed him, and he was going to prove himself worthy.

———

"RIGHT THIS WAY, MISS SYKES." Lauren looked up from where the hostess was checking her lists to see her best friend striding towards her. Cash put a hand to her elbow and led her away quickly. Under his breath, he added, "You don't have a reservation."

"What?" Lauren hissed. "I thought you said you could get us into your restaurant today."

"I said I could get *you* in and in you are. Looking stunning, by the way."

"I sense a *but* coming." Lauren crossed her arms in front of her, and Cash tripped over the carpet. He wasn't usually clumsy, but he seemed a bit flustered. Had her favor put him in a bad spot?

"*But* we've been booked solid for weeks, so you can sit at an empty table and take your photos until the 5:30 reservations show up."

"What about dinner?"

"Don't worry. I'll feed you."

Lauren took a deep breath. Cash was right. All she really needed was the picture, and he was doing her a huge favor. True, she'd been imagining how their *date* might go down since he'd suggested it. They'd hung out one-on-one more often since Alexis and Bree had gotten serious, but this dinner would have been a first.

Tamping down her disappointment, she smiled. As she'd hoped, his own smile rose in answer. She loved making him smile. His bright white teeth contrasted against his brown skin, and his whole face glowed with it. His smile went all the way up to his eyes, making them crinkle in the corners. And when he really got going, a dimple came out to play. There was just something about a guy and a dimple that got to her.

Wait, this was Cash. She shouldn't be thinking about her best friend's dimple. All of that date talk must've gone to her head.

Pictures. The favor. Focus, Sykes. Eyes on the prize.

"Lead the way."

Cash took her into the back dining room, all dark paneling and dim lighting. Every table had a bud vase with two red roses. She didn't want to think about how expensive that was to pull off on Valentine's Day. Then she looked at the price on the prix fixe menu and ceased worrying about the owner's bottom line. The restaurant was going to do just fine tonight, and hopefully some of that would trickle down to Cash.

More than half of the tables were already occupied by couples making mooney eyes at each other over their wine and first courses. Cash seated her at the corner table, which gave her a great view of the room and excellent lighting.

"You've got about fifteen minutes before the couple for this table arrives."

"Got it," she replied to thin air. Cash was already hustling into the kitchen, likely to deliver more courses to his tables. That boy was always hustling. It was a shame that he couldn't catch a break. His essays and poems were so damn good. She'd been in awe of his voice since that first class together, and she couldn't understand why he was still unpublished. He'd been submitting to different publications since they'd graduated, trying to build a reputation while he worked on his first book. All while waiting tables full time and being an excellent friend. She'd never met anyone who could match his work ethic. Except maybe herself.

Lauren pulled out her phone and got to work snapping pictures. She'd edit them later. The whole room, soft focus, *click*. The three-course prix fixe menu, excluding the prix, *click*. The classically-elegant table setting with white china, polished silver, and the splash of a red rose against the white linens, *click*. Classic Valentine's Day.

The shots were good—would be better once filtered—but they weren't quite right. Something was missing. Or someone. As

Cash bustled back through the room, arms loaded with soups and salads, she caught his eye and beckoned with her head. He nodded and carried on.

Floating from table to table with athletic grace and a brilliant smile, he delivered his plates without interrupting the romantic cooing going on between each couple. She marveled at the way his shoulders shifted, straining against his shirt while he kept everything balanced. The tendons in his hands flexed and released with ease. Had she ever noticed the strength in those creative hands before?

She shook herself. The romance was so thick in the air that it was going straight to her head. That had to be it. How could she be ogling her friend just after breaking up with another guy? She was on a break!

It was definitely Valentine's Day's fault. She couldn't say she was overly surprised that things with Devin had ended, but the timing really sucked. Cash wove his way back to her table, and she gestured to the other chair.

"Sit down a minute."

His eyes bulged wide. "You're crazy. I'm working, Lauren."

"I know but I need a date, and a glass of wine wouldn't hurt either. These shots of an empty chair feel too... lonely."

"You want... Okay. Jesus, okay. Give me five."

He ran a hand over his tightly cropped curls and down his fade to pinch his neck as he whirled away again, and she couldn't help but admire how good he looked in those black pants as he rejoined the ballet of servers tending tables full of couples in love. He could've been a dancer. She'd seen his moves. But his poet's soul spoke louder than his fancy feet. She knew that he had a few new things out on submission, but the rejections seemed to be hitting him harder lately. He was frustrated with the path to publication and the day job he had to rely on. She just hoped he didn't give up before his big break came. And she knew it was coming. He was too good to fail.

True to his word, within five minutes he was back with a glass of red wine. He sat in the chair across from her and let out a deep sigh.

"God, my feet are killing me. What do you need me to do?"

Lauren was already framing and snapping her photos, male torso now nicely filling the negative space. It made all the difference.

"Hold my hand," she said without looking up from her phone.

"What?"

"Across the table. Just hold my hand."

He stretched his right hand across the table, and she gripped it lightly with her left, almost missing the gentle caress of his fingers across her knuckles as she framed the shot with the phone in her right hand. Almost. She certainly didn't miss the resulting tingles that raced up her arm. That was new and...interesting.

"What exactly is going on here?"

That's what she'd like to know as well, her eyes jerking away from Cash's towards a very tall man in a full suit standing next to their table, who was glaring at her date. Cash stumbled to his feet. Oh shit. This was the manager. What was his name? Mr....Marinetti. Her brain supplied the name Cash had often ranted about just in time.

"You must be Mr. Marinetti. I'm Lauren Sykes with The Windy Wendy. Maybe you've heard of us?" She stood and pumped his hand in a firm handshake. "I'm doing a feature on the best places to fall in love in the Windy City, and I'd love to include Le Petit Mort on the list." She watched his face smooth into what she recognized as a service mask. No one would know he'd been seconds from losing his temper with an employee. The man was a pro.

Lauren pushed forward with her pitch now that she had his attention. "I know it's a busy night, but I convinced your server to let me take a few photos before he bothered you. If you have a few minutes, I'd love to ask you a few questions." She linked her hand through his elbow, still chattering away. "I know the couple for this table is on the way. Maybe we could move to the bar?" She waved her hand at Cash behind her, but she needn't have bothered. He'd already cleared her wine glass and was gone.

"Of course. I can answer any questions you might have. Perhaps you'd like to take some photos of our featured Valentine's Day cocktails?"

"That sounds divine. So Le Petit Mort, is the food really orgasmic?"

"Our goal is certainly to leave you breathless with appreciation."

Lauren followed Mr. Marinetti to the bar, where she dutifully asked and recorded random-ass questions about Valentine's Day in the restaurant industry and snapped pictures of each special pink cocktail the bartender made for her. She did get some great pictures, and by the end of the interview she knew exactly how much had been spent on those roses, which were a gift to the diners. She was also on her way to Tipsy Tina after sampling the fun drinks by the time Cash came back to check on her.

"Sorry to interrupt, but Tish said there was a problem with the menus printed for the second seating."

"Don't let me keep you." Lauren stood and reached for his hand and was pretty sure she didn't wobble in her high heels. "Thank you so much for your help tonight."

Once he'd made it to the front of the restaurant, Lauren let out a short laugh. "Oh God, you came back just in time. I've got to get some food in my stomach, or I won't be able to feel my knees soon."

"I've got you covered. Follow me." Cash took off towards the back of the restaurant, and Lauren was oddly disappointed that he didn't take her hand. She could still feel the way he'd caressed her knuckles, the warmth of his hand transferring to hers. His hands were always warm.

As they passed the restrooms, she gave in to her curiosity and reached for his hand again. The tingles were stronger this time, heat racing up her arm and making her heart beat faster. Or was that just a side effect of the alcohol hitting her blood stream? Either way, she wasn't letting go.

He pulled her through the door labeled "Staff Only" and into a chilly service hallway for the building. White cinder block walls met with a dingy gray linoleum floor covered in scrapes and stains from years of deliveries coming in and garbage going out. Bags of dirty linens waited for pickup, and a stack of milk crates sat in the corner behind the door.

"Welcome to The Break Room, a.k.a. Smokers' Alley." He gestured to the Emergency Exit door. "It's not alarmed so everyone sneaks smoke breaks back here." He stacked two milk crates and covered the mini throne with a napkin pulled from his pocket with a flourish. "Milady..." he bowed and Lauren sat regally before breaking into tipsy laughter. This was so not how she'd pictured her Valentine's Day. "I'll be right back."

He disappeared down the hallway at a sprint, and once again Lauren appreciated just how much he was juggling for her tonight. He really was an excellent friend. He'd never once let her down. Before she had time to miss him, he was back with a steaming plate of food.

"On prix fixe nights, we always plate extras just in case. The staff usually gets them as leftovers. You can have mine." He handed her a fork and a plate with seared sliced hangar steak artfully arranged over garlic mashed potatoes, a crab cake, and crispy fried asparagus. Her mouth watered. Cash checked his watch.

"I've got another hour before I'm off. You're welcome to hang out here, or duck out the back if you need to. I'll text you when I get off, and we can head over to the benefit."

She grabbed his hand one more time before he could run off, running her fingers over his knuckles this time. Could he feel it too, this static energy waiting to snap?

"Thank you so much for everything tonight. You totally saved my ass." Was it her imagination or had his eyes flickered down to that particular part of her anatomy? "I still can't believe you managed to get us into the ball."

"You know I'd do anything for you, Lauren." When he met her gaze head on, the look in his eyes was different somehow. She let go of his hand to reach for her phone, intent on capturing his new expression to dissect later. But by the time she raised it, he'd hidden that raw expression behind a silly grin. Typical.

"You're the best friend ever, you know that?"

His goofy expression fell, and he backed away toward the kitchen.

"Yeah. I've heard that. Listen, I'll catch you later, okay?" And then he was gone, back into the fray.

Lauren ate her meal, and pondered what she'd said to make his face fall. As she sat on milk crates in a couture gown, she snapped some selfies of her meal and the ambiance that made her grin before tucking into the delicious food. Each bite was tastier than the last, and once the fear of Sloppy Sarah had passed, she got to work.

She scrolled, filtered, captioned, and tagged her favorites shots from the restaurant with #WindyCityValentine2019 and #LoveItOrLeaveIt. She waited for the comments to start pouring in. Eating in a drafty dirty hallway that smelled like old cigarettes was a far cry from the five star treatment she'd planned with

Devin, but she could honestly say that she was quite happy with how things were working out. She had true friends she could count out. What more could a girl want? Sure, an orgasm or three on the most romantic night of the year wouldn't go amiss, but she wasn't going to split hairs.

The phone in her hand buzzed as Wendy texted her a thumbs up.

W: Photos look great! Glad to see you worked it out. Can't wait to read your feature.

Reminded that she wasn't done with her job, Lauren sat her plate on the milk crates and pulled her thoughts back from her personal struggles. She buttoned up her coat, covering her formal gown and headed off to her next photo spot. She couldn't afford to get distracted now.

——————

MILLENNIUM PARK SPARKLED as a fresh dusting of snow fell and covered the grey, grimy mounds of snowplowed ice left over from the last big storm. The city lights twinkling through the crisp cold air as dancing snowflakes swirled past, *click*. Couples bundled up in layers of scarves, hats, gloves, and each other, *click*. A pair of Chicago cops on horseback patrolling the park, their horses nickering with their noses close enough to kiss, *click*. So far, so good for the "romantic stroll through the park" segment.

When she'd pitched the story, she had imagined this would be where Devin asked her to move in with him. They'd been seeing each other exclusively for six months. Now she had to wonder how exclusive he'd been if he could drop her for an actress over night.

Thank God she'd realized that he was an asshole before she'd given up her lease. Her little one bedroom apartment might not be much, but it was hers. Being able to afford her own place had been a big deal to her, a real step towards independence. And she'd almost screwed it up. Shaken by her near miss, she resolved to be more discerning with her next boyfriend. She'd serial dated for years, hating to be single, and where had it gotten her? Alone and drifting on Valentine's Day. So she'd step back and take a break.

At least her work instincts had been spot-on. Winter at the oasis in the heart of the city was picture-perfect and full of lovers. She cued up her digital release form and began approaching couples, formulating a piece on the face of love on the spot. Old, young, gay, straight, every ethnicity that called Chicago home... She could see it becoming a visual testament to the diversity of the city she loved.

As she wandered, capturing small gestures of love with her camera phone, she felt her own loneliness more keenly. Even when she'd been with Devin, she couldn't say she'd felt the connection, the love she saw on the faces around her. Had she really been so caught up in the flashy lifestyle that his money had allowed her to experience that she'd completely missed his lack of substance? She hated to think that she'd been that shallow, but the evidence was staring her in the face.

Lesson learned. She'd pick substance over style next time. Bonus points for finding a guy with both.

She switched her camera to video as she approached the Bean, hoping to get a good clip of lovers strolling. Maybe she could do some graphics or voice overs, put together a little piece. Video was good on social media.

Formally known as Cloud Gate, the Bean was a mirrored landmark in the shape of a kidney bean and was a favored backdrop for Chicago skyline photos. As she got closer, a young man and woman strolling arm-in-arm, pulled to a stop at the center of the platform. Lauren watched on her screen as the man dropped to one knee and pulled a small black box from the pocket of his black peacoat.

Oh. Oh, how sweet. She was too far away to hear what they said, but the way his girlfriend was nodding frantically and tugging at her scarf was clear enough. In the heart of this bustling metropolis, he was offering his into her keeping. From the way the girlfriend pulled him off his knees into an exuberant kiss from her now bared lips, Lauren judged the feeling was mutual.

Her own heart squeezed in her chest. That's what she wanted. Suddenly, she felt every gust of wind coming in off the lake, the wet wind chilling her to the bone. The couple tugged off gloves so he could put the ring on her finger to the applause of the strangers surrounding them. Lauren snapped a few stills and approached them as they laughed and waved to the crowd.

She showed them the video and offered to email it to them. She made a mental note to reach out to them for a follow up, another feature brewing in her mind. She had trouble turning off her ambition. Story ideas constantly bombarded her brain. Tonight, however, they weren't quite enough to distract her from the reality that in a city full of lovers, she was flying solo.

She wished the couple well, promising to be in touch, as she headed for the Park Grill, desperate for some hot coffee to sober her up and save her from her maudlin thoughts. She'd forgotten that it was right next to the skating rink. She dutifully snapped more pictures of couples in love doing cute things. When she'd pitched this assignment, she hadn't realized the torture it would be. Warming her hands on her cup of coffee, she found herself wishing for a warm pair of hands to heat them with instead. God, she wished Cash had been able to come with her. Her resolve was fading fast. It wasn't even seven o'clock, and she was already dreaming of being home in her jammies wrapped up in bed with a "good cry" romance. Cash would have cracked a joke and made her laugh at herself or at the lovebirds awkwardly trying not to fall on their asses on the ice. Or maybe he'd just have held her hand again. When had she started craving that?

She fished her phone back out of her pocket and called Alexis.

"Hey, how's the plan going?" Alexis asked.

"Lovers in love and the other's run away. It's great, and crushing my soul at the same time. Why did we think this was a good idea?" Lauren watched as a woman in a knee length body-con dress stumbled past on rented skates, clearly wondering the same thing.

"Because you wanted to save your feature and Cash is brilliant?"

"Right. Saving my job. I don't get why I feel so upset. I mean I'm well rid of Devin, and I know that. So why do I feel like I'm missing him right now?"

"Have you ever spent a Valentine's Day alone?" Alexis said something to someone in the room with her, and Lauren felt like a heel. For the first time in a long time, her best friend was NOT alone on Valentine's Day, and here she was interrupting.

"Not since high school."

"Well, there's your answer. You don't miss him. You miss the idea of him. But don't despair. Cash is almost off work, isn't he?"

"Are you suggesting that I treat my best friend as a stand-in for a boyfriend just to pacify my insecurities?" That sounded terrible even to her ears, but Alexis's extended pause left her room to think.

"You could do a lot worse than Cash. In fact, you have. Why not give him a chance and see how it goes?"

"What? What are you saying?" The idea of Cash as her boyfriend burrowed into her brain, tunneling through his firmly established *friend* identity, and breaking it apart with potential. "Why would I mess with a friendship that means the world to me?"

"You're right. Why on earth would you want to date a guy who knows you inside and out and still likes you? I don't know what I was thinking." The sarcasm broke thickly through the phone. "Listen, Bree and I are gonna be late for our movie. You'll be just fine. Just stick to the plan."

"Yeah, okay. Have fun tonight. Love you."

"Love you, too, babe."

She couldn't say she felt better after the phone call, but she sure as hell wasn't thinking about all of the couples in love surrounding her anymore.

Cash? As a boyfriend? The more she thought about it, the more she couldn't stop thinking about it. Why hadn't they in all the years they'd been together? Sure, there had been moments where she'd wondered, but she'd never gotten that vibe from him. Had she missed it? Should they? Could they? And what if it all fell apart? She didn't know what to make of all the deep thoughts ricocheting around her skull, but she sure wasn't miserable anymore. Mission accomplished.

———

FINALLY OFF SHIFT, pocket flush with tips, Cassius ducked into the now empty back hallway. He picked up Lauren's plate in one hand and his phone in the other, texting her to see where she was. He grinned again as he slid her plate into a dirty tray, thinking of the cover story she'd spun to cover his ass. Quick thinking.

Sure, he'd gotten chewed out by Mr. Marinetti for not clearing it with him first, but at least he'd kept his job. And he needed to keep this job. Waiting tables wasn't a job he wanted to turn into a career, but he had bills to pay and student loans to cover. He didn't mind it, and it was decent money. Plus the hours spent on the el or the bus gave him time to think, time to write. Now, if he could just get someone to buy his writing...

It was hard seeing people he graduated with getting jobs, getting married, moving on with their lives. He was stuck in the college lifestyle. Same job, same roommates, same friends. He was ready to move on, too. He needed something new.

His phone buzzed in his hand, and he grinned at Lauren's selfie with her coffee in front of the igloos by the skating rink. Lauren was another part of his life where he was tired of feeling stuck. She was one of his best friends, and he wouldn't change that for the world. He could admit, if only to himself and apparently Alexis, that he wanted more than that from her, but he was terrified to lose the one voice that had always believed in him. There were days that her support was the only thing that sustained him. She was the voice in his head when doubt reared its ugly head.

He'd gone back and forth in his head over what he should do. If he made things awkward by asking her out, well, that would suck. He also didn't think he could stick around and watch her date another asshole, either. He needed to move forward or move on. Holding himself in limbo for the last year had been exhausting. No longer. Tonight was a sign. She was alone and in need of a knight in shining armor. He was going to be that and more. And if it all fell apart, well, he'd have his answer and be free to go.

Suitably buoyed, he pulled on the tux jacket he'd borrowed from the catering manager over his white server shirt, and straightened the black bow tie from his uniform. Show time. Grabbing his puffy coat, he stepped out of the restaurant and hailed a cab for the park. He had a date with destiny.

———

AS THE TAXI pulled away from the curb by the park, Cash's

nerves came flooding back. Picking up Lauren had been easy. But the moment she sat down in the cab, she spaced out with her phone. His own phone was buzzing in his pocket since he'd set follow alerts for her accounts. He knew she was working. That was the whole point of this stupid evening, but it was seriously shaking his resolve.

His heart was invested in this date, but she was all business. The cab wove aggressively through Michigan Avenue traffic, and she didn't even flinch. He didn't stand a chance in hell at winning her attention.

"How are the photos from earlier doing?" he asked, determined to meet her where she was.

"Picking up steam. Wendy gave them the thumbs up."

"So what shots do we need once we get inside?" Cash waited to see how she'd react to his use of "we." God, he wished he could turn off his sensitivity to words for even a minute.

"We need décor, ambiance, the organizer, maybe some action shots. I won't know for sure until I see the layout and lighting, but we want to promote an atmosphere that balances romance and philanthropy." She hadn't looked up from her phone, but she'd used his "we" in return. He'd take it.

He took out his own phone and texted his buddy at the Peninsula that they were almost there and sighed. Not the most reassuring start, but once they were inside he'd find his opening. He patted his coat pocket, feeling the reassuring weight. Yes, he was ready. He was not throwing away his shot.

The taxi stopped in front of the hotel, and the doorman opened Lauren's door, extending a hand to help her out of the car. When she followed the doorman towards the front door, Cash had to stop her. "Wait. We're heading this way." He avoided the doorman's gaze and took her hand, leading her up the block.

"But the benefit is…"

"I know. But they are checking tickets at that door to the ball-room. My buddy, Dwayne, is going to let us in through the service entrance. We just need to cut through the mall." The concierge was a man of his word, and had texted Cash directions to let them in through the warren of hidden passages that were concealed behind the walls of the hotel.

As they passed Tiffany & Co. on the corner, Lauren's steps slowed, her gaze caught on the sparkling diamonds that the employees were removing from the window displays for the night.

"Someday," she sighed, and Cash's insecurities doubled. She had expensive taste. Even if his writing did take off, he'd never be Tiffany's rich. If that's what she was hoping for, he wasn't going to be the guy to give it to her. That pinched his pride. Maybe this risking-her-friendship-for-more plan wasn't such a great idea.

"Isn't that pretty?" she asked, pointing to a glittering heart pendant.

"It sure is, but it can't compete with the sparkle in your eyes."

At least his words hadn't deserted him. She laughed and squeezed his hand tighter, a speculative glint in her eye. What did that mean?

"You sweet-talker, you."

She followed him without further comment into the mall and down a side corridor. Cash knocked three times on a gray door and smiled when it opened to reveal Dwayne.

"Come on. My break's almost up."

Lauren leaned up to whisper in Cash's ear. "You're my hero. You know that, right?"

Her hero. He liked the sound of that. Confidence restored, he vowed to hold on to his courage like a real hero. No matter how the night went down, it would be worth having that memory engraved on his brain.

———

LAUREN SHED HER COAT, phone in hand, and tucked it behind a service table with Cash's in the grand ballroom since they'd had to skip the coat check. The massive space was filled with Chicago's movers and shakers, the crystal chandeliers overhead creating just enough shadow for business as usual to continue unimpeded. The alcohol and gossip flowed freely, and Lauren did her best to get her pictures as inconspicuously as possible. The low lighting guaranteed that most of them would be blurry without a flash but hopefully a few would be usable. Otherwise she'd just filter the hell out of them.

Cash stepped up behind her with two gin and tonics. When he offered her one, she declined. "I should probably stick to wine. I've already had a few tonight."

Tossing back her drink in a few gulps, he grinned and then casually sipped his own. "No worries. More for me." She had to grin. He was such a goof sometimes.

"Come on. Let's dance." She took his hand in hers, getting more comfortable with her reaction to his touch, and led him through the tables. Alexis's suggestion was like a burr on her brain. She couldn't stop picking at it. He paused on the edge of the dance floor, drained the last half of his drink, and dropped it on an empty table, before tugging her hand back and spinning her into his arms with a grin.

"Anything you want."

Lauren gripped her phone as he spun her back out, and raised it to capture one of those action shots she wanted. Instead of a silly mugging grin, she caught his sincerity instead. What did she want? She'd always been able to trust him with her thoughts and plans. Could she trust him with her heart and body as well? It was a tempting thought.

Tucking her phone into her bra, she let him lead her onto the dance floor. The strains of *Today Was A Fairytale* faded, and a slower song with a deep funky bass and a steady drumbeat took its place.

"Seriously?" Lauren placed her hand on Cash's shoulder with a smirk. "Let's Get It On?"

He just grinned and pulled her further onto the floor.

"You can swing right?" he teased. He knew damn well she could swing, as she'd dragged him along to the beginner's class at the coffee shop in college, so her nod was a formality. "This is a song for steppin'. It's similar but not. Just follow my lead."

Holding her frame, she realized that he was one of few people in the world she trusted with her lead. As Marvin crooned about there being nothing wrong with love, Cash led her into a slow and sensual two-step. She couldn't help but let her hips sway into the rhythm. He pushed her out into a spin and back in close, teasing her with his hips bumping against hers, before putting an arm's length distance between them again.

When he moved his hand to her lower back to lead her into a turn, she felt the heat blaze through her, setting her on fire. Each casual touch ignited more flames until she was burning with a desperate desire. For Cash. For her friend. She tried to cling to the safety of that word, but all hope incinerated in the blaze his eyes lit as he watched her hips sway between his hands.

She'd never found her rhythm like this before, giving herself over completely to the music and the strength in his lead. He clearly knew what he was doing, and she was able to let herself go and just enjoy the dance. He was tempting her to let go and enjoy a whole hell of a lot more.

She stared into his dark eyes, mesmerized, as she shimmied closer to him. She didn't know what was happening between them. He'd always just been a solid friend. Where had all this attraction been hiding? The song ended far too quickly, with the DJ deciding to segue into *I Say A Little Prayer*. The spell between them was broken as the dance floor flooded with people eager to bop along to the drag classic.

Pulled from her haze, Lauren tried to remember why they were there. Pictures. Job. Ex-boyfriend. She turned to survey the dance floor, looking for Devin, who she still hadn't seen, deliberately breaking eye contact with Cash. What had just happened? She couldn't begin to process the bubbling energy she'd felt coursing through her. Overwhelmed by her own reaction, she backed off.

Cash stepped back, dropping her hand, his friendly face carefully devoid of any of the heat he'd just been pumping off.

"You must be thirsty. I'll get you some champagne."

"Thanks, Cash. You're the best." She smiled shyly at him, still trying to put away the feelings he'd pulled from her on the dance floor and fumbling with them. He turned to go, leaving her awash in her emotions and drifting.

With a deep breath, she fished her phone out of her bodice and tried to find her balance. She took refuge in her work, documenting the fundraiser for heart disease research.

Rose gold and white décor, *click*. Artistic shot of a passing tray of appetizers, *click*. Appetizer, *chomp*. Couples enjoying the dance floor, *click*.

She scanned the room for any sign of her brocialite ex-boyfriend. God, Cash had been dead on with that one. She didn't see Devin, but the actress he'd ditched her for, Monica Delancey, was currently swaying in the arms of the mayor. Her stomach flipped. If *she* was here, *he* was here. Maybe he wouldn't see her. Maybe she wouldn't have to speak to him. She'd be professional, do her job, and keep her cool. Then she and Cash could leave and explore the strange sparks between them more privately.

She just needed to find the woman who had organized the event. Lauren believed in showcasing women in the city who did amazing things, and she'd love to get a picture of Mrs. Robyn

Carver in front of the silent auction she'd arranged to raise money for heart disease research after her husband's sudden and catastrophic heart attack the summer before.

She scanned the crowd again, looking for the woman she only knew by thumbnail image.

"Looking for me, sweetheart?"

Fuck it all straight to Gary. Of course, Devin would find her first.

"First of all, I'm not your sweetheart. Secondly, no. I was looking for Mrs. Carver."

"Do I want to know how you got in? Pretty sure I didn't leave a ticket for you."

"That's right. You didn't. You decided that some pretty actress was more important than your girlfriend. Where is she, by the way? Last time I saw her, the mayor had his hand on her ass. Mrs. Mayor didn't look too happy about it."

Devin shrugged. "We got the red carpet pictures we needed. It was all about the publicity anyhow. I tried to explain that to you. I thought you'd understand." He gestured towards her phone with his whiskey sour, sloshing the icy liquid over the edge. She stepped back to avoid getting her dress stained. He followed, seeming to enjoy her retreat. Something sickening clicked into place in her mind. Before she could think better of it, the ugly words came spilling out of her mouth.

"Is that why you dated me? Publicity? A quick fame fix anytime you wanted it just by taking me out somewhere fancy and me posting it for the magazine?"

"Of course not." Devin sipped his drink, and she let out the breath she'd been holding, but then he kept talking. "That's why I asked you out. But I dated you because you're great in bed. So fucking eager."

He leered at her, his eyes raking over the dress she'd thought to wear for him, and Lauren felt the gorge rise up in her throat.

"Well, that's frank. Nice to know you valued me for my body *and* my social media access."

"I wouldn't want you to overlook your strengths. Your posts for the Windy Wendy really helped. Mom showed Monica pictures from our dates when she was pitching this date idea. The foundation is a major supporter of this charity, and a little star power never hurt anyone."

"It hurt me, asshole, but not nearly as much as it should have. Thanks for opening my eyes before I did something stupid."

Lauren wanted to vomit, but she couldn't afford to lose the cleaning deposit on the stupid designer dress she'd rented from the runway back when she'd thought she would be on his arm for the red carpet. How *had* she been so stupid? She knew. She'd been flattered by his attention, blinded to his faults by all the shiny new experiences he'd treated her to. Now, she could only be grateful that he'd shown his true colors before she'd let her heart get too involved.

Monica stepped up and slipped her arm through the triangle of space at his elbow, clearly marking her territory.

"Who's this, Devin? A friend of yours?"

Lauren jumped in with an answer before he could, not trusting what he might say.

"No, I'm a reporter for The Windy Wendy, a millennial women's lifestyle magazine here in Chicago. Do you mind a quick picture?"

"Of course not. Just use your flash. The lighting in here is dismal." She and Devin both tilted their heads at odd angles and fake smiled straight at her, two beautiful people presenting a perfectly false facade to the public. Lauren knew just what to do with the photo. A little revenge Photoshop never hurt anyone.

Monica's expression changed from professional smile to sultry smirk at the same time that Lauren felt an arm slide across the small of her back.

"And who are you?" Monica stepped forward, hand extended. Cash just gestured with his hands full and stepped closer to Lauren's side. Smart man. He'd always been good at reading people.

"I'm Lauren's date, Cash. Nice to meet you. Here you go, babe." Lauren turned to look up and found herself falling into Cash's deep brown eyes, so grateful for his timing, so intrigued by the intensity of his gaze, that she didn't pull away when he dropped a kiss on her lips. Warmth flooded through her, drawing a straight line from her mouth, south. The flute of champagne pressed into her limp fingers, and she barely managed not to drop it. Where the hell had that kiss come from? More importantly, where had her reaction to that kiss been hiding? She squeezed her thighs together, both for balance and to hold on to the sensation a bit longer.

Instead of being worried about the situation brewing in front of her, all of her attention was pulled to her warm tingling lips and weakening knees. He'd reawakened all of those tumultuous feelings from the dance floor. The ones she'd only barely managed to contain. Her first impulse was to lean back in and explore Cash's full lush mouth in further detail, but out of the corner of her eye she saw Devin step forward, face red and spluttering.

"What? What the fuck is this?"

Reluctantly, Lauren turned away from Cash, not wanting to lose the moment but also not wanting company for the fascinating conversation about hidden desires she felt sure they were about to have. Just as soon as she got rid of Devin.

"What's wrong, Devin? Like you said, we both got the pictures we were looking for."

"You little slut. How dare you cheat on me? And with him? A Michael B. Jordan wanna-be, with his too-tight tux, and are those gym shoes? What's wrong? You couldn't find a real man so you dragged your poor little "friend" in to punk me?"

Cash took a step towards Devin, who wisely flinched back, but Lauren stopped his forward momentum with a hand to Cash's chest. She could feel his heart beating wildly under her fingertips. As much as she appreciated his anger, she'd just as soon fight her own battles.

"Don't you dare talk about my friend that way."

She grabbed Devin's elbow and dragged him away from Cash and Monica. This was her chance to say all of the things she'd been bottling up since she'd been ambushed at work. She wanted his undivided attention.

"Listen, asshole. I'm a writer, and pretty good with my words. A slut is someone who has low morals or a sexually promiscuous nature. If either of us fits that description, it's you. I never cheated on you, not once, but after this little actress stunt, I seriously doubt you can say the same. Luckily, I have good friends who can back me up in a crisis, like being dumped the day before Valentine's Day for a chance to fuck a starlet."

"So he is just a friend. I knew it."

That statement rang false in her ears. Cash was so much more than *just a friend.* She was only just beginning to realize how much more he had the potential to be. But no way was she giving this jackass more fodder for his ugliness.

"He's a friend who has more honor, more talent, and more compassion in his little finger than you will ever have. I choose him over you any day. We are so done."

"You'll be back. I can give you what a "friend" can't." He stepped forward to touch her face, brushing her hair back, and she recoiled. "He sure can't give you the O's like me. You know we're good together, baby."

"Oh, that's cute. You thought those were real? You're crazy if you think your performance was enough to tempt me. I will never come back for more of your bullshit."

"You bitch," he spat at her. He lashed out when threatened, and still assumed he'd get his way. What a winner. Lauren was just about out of patience.

"You lost the right to judge me when you... Oh, wait. That's right. You've never had that right. I'm so over this. Good-bye, Devin."

"Don't you walk away from me."

He grabbed her arm, and she yanked it back with a growl, tossing her full glass of champagne in his face in the process. Turning on her heel, she stalked off.

It would go down in her personal history book as her best exit ever. Only two things marred her triumph: now she was out of champagne, and Cash had disappeared. All she wanted to do was get out of here and spend the rest of the night hanging out with her best friend, and she had no idea where he'd gone.

———

CASH STALKED to the el and caught the Red Line north, his head spinning from three strong drinks on an empty stomach and Lauren's reaction. He was desperate to get home, even if home was a two-bedroom apartment in Wrigleyville that he shared with three other guys. It was away, and that was what he needed.

He breathed in the filthy air of the subway and shivered on the platform, trying not to lose it. He'd left in such a rush that he'd forgotten to grab his coat, but he hadn't been able to stomach watching her talk to that asshole one more minute. Hell, his gut was still flipping over it.

It was bad enough that after their dance together, a dance he'd poured all of his longing into, she'd immediately looked for *him.* She hadn't even let Cash stand up for himself when Devin had looked down his smug nose at him.

True, the last thing this complete failure of a Valentine's Day needed was an assault charge, but still, a man had his pride. Cash could respect that she wanted to confront Devin herself, but the impotence he'd felt was choking him. Punching out that asshat would have been worth it. At least he'd have gotten some of his frustration out instead of bottling it all up inside.

And then, on top of it all, he'd had to listen while she defended him as her friend. It had been the straw that broke him. After everything he'd done, he was still just her friend. Rage, some for Devin, some for Lauren, some for himself, pressed at the inside of his skull, throbbing until he dropped into a chair on the train and clutched his head. It was too much. He was going to do or say something he'd regret. He needed some space.

He'd watched her bounce from boyfriend to boyfriend for six years now. Some of them had been jerks and hadn't lasted long. Some had been tolerable and had hung around longer. None of them had deserved her.

This Devin fool had been the worst, because on paper he looked perfect, which meant he'd lasted longer than Cash's bull-shit meter would have predicted. But he'd held his tongue, because Lauren was an adult and capable of picking her own partners. Through it all, he'd stood by her side with a joke or a hug at the ready, a true friend.

Now, when he wished she'd pick him, everything felt differ-ent. He didn't know if he could cheer her up with a smile and a laugh when his own heart was breaking. He'd given it his best shot tonight, but apparently it hadn't been enough.

And he didn't think he could stick around while she searched for a new stranger to give her the love she deserved, the love he desperately wanted to give her, the love she didn't want from him. Before, he'd managed, because he'd had hope. Without it, years of misery stretched in front of him.

He let his mind toy with the fantasy of leaving. He had friends in Nashville, L.A., Seattle...he could couch-hop for a while until he found his feet. He could wait tables anywhere while giving his heart and his muse some room to breathe.

Right now, he needed to give his rage and defeat a path out of his head. He reached for his ever-present journal to spill his ugly thoughts onto a blank white page, trapping them and making them stand still long enough to be dissected. But as he patted his pockets, panic simply joined anger and regret for the pity party. His journal wasn't here on a Red Line train hurtling towards his cramped, crowded apartment. It was in the pocket of a puffy coat he'd abandoned in a fancy hotel along with his hopes and dreams for love.

Damn.

He stared out the window as the city at night flashed past, and mourned his losses. Could this day get any worse?

His phone vibrated in his pants pocket. At least he still had that on him. He pulled it out to find a message from Lauren.

Lauren: We need to talk. GN. Half an hour.

A second text quickly followed with a picture of his coat and journal in her hands.

Well that answered that. It could indeed get worse. It looked like he wasn't quite done being tortured for the night.

He hopped off the train and instead of heading east for his apartment and oblivion, he turned west for the cold trek to the Golden Nugget.

———

LAUREN, having sprung for a cab, made it to the Golden Nugget before Cash. Open 24 hours, it had been their end-of-the-night, carb-loading and caffeine-bingeing hangout.

Sliding into the golden vinyl covered booth, she sighed. She missed those easy days, laughing and studying together, just the three of them. Lauren, Alexis, and Cash. They'd been inseparable at Loyola. College had seemed like such a struggle back then, but it felt like a cakewalk compared to this adulting bullshit.

How had everything gotten so complicated?

She toyed with the worn edges of the leather-bound journal in front of her. She'd given it to Cash as a graduation present. He'd clearly been putting it to good use; the pages were wrinkled and worn. She felt a bit of pride that he'd valued her gift, and that he hadn't given up on his writing. She was mighty tempted to peek inside and read what he was working on, but she wouldn't.

Cash had always been very particular about what he'd share and what he kept private. She wouldn't break his trust like that.

When he stumbled through the door, half frozen, she rose from the booth to greet him, but he just dropped heavily onto the bench across from her. No hug of greeting. Not even a hello.

Just bleary eyes focused intently on the journal she now clutched to her chest. He pulled her coffee across the table and drank deeply before he asked, "Did you read it?"

"No. Of course not. I would never, not without permission."

She tried to hand it back to him, but he just stared into his pilfered mug. What the hell had gone wrong?

"Are you okay, Cash?"

"Sure, I'm okay. I'm always okay, aren't I? Isn't that the role I play in your life?"

"You're drunk."

"Nah, I'm only up to Honest Harry."

"Sounds more like Pissed Off Pete to me."

"You might be right. So? What do you care?"

Lauren flagged down a waitress and ordered another coffee and the Bonanza special that they'd been splitting since college.

"I care because I'm your friend. I care because I don't know what I did to make you run off, and the thought of losing you scares me. So eat some fucking food and sober up, because neither of us are leaving here until we get this straight."

Cash slouched sullenly in the booth, refusing to meet her eye until their food arrived. She waited until he'd finished half of his short stack of pancakes, picking at the ham and eggs herself. She'd been starving when she sat down, but now her stomach was tied up in knots by his uncharacteristic silence, and she could barely chew.

Lauren's phone buzzed with an incoming text from Alexis.

Alexis: How did things go at the benefit?

Lauren sent her a picture of their meal and Cash's hands gripping his coffee cup.

Alexis: Before midnight? That rough, huh?

Lauren: Working on avoiding Pete.

Alexis: Good luck.

When he drained his coffee, she broke the silence.

"Are we going to talk about what happened back there?"

"Which part? The part where after everything I tried to do for you tonight, you still dissed me to that guy?"

Lauren sat back against the seat, her shoulders sticking to the vinyl. There was a lot to unpack in that statement, starting with what?

"What?"

Apparently that was as far as she was going to get in her rational breakdown.

"That's really why you were so concerned about the ball, wasn't it? It wasn't about saving your feature. Or not entirely. You wanted in so you could get back at that jerk."

"No, the purpose of tonight was to save my reputation. Did you expect me to ignore the filth he was spouting?"

"I sure as hell didn't expect you to leave me standing with Monica fucking Delancey while you dealt with all of his shit alone. But I guess you just want me there to pick up the pieces. You don't want me standing by your side."

"That's not..." Lauren tried to find the words to explain.

"I just wish you could see that you deserve so much better."

Her temper finally snapped.

"And who's gonna give me what I deserve? You?"

That shut him up.

"Listen, I pulled him aside because I didn't want to cause a scene. I also didn't need an audience for my embarrassment. I told Devin he was a jerk and that we were through for good. That he couldn't hold a candle to you. And then I turned to find that you were gone."

"Didn't think you wanted me there. You told him I was just a friend." Cash mumbled to the table. Lauren would dissect why that particular statement sounded like it broke his heart once she got the rest of her anger out.

"I also threw champagne in his face. Oh, wait, that's right. You missed that part because you fucking ghosted."

More sullen silence. He poked at the pancakes with his fork until she gripped his hand to still it.

"So are we going to talk about what happened back there?" she asked again.

"Thought we just did."

"Contrary to what you might think, my stand-off with Devin was only the fourth most interesting thing to happen to me tonight." He finally looked up at her, so she kept talking, desperate to get him to open up. "The third most interesting thing was when my best friend held my hand and sent chills up my arm. That's never happened before. Then Alexis suggested that I might want to look at my best friend for my next boyfriend. Completely out of left field, right? That's what I thought, but then I couldn't get it out of my head." He looked up at that, but kept his lovely lips pressed into a firm line. She pressed on.

"But no, that only took second place. I want to talk to you about the most interesting part of my night. Any guesses?"

He shrugged. Irritating man.

"How about discovering that my best friend is capable of flipping every switch I have with a dance? That he can turn me inside out with one hot look? And then finding out that he can kiss me and just walk the fuck away? How about we talk about that?"

He stared at her, jaw clenched. At least she had his attention now.

She couldn't have been the only one to feel that chemistry sparking on the dance floor. The more she thought about it, the more she wondered how much more he was hiding beneath his usual happy-go-lucky exterior.

"You're sure you didn't read any of this?" Cash tapped his journal.

"No. I didn't."

"Maybe you should." He flicked past the pages filled with slice-of-life essays and poems about race and class that she had helped him critique, settling on one, dog-eared and smudged. "How about this one?" His deep voice trembling, he began to read.

> *It's just a crush, they say.*
> *It'll fade, they say.*
> *Never date a friend, they say.*
> *Date someone else, they say.*
> *It'll get better with time, they say.*
> *The fuck do they know?*

Lauren's jaw dropped. He'd written about her? He flicked further through the book, searching for another one. Before she'd regained her equilibrium, he was shaking it further with more tender words.

I hope you feel the sun warm and loving on
   your face.
The wind ruffling your feathers with stealthy
   laughter.
The cool moonlight glittering in your eyes.
The rain washing away the tears he left behind.
The rainbow chasing your smile.
The world reflects the best of you.
I see you everywhere.

Tears began to flow down Lauren's face as he kept reading. When his voice trailed off, she snatched the book from him and kept reading, captivated by his scrawling handwritten poetry. There, between the words he'd shared with her, the words for the world, lay his hidden emotions.

That skirt
Worn to flirt
Worn to tempt
Worn to touch
So soft
So many wearings
So short
Does she know what I see?
Does she care if I do?
Or is it as ever not for me?
Look but don't touch.
Long but don't speak.

I can't. I won't. I shouldn't.
That skirt tho.

That was her second date skirt, short, denim, and flirty. She'd had it since high school and was proud that it still fit. But it was hers. These poems were speaking directly to her.

"These are beautiful. Have you thought about publishing them along with your other stuff?"

"No one wants bad love poems."

"I do. I want them. Are they all... are they all about me?"

He nodded holding her gaze.

"But you never said anything."

"You never seemed interested."

"I've always been interested in your thoughts and feelings. For crying out loud, you're my best friend."

He leaned forward, his voice intense with suppressed emotion.

"And if you had secret longings that could ruin that friendship, would you share them? Or would you bury them down deep, afraid that they might change things forever and you'd lose the one person in the world you really need? As much as I wanted you to be mine, I couldn't risk losing what we already had. You mean too much to me, Lauren, and the thought of losing you scares me to death."

"Cash. I... I didn't know."

"It's okay. I told myself it was a crush and that I'd get over it. But I haven't. I love you, Lauren, enough to let you go."

"What?"

"It's okay," he repeated, as if he weren't spouting nonsense. "That's what I decided tonight on the train. It's time to move on, start fresh. Our friendship can survive the distance, and hopefully the rest will fade away. And someday, when this has all blown over, we'll have a good laugh about it."

Lauren's heart stuttered in her chest. What in the fresh hell was this? I love you, but I'm leaving? Panic pulsed in her chest, and she pushed back hard against his words, hoping to goad him out of this insane plan.

"Hold up. You're just going to drop all of this on me, and then snatch it away? That's not the Cash Hendricks I know. I think you like the idea of love, but doing the actual work of being in love is what's really scary, isn't it?"

"Pffft. What do you know about it?"

"I'm just calling it like I see it. One kiss, and you're ready to bail. My very own love it or leave it."

"That's not... I didn't..."

"There's only one way you're going to convince me you're not afraid to love me."

His head snapped up at the challenge in her voice.

"Oh yeah, what's that?"

Lauren leaned over the table and grabbed his hand, linking her fingers through his.

"Stay."

The glimmer of hope in his eyes when he looked at her sideways melted her into the seat. And when he smirked and tilted his head to the side, she couldn't help grinning over her win. To hell with taking a break. This felt right.

"So you think you can handle being my lover?"

His cocky humor was back.

"Only one way to find out," she tossed back, dropping a twenty on the table and turning for the door of the gritty diner in her fancy dress and stilettos, still holding onto the hand of her best friend.

———

THE TAXI WASN'T DRIVING FAST ENOUGH. Lauren

leaned against Cash in the backseat, conscious that everything felt different. She had leaned on his shoulder a thousand times. She had always felt the firm muscles beneath her cheek and appreciated them for its unwavering support. But tonight she was aware of every inch of her body that pressed against him. Had he felt this overwhelming awareness, too?

She shifted, burrowing her nose into the crease of his neck, inhaling his dark, woodsy scent, realizing that she could already identify it as *his*. She'd stolen enough of his sweatshirts to associate it with comfort and care. Pressing a kiss against the pulse racing at the base of his throat, she knew she would feel a layer of lust on top of that the next time she stole his shirt. She groaned when he caught his breath and swallowed audibly.

"How did you do it?" she asked against his skin.

"Do what?" he managed.

"Ignore this need? I've only just started seeing you this way, and I can't keep my hands to myself."

"Don't."

Lauren leaned back at the harsh command. Cash grabbed her hand and put it flat against his racing heart.

"No. Don't keep it to yourself. I need this. I need you," he gasped, pulling her closer to kiss her fiercely.

She lost herself in the sensations he built with his hands, his lips. An old familiar love clashed with this strange new love to create something new, something powerful inside of her. She felt alive with it. Needs and desires twisted up inside her, and all she could do was cling to him and trust that he'd see her through the storm.

He always had before.

The taxi driver had to honk his horn to get their attention. Who knew how long he'd been parked outside her apartment, muttering about young love. Who cared?

"Will you come up?" she asked on a breathy exhale.

"Anything you want." Cash replied. He'd said that earlier, too, and countless times over the years of their friendship. How had she missed the love behind those words?

Lauren paid the still-grumbling taxi driver and left him a ridiculous tip. She fumbled to find her keys as Cash pressed kisses to the back of her neck.

She didn't want to fumble this, either. But who better to fall with than someone who'd always been there to catch her?

———

IT WAS three in the morning and freezing in her apartment. Lauren snuck out of bed, wired and unable to sleep. Cash was in her bed. That thought filled her with a quiet joy. They hadn't done anything drastic, agreeing to approach this new phase of their relationship with care. But even just kissing and touching, ending the night curled up in his arms, Lauren felt more connected, more alive. Every nerve ending was still tingling, and her brain was bursting with words. She pulled on his puffy coat over her t-shirt, loving the way his warm, woodsy scent surrounded her in the dark.

She booted up her computer to write her feature, so she could send it off to Wendy first thing. She uploaded her photos and, as she scrolled through her night, she realized she had a very different narrative to share than the one she'd pitched.

My Best Worst Valentine's Day

Valentine's Day. A day women either love or
    hate. After getting very publicly dumped the
    day before, well, let's just say I was not
    enthusiastic about it this year. I had the
    perfect day all planned out. The fancy

dinner, a stroll through the park, even a
charity ball...sounds perfect right?
Despite my sudden lack of a boyfriend, I was
determined to keep my plans. I can be pretty
stubborn. Ask my friend Cash. He'll tell you
about the time I decided that I was going to
be a singer/songwriter. It took me many
terrible open mic nights to let that go. Not my
finest hour. Maybe I should try to be more
open minded and flexible. More on that later.

Lauren inserted a picture of herself from college soulfully
clutching a guitar she didn't know how to play.

Given that I was determined to carry out my
plans, I needed help. Friends to the rescue.
Cash got me into the restaurant Le Petit
Mort. I highly recommend it for date nights.
The food was fantastic, and the drinks
potent. It certainly lived up to its name. But
even friendship has its limits in the face of a
fully booked restaurant, hence my creative
dining spot.

She selected the nicer pictures from the restaurant, as well as
her selfie on the milk crates.

A stroll through Millennium Park was next on
my list, so despite the cold, I went for a solo
wander. The happy couples everywhere may
have pinched my bruised heart, but it also
reminded me that Chicago is full of love and

that my true love might be right here if I'd
only open my eyes.

Lauren selected her favorite photos from the couples she'd
met at the bean and skating, and linked to the proposal video
with a sappy smile.

The fundraiser to support heart health was last
on my list, and I wasn't about to let losing my
ticket stop me. Cash pulled some strings, and
I got to spend a few hours rubbing elbows
with Chicago's rich and famous. I'm sure lots
of money was raised, as well as a few
eyebrows over my spectacular exit. Side note:
he deserved every drop.

She found some useable photos from the hotel and the gala.
She also included the one of Devin and Monica, deliberately
cropped to remove most of her asshole ex. She'd be damned if he
got one more ounce of publicity out of her.

You might be reading this thinking that spending
Valentine's Day chasing plans I'd made with
my now ex-boyfriend sounds depressing. But
it wasn't. Far from it. Because I had my friend
by my side, supporting this crazy plan all
the way.

Choosing which pictures of Cash to exclude was impossible,
so she used them all.

He bent over backwards to help me out. He made
me laugh over the absurdities of the evening.

He held my hand and told me I was
beautiful. He gave me the words I hadn't
known he was hiding. And by the end of the
night, I realized that love really was right in
front of my face. Here was someone who
knows me inside and out, and loves me
anyway. I don't know how I missed it all these
years, but I'm sure glad I opened my eyes and
my mind to the possibility of us. That's what
made this the best worst Valentine's
Day ever.

Happy with her first draft, she clicked over to Instagram and loaded the photo of him holding her hand on the dance floor. Looking at it now, she could see the truth of his love and desire clear in his eyes. The future looked bright indeed. She tagged the photo #LoveItOrLeaveIt and went back to bed.

Hours later she woke to his kiss on her shoulder, and she reached for her phone on auto-pilot. Her notifications were blowing up, and she had her first published byline. There was also an email from Wendy congratulating her and asking if she had any more feature ideas. Inspiration swirled through her. The proposal follow-up, the faces of Chicago piece, maybe even a profile on Cash and his work...

Cash pulled her back into his arms and kissed her gently. The rest of the world faded away, leaving only her best friend and her lover in her arms. Everything else could wait.

"RIGHT HAND MAN" BY KILBY BLADES

A WORST DAY EVER SHORT

January 29th - The Ostler Wedding

"BRIDESMAID DOWN."

Tori's whispered words were delivered swiftly and too softly for the others in the room to hear. I'd surely have seen the remnants of a calm smile on her face had I looked up to gratify her comment with a response. But I didn't look up—didn't turn my eye from my viewfinder and didn't turn my lens away from the mother of the bride. Because I was a professional. And so was Tori. And we knew what had to be done.

Finishing up the shots I was getting of the bride's mother in the make-up chair, I stopped long enough to smile at the bride, Lena.

"Your train will be gorgeous flowing down the grand staircase near the reception hall. We should get some of you and your parents, before the guests arrive."

"Oh!" Lena blinked. Because, not fifteen minutes before, I'd told her that, after hair and makeup, we'd shoot the bridal party on the lawns. David cast me the subtlest of questioning glances as he patted the up-do he'd just sprayed in place.

Change of plans, I telegraphed with he subtlest of answering eyebrow arches.

"That will be absolutely elegant," David chimed in, then nudged Lena conspiratorially. "And breathtaking with your cathedral-length veil."

"Five minutes?" I asked Marla, the makeup artist who was working on Lena's mother. As with David, Marla and I had worked together at weddings a dozen times. As soon as she nodded confirmation, I looked between Lena and her mother excitedly. "I'll get the room ready for the shots I'll take of you putting on your dress."

I was the picture of calm confidence as I turned on my heel and made the short walk to the door that separated the adjoining rooms. Hotel suites were rarely ideal for dressing, primping, and photographing when your bridal party was large. Today, it would save our bacon that the dressing suites were so small that we'd hustled the bridesmaids out as soon as their makeup was done. All that Tori would remember was tender moments putting on her gown with the help of only her mom.

"Bridesmaid down," I whispered calmly when I got close enough to Nellie and out of earshot of all the others. I surveyed the lenses and lighting equipment she'd laid out on the bed. By then, she should have been ready with the the lighting, lens and camera go-bags we'd need for the ceremony and the reception hall.

Flattering shots of decorated venues were among my new assistant's fortés. When the time came, I'd shoot candids in the ante-room where guests would be having hors d'oeuvres. Nellie could shoot the main house with its double-tiered, mirrored-twin marble stairs and the receiving-room-turned-chapel on the lower floor.

"Oh my god! What happened?" Nellie practically shouted.

But I was close to the door, so I moved to shut it. Had I been closer to Nellie, I may have clapped my hand right over her mouth. Eight weeks before, I'd have fired her for her antics already. I'd been through three new assistants since the day Cal quit.

Cal had interviewed his replacements himself. His top pick had been Melanie. She'd shot beautifully and was good with people, but retouched at a snail's pace and didn't do it well. I'd ended up pulling all-nighters and sacrificing much-needed days off to pick up her slack. I'd fired her after just a week.

Finn had lasted two. He'd been proactive, organized, and talented and for a fleeting moment, I'd let myself hope that it would work out. My hopes were shattered when I'd found him hitting on the groom at the Primus wedding. I treasured my hard-earned reputation too much to expose my studio to risk like that.

My studio was my baby. I'd moved to Lassen five years before because I wanted to shoot weddings my way and it was this cute little town seated in the most charming part of upstate New York. I'd discovered it on a shoot I'd been on with my old boss: the wedding of a bride from the city who'd broken ranks and traded Gotham Hall for an intimate affair in a rustic country barn.

I'd moved to New York at seventeen to go to the New School and get my BFA in Photography. My classmates had looked down their noses at me for photographing weddings. As they'd vied for assistantships with the Annie Leibovitzes and Frans Lantings of the world, I'd worked my way up, apprenticing for a few of the greats who shot Manhattan's elite. I'd slowly but surely made a name for myself—even had my work featured in some of the bigger bridal magazines. Then it had happened: Lassen had been named the #1 Most Romantic Town in America by a big travel magazine. The piece had featured an indulgent photo spread of a Valentine's Day wedding. I hadn't shot it, and if you ask me, the affair came off as a bit kitschy in the piece. It didn't matter. People loved it and began to flock to Lassen in waves.

Cal had joined me the year before the article was written. We were already an amazing team—were already building something far better than what I'd started. For three blissful years, I'd adored my job and business had been great. Until, out of the blue, Cal had given his notice and quit.

That was how Molasses-Slow Melanie and Flirtatious Finn had found their way to my doorstep. Clumsy Claudia had been fired after only a day when she'd accidentally kicked a go-bag full of equipment off of a bridge where we were shooting to die a watery death in the creek below. Now, here I was with Nervous Nellie. Her portfolio was beautiful. It was rare to find a girl in her early twenties who composed and lit shots with such distinctive style. Nellie had talent. And perspective. She reminded me of a younger me. Problem was, she didn't really think before she talked.

"What happened..." I began calmly, even as I felt frustration heat my face. "Is that one of the bridesmaids is drunk. Can you guess which one?" I quizzed.

This was my fourth week and the fourteenth wedding I'd done since hiring Nellie.

"The one in the green dress?" she finally replied.

I let my hand fall to my side and placed the camera on the bed. I took a few seconds to stretch my neck and rub my temples. I was exhausted from eight weeks of pulling so much more than my own weight. If Cal were here, the go-bags would be packed and we'd have Lena halfway to the new location. He'd have made sure my bag had water, and he'd have probably slipped something in there for my headache. When I shot for too long and strained my eyes, both my head and my neck got sore. All the shoots these past weeks had shown me just how much I'd depended on Cal.

He was a brilliant photographer. But, to me, he'd been so much more.

Nellie didn't now and probably never would have this sort of intuition, let alone such attention to detail. Had she really not noticed that *all* of the bridesmaid's dresses were green?

"You gotta pay attention," I scolded her lightly, and not for the first time. Because lots of people could take pretty pictures. What lots of people *couldn't* do was keep the shots looking good when a wedding was turning to shit. No couple wanted to look at their wedding album for years to come and always be reminded of how drunk their sister was, or how badly their divorced parents hated each other. No one wanted gritty, painful truths.

"It's Bridesmaid #3. The blonde who's been drinking since ten o'clock. Tori's handling her now."

"*Handling* her?" Nellie hissed at a much wiser volume.

You had to learn to be a human breathalyzer in this job. It was hard to shoot groups, let alone shuffle the schedule if need-be, if you didn't know who'd had how much to drink.

"Letting her get it out of her system. Giving her a coffee and a Zofran. Sobering her up."

Nellie blinked. "Is that even legal?"

I had to smirk a little at that. I'd seen some things, but Tori could write a book. But we needed to get on track.

"Do you know what I need for the staircase shoot?"

Nellie's eyes answered with a definite "no".

"Yeah," she squeaked.

"Do you have the shot list printed?"

This time, the "no" in her eyes matched the "no" in her spoken words.

How the hell did I let this happen?

It was the question I'd been asking myself non-stop since he'd given notice. Hell—I'd even asked *him*. Made him counter-offers.

Practically begged him to stay. Eight weeks later, I still had no clue why he'd gone.

What did I do to make Cal quit?

———

January 30th - The Tucker Wedding

MY STOMACH DID WORSE than growl when I walked into Wolfgang's to pick up dinner. It roared a warning that it needed food—now. Keeping power bars and almonds in my camera bag didn't mean much if I never had time to eat them. Even on a light day, I was on my feet for eight hours.

Today had not been a light day. Nellie had forgotten to charge the backup batteries at the Tucker wedding, which I didn't discover until five minutes before cake-cutting time. I'd already been shooting for five hours and had run out of juice on both of my DSLRs. By the time I'd hoofed it to my car for the old 35mm I used for my own personal shooting, old Uncle Bob had shown up and taken my spot. Every wedding had an Uncle Bob— a hobby photographer who showed up with an entry-level Nikon and tried to bogart all your shots. Yes, I told myself. It had been a shitty wedding all-around. But Nellie was getting better...right?

At least it was Sunday, which meant the weekend weddings were officially over. I wouldn't start this madness again until Thursday night. Weekdays were mellow and I really liked the couple I was scheduled to meet with tomorrow, the soon-to-be-Bedrossians. Their wedding would be at my favorite venue—the most sought-after but hardest-to-book spot for miles around.

Erin McKay was fiercely protective of Kilroy House, the old stone beauty in Berridge. Couples spoke their vows in what had been Erin's ancestral family chapel and received guests in a gorgeous, rustic barn. It was ideal for small weddings, and those who married there loved it most for the guest accommodations: twenty bedrooms between the classic estate home and the converted carriage house.

Weddings at Kilroy House were a weekend-long affair. The Bedrossian family would pay me an ungodly amount of money to have me photograph clean-through from when guests arrived on Friday to the post-wedding brunch on Sunday morning. The last wedding I'd shot at Kilroy House also marked the last time when things had been good between Cal and me. Better-than-good, I recalled. We'd always been in sync, but I'd felt more connected to everything that weekend.

The Bhojani wedding had been magical. Every wedding was a gift but this one had that rare extra something—something ethereal and palpably divine. It had been heartfelt. Unencumbered. Un-self-conscious. After we'd finished taking pictures each night, I'd barely been able to sleep. I'd felt inspired and rejuvenated. The grounds had been beautiful and the early November evenings had been unseasonably mild. Both nights, Cal and I had stayed up for hours and just talked. When I looked at the pictures we'd taken days later, I wasn't surprised that it had yielded some of the best work we'd ever done.

"What happened? You don't like me anymore? I haven't seen you in two weeks."

Wolfgang always ribbed me and I always let him. Wise decision, seeing as how he stayed open late and served the best comfort food in town. He also catered some of the higher-end weddings with traditional dishes from his native Austria. I ran into him on the occasional job.

His restaurant was so renowned for its imported coffee, apple strudel, and Sachertorte, that he attracted a better-than-decent afternoon coffee crowd for his baked goods alone. His typical gasthaus dinner menu kept the people of Lassen deep in Wienerschnitzel and red cabbage. I came for the bread dumplings and beef goulash.

"I don't even know if I like myself anymore," I grumbled, only half-joking. "I can't take another two weeks of this."

From the way I said it, I knew he'd understand. He crossed his arms and fixed me with a look of mild scrutiny.

"The holiday that shall not be named?"

He still had hints of an accent, stood tall with light brown eyes and straight, dark hair, and his tone held the subtle commanding quality that I'd only ever seen German-speakers pull off.

"I need an invisibility cloak," I complained.

I fished into my pocket and handed him my credit card. I rarely carried a wallet. Purses were too hard to keep track of at a wedding, and I didn't like to keep my wallet in my car. It had occurred to me more than once that if I ever got in an accident and had to be rushed to the hospital, they'd have to frisk me to figure out who I was.

"Hey..." I just remembered something I'd been meaning to ask. "...speaking of the 14th, are you working the Dryer wedding?"

"How do you know?" He stuck my card in the reader.

The truth was, I'd warned them off of Spiriani's and suggested they consider Wolfgang's. Spiriani's had really gone down since the mother had stopped running it. Wolfgang's food was amazing and his plating really held up.

"Lucky guess." I smiled. "What's on the menu?"

"We're doing Tafelspitz and vegetable strudel. But I'll be sure to bring you a bowl of goulash."

A smile more genuine than any I'd sported all day spread across my face. "See? How could I ever fall out of like with you?"

He swiveled his iPad around and I used my finger to sign the screen. When I went to lift it, my to-go bag felt suspiciously heavy.

"Jeez, what'd you put in here? You know it's just a single order, right?"

"It's enough for dinner tonight and lunch tomorrow. And I put in a bottle of Weihenstephaner. You need to drink. And eat."

I raised my eyebrow and smirked, but inside I felt warm. After my past-few-weeks of hell, it was nice to have someone looking out for me.

"Beer first, huh?"

"You look like you could use a bottle or four."

What I could use was a time machine to rocket me to February 15th, and a vacation. But I didn't like to wallow. So I tucked the bag in the crook of my elbow and smiled a genuine smile.

"Seriously, Wolfgang. Thanks."

———

I STILL ADORED my artist's loft, though I'd long-since ceased to live in the bedroom at the top of the stairs. My century-old space sat at the far end of Main Street in town. The old ware-house had been renovated, but maintained the character of its industrial roots.

It had been sub-divided into three parts. The unit in the middle held writing classes and sold books. On the far end was a wine-tasting room. What had once been loading docks in the back had been enclosed and refashioned into a large garage. Lassen was a safe town, but carrying $40,000 worth of camera equipment in my car at any given time made not having to unload it every night invaluable.

Leaving everything except for my memory cards was exactly

what I did. With my food in my left arm, I used my right to key in the security codes. Cal was a master contingency planner. The system had been his idea. So had cloud infrastructure that created redundancy and back-ups for all of my work. So had the iMac I'd come to use to show my portfolio and plan out shot lists with my clients. That last suggestion alone had cut my sample portfolio expenses by 90%. Every streamlined innovation was one I owed to Cal.

The downstairs was where I met with prospective clients. A high table of reclaimed wood held the iMac and was seated with six gray leather stools. Upstairs was the living area: my enormous desk with its double monitor and the leftover bedroom furniture I'd never bothered to move.

It was my favorite place in the loft and where I did the majority of my work. But it was still an industrial space—still winter—and it got its drafts. The accent pieces up here were faux-fur—from my faux-sheep area rug, to the faux-fur-gray-and-white-ombre throw that sat atop the bed. Flipping on the space heater next to my desk, I set my food on the table and fished out the first of two memory cards. I opened my syncing program, stuck the cards into their drives, and confirmed that both cards were uploading to the cloud server.

Only then did I crack open my half-liter of Märzen and start to drink straight out of the bottle. Catching up on Hulu shows would take up too much bandwidth if I wanted the upload to go fast. So I opened my container of goulash and set in to catch up on everything I'd missed on my phone.

Never being free on Fridays or Saturdays meant living "normal" vicariously. I hit up social media to keep tabs on what my friends and family were up to, and to be a voyeur to whatever occasion I had missed. Cal had been on my feed a lot lately. His Instagram posts always showed up close to the top because of how much engagement he got from his fans. His account featured his own superb work that had nothing to do with the work he'd done with me at the studio.

Seeing his postings never got easier, though, in the quiet of my own studio at a quarter to midnight, I could admit that I got some sick pleasure from stalking his feed. Sure enough, today's photo topped the one from yesterday: from a long sunrise shot of the signature peacock pillars in the Mumbai airport, Cal had literally flown to paradise. He'd posted a breathtaking selfie of in an overwater bungalow in the Maldives.

He sat on the lowest part of the platform—a sitting dock just above clear blue-green water. A staircase rose behind him leading to the thatch-roof bungalow above. The perspective was astounding. Somehow, he' gotten a wide view of the water, and gotten enough loft that you could see up to the bungalow's roof. He was perfectly-aligned in the center—his perfectly-silky black hair and perfectly-tanned skin framing the perfect dimple on his perfectly-angled face. How easy it seemed for him to show the world a perfectly-impish smile that I'd naïvely believed he'd shown only to me.

It shouldn't have hurt that he'd gone off to show his special to the world, and it was no surprise the world had taken it. His work had a wow-factor that was hard to fake. The bungalow selfie was an epic photo to begin with, but the way his sunglasses reflected the open ocean from behind his camera...that shot—it was just...beyond.

I hate you, I private messaged him, not feeling even a little bit guilty. He'd never believe it anyway and there was no point in mincing words. I'd been nice enough about his earlier shots— asking him whether he'd used a panoramic fish-eye to get the jaw-dropping shot he'd taken of the Taj Mahal and telling him his stunning capture of a child playing in front of a colorful temple in Chennai was beautiful—but The Maldives? This one took the cake.

By the time I was halfway done my beer, I was all the way done my goulash—or at least as much goulash as it was wise for me to eat. If I didn't pace myself after not having eaten for so many hours, I'd be up all night with a stomachache.

I was busy sealing the to-go container when my computer made the sound it did when I was receiving an incoming text. Instead of looking on my phone, I clicked on my iMessage. Cal had sent me an image: it was a meme with the two old dudes from *The Muppet Movie*; its caption read *Haters Gonna Hate*.

It made me smile. And damn if I didn't hate him a little for real, for knowing that it would. I hated myself even more for wanting him to cheer me up, for wanting him here, period. He was responsible for my predicament, after all.

I tapped out a response on my keyboard with the hand not checking the seal of the container.

Does paradise never sleep?

Was it possible for a tone of bitterness to ring loudly and clearly through a text? Yes, I believed. It could. I wouldn't be so jealous that he was drinking alcohol out of coconuts in South East Asia if he'd given me a remotely good explanation for why he'd left me in the lurch.

No. That wasn't true. I'd be every bit as jealous. Being away from Cal, it felt...wrong. Twice as wrong as finally admitting to myself that I had feelings for my best friend. Three times as wrong as it had been to wait until he left on his own and everything fell apart.

Sunrise was at 6:20. It's nearly 10:00.

He was telling me he'd been up for hours. Photographers did crazy things like get up at sunrise because that was one of the best times to shoot. People thought fancy cameras were the trick. Really, it was the light that did all the work.

I wanted to ask how he was. How he *really* was. What he was *really* doing there. What his decision to drop everything and travel the world was really about. But I didn't do any of that. Couldn't do anything if I didn't even know where the hell we stood.

How's Nellie working out? He finally shot back.

If you're asking whether she knocked a bag containing $7,500 worth of equipment into Lassen Creek, that's a no.

So, better than Claudia? He punctuated his question with a concerned-looking emoji.

Only slightly, I returned.

When I'd admitted a month before that I'd fired Claudia and was currently without an assistant, he'd gone back into the applications and come back to me with a few more choices. His gesture was just the sort of thing that complicated this even more. Because he'd left with such swiftness and conviction that he couldn't have been more gone. So why did he still take care of me like he was here?

Be easy on her. I think she could be good.

What?! I'm easy, I shot back with indignation.

I scoffed when he sent back three emojis laughing so hard they were crying, and I started typing back my retort.

I don't hear the clients complaining, I pointed out.

Like Cal was one to talk. Not when so many of the studio's best-loved and most iconic shots had been taken by him.

Candace. You're a perfectionist.

Dancing dots told me he was still busy writing. All the better for me to lick my wounds. He was making me sound mean. Is that why he'd left? Had I been delusional to think we were in a good flow when all along he'd seen me as some sort of Boss-zilla?

It's not going to be smooth with someone new overnight. It took you years to train me. For me to learn how you work.

But that was just it: it didn't feel like I had ever trained Cal Jamison. From the first day he'd started, it had felt like he'd completely and perfectly filled a void. He'd anticipated every need and solved every problem and done it with efficiency, style and grace. I'd never wanted for anything. He'd always just been there. And it wasn't just the assistant work. Cal delivered the full package, and was the real deal: he had the precision of a flawless assistant, the sharp eye and raw talent of a great photographer, and the technical skill to get it all done.

I didn't train you. You were born with it.

I shot it off like it was nothing, but it was the first time I'd lavished that praise. My flattery-leads-to-hubris mentality had always made me stingy with giving credit.

He didn't answer right away. Maybe I'd said too much. Maybe I was just feeling sentimental. I'd never been comfortable with him referring to me like he was my pupil.

Okay, Miss "let the light do the work."

Alright. He had me there. I'd said that to him at least two-hundred times.

Shut up, Mr. "Breathe through the shot."

He'd taken me to the gun range every day off for two straight months. I'd never forget the feeling of his arms guiding me into shooting position—his breath on my neck as he'd instructed me what to do. He'd told me that shooting guns was exactly like taking pictures and he'd proven to me he was right: if you held your breath, you'd never get the best shot.

She'll get better, he rejoined, bringing me back to the original topic. *Do her like you did me. Just give the girl a chance.*

———

February 5th - The Sweetwater Wedding

"HEY, CANDY GIRL"

I heard Dev's voice before I found him in the room. He stood next to a counter in the corner, hands busy arranging pencils and glosses and all sorts of makeup-y things. Dressed in his standard all-black uniform of a stylish v-neck, fitted slacks, and a pocketed apron, he looked every bit the professional; but it was the details that always made him stand out. His pants had a bit of sparkle. Diamond studs shined in the lobes of his ears. And his bejeweled ring made him look like an African prince. And I wouldn't have put it past Devereaux Jones to have a shocking secret past or even a shocking secret present. His VIP client list was rumored to be a mile long.

"Hey! I thought that was you..." I trailed off, referring to the Range Rover parked next to mine, outside. That was an understatement. No one else in town had a pearl white chameleon custom candy-painted car.

I scanned the room quickly, eager to set down my armful of lighting equipment and one of my three camera bags. It had good light, was elegantly-furnished and spacious. It had plenty to work with for shots I could take of the bridal party getting ready, but it was light on work surfaces.

"Half and half?" Dev had already splayed out what looked to be dozens of compacts and brushes on the marble island of the only good working space—the kitchen. Seeing my predicament, he reached out, shifting his setup to accommodate mine.

"Thanks." I threw him a grateful smile and walked carefully with my precarious load. He relieved me of a tripod bag that would have certainly hit the floor had he not stepped in exactly when he did to save it. I set the rest down eagerly and gave a sigh of relief when I did.

Brushing my hands off a little, I stepped forward to hug him and stood on my tip-toes. Dev was tall. Like, male runway model tall. But I only wore sensible flats to jobs.

"You know you do *not* need to be carrying all of that yourself," Dev scolded.

"My assistant's running late." I gave him a put-out look and started unzipping the first of my equipment bags.

"Your *assistant*?" Dev crossed his arms, speaking the title as if it were a dirty word. "What happened to Cal?"

Shit. He doesn't know.

Thinking back, I realized that Dev and I hadn't been on a wedding together in weeks, maybe even a couple of months. Between that and his jet-setting it was, indeed, possible that Dev was the only person in my circle who hadn't heard about Cal.

I was tired of telling the story and still raw from the reactions some people had expressed: "Cal was amazing." "You were an incredible team." "How could you have let him go?"

"Cal is on an epic journey that doubles as a permanent vacation." I said it with a practiced mix of humor, irony, and admiration. It was the perfect misdirection. It made me sound begrudgingly happy for him. It was also carefully-chosen phrasing. It wasn't a lie. It let me avoid coming out and saying, "Cal quit."

Anyone who knew anything knew that he'd been more than my assistant. That was why Dev had bristled at the word. It might have been my initials that made up the company name, but Cal and I—we'd been an unstoppable team.

"He left you during Valentine's season?"

"He stayed through Thanksgiving," I said a bit defensively. We'd done eight weddings that week. He'd stayed on to help with post-production—had done all the retouching and sending out of approval proofs to the brides. He'd even done a full sweep of our equipment inventory and stocked replacement parts so that I wouldn't have to worry about that piece for awhile. He'd done first-round interviews for the candidates. And on December first, he'd been gone.

"I'm so sorry I'm late!"

Nellie's panicked voice saved me from further explanation.

Though, when I laid eyes on her, I was less appeased. It was good that she'd arrived. With the bridal party coming in less than half an hour, we had a lot to do. What wasn't so good was her frazzled appearance: her clothes were wrinkled, her glasses were crooked, and her hair was in disarray.

"I don't know what happened. I set the alarm. But for some reason, it didn't go off. Then I was halfway down the road when I realized I hadn't fed my dog..." By the time Nellie had traversed the room and set her heavy purse down on the counter, she was still deep into an account of how her tiny Yorkshire Terrier, Buttons, needed her food heated up and a special anxiety medicine mixed in.

"Nellie." I interrupted in what Cal called my "mom voice"— the perfect mixture of sharp authority and calm. She stopped talking and appeared to be somewhat out of breath. I allowed for a deliberate beat of silence. Two beats. Nellie was getting better at most aspects of the job, but she still needed to calm the hell down.

"Yes?" she said finally, still seeming a bit out of breath.

I smiled and motioned to my side. "This is Devereaux Jones. He's the platinum standard of talent in the glamour business."

Nellie needed to learn to stop—to be sensitive to people and to the climate in the room—to being a calming force instead of adding to the drama. Tensions were high enough at weddings. A photographer who couldn't help people relax was a photographer who couldn't get good shots.

"Oh. Nice to meet you, Devereaux," Nellie said politely, straightening her glasses with her left hand while extending her right hand across the kitchen island. "I'm Nellie."

"Charmed," Dev returned. "You've got gorgeous bone structure, darling."

The corner of my lips turned up. Because Dev was working his own magic. I'd seen him pay the same compliment to countless brides when they'd shown up with the same nervous energy. Dev was helping me calm down my wet-behind-the-ears assistant. Yet another reason why I loved working with him.

Nellie blushed. "Thank you. I get it from my mother." Her tone had changed from panicked to one of flattered flirtation.

He's gay, honey, I thought pitifully. Though, I mostly pitied myself. She needed more sensitivity training than I may have been equipped to provide if her gay-dar was that broken.

"Come on," I said, going around to the side that she stood on and pulling one of the bar stools out. "We've got less than twenty minutes to go over the shot list."

As I went to sit, my phone buzzed in my pocket. It was a number I didn't recognize, from the city. No matter who it was, now wasn't the time to pick it up. Receiving the call was a good reminder. The wedding was starting. Time to turn on the Do Not Disturb.

———

February 8th - The Couple with the Dogs

I COULD'VE FILLED my book two years in advance with people ready to sign with me, sight unseen. And I'd learned my lesson years before. It added to my plate, to meet with every couple personally before even offering the possibility of a contract. But no sum of money was worth the wrath of an unsatisfiable bride.

To be fair, it wasn't always the bride who had the loftiest expectations. Sometimes it was the mother of the bride or whoever was writing the check. My goal for any first meeting with a couple was 10% understanding what they were looking for and 90% figuring out whether I wanted to work with them at all.

"What's your vision for a perfect wedding?"

I smiled across the table at Claire and Nicholas, taking a long sip of steaming herbal tea after voicing the same first question I always asked. The heat hadn't kicked in just yet and my loft was drafty. Nicholas had already won points with me when he'd taken off his gray cashmere blazer and placed it across Claire's shoulders as if he'd done it a thousand times before.

The "perfect wedding" opener was a trick question. People who believed in the lie of perfection answered too quickly and with too much precision. Anyone who described in wistful detail their perfect sunny day or the expressions that would be on their guests faces was an automatic "no". I wasn't in the business of engineering idealized images—I was in the business of capturing magic when it happened. I didn't work with any couple that didn't have enough of that.

"We want the dogs to be involved," Nicholas said quickly.

I nearly choked on my tea. "The dogs?" After so many years, I thought I'd heard it all.

"We have nine of them," Claire chimed in proudly. "That's how we met. I didn't know there was a hole in my fence and that my dog, Klaus, was getting out at night. His dog, Lulu, got pregnant, but he couldn't figure out how. Then the puppies were born. Everyone knows I'm the only one in the neighborhood with a Pomeranian. One day, he showed up on my doorstep with a box of Pomskies."

"Pomskies?"

"A mix between a Pomeranian and a Siberian Husky. They're just about the cutest puppies you've ever seen."

Claire produced her phone from somewhere and tapped it on so that a screen saver popped up. It was a photo of she and Nicholas laughing in a field, lost in a sea of indeed-very-cute dogs. Despite each of them being jumped-on and licked and fawned-over by what seemed to be very eager puppies, their gazes were locked in a look so expressive that it was clear they were truly in love.

"So cute," I cooed, not really knowing whether I was talking about the dogs or talking about them. The romantic in me never got tired of this—never got tired of couples like this. "You kept them all?" I asked, hoping that I would like the answer and that this would go down as one of my all-time-favorite"how we met" stories.

"Oh, no," Nicholas interjected. "We have a lot of relatives. We gave all but two to family. We only have four."

Four dogs is still a lot, but okay.

"How many people do you expect at the wedding?"

"About a hundred." Something in Claire's voice changed when she said it and I didn't miss the sad look she gave when she looked at her fiancé. "Each of us has so many siblings and nieces and nephews, that family-only is really all we can afford."

Nicholas covered his hands with hers before leaning in and looking up at me. "Your portfolio is gorgeous, but your website doesn't list prices. Assuming you have availability, how much would you charge for an October wedding on a Sunday afternoon?"

Couples like Claire and Nicholas were precisely why I didn't post prices. My best-kept secret was that I charged on a sliding scale. The fact that the city folk practically threw money at me because paying top-dollar convinced them they were getting the best made it so that I could give at least a few couples a month a great deal. I liked Claire and Nicholas. They seemed like the real thing and I wanted to shoot their special day.

"Don't worry about that. I can work with you on the price."

Forty-five minutes later, I'd answered even more of their questions and shown them photos from weddings I'd shot at the venue they'd chosen. We set up a date to do a tour of the venue together so that we could solidify their plan. I was just promising to send over a contract before the end of the day and escorting them out the door when Claire lobbed a final question.

"Your assistant's name is Cal, right?"

The question took away a piece of my contentment, which was unfortunate, because I'd made it half the morning without thinking about him.

"He's my former assistant, actually. He's no longer doing weddings. He's decided to focus on other things."

The words tasted bitter in my mouth, even though they had been his. He'd been quick to assure me that he had no plans whatsoever to hang up his own shingle or in any way compete with me. I hadn't liked the connotations of the vague "other things" he'd left so abruptly to work on. It all felt very, "it's not you—it's me."

I'd asked him whether he wanted more money. I'd asked him whether he wanted more recognition—I already referred to him as my partner and I'd asked him whether he wanted to do something official, like take the job title of his choice. I'd even done what I hadn't thought I'd ever do—offered him not-a-small-percentage of the business. But he'd been immoveable, turning down even that.

"That's a shame. So many people talk about how wonderful he is in the reviews. We were hoping we'd get you both."

"That's sweet—I'll let him know that people are asking for him."

I ushered them out the door then, mood killed and resentment creeping. Too many people lately had unintentionally insinuated I couldn't do the job right without Cal. Locking the door behind them, as they were my only appointment of the day, I went back to my loft. To sulk.

Two voicemails. One was from my album printer and one was from an unrecognized cell phone number in New York. I called the latter number back first. Unknown numbers from New

York City were almost always brides wanting to know about availability and price.

"Candace Burton, Photographer?"

"Yes?"

"This is Riley Cooper, from The New York Times Magazine. I was wondering—"

"Oh, no thank you. I'm already subscribed to the digital version. You can probably take me off of your calling li—"

"Ms. Burton," the impatient-sounding man said sharply. "Though I'm thrilled to learn that you're a loyal subscriber, that's not why I'm calling. I'm an editor for the Arts section of the magazine. We'd like to do a feature article on your studio—"

"A feature?" I interrupted, because that's what I did when I was nervous: interjected with echoing questions.

"Your photography is extraordinary. We'd like to follow you as you work one day—to shoot your team as they shoot a wedding."

My mind was still racing. "We'd have to get permission from the bride and groom."

I could practically hear him smirk over the phone. "In our experience, many couples would jump at the chance to be featured."

I spent a dazed five minutes jotting down notes about how to arrange the logistics—they wanted it to be an intimate wedding and, ideally, the shoot would be in June so they could run it in September. I knew just the wedding: a forty-guest affair at the Kilroy House. The Ramirez wedding. On top of what magic I could do at that venue, the bride, Leah, had impeccable taste.

For the first time in weeks, I felt optimistic, energetic, excited. *See? I don't need Cal.*

This was big news: the New York Times Magazine wanted *me.*

Riley Cooper had promised to send out more information

that afternoon. I wanted to celebrate. I pulled out champagne. I opened it and toasted to me. I stared at the details I'd e-mailed to myself. For ten minutes, I googled the magazine archives for previous features of weddings. I thought again of how floored I was.

But the second glass of champagne wasn't as sweet as the first. Suddenly, I felt silly for it being a Tuesday afternoon and me being here, drinking all alone. The third glass tasted neither bitter nor sweet nor sour—it tasted of sadness. Because there was only one person I wanted to call.

NYT Magazine just called me and wants to feature the studio. So excited I'm day-drinking.

After that, I googled what time it was in Sydney.

Eek. 4:00AM. Slim chance he'd be up, and, if he was, I wasn't sure I wanted to know what he was doing or with who. Cal was smoking hot, artistic, and he was on an aimless international vacation. And I had to stop thinking about him right-this-instant because I was more than a little drunk.

There would be no fourth glass—only the champagne bottle going back into the fridge and me turning my monitor to let the loft fall into darkness. When I went to put my computer to sleep, I saw Riley Cooper's name in the "From" field of my e-mail. His promised instructions had arrived.

> *Dear Ms. Burton and Mr. Jameson,*
> *We're thrilled to hear that you're open to having*
>   *us on your shoot and we look forward to*
>   *interviewing you both...*

I didn't read anything after that.

More like, couldn't read. Because my vision became blurry and I no longer had the motivation to put my computer to sleep. Instead, I sat on my bed and half-drunkenly cried.

_____

February 11th - Two Bombs

HEY. If you have time after the weekend, I really want to talk.

I sent the text out into the ether. It had been brewing all week. I'd broken it to Cal in earlier texts that I'd declined the Times feature. But I had to face him—face *someone*—about why.

Not that my courage was real courage—it was more like a sense of dread. Real talk was inevitable. Now it just had to happen. And since he was halfway around the world and I didn't know whether or when he was coming back, no time was as good of a time as now.

I nearly jumped out of my skin when, two minutes later, my phone buzzed. This was why I'd chosen a Friday morning to send the text. If I'd done it on a day off, I'd have spent the time obsessively checking my phone. Sending it off when I was walking out the door to get to a wedding would make me too busy to wait for —and overanalyze—his reply. He must have been right by his phone for as quickly as he'd answered. Was he alarmed by what I was asking? "We need to talk" is never good... Before I could speculate on what he might be thinking, I glanced down at the text. A text that wasn't from Cal at all.

Candace. It's Lacey. Can you call me? It's kind of an emergency.

Uh-oh. My Valentine's Day bride, Lacey Dryer, was level-headed and laid back. Which meant that an emergency by her definition was really an emergency. I'd just pulled the car out of the garage and could have easily remained stopped in my fenced-in parking area to text her back. Instead, I gave her a call.

"Lacey, honey? What's going on?"

I'd seen an emergency or ten. The ones that came a few days before the wedding were rarely good. Once or twice, a relative had died in the days leading up to the nuptial—the mother or father of the groom or the bride. Those circumstances were always the saddest. More often than not, the "emergency" a few days before the wedding was a break-up between the bride and the groom. With all the bachelor-party-gone-wrong and left-right-before-the-altar stories I'd seen firsthand over the years, it was a miracle I still believed in love.

"I have a huge favor to ask."

It didn't sound like she was crying, so that was a plus.

"My sister just got engaged," Lacey continued.

"Which one?" She had two. Michelle was the eldest and Casey was her twin.

"Casey. And you're not gonna believe this. It's to Daniel's brother."

My aw dropped open. Daniel was also a twin.

I was speechless as Casey launched into a rambling story—something about a joint bachelor and bachelorette party the week before in Jamaica and the two of them getting very close.

"Do they need engagement pictures?"

Please say yes. Please say yes. Please say yes.

Because there was only one other place this story was going if this was the emergency and Lacey wanted a favor.

"Well...yes. I mean, no. I mean, if you're willing to photo-graph us all, we're trying to pull together a double wedding!"

I'd always imagined that the moment a photographer was asked to do a double wedding felt something like the moment when expectant moms and dads found out their babies were twins. This wedding would happen, but double weddings could add up to three times as much work.

"We'd pay you more, of course. For if you needed an extra assistant or whatever. Or even if you didn't. I mean, I know the wedding's only three days away, and that something like this is a huge change."

I laughed, not out of excitement, but from a sheer feeling of crazy. Because this would be my busiest next-three days of the year.

"We'll make it work," I said with a bit of giddiness. "Though we'll have to go through a mini-version of our walk-through again. Oh yeah, and I'll need a way to tell everyone apart."

Twenty minutes later, I'd hung up with Casey and was pulling up to the day's first wedding. It was the most grueling Valentine's Day weekend schedule I'd ever taken on. Due to the timing of everything, the 11th was a Friday, which made Valentine's Day a Monday. It made for four wedding dates that were highly in demand.

I rarely did two weddings in one single day, but for Valentine's Day, I made an exception. It was a premium weekend, which meant it brought in a lot of money. The better I did on weekends like this, the better a position it put me in to accommodate couples who needed to pay on the lower end of the scale.

I had two each on Friday, Saturday and Sunday and the Dryer wedding had always been the only one on Monday. Even though Monday was Valentine's Day proper, it was less in demand and I'd thought that after the weekend, I'd be too exhausted for two. Looks like I was getting two out of that one anyway.

Reflexively, I checked my phone before I got out of the car. Once wedding festivities swept me up, I'd be gone. There was only a text—from Cal—and it made my heart race.

I want to talk, too, he replied.

But I didn't have time to think too hard.

Tuesday? I shot back. I'd already told him that after the weekend would be best.

Before Tuesday, he returned right away.

You know what weekend this is, don't you?

He was lucky I hadn't shouted it in all-caps.

Of course I know. An I need to talk to you, C. This is important.

I frowned at the screen, awash in all kinds of confusion and annoyance. Forty minutes ago, it had been me summoning him. Now it was him somehow summoning me? But I couldn't do this now. Because I was working. And I couldn't make promises.

About to walk into a wedding. I'll try to call you on the margins.

And, with that, I turned my phone all the way off.

————

February 14th - The Dryer Wedding

FRIDAY NIGHT I'd forgotten to call, had been exhausted from the two weddings, and I hadn't gotten home until one. Saturday, Nellie's car had broken down. Since I had no plans to hear whatever Cal had to say to me on Bluetooth in front of her, I didn't have a chance to call him again until Saturday night. No answer, of course. Only texts here and there. Mixed calls from him, too. If I hadn't been so exhausted, I might have laughed at our failed exchanges. Two-and-a-half months had passed with nothing more than texts, e-mails and calls, and, all-of-a-sudden, each of us was clamoring to talk.

If I made it out of this Dryer wedding alive—and that was a big *if*—I would wait until tomorrow afternoon to try him again. Some part of me was glad we hadn't caught each other any of the times we'd called. I should be rested and coherent to say what I had to say. And it wasn't just that I was angry. I owed it to him to say that I'd been wrong—that I should have offered everything I did at the end without it coming to this.

I wasn't quite sure how Casey and Lacey had pulled off identical wedding gowns at such short notice, but it was helpful that each had a different-colored sash tied at the waist. Casey's was a brownish-green and Lacey's was a bluish-gray and I was thrilled to pieces that they hadn't taken the Valentine's Day thing too far with pinks and reds.

Nellie was getting better at handling the processional and was poised to get shots of the wedding party as they took their places. I stood in a strategic spot off to the sides. My job, for the moment, was to take shots of guest as they shuffled in and to eventually get the frontal view of brides walking down the aisle. Raising my camera into position, I did a practiced sweep. Slowly and methodically, I scanned for moments among the guests. If I was patient, I always found a few worth taking.

First was a stately older woman wearing a hat so exquisite she may as well have been attending a royal wedding. I smiled as I snapped a few shots of a drooling toddler falling apart with laughter every time a middle-aged man pulled funny faces. Next was Cal.

Wait...what?

Cal was at this wedding. Cal was somewhere in Asia Pacific.

No. It can't be him.

Except it was. Because I'd know him from any angle and in any light. From far away or close up, no matter the filter or lens. It had been ten weeks but I'd know Cal in ten years. I knew every last one of his lines.

I froze, unable, somehow, to stop staring at him through the view finder. My finger slackened, as if unwilling to shoot. Was I so relieved to see him—so furious with him—so hurt by him that I couldn't even snap his picture? Did the mere sight of him make me so unhinged that I couldn't even do my job?

His image went blurry. Muscle memory sent my finger back to the shutter release, commanding it to refocus with a light tap. I tapped again. I wanted to see him, but my lens didn't correct.

That's when I realized—the blurriness that had clouded my vision was my own tears.

Muscle memory kicked in again a few moments later when the first notes of *Pachelbel's Canon in D* came from the direction of the string quartet. The unmistakable cue signaled that the bridal party was ready to march. I kept my camera in position as I swiveled my torso to get a clear shot of the aisle. That the movement of bodies and the creaking of chairs could be heard as guests turned to watch. By the time the guests were on their feet for the brides and Wagner was playing, I was shooting again, tears wiped, and game face securely on.

Of course he was bound to show up for some local weddings. He'd been invited to at least a dozen that the studio had been hired to do. He'd always stood by my side—always chosen his job as my partner. Since he didn't work with me anymore, that meant he'd start going to weddings like a normal guest.

But, why this one?

Or, why not? It seemed there was much I didn't know about Cal Jameson. It was easy to forget, sometimes, that he'd grown up in this town.

The only thing that got me through the next forty minutes— through the vows and the passage readings, through the crowd's delighted laughter as the brides and grooms spoke their "I dos" in unison, through the soloist and her song—was the shield of my camera covering my face. I'd planned every shot meticulously, but I knew in the back of my mind that, if they had to, my instincts alone could get me halfway through. By the time the recessional had been played, Cal had disappeared. Had it been my imagination, to have felt his eyes on me the entire time?

Outside, the weather cooperated. The wedding party was compliant and even kind of fun. I had underestimated the patience of two families with multiples, though halfway through, the realization clicked: they were accustomed to doing everything twice. They had asked for the traditional shots, and I's got every permutation and combination of them all: the sisters, then the brothers, then both couples, then each couple with each set of in-laws, then flower girls and ring bearers, and then all of it in reverse. The family was all smiles—even the ones who waited on deck as I got different shots.

A week before, I would have been ecstatic about how unobtrusively Nellie had fallen in to get some of the candids, shepherding the wedding party only when she needed to and being invisible the rest of the time. But I wasn't happy—not when I nailed the gorgeous fish-eye shot I'd wanted of both couples descending the staircase simultaneously. Not when I'd gotten the perspective right on the speech of the father of the brides as he'd tearfully addressed both of his daughters. Not when I'd gotten dozens of other shots that could have been a disaster—shots that had kept me up at night and made me rue the day I'd acquiesce to a double-wedding job. Because knowing he was there—feeling the electricity that had been ignited by his sheer presence—electricity that I hadn't felt in weeks, confirmed my fear. Without Cal, my mojo still felt lost.

But it was even worse than that: because my game face worked only on strangers, and since he left, I'd been mostly getting by. Everyone else at this wedding—even vendors I'd been working with for years, and even Nellie who had seen me at less than my best...everyone else at this wedding would believe my facade of being in control. Everyone except for him.

It tapped my every insecurity, my every bit of rage, and my every oozing sore of hurt. Cal would watch me stumble and see clean through to what was wrong: I couldn't do this without him.

The day was winding down—or, at least it was for me. After the big speeches and the big dances, the photogenic nature of pretty much everyone at a wedding was cut in half. People were tired. And drunk. Some of them were sweaty from dancing. The women's makeup no longer looked fresh and brows furrowed from too-tight shoes and feet that hurt. This was the time of evening when I finally got to pee, when I started packing up the equipment I didn't plan to use anymore, and waited around to get the final shots of brides and grooms driving away.

"You haven't eaten all night," came the deep baritone I'd been waiting to hear. He'd been invisible, steering a wide berth and giving me my space, but some part of me knew he hadn't left.

I'd known this moment was coming, but I was afraid to turn around, certain that if I met his eyes, I'd never be able to look away. I'd seen everything in the dozen loaded gazes we'd shared throughout the night—the glue that had always held us together and proof that something I didn't understand had torn us apart.

But I did turn around, because nothing real that we had to say to each other was going to be said here, and because, above all else, he was still my friend. I wasn't stupid—I knew I was only so mad at him because he'd hurt me so much, but that didn't mean I got to ignore him or hurt him back.

I was saved from having to think up a witty retort when the vision of him sent different words spilling, unbidden, from my mouth. He still wore his tuxedo jacket, but the bowtie had been undone, and in his hand was a steaming plate. Its held a steaming pile of beef goulash and a pile of noodles next to it.

"How is that even hot?"

He shrugged. "I know people."

I'd been so busy with the double wedding—so preoccupied over Cal—that I hadn't seen Wolfgang all night. Cal didn't move to come farther into the room. I appraised him, looking him up and down in his tux with exaggerated scrutiny etched on my face because I was afraid to stay too long in his gaze.

"Guesting or crashing or...whatever you're doing becomes you," I complimented. "Though I'm surprised you interrupted your nomadic journey to fly 3,000 miles for a wedding."

"I didn't come back for the wedding. I came back because I wanted to talk to you."

He stepped toward me then and the rate of my heartbeat tripled—because what the hell did that mean and why now? And why was he even telling me this? He knew that I wasn't done.

"You can't back out of the feature. It's the New York Times Magazine."

He set the plate, a cloth napkin, and cutlery down on an empty corner of my work space. Whatever appetite had arisen from the smell of the goulash was dampened by the thought.

"They didn't want me. They wanted us."

He was close now—close enough to smell and close enough for me to feel his body heat. He paused in front of me long enough to breathe him in.

"Here I am."

I gritted my teeth. "You quit."

"So hire me back for the feature."

I felt my breath quiver as I let out a slow breath. "That's not how this works."

"Oh, good—there you are." Nellie's young voice interrupted our staring contest. Or, at least tried to, because I didn't break our stare. From my peripheral vision, I could see her looking back and forth between Cal and me. "O-kay." She backed away. "I'll just shoot the final exit myself."

"It works however you want it to." Cal said it the second Nellie left. Now it was his turn to clench his teeth. "I'm not gonna be the reason why you throw away this opportunity."

"You're missing the point."

"What am I missing?"

"That, with you gone, I have to rebrand. Because half of my brand has always been you."

He frowned and took a step back.

"What do you even mean by that?"

"I mean, it's not just the New York Times. Brides who want to book with me...vendors I run into on jobs...everyone who asks for me thinks they're getting you."

Comprehension dawned on his face and he looked at me with pity, but I didn't want that. "And, believe me, Cal, I understand. You *have* been half of this operation, but if you're not anymore, I have to own it. I don't want to mislead the New York Times."

He stepped closer to me and for a moment I thought we might actually touch. He looked almost like he wanted to hug me. Instead he stepped close into my space.

"I'm sorry. I know how bad you wanted it."

I tamped down my tears.

"I'm sorry you flew halfway around the world just to hear that."

———

February 15th - Best Valentine's Day Ever

SEEING his car in its regular spot made me want to abandon ship, or at least to pretend everything was normal until tomorrow. I'd taken for granted all those nights he'd beat me back to the studio, gotten food ready for us, and had the foresight to have already downloaded something entertaining for us to watch.

But our time had come, for what I didn't know. But this wasn't sustainable: flying around the world to escape, then get back to me, fighting about newspaper pieces...this wasn't how it was supposed to be. At least we'd gotten half of it over with at the wedding. And at least Nellie had chosen the exact right moment to learn her personal sensitivity lesson. But now it was time—high time—to deal with the rest.

I climbed the stairs to the loft slowly. He stood facing my bed, his back to the showroom below, and his back to me. His jacket was still on. So were his shoes. His bowtie hung loose in his hand. I wanted him to take his shoes and socks off. Shoes on in the loft meant that you were about to leave.

Finally, he turned to me, as beautiful as ever. It wasn't easy to stop my dismal thoughts. I wanted to hug him, to memorize him, to *photograph* him like this, in case things got weirder. In case this was the last time.

"I fucked up."

He said it at the very same time as I asked, painfully, "Why'd you leave?"

He brought his hand to the back of his neck, but didn't break my gaze.

"Because I fucked up."

This wasn't the Cal I knew. The Cal I knew was my rock—unmoving even in the fiercest of storms. Tonight, his dark eyes were stormy and his pain mirrored my own.

"Are you, like, in trouble with the law?" I didn't understand. That might explain why he'd left the country. But if he was in real trouble, why would he come back? He'd always been a bit too sexy to be a photographer's assistant, and uncommonly tech-savvy at that. Maybe this was where he was going to tell me he was an international spy.

"Something happened. At Kilroy. Do you really not remember?" He stepped toward me and his eyes searched mine. "Like, anything? Do you remember, literally, anything from Saturday night?"

Of course I remembered that night. Thinking of that weekend with him took me to my happy place.

"I remember the reception ending and me not wanting to call it a night. I remember us bringing a bottle of wine down to the lake. I remember we'd brought the wine glasses but we forgot to bring down an opener, so you did some trick to get it open with your pocket knife."

I spoke softly, and even more softly then when I realized it was calming him down.

"I remember that we drank half the bottle and we talked about shooting at night. And you told me a story about your mom..."

I quieted then, thinking of the story, then thinking of afterward, as we'd sat with our arms linked and my head on his shoulder.

"And then we hiked back and we each went to bed and I woke up the next morning under a down comforter and 1,000 thread count sheets."

"So you remember walking back?"

I blinked. "I think so." I narrowed my eyes. What was to remember about a dark trail?

"Do you remember bumping into Satya and Siva?"

Satya and Siva were the bride and groom. And, no, I didn't remember bumping into them.

"Do you remember holding hands on the way back to the cottage, and you tripping and me catching you right before you slid down that little hill?"

What was he talking about?

"What are you talking about?"

"But you do remember seeing Satya at Sunday Brunch, and thinking that something she said about seeing you the night before was weird."

Shit. I did remember that. She'd asked me how I'd liked my walk. I'd answered politely that it had been lovely, but had wondered how she'd known.

I nodded confirmation. "I still don't understand. What does this have to do with...anything?"

He winced a little. "You were drugged."

"What? By who?"

He fisted his hand in his silky hair and tried to explain. "By no one. By yourself. By me."

I shook my head, meaning to ask for a little more detail, but the words wouldn't even come out.

"The pills were mine. You thought it was headache medicine. It wasn't."

"You had pills? What kind of pills?"

"Old pills I packed for sleeping. It's always hit or miss for me, sleeping in hotels. And I'd already had some trouble that week 'cause—"

"—it was near the anniversary of your mother's death," I interrupted

I sighed and looked toward the window, working it all out as it came together in my head. I'd had a headache and he'd told me to look for a bottle of aspirin in his bag. We'd stopped in his hotel room and he'd been in the bathroom, changing. I'd taken two pills and popped them into my mouth.

"You threw your sleeping pills in your bottle."

He nodded, looking more ashamed than she'd ever seen him.

"I always packed yours in the camera bag. I never planned on you being in my stash."

"Why didn't you just tell me? We could have laughed about it..."

"'Cause you don't remember what we did." He said it a bit forcefully.

"Alright, you're scaring me. You're making it sound like we killed somebody."

He stepped closer and I did hold my breath then, because his eyes were blazing. "We kissed." He seemed out of breath. "For *awhile*."

Now it was me who didn't breathe. I did manage to swallow. "How long is awhile?"

His eyes changed yet again, to something apologetic. Suddenly, he seemed tired. "Long enough, and sweet enough, and sexy enough for me to think that you wanted the same thing I did and that, come morning, things between us would change."

Then I woke up.

And I didn't remember any of it.

But he couldn't handle that he did.

Or that we worked together.

That's when things got weird.

That's when he resigned, and he ran.

"You were my boss—" he continued, but I cut him clean off.

"I missed our first kiss?" That it might have been the stupidest question that could ever have been asked in response to this fiasco didn't faze me. My eyes still smarted with tears. For me, for him for this fucked up situation. "What was it like?"

I read the cautious hope in his eyes. He shook his head and said it on a sigh: "Epic."

"Wrong answer."

His eyes narrowed for a millisecond before widening in understanding. I wanted him to show me.

I was halfway to swooning in toward him when, in the least-expected of moves, he sidestepped to my bed, and snapped up my faux-fur blanket. He took me gently by the hand and turned off the floor lamp before walking me toward the window next to my bed. He settled me in front of him and draped the blanket around his shoulders until he'd buried both of us inside it, my back to his chest. He held me tightly, and it felt familiar—not like I'd merely day-dreamt of this—like I'd actually done it before.

"We'd gotten back to your room. Yours had a balcony and a view of the lake. We still had a third of a bottle of wine, so you invited me in."

His cheek was against mine and my eyes were already closed

and I was taking in his voice's vibrations. He looked like sunshine but he smelled exactly like himself.

"The back of the sofa in your room had a thick fleece blanket. We grabbed it and went outside to look at the stars, just like this."

Except I wasn't looking at the stars. I wasn't looking at anything. I was just taking in how I felt in his arms.

"And you smelled so delicious and your skin was so soft, and I'd waited so many years to do it that I just..."

His lips lowered down to graze my jaw.

I turned in his arms then, not caring anymore how it had happened that night—only caring how it would happen now—only caring that we didn't wait another minute. Because he was here. He'd come back. And I couldn't let him go. Not ever again.

His lips were as soft as they'd always looked, and his tongue every bit as deft, and his arms every bit as strong as they held me. His eyes had concealed every bit of passion, his breath every bit of need, and his pounding heart every bit of love that I'd ever dared to imagine.

And in that kiss, I saw it all: I saw more starry nights and more bottles of wine; and more snuggles in many more cozy blankets; I saw the wedding we'd have at the Kilroy and the photos we'd take together as we traveled the world; the little darkroom we'd build, and the pride we'd share when we taught our daughter her to develop her first picture. I saw our future together. And it was epic.

"WOLF AT THE WEDDING" BY ERIN ST. CHARLES

CRAZY IN LOVE

Vanessa Miller braced her maroon dyed-to-match shoes on the floorboards of the golf cart as Bubba Cermak executed a sharp turn that almost had her spilling out of the open passenger side. She grabbed the bucket seat and the side of the cart with hands that were stiff from the cold.

"Can you please slow down?" She panted, glaring at Bubba.

"We don't have time to waste, City Mouse," he told her, his brows together as they navigated around the sand traps. He glanced over at her after he spoke, and had the same self-satisfied expression on his face that he sported most of the time.

The fact was that Bubba seemed to enjoy annoying the fuck out of her with liberal use of terms of endearment, when she'd repeatedly asked him to knock it off. But then, Bubba wasn't the kind of guy who much respected boundaries.

"We'll have even less time to waste if the best man or the matron of honor winds up in a hospital because of your insane driving," she ground out from clenched teeth.

"Off-topic, but since you've never been married, are you sure you're not the maid of honor? You're too young to be a matron."

Her lips twitched in an involuntary smile, which she covered up with another glare. "Why do you say things like that?"

He chuckled.

"It should be obvious. I'm flirting with you. Trying to make you laugh." He said this with a silly grin plastered across his stupid, good-looking wolf face. She resisted the urge to melt at his attempts to impress her.

"Listen, just focus on your driving. Don't waste time trying to impress me."

As they drove, Vanessa scanned for anyone looking out of place at a golf course on a Saturday evening. Someone like, say, a preacher who should have been at the chapel at this very moment, instead of wherever the hell he was right now. The man was a Luddite and did not use an Omni. They had been trying to reach him for the last half hour, without success.

After an unconventional and somewhat roundabout courtship, Diana Miller and Mac Bodie were set to marry this fine Valentine's Day evening. Unfortunately, the preacher was MIA, so of course Vanessa, as the matron of honor, had volunteered to find the wayward preacher and bring him to the chapel. Bubba immediately jumped in, claiming the best man should help. Now here they were, charging around on a golf cart. She should have stayed at the chapel.

Diana, her sister, a hard-charging career woman, had morphed into a bridezilla during the wedding preparations. When Diana and Mac finally announced a wedding date, fully a year after their twins were born, Vanessa had naïvely assumed her sister would want a low-key wedding.

Vanessa had been wrong. So very wrong.

Diana, a social worker who looked after the sex workers in Dallas's red-light district, seemed to have invited everyone she

knew. Every client she'd ever had was on the list. Her pimps and
hos, amazingly, managed to dress wedding-appropriate.

Right now, Diana and Mac's professional contacts, as well as
family members, friends, and plus-ones all waited patiently at the
adorable wedding chapel that pre-dated the country club.

Diana tried, and failed, to keep from losing her shit as the
minutes ticked by without the preacher. Their mother had
unhelpfully suggested that had Diana and Mac decided to marry
in a Catholic church, the priest would not have been late. It was
possibly true, but again, unhelpful in the face of the current
dilemma.

The wedding planning experience had frayed Diana's nerves
to the snapping point, and she was at the end of her rope. It was
just all too much to deal with, and only Vanessa's admonishment
not to ruin her professionally-done makeup with her tears of frustration had kept Diana's trembling lips from escalating into a full-
on ugly cry.

"You think your sister will react poorly if we can't find the
preacher and get him to the service on time?" Bubba asked, as if
reading her mind. He cocked an eyebrow at her, topaz eyes fixed
on her with an arch expression.

There was no restraint considered, no expense spared, when
it came to making Diana's wedding dreams come true. Diana's
wedding fête consisting of three hundred or so of the couple's
closest friends and family. Vanessa was frankly surprised that her
sister and fiancé knew that many people.

The location had to be perfect, too. And that was why they
were now bumping along the fairway or whatever they called the
rolling golf course of the posh country club Mac's old money
family were members of.

"Hang on," Bubba gritted through clenched teeth. Her head
swiveled just as they narrowly skirted a water trap.

She turned incredulous eyes on him, her mouth open.

"Are you trying to get us killed?" She yelled. "Slow the fuck down!"

"Now baby, there's no reason to get testy." He placed a hand on her satin-covered thigh, and gave her a lecherous grin.

She was at first surprised by his boldness, then annoyed at his audacity. Pulse pounding with pique, she plucked his hand off her thigh and moved her leg away.

"Keep your eyes on the road...or the grass," her words were clipped. She glared at him again, then turned her eyes to the green ahead of them. The man was beyond infuriating. "I am not testy, and stop calling me 'baby'."

Vanessa had not been enthused about standing up at her sister's wedding, not because she didn't love her sister, but because she preferred to keep her distance from the groom's best friend, Bubba. The man had shown his interest in her since they'd first met more than a year ago. But Bubba was a shifter, a predator, and she'd been down that road before. It only led to heartbreak.

Vanessa had resolved after her girls were born that her free-wheeling days were behind her. She needed to focus on her girls, who were shifters themselves, to raise them in a world that still discriminated against shifters.

She couldn't let her sister down, though. For the past few months, Vanessa had been the perfect sister, arranging the engagement party in Chicago, throwing the bridal shower with the help of Diana's clients, and gamely planning the Las Vegas bachelorette party. Diana was Vanessa's twin, her womb mate, and her best friend. Vanessa would do anything to make her sister's wedding day perfect. So she'd tolerated Bubba Cermak, who had a knack for showing up at places when she least expected it.

The engagement party in Chicago, which she had been careful to schedule when he was supposed to be away on a mission? He had somehow managed to show up. Since he had been part of the wedding party, she couldn't exactly ask him to leave.

Bubba had also crashed the bridal shower and bachelorette parties, whose timing and locations had been closely guarded secrets, but Vanessa had drawn the line at allowing him to attend. He shamelessly used his considerable charms to insinuate himself into the good graces of anyone he came in contact with. This included her mother, who evidently thought Bubba was Vanessa's last hope to find a nice Catholic boy to settle down with. Vanessa's twins adored "Uncle Bubba." The women who attended Diana's pre-wedding parties also liked Bubba, while also acknowledging Bubba had a reputation as a player.

Even knowing all this about the man, if she wasn't careful, she could easily become sucked into his devastating wolf charm. The man was equally at home in jeans and a T-shirt, like he'd worn to crash the bridal festivities, as he was in the tailored tuxedo he now wore. The charcoal gray tuxedo was the perfect complement to his pale complexion. It was only enhanced by the slight stubble framing the curved lips that invited kisses and nibbles.

Yep, Bubba Cermak was a fine specimen of a man. It was equally true that Bubba was known for saying the wrong thing, his brain-to-mouth filter as leaky as a colander. Once you got past all that, it was easy to become enthralled with his broad shoulders, his flat abs, his muscular arms, and, glory be, the bulge that hinted at the promised land between his legs. The trousers of his suit revealed the man's propensity to dress left. This wasn't the first time she had noticed, either. There were many times where her eyes were irresistibly drawn to the man's groin. She was pretty good at hiding it too...

"What's on your mind, City Mouse?"

Vanessa snapped out of her salacious thoughts to find Bubba

pinning her with a knowing expression, one eyebrow cocked and wolfish eyes gleaming at her.

He didn't see me checking out his package...did he? She blinked quickly and looked into his topaz eyes. His gaze was impassive, assessing, eyeing her speculatively. He smirked, but if he had caught her checking out his package, he made no sign of having done so.

"I'm... where are we going?" She stammered, looking around and thinking she sounded like an idiot.

They had come to an area close to a massive parking lot. Beyond it was the entrance to the country club. The air held a chill that was more obvious when her mind wasn't consumed with pervy thoughts of him. She watched him, holding her breath, waiting for his answer.

Bubba stopped the cart and looked at her. His eyes took a leisurely stroll over her body, blatantly landing on her chest and her nipples, which had hardened into pebbles underneath the thin silver material of her bridesmaid's gown. His eyes, a beautiful topaz with a dark gray ring around the irises, looked into hers.

"You look cold," he told her, smirking.

He removed his suit jacket and draped it over her shoulders before she could refuse it. Like most shifters, the man ran hot, and when the suit jacket landed on her shoulders, her whole body was cradled by his residual warmth. His intoxicating scent lingered on the suit jacket as well, and she could not help but inhale it.

"Thank you," she mumbled, pulling the suit jacket around her and looking away from him. Her face burned with embarrassment.

Then they were once again moving, the little golf cart bouncing along the green, then ontp the asphalt, dodging the parked cars of club members, finally pulling up to one of the stone pillars abutting the front gate. They came upon a short man with an ambitious comb-over who was dressed in a black suit with a clerical collar. The little man stood next to a small sedan looking distressed. As they drew closer, Vanessa realized the car had evidently hit a curb, the driver lost control of the car, and it wound up nose up in a now ruined flower bed. It had to be their pastor.

Bubba parked the golf cart and rounded to Vanessa's side of the vehicle with a few long strides to help her out.

She mentally braced herself for the inevitable physical reaction she always felt when they had occasion to touch skin-to-skin. When their fingers touched, a pleasant sizzle of electricity rushed over her body.

"I'm okay," she said, snatching her hand away abruptly. Bubba's smirk returned.

Did he feel the same surge of electricity that I did?

But, there wasn't any time to waste puzzling over this.

They had a wedding to save.

Get Me to the Church on Time

AFTER DETERMINING that the little man's sedan could not be moved at the moment, Bubba hustled the preacher into the back seat of the golf cart. They ignored the car in the flowerbed in favor or getting them to the wedding as soon as possible.

It turns out the preacher had been in a hurry to get to the wedding and, already running late and unfamiliar with the country club, had missed the entrance entirely. He'd tried to make a quick U-turn, but he'd gone wide of the mark and wound up plowing into the flower bed. The man was beside himself at the damage he'd done, and wanted to stay to see to his car.

"I'll take care of this later," Bubba told the man. "You're already late for the wedding."

Bubba saw Vanessa brace herself again, as if preparing for a hard crash landing. She had her feet pressed against the floorboards as Bubba turned the cart around and went barreling back the way they came.

"Slow down!" Vanessa cried from the passenger seat, eyes bugging out at him. Her reddish brown hair was pulled back from her gorgeous face and she wore a bunch of fresh roses around the base of her tidy bun. Her hair was always wild, and he wondered what manner of wizardry had her springy locks tamed to such a degree.

She narrowed her eyes in a warning glare and he repressed his smirk. Her glares always turned him on. He supposed this was the opposite of what she was going after.

"Yes, son, please slow down," said the little man in the back seat. The little man who couldn't even drive through the front entrance of the country club without wrecking his own car.

Back seat driver Bubba thought to himself, not in the mood to have his driving criticized. *This guy has a lot of nerve.*

"I just want to get there in one piece," the man said in a rush.

The design of the golf cart had the man seated right behind Bubba, basically with his back to the front seat, and he caught a whiff of fear in the man's scent. When Bubba looked at the man, his face was flattened in fear, his blue eyes beady in his pale face.

Did I say that out loud?

Bubba glanced at Vanessa.

"No comments from the peanut gallery," she admonished.

Oops. He had said that out loud.

Returning to the chapel took much less time than retrieving the preacher, and soon they were parked in front and heading up the steps. As they entered, Bubba spotted Mac, who stood in front so as to avoid seeing the bride, who was....wherever brides hid themselves before weddings.

Vanessa stalked towards the back of the church, the back of her silver dress trailing behind her, still wearing Bubba's suit jacket.

"Nessa!" He called out, then rushed after her. When he caught up with her, she gave him an aggrieved "what the fuck" look, her pale brown eyes huge and irritated, her soft, plush lips pursed.

Once again her irritation only made him hot and bothered. A thought popped into his head. Actually, more like an image, one that involved him palming each of her ass cheeks in one of his hands, her legs wrapped around his waist, backing her into a wall as he chewed and sucked on her lips. His dick went hard in response to these wayward thoughts, her proximity, and the death glare she now directed at him. The woman was so fucking hot.

Blood drained from his brain and surged toward his man parts. He almost forgot what he wanted to say to her, but her annoyed, "What?" snapped him out of his daze.

"My jacket looks great on you, but I don't think your sister is gonna want me standing up for Mac unless I'm wearing it." He gave her the most charming smile he could muster.

She maintained eye contact, her expression challenging him. He shifted his legs, the better to accommodate his lengthening arousal, and stared right back at her. The sexual tension between them crackled like kernels of popcorn tossed in hot oil. She removed the jacket and handed it to him. Then she raised an eyebrow, turned on her dyed-to-match heels, and stalked away, her shoes making a sharp snap on the floor.

He watched her retreating backside, covered in a silvery fabric that emphasized every sway of her hips, as she walked away. He pursed his lips in appreciation and absently adjusted his cock in his pants.

"Excuse me," came a rich bass voice, snapping him out of his thoughts.

Bubba whirled around and his eyes locked with those of Mac. His best friend was glowering at him. Unlike Vanessa's death glare, Mac's disapproving look caused Bubba's dick to go soft. All things considered, it was probably for the best.

Bubba cleared his throat and nodded at Mac.

Show time.

————

White Wedding

THE OFFICIANT SMOOTHED THIS HAIR, squared his shoulders, and waited for the cue to start. The wedding march began, and Mac stood at the end of the aisle looking as cool as a cucumber.

Diana began to walk up the aisle alone, and Vanessa felt a pang of sadness over their missing father. He had been gone for half their lives, killed in the line of duty while he worked for the Chicago PD, and sometimes she forgot his absence. Then something happened and the grief came back to her, washing over her and percussive waves. Suddenly, she was transported back to when she and her twin were teenagers, and her father had just been killed. The pain, the grief, washed over her anew as if they had just lost him.

Vanessa rallied. This was her sister's special day and she was going to make sure Diana had a beautiful wedding.

————

Forever My Lady

"LADIES AND GENTLEMEN, I present to you, Mr. and Mrs. Bodie!"

The diminutive preacher stretched his arms out as if to air cuddle the newly married couple, and addressed the congregation. Applause, howls, and ululations erupted from the crowd. Diana and Mac grinned stupidly at one another as they made their way out of the church, hand-in-hand. The wedding party followed right behind.

They moved to the side, and Bubba watched as the guests filed out of the chapel and headed over to the event hall, just a few yards away, where appetizers and an open bar awaited the guests. The wedding party milled around and waited for the photographer.

It was then that Bubba saw the two Dallas Police Department uniforms making their way up the hill on a pair of motorcycles. And out of the corner of his eye, he saw Vanessa stalk over to head them off. He jogged over to the three of them to intervene.

As he got closer, he heard them telling Vanessa that they had run the car's registration and discovered the owner was a pastor who lived on the other side of town. They put two and two together, deduced that the man was there to perform a wedding, and had tracked him to the ceremony.

They were now ready to take the pastor's statement and/or apprehend him for causing damage to the club and fleeing the scene of the accident. Vanessa somehow managed to convince them to wait until after the photos had been taken.

For the better part of an hour, the wedding party took photos together. Bubba made sure he appeared in as many photos as possible with Vanessa and her twins, Scarlett and Charlotte. He kept the girls giggling and loose throughout the photo shoot, instead of frisky and sullen.

After the photos were taken, the preacher was taken away by the police.

He held hands with the girls and they strolled into the reception.

Don't You Want Me Baby?

AS BUBBA LED her daughters into the hall, Vanessa frowned at his high-handedness. He wasn't their father, after all. But she had to admit he took good care of them. Watched out for them.

Hell, if Vanessa was completely honest with herself, even *she* liked Bubba. However, that didn't mean she needed to date him. Or sleep with him. Vanessa only wanted to like Bubba in a platonic, friend-zone way.

Bubba had made it super-clear that he didn't want to be friend-zoned. He flirted without mercy, showed up wherever he thought she would be, and—she suspected—had enlisted her mother in his plan to win Vanessa over, these past couple of months. He was fixated on her. She could do nothing to dissuade his attentions. He had even begun to insist with sincerity in his topaz eyes that they were mates.

Vanessa had heard this line before, from Ben, the twins' coywolf shifter father, when she had informed him of her pregnancy.

She thought about that grin Bubba gave her, his teeth flashing white and the scar bisecting his eyebrow and trailing down his cheek giving him a rakish look. Vanessa had often wondered how he got the injury. As a wolf shifter, it should have healed with a less noticeable scar.

She had wondered, but hadn't asked. She didn't want to encourage him, and she knew he would consider personal questions encouragement. Bubba made no secret that he had a "thing" for Vanessa, had since they'd first met at her sister's barbecue.

But Bubba was a player, and she didn't want to go there with him. She had two little girls to think about, and she didn't have time to play games. He kept hinting that he wanted more from a relationship. But Vanessa have been around the block with Ben, the coywolf who had fathered her children. Ben wasn't built for commitment, and she didn't want to mate him just because of her pregnancy.

But Bubba was a whole lot of sexy.

Wall-to-wall sexy.

She could look, but not touch. As he walked away, she reminded herself again.

Look, don't touch.

———

Why Did Love Put a Gun in My Hand?

VANESSA EYED Bubba's outstretched hand doubtfully. Around her, the guests ate at their tables and cheerfully chatted. Diana, the bride, was making calf eyes at Mac.

And Bubba had just informed her it was their dance. In order not to make a scene, she placed her hand in his, and followed him to the dance floor.

She doubted very seriously that there was an actual, real tradition involving the matron of honor and best man dancing. She was pretty sure the so-called tradition was just some shit Bubba made up in order to get her on the dance floor and cop a feel.

Nevertheless, when he asked her to dance in front of every-one, citing the tradition that no one had heard about, it was easier to just go along with it. So while three hundred of Mac and

Diana's closest friends and family looked on, Bubba had taken Vanessa by the hand and led her to the dance floor.

When they were out of earshot of the mostly non-shifter guests, Vanessa placed a hand on Bubba's bicep and leaned close to whisper in his ear. To most, it would look like a friendly, intimate gesture. But what she said to him was anything but.

"Make sure you keep your hands where they belong," she smiled and whispered between clenched teeth. He placed his large hands on her waist, and pulled her close to him. She tried not to respond to his nearness, employing the mantra she'd been using around him for the past 18 months.

Don't fuck the shifter. Don't fuck the shifter.

It mostly worked. She had to admit, though, that it was difficult when he was so close to her. They stood like that, in the middle of the dance floor, waiting for the music to start.

"City Mouse, I won't do anything you don't want me to do."

Bubba looked into her eyes. His mouth was saying the right things, but his eyes were fucking her. Fortunately, the guests were too far away to know what he was up to.

"I told you, I really do not care for all the nicknames."

The music isn't starting. Why isn't the music starting?

"Oh, you are so prickly these days. Everything okay with Gaylord?" Bubba's eyes looked at her with the predatory gleam.

"I've told you many times, his name is Gavin," she said, invoking the name of her usual plus one, who was unavailable to be her date for Diana's wedding. "Gavin couldn't make it. He had a business trip."

"If you were my woman, I wouldn't let you attend your sister's wedding alone."

His voice was a sexy growl that made her catch her breath and sent shivers skating over her skin. It vibrated through her body and went straight to her clit. His voice and his palm planted at the small of her back, just on the right side of decency, almost made her forget her resolve to keep this man at arm's length. She'd had bad experiences with shifter men.

The music started just then. Dorothy's *Gun in My Hand* blared from the surround sound. *What on earth?*

"Who picked the song?" She asked, thinking this particular song was highly inappropriate for a wedding dance.

"What, you don't like this?" He asked her, flashing that smile of his again. The man was far too good-looking for words. She wanted to trace his scar with her fingertips...

Nope. Nope. Nope. Not gonna go there. Nope.

"Don't tell me you picked this out?" She drew back and looked at him, incredulous. "Did you know that children would be here?"

The thought had her scanning the crowd for her girls. Bubba must have caught her glance, because he leaned and whispered in her ear.

"Relax. They're fine. They're having a good time."

And at just that moment, Vanessa's eyes landed on her twins, who were playing pat-a-cake with Diana's twins, watched over by their grandmother. Vanessa let out a sigh.

"So they are," she acknowledged.

"So... about Garfield..." He started, steering her back to the subject of Gavin.

She rolled her eyes at him. "You mean Gavin? What about Gavin?"

"When are you going to dump that guy, and ride off into the sunset with me?" His topaz eyes looked into her caramel ones.

"I'm not. Gavin is a great guy. I have no reason to dump him."

Also, she and Gavin were just friends. She decided to keep the information to herself. She just didn't want to get into it with Bubba again. She'd been with a wolf shifter before, only to have it not work out. She wasn't going to put her daughters through a process of getting to know someone, getting to rely on them, only to have them go away. Bubba was a player, and she didn't want that kind of heartbreak for her daughters—or for herself.

"I can think of several reasons why you need to dump him," Bubba said, sliding his hand over her back. His hand didn't move more than a couple of inches, but her back snapped up straight and she found herself arching into him subtly. Annoyed with herself, she relaxed her shoulders again.

"Everything okay, baby?" He stroked her back again, the same subtle motion that practically had her creaming her underwear a moment before. He knew exactly what he was doing to her, the bastard. Most wolves had a sort of native charm, even the ones that barely had any game. Bubba was an alpha wolf, and had that seductive charm in spades.

"Everything's fine." The fact that her voice came out in a squeak that undermined her assertion made her clench her teeth. Oh she was fine, just a little too fine.

"You want to know what I think?" Bubba asked.

"Think? About what?" The words were supposed to come out smooth and calm. Instead, they came out rushed and high-pitched.

He stroked her back again, and she almost came out of her skin.

"Relax, sweetheart." This time, he combined that back-stroking with a whisper in her ear. His lips grazed the shell of her ear, and she let out an involuntary sigh.

"I think you use poor Geoffrey as armor. Against me."

"Wha-what do you mean?"

He stroked her again, trailing his fingers to the small of her back and applying subtle pressure there. She, in turn, did a subtle arch into his body. She felt a little light headed.

"I make you feel good, and that scares you. With Gaylord in the picture, you have a reason not to give into me. But you forgot something important."

She frowned, her hackles raising. "What are you talking about?"

"I'm a wolf." Again, he whispered in her ear. "I know what you smell like. You don't smell like him. I don't think he's even gotten to first base with you."

Yeah, that was true. But she was not about to admit as much to Bubba.

"It's none of your business," she told him.

He chuckled. "It's absolutely my business. We've been at this for eighteen months."

"Been at what?" she feigned ignorance.

"Our courtship," he said simply. She tried to pull away from him, but his hands were like steel bands around her, holding her in place. It was frustrating...and a little exciting. He took advantage of her captivity to bring her a tad closer so that she could feel his...

Jesus, Mary and Joseph. The man must have stuffed a cucumber down his pants...

"No. This is not a courtship. I'm not even sure it's a friendship," she told him in a sputtering stream of outrage.

Goddamn good-looking cocky bastard!

The song ended, then Michael Jackson's "Give In To Me" started up.

"Let me guess. You picked this one too? Could you be more obvious?"

"This is definitely a courtship," he said smoothly. "But I have to tell you, I'm about out of patience. If we were in the old country, we wouldn't even be having this discussion."

"Oh, is that right?" This man really did take the cake. Vanessa didn't care how big his dick was. She wasn't buying what he was selling.

"The first time I saw you, I knew you were meant to be mine."

She scoffed. "Oh no, that's not stalkerish at all."

"Vanessa."

She tried to ignore the way he said her name. His voice was too deep. Too intense. Too... everything. She didn't want to feel this way about any man, and especially not Bubba Cermak.

"Bubba, what is it?" The moment this song was over, she was out of there. He pulled away from her, but kept them both swaying to the music. He looked deeply into her eyes. She saw lust in his eyes, along with something else. *Longing*. He had longing in his eyes. And she didn't like it. It scared her. It scared her because she thought she knew how he felt.

"You are my mate. I knew it the first time I saw you. I've tried to let you set some of the pace. I know you've been hurt before. But I'm getting to the point where I can't wait anymore. There's things I need to go home and take care of, and it will be much better if I have my mate with me."

After he dropped that bomb on her, and before she could think straight, he had her back in the steel trap of his arms again.

"I don't do mates," she told him, coldly. "My girls' father wanted to be mates, but I refused. I don't believe in that shit. And I don't believe that you do, either."

He frowned at her. "What are you talking about? To wolves, the mate bond is the most sacred thing there is. You think I'm joking?"

His emotions had turned on a dime. Instead of the passion and longing of a moment ago, she saw pure anger in his eyes. But she wouldn't let him play with her, pretending that his desire to get her in the sack was anything more than pure animal lust. He could never convince her that he was anything other than a player and she was angry that he seemed intent on trying. She was furious at how he tried to play her emotions.

"Whatever you need to do with your pack, kindly leave me out of it."

"Vanessa —"

She ignored the way hearing her given name on his lips made her feel. All shivery and tingling from wanting him to say her name, and having him do it. He was dangerous, and not just because he was sex in a tux.

Time to get out of here. She didn't care how it would look if she left him alone on the dance floor. This was all about protecting herself now. Protecting her daughters from disappointment. Protecting herself from empty promises. She clenched her jaw and met his angry eyes with her determined ones. She gave him a peek at her emotions, her irritation. Her anger.

"I have to go," she told him through clenched teeth.

"Vanessa --" he laced the fingers of his left hand with her right. She looked at their entwined fingers, hers slender and brown, his pale and strong, with veins through the webbing.

We are one.

She heard his voice, but his lips didn't move. *What the hell?*

We are intertwined already. You can't just walk away from it.

"I'm not the one for you, Bubba. So just move on. Find someone else."

Then he did let her go, his fingers releasing hers and she felt a sense of loss, because she missed his warmth. But she didn't want him, right?

She booked out of there like Cinderella trying to beat the clock before it struck twelve. But her prince just stood in the middle of the dance floor, watching her go.

He'll move on, she told herself as she made her way off the dance floor. Thankfully, the dance floor had quickly filled up, and half the guests were shifters, so a tall woman rushing from the dance floor didn't attract as much attention as she might have otherwise. She was shaking all over, and breathing so hard she felt about ready to faint. Perspiration gathered on her upper lip. Her makeup would surely need to be touched up, so she headed for the ladies room.

The bathroom was empty, thank God, and she was able to press cool, wet towels to her overheated skin in peace. She locked herself in a stall and put her head between her knees to catch her breath.

When she emerged, the party was in full swing. She stood in the corridor outside of the ladies room, her eyes closed as she listened to and swayed with the music. As one song ended and another began, she felt an awareness creep over her skin in the form of an all-body blush. She got goosebumps all over, her nipples went painfully hard, and she knew before she opened her eyes who would be there. Watching her.

She let out a shaky sigh, and resolved to get it over with.

When she opened her eyes, it was to a pair of topaz eyes. His eyeshine glowed green in the half-light.

Bubba.

———

Brown-Eyed Girls

SHE SHOULD HAVE KNOWN BETTER than to try running from an apex predator. Hell, the woman had known him for a year and a half—surely she'd know something about him by this time.

With the wedding now behind them, and her sister settled into domestic bliss, Bubba was about done with pussy footing around. He had long-since gotten past why she was making this so hard for him—and thus, for them. She wanted him, this he knew with certainty. And he wanted her too.

She liked to pretend that he was nothing more than a pest, but Bubba knew better. Bubba was steeped in the way of wolves, but also knew a little about the way of humans. Mac, his best friend, had mentioned that Vanessa's sister Diana was hard to get.

She didn't play hard to get. She *was* hard to get, as were apparently all of the Miller sisters. But Bubba was confident in his abilities to win Vanessa over, and claim her eventually. He had time. They both had time, and it was better to make her all into the idea, rather than try to talk her into something she wasn't sure about.

These thoughts swirled in his mind as he followed her scent trail to the corridor of the country club that led to the rest rooms. His nose led him to the ladies room. A female icon on the door, along with a concentrated scent signature, confirmed that he had caught up with his mate. He leaned against the wall opposite the closed door and waited.

Several women exited the restroom, startled at the 6' 5", scarred yet handsome strawberry blond shifter male who seemed inordinately interested in the women's restroom. He got a couple of double-takes and disapproving frowns, as women walked by where he stood, looking for all the world like a pervert interested in the toilet habits of strange women.

After a few minutes, he started to wonder whether Vanessa planned to come out again. It was past-time to move this courtship along. Hell, his cousin Phelan had met his fated mate, moved in with her, and gotten her knocked up. And Phelan didn't have half the game and his whole body than Bubba had in his little finger.

Her eyes landed on his, then narrowed.

"What do you want?" she huffed.

Pussy? Fellatio? Maybe even doggie-style? He thought.

"Another dance?" He said.

Even though what he wanted was a full mounting, shifter style, with her pretty, high ass in the air, his large hand wrapped firmly around her neck, but not enough to cut off her ability to breathe. The dress was a little tight...but he believed he could work around it in a pinch.

He could steer her back into the ladies room, lock the door, and fuck her in front of the sink, so that their eyes could meet in the mirror, and he could make her look as he claimed her.

Goddamn, the woman was hot!

His lascivious internal monologue must have been all over his expression, because she twisted her pretty face into a scowl, and made a beeline around him, headed back to the ballroom.

She got a few paces from him, and he had to jog to catch up to her. But he didn't move too fast, because honestly, he wanted to enjoy looking at her firm ass for just a few moments more. Vanessa Miller was beautiful, sexy as fuck, and a great mother—she was the perfect mate and wife for an alpha wolf like himself. What was more, he had great affection for Charlotte and Scarlett, Vanessa's twin girls. And the girls loved him.

She was smart and capable, extremely tenacious (as evidenced by her continual rejection of his courtship).

And beautiful, and sexy, and...

Vanessa whirled around and confronted Bubba.

"Why are you following me? We already had our so-called dance. I'm done with you. Go away."

She made shooing motions with her hands, turned on her heel, and stalked away. He stood there, baffled, and she strolled her hot ass back into the ballroom. He was only a few paces behind her. Maybe it was a little stalkerish to not give her any space. He was willing to make some concessions to her wishes, but in the back of his mind, he kept a tally of all the spankings he owed her as a result of the insolence she'd shown in the throes of their courting.

Yes. She would pay. He chuckled to himself.

Bubba arrived at the ballroom and looked around, trying to spot Vanessa. His eyes landed on her just as she dragged one of his men from the agency onto the dance floor. Blake LaTour, a big, blond minotaur shifter, looked deeply unhappy to be socializing. But his good Southern manners prevented him from turning Vanessa down.

Vanessa smiled pleasantly at the man, not even glancing in Bubba's direction. He decided to leave well enough alone in favor of socializing with guests. He made his way to the head table. Sitting with the rest of the wedding party would afford Bubba a good view of the dance floor, where Vanessa was dancing with Blake. The other man placed a meaty hand on Vanessa's slender waist, while she beamed up at the man. Vanessa was about six feet tall, and in heels, she was just about eye-to-eye with Bubba. Blake had a powerful minotaur build, wide shoulders, a heavily muscled, "beefy" body that strained the confines of his charcoal suit.

Bubba took a seat next to Leona Miller, mother of the bride and the matron-of-honor. He liked Leona. She was blunt, straightforward, and she liked Bubba.

He nodded at the woman. "Beautiful service," he said to Leona, but he kept his eyes on the dance floor.

"Would have been even better had they held it in a church. With a priest," Leona said, with a huff.

"Don't worry, ma'am. When Vanessa and I get married, it will be in a church, with a priest. There's a nice parish in my hometown, Perdition, and it's a nice place to live too." His eyes narrowed and his beast growled in the back of his mind as he watched Vanessa and Blake dance. *Did he have to hold her that close?*

"Oh!" she said, smiling and raising an eyebrow at him. Along with their similar complexions and the fact that they all smelled like coconuts, the Miller women were each one of a type and their relatedness was obvious. Even the little girls smelled like coconuts, and they all had confident, vibrant personalities.

Bubba had often announced his intention to mate and marry

Vanessa. Leona was one of the few people who actually believed him.

"And how is the campaign going?" Leona asked eagerly.

"She wants me," he gave her a confident smile. "It's only a matter of time. Don't worry, I have this under control!"

Leona raised her eyebrow again, then tilted her head to one side.

The song was coming to an end, and Bubba, his eyes still on Vanessa, expected her to say goodbye to her dance partner and head for the head table. Instead, she continued to smile at him as if he were a long-lost friend. Blake's expression remained unmovable. The music started again, and Bubba got to his feet.

Time to put an end to this. Vanessa could dance with anyone she wanted to. Within reason.

As he made his way to the dance floor, intent on cutting into Vanessa's dance, he was suddenly waylaid by arms around his waist. He looked down into a pair of brown faces, with eyes as black as night and a smattering of freckles across their noses. They beamed at him, and he went to ruffle their curly heads, but they burst into giggles and evaded him. It was an old game between the three of them. They didn't want their hair touched, so he always made a point of pretending to do so.

"Dance with us, Uncle Bubba!" Vanessa's six-year-old twins, Scarlett and Charlotte, demanded in unison, then burst into giggles.

And really, how could he say no? So he picked up the little girls, one dangling from each arm. Despite the girls wearing formal white junior bridesmaid's dresses, they attempted to climb him as if they were a pair of baby goats.

"Girls, knock it off!" He admonished them, laughing. "You're going to get your dresses all messed up, and what would your mother say?"

"I don't care! She's not the boss of me!" Charlotte exclaimed, kicking her legs.

"I'm pretty sure 'Boss of you' is number one on the list of qualifications to be your mother," he told her. Charlotte was the spunkier, more impudent of the two girls, her mother's mini-me if ever there was one. The alpha in him recognized Charlotte's dominant tendencies. Which was only one of the reasons Bubba would make a great father to the girls, someday.

Vanessa was never married to Ben, the coywolf father of her daughters. Ben had been a soldier, and was killed during a training exercise. Bubba had made it a point to find out all those details. He was ready to step in to be the father the girls needed. He had a vision of the four of them moving back to Perdition to raise the girls there where they could roam free and explore their animal natures.

In his opinion, the girls were more wolf than coyote, and therefore better off living in a country town like Perdition, where he could take them on runs and they could live with a pack. In fact, Perdition would be perfect.

There was only one problem with moving to Perdition? He'd been banished for life. So that town wasn't really an option. He frowned, remembering the series of events that led to him being banished and forcing to go into foster care with various shifter families in the Waco area.

But the girls were with him now, and this was not the time to get all into his feelings. He was responsible for them at the moment, so he needed to put his feelings aside.

The music started up and he put the girls on their feet. He twirled them around, swept them off their feet, and taught them a couple of new dance moves. The girls learned how to do the bump, and they did it together, bumping hips and falling into fits of giggles as they bumped their hips together, which quickly evolved into bumping shoulders, chests and backs, hooking their elbows together and twirling until they made themselves dizzy.

They went faster and faster, and Bubba was about to break it up before they did each other physical harm, when Leona and Mac's mother, Anita, swooped in and scooped up the girls, hustling them off the dance floor with promises of more cake.

The music stopped just then, and the partygoers began to drift away to find their seats. Bubba felt eyes on him, along with a presence that caused him to swivel his head, even though he knew already who would be there, watching him with a cold stare.

Vanessa.

————

You Can't Hurry Love

VANESSA'S EYES narrowed on Bubba. The man was always around. She clenched her jaw when he stuffed his hands casually in his tuxedo pockets and strolled up to her. Blake, the handsome, blond minotaur she'd snagged for a dance, excused himself to go sit with his date.

"Can I buy you a drink?" Bubba asked her.

"It's an open bar," Vanessa pointed out.

"What can I get you?" He asked, giving her a rakish grin.

She sighed. One little drink couldn't hurt, she supposed.

"Let's see what they have," she mumbled.

At the bar, she ordered a Shirley Temple, and he ordered a Lone Star.

"You're not drinking?" He asked, motioning to her non-alcoholic drink. "You should unwind."

"I'm still a mom tonight," she told him, nodding at her twins, who were currently scarfing down large wedges of the bridal cake under the indulgent gazes of two grandmothers.

"Let's go outside," he said. "The girls are good right now. And I could use some air." His smile was easy, and at least for the moment, he wasn't leering at her.

She gave Bubba a sidelong glance, then said "Sure."

She pursed her lips and followed him out of the ballroom. She could use some air herself. After weeks of wedding planning with Diana, she was ready to relax. The wedding party and out-of-town guests had booked rooms at the hotels adjacent to the country club. The grandmothers had booked adjoining suites and would be keeping both sets of twins, Vanessa's girls, as well as Diana's babies. Vanessa's plan was to crash after the reception, and attempt to sleep in. As a single mother, sleeping in was a luxury she seldom indulged in.

After all the prep that went into the wedding, it felt good to have not a single thing to worry about. Outside of the ballroom, on impulse, she kicked off her pumps and sighed deeply as her feet and calves relaxed. She closed her eyes to savor the relief and when she opened them again, Bubba's eyes were on her, watching her intently. She ignored the ripple of desire that coursed through her, and turned away from him to head for the outside door, leaving her shoes parked right outside the ballroom door.

"Hey, you gonna leave these?" he asked.

"Nah, they aren't going anywhere," she said, shrugging.

He bent to pick them up by their slingbacks and followed her. Without her shoes, he towered over her. He had a good five or six inches on her. Outside, she inhaled the cool evening air and rolled her shoulders.

Despite what she'd said earlier, she was actually curious about what was going on in Bubba's home town.

"Where are you from, Bubba?" She took a sip of her Shirley Temple and looked out on the golf course.

"A little town near Waco called Perdition," he said, looking both wistful and pained at the same time.

She wondered at the look that crossed his face when he mentioned his hometown. He looked sad.

"What do you need to do there?" She took another sip, and felt goosebumps break out over her body, unsure of whether they came from the cold, or the thrill she always felt around this man. She shivered.

Without a word, he removed his jacket, and for the second time that evening, she found herself enveloped by his warmth indirectly. She took a deep breath of his scent. Like her sister Diana, Vanessa had the psychic gift of sensing when someone has shifter abilities, through scent. Bubba had a scent that her brain interpreted as burning leaves.

My God, this man smells sooo good...

Her eyes drifted close as she inhaled his scent. She wavered a bit on her feet, suddenly feeling the months of wedding preparation

"Just some things that are long overdue..." he trailed off, looking evasive. Reluctant to continue. So unlike his normal, gregarious self. She searched his face for a hint of what might be causing that expression.

"How long are you staying?"

"That depends."

"On...?"

"On you, of course," he said. He towered over her, and she loved the way he smelled. Burning leaves. And spice. But she needed to keep her wits about her. His eyes had softened on her, and she detected a hint of vulnerability.

"What do I have to do with it?" She tried to keep her voice light and teasing, but something in his eyes looked deadly serious. She wasn't used to this version of Bubba.

"You have everything to do with it," he said, giving her a faint smile.

She squinted at him and cocked her head, confused.

"What are you trying to tell me, Bubba?"

"The same thing I've been trying to tell you for the last eighteen months." He looked straight at her, his expression tender. Vulnerable.

Vanessa's lips twitched.

"We're friends," she said, turning away from him. Excitement buzzed through her body, despite all her conviction that he was not the man for her.

"Vanessa," he said to her back. "We're not friends."

Another shiver ran over her body. Vanessa thought turning around to face him was a bad idea. Turning around to the serious discussion he wanted right now, to questions she couldn't answer...at least not the way he wanted.

She jumped when she felt his hand on her shoulder. She was pulled into his hard body, her back to his front, and she sucked in a breath. This was the closest she had ever been to him. Ever.

His arms encircled her from behind and he shifted his weight from foot to foot, pressing his...cucumber against her back.

"Wha-what what are you doing?"

He held held her in his arms, breathed in her scent, and whispered in her ear. "What do you think I'm doing?"

His voice was a dark, rumbling thing that started deep in his chest. She could feel the vibrations from his chest against her back. His lips ghosted over the nape of her neck, prompting an all-body shiver and a roll of her hips. She backed into his groin and made a subtle grind against him. His scent enveloped her, his heat surrounded her and she just about lost her mind.

She thought of her girls, and the two grannies keeping them. She thought room service and sleep sounded great, but something else sounded even better at the moment.

"We can't do this right now," she said, turning around and flattening her hands against his chest. His eyes were fully dilated, reflected eyeshine around the irises. The expression on his face was no longer laughing. When she put a hand on his cheek, his skin almost scorched her. The dusk that closed in on them cast his face partially in shadows.

Lust was heavy in his voice when he said, "When do you suggest we do it?"

"I'm not going to mate with you," she told him. His gaze on her remained hard. Determined.

She pulled his face down to hers, brought her lips to his ear, and whispered something for his ears only.

Then she left him outside.

Don't You Forget About Me

ALONE IN THE COLD, he watched her go. She was still wearing his suit jacket. He thought about what she'd whispered in his ear.

"Room 1223. Two hours."

She'd told him, although he already knew the room number. Because he made it his business to know everything he could about her.

He reflected on the fact that it had taken him this long to even get to first base with this woman. But good things come to those who wait.

After a few minutes, he re-entered the club, and went to mingle with the dissipating crowd while Vanessa said goodnight to her girls and excused herself for the evening.

Yes, good things come to those who wait. It seemed his wait was nearly over.

"VALENTINE'S DAY FROM HELL" BY R.L. MERRILL

AFTER TWO DELAYED FLIGHTS, a five-hour layover, and an Uber ride through the hell that is Bay Area traffic on a Thursday afternoon, Orrie Jones was relieved to be home. He burst through the door and called out for his fiancé, Dalton Bishop.

He was greeted with silence.

It was after six and Dalton was usually home by then. Orrie figured he would just dump his bag upstairs and take a quick shower while he waited. Perhaps Dalton would arrive in the middle and they'd both enjoy a surprise.

Orrie had finagled a quick trip home before heading back out for a Saturday performance. The extra travel was a drag but getting to spend Valentine's Day with Dalton for the first time made it all worth it. Last year he'd been on his way to Europe and hadn't been able to come home, so they'd settled for FaceTime. It had definitely been hot, but nothing like what Orrie had planned for tonight.

He'd told Dalton to be ready for a romantic evening, but his last-minute plans had almost been derailed by delays, and he'd called Dalton and let him know that was a possibility hours before. Hopefully Dalton hadn't decided to do something else?

The shower temperature cooled and still no Dalton. Orrie got out and dried off, thinking it was time to send out a text. It wasn't like Dalton to be late

Guess who's wet, naked, and ready to greet his Valentine?

Dalton didn't respond in the time it took Orrie to dress, fix his hair, and grab a sandwich in the kitchen. Now Orrie was worried. He texted again, but after five more minutes with no response, he decided to call. It seemed unlikely Dalton would be in a business meeting at this time of day, so Orrie dialed his cell. No answer. It definitely wasn't like Dalton not to answer his phone when Orrie called. Orrie's last option was to call Sanjay, Dalton's personal assistant and close friend. If he didn't answer, Orrie was going to lose his shit.

"Orrie! Did your flight land already? I'm sorry, I was supposed to text you."

"What's going on, Sanjay? Dalton's not home and he's not answering. I'm starting to freak out."

"Shit. I am so sorry. Dalton's going to be pissed. Look, your sister called him this afternoon, frantic. Their babysitter canceled and they had tickets to see a show in the city. Your mom has the baby and Dalton told them not to worry—that he'd take the boys. I was supposed to let you know where to meet him in case you made it home."

"You're lucky I wasn't out checking emergency rooms. Jesus, I was scared half to death."

"I screwed up. I'm so sorry. Let me try to fix this. Are you at home?"

"Yeah."

"I'll come get you. They're across the bay at some wildlife place."

Orrie sighed. "Sulphur Creek?"

"Yeah, that's it. You know it?"

He most certainly did. Olive had held Hendrix's birthday there last year. Orrie had heard all about how Clapton had held a snake and how Hendrix wanted a pet tarantula. He'd been devastated to miss it, but Olive let him know that Hendrix still talked about their trip to Disneyland in December as the greatest time in his life. "I do. Now, are you coming? If not, I'll get a Lyft."

"No! Don't do that. Please. Dalton's already going to make me suffer for screwing up. If I let you Lyft, I'll be done for."

Orrie chuckled, his worries fading now that he knew Dalton was safe. "How will he make you suffer?"

Orrie heard a horn honking in the background and Sanjay cursed.

"I just almost got run over by our receptionist. You know how he makes me suffer? He makes me work the front desk so the admin up front can take a spa afternoon. Do you know how much stupidity they have to put up with? I'll be there in ten minutes."

Sanjay disconnected and Orrie sighed. He stood in the living room, stunned for a minute. There went their romantic evening. But how could he be upset? What a wonderfully sweet thing to do, to offer to watch the boys. It was the kind of thing that made Orrie love him even more. Orrie called and cancelled the reservation he'd made at the Claremont in Berkeley. All hope was not lost. The boys might fall asleep early. It could happen...

———

"HENDRIX, honey, please stop kicking my seat."

"Sorry, Uncle Dalton."

Dalton white-knuckled the steering wheel as he was cut off once more on Mission Boulevard in Hayward. He was paranoid of having an accident with precious cargo in the back seat and dealing with rush-hour mania wasn't helping his blood pressure. It would be so much easier if Orrie were here.

God, he missed Orrie. He hadn't seen his fiancé in over a month and his heart hurt. The two bundles of joy in his backseat would have to suffice, though. The last he'd heard from Orrie was that his flight was delayed and he wasn't sure he could make it for a last-minute Valentine's Day rendez-vous. He'd seemed off during their last few conversations and from their FaceTime chats; he could tell Orrie wasn't getting enough rest. Dalton had even called Joshua, Orrie's manager, to make sure he was eating right and taking his medication for his anxiety. Joshua took great care of Orrie out on the road, which is the only reason Dalton hadn't flown out to meet him. His decision to come out for just a night, though, had Dalton worried.

Dalton looked in the rearview mirror at the two mops of curls currently headbanging to *Sad But True* by Metallica—their request. He hadn't taken the boys out by himself before, but when Olive called to see if he might possibly be able to help, Dalton had leapt at the chance. Anything to keep his mind off the absence of his beloved on Valentine's Day.

"Are we almost there?" Hendrix asked for the third time.

Dalton looked at the map on the screen of his Tesla and sighed, reminding himself that this had been his idea. Well, his and his dear brother Terrence's.

"Waze says we'll be there in twenty-three minutes, buddy. We just have to pick up my brother first and then we'll be there."

"You has a brudduh? Who you brudduh?"

Dalton could listen to Clapton talk for hours. The little guy had the cutest speech impediment. Dalton's youngest brother, Stanley, had talked just like that when he was little, and he didn't get help for it until he was in middle school. Dalton and Terrence had chased off many a bully for teasing poor Stanley. Of course, then Stanley hit his growth spurt and ended up a starter on the

Castro Valley High School varsity football team his freshman year. Terrence had been just as big and an even better football player. Until he'd started drinking.

"I have two brothers. Stanley and Terrence. You met them at Christmas, remember?"

"The guys who yelled at the TV, remember?" Hendrix asked his brother.

"Ohhhh. You brudduhs aw noisy."

Dalton chuckled as he pulled into the driveway of his father's house.

The boys were back to singing and rocking out while Dalton debated whether he should take them out of their car seats and into the den of slack, or if he should just honk. Honking might be considered rude. There were elderly folk on this street.

He settled for texting.

Your chariot awaits.

Three minutes later, Terrence came dashing out, tucking in his volunteer polo shirt as he went.

"Thanks, Dalton," Terrence said as he slid into the passenger seat. Movement in the backseat caught his attention. He turned to look over his shoulder and snickered.

Hendrix and Clapton bobbed their heads together in time to Korn's *Falling Away from Me.*

"How'd you end up with babysitting duty?"

Dalton backed out of the driveway after double and triple checking and followed the directions on the screen back to Foothill Boulevard.

"Babysitter cancelled. I was just going to feed them pizza and watch movies, but then you mentioned the program and I thought it would be fun."

Terrence had been doing his community service at Sulphur Creek in Hayward, a wildlife rehabilitation and education center in the East Bay. He'd mentioned that, for Valentine's Day, they were having some sort of a kids' program about animal mating habits. Sounded...interesting? He figured if it would keep the boys occupied for a bit, it would help make his first solo babysitting gig a success.

He just wished Orrie were here.

"I want you to meet Tasha. She's great. She knows so much about all of the animals there."

Dalton raised an eyebrow. "Tasha?"

Terrence frowned and crossed his arms over his chest. "She's in charge of the volunteers. She signs my timecards."

"She's great, huh?" Dalton only teased because Terrence was usually much more likely to describe a woman's physique than give an overall "she's great."

"Yeah," Terrence said, staring out the window. "She's different. Like, she's doing important work and she's really passionate about it. I admire her."

Dalton fought hard to silence the smart-ass remark he was ready with. It was a genetic predisposition that he hated. Their father, grandfather, and uncles were all smart-asses, and Peter Bishop had schooled his sons well in the art. Luckily, once Dalton had gotten away from the other Bishop men, his need to bite back had subsided and he could actually hold pleasant conversations. Was it possible that his middle brother could do the same?

"I'm looking forward to meeting her."

Terrence nodded and Dalton sighed happily. It wasn't often that he and his brother could sit in an enclosed space for a length of time without one of them leaving pissed off. Maybe things were changing for the better. Terrence getting a DUI had been awful, and Dalton had laid into him about it, but it could have been much worse. Perhaps it was the rock bottom he'd needed to hit and he could climb from there.

"Are we gonna be there soon?" Hendrix asked just as Dalton turned into the parking lot for Sulphur Creek. It was dusk and the

Hayward Hills around them were dark against a delicate pink and purple sunset. Dalton took a moment to step out of the car and gaze at the colors before unleashing the hellions from the backseat.

He and Orrie frequently took walks at this time of day and talked about anything and everything. Walking seemed to loosen Orrie's tongue. When he was physically active, he was even more open with Dalton about his feelings.

It had been during one of those walks that they'd had a conversation that had stuck with Dalton.

They'd spent a lot of time at Coyote Hills in Fremont over the past summer. It was between their house and Orrie's family's house. Often, they'd walked at sunset and then joined Orrie's mom or Olive and Patrick for dinner. On that particular day, they'd been talking about the boys and a recent trip to the zoo they'd taken with the boys and Patrick

"Patrick is amazing, how he handles both of the boys at the same time. It's like he has a sixth sense and just knows where they are at all times."

Orrie squeezed his hand. "My father never took us anywhere because he always said he was afraid of losing one of us. He claimed we never listened to him."

Dalton heard the hurt and disappointment in his voice. "I think you're just as wonderful with the boys as Patrick, regardless of whether your father took you anywhere. You are so good with them."

Orrie shrugged. "I miss them a lot when I'm on tour. Sometimes I wish I could have been, like, their manny or something. But then I figure they're better off with someone who knows what they're doing."

"I understand. My dad was best at teaching us to fight, both directly and indirectly by allowing our roughhousing to go unchecked. I would never want to do to a child what he did to us."

Orrie cleared his throat. "You wouldn't, babe. You'd be a great dad."

Dalton shook his head. "I'm too afraid to try. I love kids, but you see how hard it is for me to get along with my brothers. Bickering is like a reflex when I'm around them. What if I was like that with my own kids? I can't take that chance."

"I guess we'll just settle for spoiling Hendrix and Clapton then." Orrie laughed, but it was a sad sound, one that let Dalton know Orrie was disappointed.

Dalton had apparently been too long with his thoughts, as he heard a noise. He turned to see Hendrix's face smashed against the window of the car, his nose pushed up like a little piggy, leaving behind marks consisting of some body fluid Dalton didn't even want to contemplate.

"Out! Out! Out!" the boys chanted.

"I'll grab Clapton," Terrence said, and Dalton gave him a sharp look.

Since when did Terrence offer to help with anything?

"Thank you," Dalton said when he realized he'd been staring quietly for too long. Hendrix had already unhooked himself from his car seat. He jumped up and down on the floorboard, making the whole car bounce. Dalton hurriedly set him free from the backseat before he did any real damage.

Hendrix grabbed for his hand like a reflex and the amount of trust in that one movement made Dalton's eyes well up. He reached for the go-bag shoved between the seats and took a moment to compose himself before locking the car.

"You ready to learn, boys?" he asked as they moved as a group toward the steps.

"I wanna see da aminals," Clapton said. He fought Terrence's hold on his hand as they descended the steps.

Terrence stopped and bent down to his level a bit.

"Hey, buddy. You gotta hold my hand because it's easy to get lost here and the steps are really steep."

Clapton brushed his hair out of his eyes and grabbed for Terrence's hand.

"You take me to da aminals?"

"Yeah. We'll go see Miss Tasha and she'll teach you all about them."

Dalton snorted and Terrence turned around.

"What?" Dalton grinned mischievously. He couldn't help it. He was happy for his brother, but it was too good of an opportunity to pass up.

"Don't be an ass," Terrence muttered.

"Ooooooooo," both the boys said, and then they giggled.

"Sorry." Terrence seemed thoroughly admonished for his lapse.

Terrence remained quiet on the rest of the walk down the steps and past the compound. The boys pulled at their hands, trying to get to all of the different cages to see the animals. Dalton and Terrence held on for dear life as the two whirlwinds darted back and forth and stopped on a dime before rushing forward.

They made it to a classroom without further incident and found more boys and girls around the same ages as Hendrix and Clapton. The buzz of activity seemed to jump to a higher level when they entered, and Dalton was immediately rammed in the leg by two little girls chasing each other around the tables.

"I'm so sorry," the desperate mother said as she pushed past him to grab the girls.

Dalton was relieved to see he wasn't the only one struggling with his charges.

"Boys, let's grab a seat up front so you don't miss anything."

Dalton looked for three chairs together and sat down in the middle, assuming the boys would sit on either side of him.

Instead, the boys began shoving each other and fighting over who would sit on Dalton's lap.

"Hey, guys, I have two legs. There's room for both of you."

They immediately stopped their fussing, each climbed on a knee, and sat up straight, waiting for the class to start.

Dalton was shocked that they'd settled down and once more had to get his emotions under control. These boys had come to mean so much to him in such a short time. And if he were being honest, being with them was nothing like being with his brothers. He never felt the urge to tease or—more accurately—belittle them. Maybe it was strictly a Bishop family defect, one that wouldn't continue?

Terrence stood near the front talking to a woman in a khaki park ranger uniform and worn hiking boots. She had long, dark hair in two braids, big brown eyes, and an enthusiastic smile just for Terrence. He leaned close and said something near her ear, and she laughed before shooing him away, presumably so that she could get started. Terrence gave a wave before heading outside.

Clapton wiggled on his lap. "I gotta pee-pee," he whispered loudly.

Oh Lord.

Dalton collected the boys and headed for the restrooms, praying once more he wasn't in over his head with these two balls of energy.

———

SANJAY MADE three wrong turns before finally turning into the dark, wooded parking area at the top of the hill.

"Good to see you, man," Sanjay said as they shook hands. "Please tell Dalton it's all my fault you're late."

"Don't worry. I'll tell him you secretly like working the reception desk."

"No! Then he'll put me in charge of the Secret Santa exchange again. You know how hard it is to get people to follow directions?"

Orrie waved to Sanjay as he drove off and looked around.

"Hello, murder scene." Orrie figured if he made it out of here alive, he'd write the perfect song about it.

The lone streetlight shone down on gravel-covered stairs that led into darkness below. He spotted Dalton's car at the far end of the lot so he knew it was the right place. It still gave him heebie-jeebies, though.

The stairs led down to a wooden bridge that spanned a ravine. He heard running water so he assumed there was a creek under him, hence the name. The bridge was lit at either end and stairs led farther down the hill. There were lights far off to his left, so he turned that way at the bottom of the stairs. He heard rustling sounds all around him, as though he were under sheets, which was where he wished he was...with Dalton.

As he neared the lights, he saw that the rustling was coming from a series of large cages. Something with a large wingspan *whooshed* down to the ground in one of them, and Orrie walked closer to check it out. A giant brown bird looked over its shoulder and, as Orrie walked past, he saw it had something furry clutched in its talons.

"Sorry, dude," Orrie whispered.

The bird watched him as though he were next in the buffet line, or would be as soon as the giant feathered beast figured out how to leave his cage.

"That's a golden eagle."

Orrie jumped out of his skin and gave a decidedly unmanly squeak.

"Jesus, Terrence! You gave me a fright."

Terrence cackled. "You should see your face right now."

Terrence was Dalton's middle brother, and Orrie remembered Dalton telling him he was working here doing community service for a DUI. It had happened a week after Thanksgiving, and thankfully no one was hurt, but Terrence had spent the weekend in jail and came out ready to make some major changes. He'd started going to meetings and was doing his community service like a good boy.

Didn't change the fact that Orrie thought the guy was a selfish ass who took advantage of his brother.

Dalton had said that Terrence loved working here and may have actually found his calling. He loved the animals and the children's programs and was thinking of trying to get a job with the park service or rec department once he was finished serving his time. It seemed out of character in Orrie's mind, but Dalton always tried to see the positive.

"It's dark as fuck out here. What the hell are you doing?"

"One last check on the animals and cleaning up trash from the day. Dalton's inside with the boys. I told him there was a fun program tonight for the kids, so when he took on uncle duty, he brought them here. Tasha is leading it."

Ahhh. There was a chick involved.

"Rad. He doesn't know I'm here. My flight was delayed and last I told him I wasn't sure I could make it."

"That's cool," he said, and then he chuckled. "It's probably a good thing you came. I think he's in over his head."

"I'm sure he's fine," Orrie said, though he was sure Dalton would appreciate the help. "Point me in the right direction?"

"I'll take you. I should see if Tasha needs anything."

Terrence led him down the path, past a building, and around the back of another one.

"This is the classroom," Terrence said as they turned the corner.

Orrie peeked in the window and his heart stuttered as he spotted his beloved.

Dalton Bishop was the most adorable man on the planet, especially with Orrie's nephews sitting on each knee. The boys were listening intently to the teacher—Tasha, apparently—talk about the tiny owl she had perched on her arm. Dalton had his arms protectively around them, probably more to keep them from launching themselves at the bird.

"Owls mate for life. Once they find a mate, they'll breed and watch over the nest together. The male will bring food to the female as she stays with the eggs. Barn owls are even known to cuddle together and show affection."

Orrie watched from just outside the screen door, waiting for a good moment to step in. The boys giggled together, and Dalton tried to keep them focused on the teacher. Anyone watching from the outside might think they were Dalton's boys, as good as he was with them.

Hendrix and Clapton Donnelly made Orrie's world a better place. At 5 and 3, respectively, they both sported long, dark blond, curly hair, rock shirts and attitude. They were brilliant and already showing musical aptitude. Orrie had bought them a drum set for Christmas and Hendrix could already keep up with some of his favorite songs. Clapton sang all the time, especially when he was using his froggy potty. Before Olive started potty training him, he used to hide in Olive's closet to poop, all while singing at the top of his lungs.

"You coming in?" Terrence asked him.

Orrie nodded. For a split second, he wondered if maybe he should wait, but he couldn't stay away from Dalton and the boys for one more minute. If he just snuck in the back...

The screen door creaked as he pulled it open.

"UNKIE OH-WEE!"

Orrie immediately realized the folly of his decision.

Clapton saw him first and launched himself off of Dalton's

lap, knocking Hendrix over and racking poor Dalton's groin in the process.

"Boys! Remember that Orville the Owl likes quiet—"

The poor owl took off from the woman's arm, where thankfully it was tethered, and flapped around her head. Orrie couldn't tell which was louder, the screeching of the owl or the ten or so other kids shrieking.

"I'm so sorry!" Orrie said as he knelt beside his poor red-faced Dalton. He took the boys into his arms and tried to shush them. "Surprise?"

Dalton winced and tried to smile. Clapton's foot must have really connected. "It's good to see you," he groaned.

Terrence tried to help the instructor get Orville settled back down. Thankfully he seemed to have the magic touch.

"Thank you," the flustered woman said. "We're going to take a quick break to put Orville away. Say goodnight, kids."

They all shouted good night and the poor owl shrieked again. It wasn't very big, smaller than a pigeon actually, but the thing was loud.

"I didn't think you were going to make it." Dalton leaned in for a kiss, which meant getting their cheeks simultaneously kissed by the boys.

"It was either spend two days off in Dallas, or finally get to spend Valentine's Day with you."

"I can't believe you flew all the way home. I know you hate taking these short trips."

Orrie needed to express his fears to Dalton, but this wasn't the time. "I needed to see you." He sounded more cryptic than he intended. He hoped that Dalton would understand when they finally spoke.

The boys watched their exchange with interest, probably waiting to be sure they were part of Orrie's decision-making process.

"And to see my boys, of course. I couldn't let them have all the animal fun without me, now could I?"

"Unkie Oh-wee! They gonna has tranchula!"

"Really?" Orrie said, swallowing back a little bile. "That's...something."

Dalton gave him a sympathetic smile, but he frowned slightly —as though he had questions.

Tasha came back, followed by Terrence sporting puppy-dog eyes. "Okay everyone, we put Orville back to bed. I would like to introduce our next night-loving friend, but I need you all to promise you'll stay seated and quiet, otherwise we won't be able to see any more friends tonight."

Orrie sat on a small chair next to Dalton and took Hendrix onto his lap. His nephew's little body was vibrating with the need to wiggle, but he was trying so hard to stay still. Poor kid. Orrie'd had similar struggles as a young boy. He'd been in a constant state of motion. Luckily, Hendrix didn't seem to have worries like he did. By his age, Orrie was already perseverating. It had taken therapy and patience from his mom to help him make it through the challenges of school.

"Our next friend is Tallulah the Tarantula."

Orrie immediately broke out in a sweat. *Spiders.* The object of his ridiculous phobia. Now Hendrix wasn't the only one vibrating.

"Tallulah, like most female tarantulas, spends most of her time living in her den. During mating season, at dusk, male tarantulas go out walking around, looking for love. Sadly, males don't usually live very long, and oftentimes they only get one chance to mate. Tallulah was rescued by local firefighters who discovered her den while cleaning up after a house fire. They brought her to us for safekeeping, and she's been with us about three years now. The delicate hairs on her body had been singed and the firefighters were worried she might not be able to fend for herself.

Female tarantulas can live for many years, so we hope to have Tallulah in our education program for a long time to come. Now, would any of you like to get a hug from Tallulah?"

Both Hendrix and Clapton shot their hands up, and Orrie tried not to panic. *A hug?*

"Babe? Are you going to be okay?" Dalton whispered.

Orrie nodded, unable to speak around the dryness in his mouth. Dalton had rescued Orrie in the bathroom one morning when Orrie had disturbed a spider in the bottom cabinet. The brown wolf spider had popped out and Orrie had hopped on top of the counter, naked and afraid.

Orrie had known Dalton was the man he'd spend his life with when the gentle ginger had rescued the spider, carried it outside, then come back and helped Orrie down without laughing once.

"Phobias may be an irrational fear of something," he'd said. "But the fear itself is real. I'm sorry, babe. If you want me to call the exterminators to make sure we don't find any more—"

Orrie'd cut him off with a kiss, thanked him profusely, and then showed his appreciation the rest of the morning. That memory was almost enough to get Orrie through the next few minutes.

Tasha brought the hairy arachnid around the circle and instructed the kids to hold their hands out flat.

"Tallulah will give you a little hug with her front legs. Are you ready?"

Orrie tried to breathe normally while Tasha brought the creature closer.

Hendrix looked over his shoulder at Orrie and frowned. "What's wrong, Uncle Orrie?"

"Nothing, baby. Go ahead. Hug the little spider."

Sweat ran down the side of Orrie's cheek despite the chill in the room.

"Unkie Oh-wee why you face red?"

"Um..."

"Now just hold really still, and Tallulah will—"

Hendrix yanked his hand back and held it close to his chest. "Uncle Orrie?"

"It's okay," he said, not meaning a damn word. The proximity of the spider had him nearly hyperventilating.

"Maybe you could place your hand under his to keep him steady," Tasha said to Dalton, raising her eyebrow knowingly at Orrie.

Dalton smiled at him—and just like that, Orrie was back in the bathroom, and Dalton was saving his life.

"Here, Hendrix. Put your hand out and I'll help you, okay?"

Hendrix gave Orrie one last fearful glance before placing his trusting hand in Dalton's.

"There we go, now just hold still."

Orrie held his breath as the delicate demon crept closer to his sister's oldest child as though she were tasting her next meal. Hendrix sucked in a breath, and Orrie gave him what he hoped was a reassuring squeeze.

"Ow, Uncle Orrie, that's too tight."

"Sorry."

The tarantula held its front two legs in the air for a moment before gently tapping the tips of Hendrix's fingers. He gasped, and then a huge a smile lit up his face. Orrie was so proud of him. He wished he could be so brave—

"Me turn!"

Clapton stuck his hand out next to Hendrix's a little too quickly for Tallulah's liking. She scurried back onto Tasha's hand and curled her legs in.

"We need to move very slowly around the animals, remember?"

Clapton nodded, wide-eyed and repentant. "I sowee

Tawuwah." He reached his hand out so slowly it was comical and placed it in front of Tasha. "Pweeze?"

There really was no resisting his cherubic face. Orrie knew he was going to be harder to resist than his brother. His sister Olive was going to have her hands full for sure.

Tasha held Tallulah out once more and Clapton focused all of his three-year-old energy on being still. Dalton and Orrie made eye contact, and that kept Orrie from losing it in the presence of the furry fiend.

She truly was a beautiful creature. Up this close, Orrie could appreciate how delicate each of her legs was and the graceful way the spider moved. Tallulah uncurled and crept forward, her beady little eyes focused on Clapton's chubby fingers. She moved slowly, letting one leg dangle in the air for several seconds before taking two steps onto Clapton's fingers.

Clapton's mouth opened in a silent O and he sucked in a breath. And then he smiled.

"She's pwetty," he said and smiled up at his uncle.

"Very good," Tasha said, and she quickly scooped the tarantula back into her hands before the boys freaked out again. "Does anyone have any questions about Tallulah before I put her back in her den?"

Hendrix's hand shot up and Orrie squirmed, wondering what the precocious child would say this time.

"If you keep Tallulah in a cage, how is she going to find her true love?"

Orrie sighed. He recalled Olive mentioning that he seemed overly fixated on people finding their true love these days. She'd had to gently advise him that he didn't have to find his true love in Kindergarten, that he had plenty of time, but he was convinced everyone had a true love and they needed to find it right away. He wondered if he and Dalton getting engaged had anything to do with it.

"Well, Hendrix, we're not sure she could survive on her own. That's why we keep her here at Sulphur Creek."

"But can't you *find* her a true love?"

Tasha smiled at Orrie and Dalton like this was the most adorable thing ever.

"I don't think someone else can find your true love for you. Even tarantulas need to have a choice. It might not work out too well if we put a male in with Tallulah." Tasha's smile dropped, and she snapped her mouth closed as though she'd almost spoken out of turn.

"How come?" The ever-persistent Hendrix continued questioning her.

"They just might not get along and that's not safe. Now, for our last visit tonight, we're going to meet a mated pair who *have* found their true love. Does that sound good, Hendrix?"

He nodded vigorously, his curls bouncing into his eyes.

"Alright then, everyone follow me outside. You might want to put your coats on; it's a little chilly."

The kids all jumped up and dashed for the doors while parents scrambled to catch up to them. Clapton and Hendrix were at the back, so Orrie figured he had a moment.

"Can I give my best guy a hug?"

Dalton turned to embrace him and sighed happily. "It's so good to see you," he whispered.

Orrie inhaled Dalton's cologne and his mouth watered. He hoped this program was over quick or he was going to explode.

"Are the boys spending the night?" Orrie asked.

Dalton pulled back and his expression was regretful. "Yeah, I told Olive I'd keep them since it looked like you wouldn't make it. I feel bad; you came all this way."

"Babe, you taking the boys is awesome. I'm grateful you did. Me and my needs can wait. I'll just reschedule the getaway I had planned."

Dalton sucked in a breath. "A getaway? Oh, honey, that would have been fantastic. I'm so sorry! We should be done here soon. They'll be tired, right? Like, they'll go to sleep? Eventually?"

Orrie didn't want to jinx it by saying yes. "We can hope."

Dalton linked hands with Orrie and led him toward the door just before the boys dashed outside.

"It's hella dark out there. I don't want to lose them."

"Good call," Orrie said.

There were a few more lights at this end of the compound but it was pitch black not too far from where they were.

"If you'll all follow me, we'll visit our lovebirds. Catrina and Cass are a mated pair of coyotes—"

The boys darted into the darkness ahead of Tasha, and Orrie heard them squealing in delight.

"Lord, don't let your nephews get eaten by coyotes on my watch." Dalton quickened his pace and Orrie trotted to catch up with him.

"I don't see anything," Hendrix said. "Hello?" he called into the darkness several times, until a flash of golden fur darted past him. He shrieked and pulled Clapton back from the fence with a jerk that sent them both tumbling to the ground.

"Boys!" Dalton reached them first and did an initial assessment. Some dusting off was all that was necessary, thankfully. Dalton always worried, but Orrie knew they were pretty tough little dudes.

"Would you all like to say hello? Catrina and Cass like to have boisterous conversations. All you have to do is call to them."

Tasha demonstrated how to make a coyote sound and soon all of the kids did their impressions. It wasn't quite a howl, more like *Oooo*, and after several moments of the group calling, the coyotes darted forward and threw their heads back, answering with calls of their own.

"Coyotes, like a few other species, actually mate for life. Cass and Catrina haven't had any offspring, but it's always a possibility. Can anyone tell me some other creatures that mate for life?"

The other kids shouted out answers.

"Wolves."

"Barn owls."

"Bald eagles."

"Penguins!" Hendrix said. "There are even boy penguins that find true love together. And there's a kind of penguin that brings special rocks to each other. My mommy told me about it."

Dalton and Orrie shared a look of *OMG could he be any more precious?*

"That's correct!" Tasha bent down to speak to Hendrix. "I just read that in Australia, there is a same-sex couple of penguins that have been fostering an egg together. Pretty cool, huh?"

"And Tango Makes Fwee." Clapton hopped up and down, clapping his hands. "We has that book."

Olive had bought the book for the boys for Christmas this past year. Orrie was so grateful his mom and sister had been so supportive. Since he and Dalton had been together, they'd gone out of their way to encourage their relationship. They knew how happy Dalton made him.

I just hope it stays that way.

Orrie really hated to worry, but anxiety was part of his makeup. The more he tried to change, the more he perseverated. His tour manager, Joshua, was great about tending to his idiosyncrasies while out on the road. Joshua had been with him since he got signed to a major label and he took very good care of Orrie. He also made sure to keep Dalton apprised of Orrie's plans, which Orrie very much appreciated.

The group moved back inside to make a craft and have hot cocoa. The boys were more interested in the marshmallows than the craft or the hot chocolate, and soon Clapton had the gooey mess in his hair.

"Peanut butter will get that out," Orrie said, and the boys giggled.

"Siwwy unkie, you no put peanut buttuh in hayuh." Clapton couldn't control himself and ended up rolling on the floor, getting his hair even more tangled and landing him a case of the hiccups.

"I think it's about time to go home," Orrie said, ready to put them to bed and at least have some cuddle time with Dalton.

"Let me see if Terrence needs a ride home," Dalton said. "We picked him up, and I told him I could take him home if need be."

"It's fine," Orrie said with a sigh. *A night of endless cock-blocking.*

"Unkie Dawton, I wanna make a buhdie feeduh pweeze?"

Tasha had set out seed, peanut butter, and pinecones for the kids to make natural feeders. The boys struggled out of Dalton's grip and pulled on his hands to get him to help.

"We have time?" Dalton looked so touched that the boys wanted his help. They usually only asked Orrie for help.

Orrie smiled. He could never say no to Dalton.

"No problem. You guys make some feeders. I'll go see if I can find Terrence."

Dalton blew him a kiss, and Orrie felt that warmth in his chest that he'd been missing while on the road. Yeah, he'd needed to come home, even if it was just for a night. He was on tour through May this time, and then he'd spend the summer in the studio. He couldn't wait for the time off the road.

"Be right back, okay? And then it's time to get you crazy kids to bed."

The boys paid no attention to his stern voice. He was going to have to work on that.

Orrie went to the back of the classroom, where he'd seen Tasha and Terrence minutes before. He heard voices through another doorway and followed them. He entered a room with aquariums set into the walls and murals painted around them. He followed the sound of laughter and found Terrence and Tasha talking quietly in a corner. Terrence had his arm up on the wall over her head, and her smile said she was perfectly fine being this close to him.

"Then the owls just get busy?"

"Well," Tasha said. "Owls have what's called a cloaca. They take care of all of their business in one spot. Male owls have testes, but yeah, it's different."

"So no owl boners, huh?"

Oh my god, Terrence.

Orrie cleared his voice before their discussion got any creepier.

"Oh, hey, Orrie. Tasha, this is my brother's fiancé, Orrie Jones."

Her eyes bugged out. "*The* Orrie Jones? Like, *Be Your Man* Orrie Jones?"

Orrie smiled and held out his hand. "Guilty. Nice to meet you. That presentation was great, by the way."

"Thanks," Tasha said, blushing. "I love the kids, but it's more fun to give that talk to the older crowds."

"Why is that?" Terrence asked.

A mischievous glint sparkled in her eye. "Well, with the littles, as soon as I start talking cloacas, they lose it. And with older kids and adults, I can tell them the real reason Tallulah won't be having a mate."

"Oh yeah?"

"Yeah. Because female tarantulas frequently kill the males, either if they don't want to mate with them, or sometimes after they mate, they use them for a snack."

Terrence swallowed hard. "Wow, uh, yeah. I can see why you wouldn't tell the little ones that story."

She leaned in a little closer, her eyes wide with excitement. "Other insects kill their mates as well. Like praying mantises? The female eats his head. Isn't that cool?"

Orrie couldn't tell if all this mating talk was making Terrence amorous or squeamish.

"Hey, Terrence? Dalton wanted me to ask if you needed a ride home?" *Please say no please say no please say no.*

"Oh, well, I was going to stay and help Tasha clean up."

She totally melted. "That would be great. You know, I could always give you a lift."

Perfect.

"Thank you, uh, I better ask Dalton—"

"Totally fine," Orrie cut in. "I'll let him know. You can just, uh, stay here. Learn some more. We should really get the boys to bed, anyway."

"Yeah," Tasha said, her excitement growing. "It's no problem. I don't mind at all."

Terrence, for once, was speechless. Orrie was waiting for one of his smarmy lines or asshole moves, but he seemed to genuinely be into this girl. Perhaps Sober Terrence was new and improved for real?

"Great. Well, thanks again."

"Sure." They were soon back to their conversation about owls and multi-use ports for entry and exit functions.

Orrie shuddered. Who knew what other animal mating facts she had up her sleeve? *Terrence better know what he's getting himself into.*

Orrie reentered the classroom and found the boys and Dalton covered in peanut butter and birdseed.

"Did you get any on the pinecones?"

His answer was little boy giggles that never ceased to warm his often-cold heart.

"You ready?" Orrie asked Dalton.

Dalton gazed at him with that *I'm trying really hard not to cry right now* expression. Orrie hoped it was just the dose of the nephews that had him in this state and not that something was wrong.

Orrie thanked Tasha's assistant and gave her a hefty tip as a donation. She thanked him profusely and assured they should just leave their stations as they were. He placed the finished bird feeders in the provided paper bag and scooped up Hendrix. Thankfully he'd been hitting the treadmill hard to stay in shape for this tour or he would have been dying by the time they reached the top.

Dalton carried a fussy Clapton up the steep hill. "My thighs are going to feel this tomorrow," Dalton said with a shy smile as he unlocked the Tesla's doors.

"I have several comments that will remain unspoken, as none are appropriate in present company."

"Who's Present Company? Are they a band, Uncle Orrie?" Hendrix asked, his eyelids already drooping now that he was in his car seat.

"No, but that's a good band name."

"I still like Boney Jones. Can that be my band name?"

"I think it's a great band name."

"I wanna be Boney Jones tewwwww," Clapton cried.

"You can be in my band, buddy. You just gotta practice."

"I pwactice aw da times."

By the time Dalton pulled out of the parking lot and onto D Street, the boys were singing one of Orrie's songs together, and when they reached the freeway, they were sound asleep.

Orrie reached over and squeezed Dalton's thigh.

"That was real sweet, you bringing them tonight. I think I ovulated watching you with the boys."

Dalton barked out a laugh and then sniffled, his eyes glassy. "Shhh. You'll wake them."

"Seriously, babe. Thank you."

Dalton smiled at him and then trained his eyes back on the road. "I can't believe you're here."

"Surprise," Orrie said, feeling nervous all of a sudden. "Was this not a good idea?"

Dalton frowned. "Of course it is! I just wasn't expecting you, that's all. I love that we get to spend Valentine's Day—well, evening—together."

Orrie breathed a little easier. "Okay. Good."

———

THEY DIDN'T TALK for a long time, and Dalton was surprised to feel tension in the car. Orrie seemed off, intense. Dalton thought maybe he'd just been tired from the tour and traveling. But then why did he come home for just a night? He'd never done that before. And he was acting like he had something to say, fidgeting in his seat in the car, picking at something. All Dalton could do was wait until they got home and for the hammer to fall.

"I made lasagna last night if you're hungry," Dalton said, knowing Orrie loved his lasagna.

"I grabbed a sandwich when I got back. Before I called you."

Dalton slumped a little in the seat. "I'm sorry I wasn't there when you got home."

"Babe, it's fine. I'm sorry. I thought it would be a good idea, but I obviously didn't think about weather delays in February."

Dalton cursed under his breath, and he felt his cheeks get hot. He exited the freeway and took the several turns toward their house. He pulled in the driveway just as Clapton woke up, talking loudly, and scared the shit out of both of them.

"And I gonna put the buhd feeduh in the twee outside my window so I can wake up to see the buhdies."

Dalton and Orrie laughed together, holding their chests to keep their startled hearts from leaping free of their ribs.

"Let's get you maniacs to bed."

They carried the boys up to their beds and helped them change into their jammies and brush their teeth in the en suite bathroom. Dalton had insisted on making them their own room, complete with bunk beds, rock posters, and lava lamps, so they'd love coming to stay with them. He'd even had custom constellations painted on the ceiling that showed the sky as it looked the nights they were born.

At the same time, he'd had the constellations from the night he and Orrie first met painted on their bedroom ceiling.

Orrie often told him he missed those stars something fierce when he was away from home. He said he fantasized about the day he'd made enough of a name for himself that he could take longer breaks from the road. He'd been on tour almost constantly for the past two years and he was exhausted. Dalton knew that their relationship made it better and worse; better because Orrie had something to look forward to when he came home, and worse because he had to be away from Dalton.

Dalton struggled when Orrie was gone, too, but at least he had a schedule. His work kept him busy, his brothers drove him crazy, and when he was home alone, he tried not to pine for Orrie. Sleeping in their empty bed was the hardest part. Waking up without Orrie made it a little harder to get out of bed, and it was a damn lonely existence.

The boys needed baths, which Orrie handled with ease, even getting the sticky mess out of Clapton's hair. Then they wanted a story and a song before they'd settle down. Dalton told them a story about a frog in a creek waiting for his true love to come and find him and give him a smooch, and Orrie sang to them until they drifted off with smiles on their faces.

Dalton stood from where he'd been sitting on the edge of the lower bunk next to Clapton and stretched his back. He smiled at Orrie and gestured with his head toward the hall and their bedroom at the other end.

Orrie followed, still oozing tension from all his pores. Dalton felt it bearing down on him as he shut the door. He prayed they weren't about to have a fight. He was emotionally raw after the night they'd spent with the boys. He suddenly wanted things he said he'd never want, and it frightened him as much as Orrie's melancholy mood.

"You need a shower?" Dalton asked. "Want anything from the kitchen?"

Orrie shook his head and ran his fingers through his hair, which had completely fallen in his face by this time of night. Dalton had noticed he'd left out his industrial-strength product. Dalton had wanted to run his fingers through it all night and feel it against his skin—

"Are we okay?" Orrie blurted out.

"God, why would you need to ask that? What's wrong?" Dalton approached him, but he didn't touch Orrie. Orrie's body language was hard to read and Dalton didn't know how to comfort him, or whether he should even try.

Orrie lifted his hand and examined a hangnail. He was bleeding more than he should from just that small wound, but Dalton thought he'd probably been worrying it all night.

"Fuck," Orrie said, his voice hoarse. "Give me a second."

He stormed into the bathroom and shut the door behind him. Dalton usually gave him his space, but something told him he shouldn't give Orrie too *much* space right now, especially if Orrie was worried about them.

Dalton opened the door without knocking. A first.

Orrie stood at the sink washing his hands a little rougher than usual under the faucet, scrubbing the blood off with soap until he was squeaky clean.

"Stings like a bitch," he said.

"Is it because of me?" Dalton crossed his arms to keep himself from touching Orrie, partly to give him space, but mostly to keep from getting hurt if Orrie pulled away. Dalton couldn't handle that right now.

"No! Fuck, I'm just... Do you still want to get married?"

Dalton's eyes bugged out. "What? How could you even ask me that?"

"Because!" Orrie tried to wrap his finger with a Band-Aid but the sticky parts stuck together and then he made the cut bleed again when he pulled it off. "Dammit."

"Here," Dalton said, his voice soft and soothing. Dalton wanted to pull him in and hold him until everything was okay, but first he grabbed a new Band-Aid and got Orrie wrapped up. He didn't let go of Orrie's hand.

"Of course I still want to get married, babe. I love you. Why would you think that?"

Orrie blew out a breath and pulled his hand away. "We haven't set a date."

Dalton tried to speak, but Orrie cut him off. "The last couple of times I've asked you, you said don't worry, we'd plan everything when the tour was over."

"Because I was trying not to put more pressure on you! You've been so overwhelmed lately, and I thought it would be better if we just waited, you know, until the tour was over."

Orrie stood with his hands on his hips. "Makes sense. You always make sense. Listen, forget it. You're tired. You worked hard tonight. I just haven't been able to think straight lately. I needed to see you to know we were okay."

Dalton stood up a little straighter, his eyes wet with tears. "I had fun tonight."

Orrie frowned. "I'm glad...?"

Dalton sucked in a shaky breath, his lower lip trembling. "I want to have kids, Orrie."

Orrie stumbled a bit. "What?"

"I want to be a father."

"But you always said—"

"I love those boys, Orrie. I love spending time with them." He couldn't believe he'd just put those feelings out there. He hadn't even been able to admit it so bluntly to himself.

"They're pretty great," Orrie said, moving closer. "I love watching you with them. But baby, you always said you didn't want to, that you—"

"I always said I'd never have kids, never subject them to my parents, never even take the chance that I might do to my kids what my parents did to me."

Dalton's admission took the wind out of his sails. He left the bathroom and plopped down on the bench at the foot of their bed with his head in his hands.

Orrie sat next to Dalton and rubbed his back. "You know I'll do anything for you. If you want kids, if you don't want kids. I just want *you*."

Dalton rubbed the back of his neck. "I just don't want to be like my father or grandfather."

Orrie blew out a breath. "I didn't exactly have good role models, either." He turned to Dalton and caressed his jaw, eventually turning Dalton to face him. "But I would do anything for you. I'll read books, take parenting classes, whatever will make you happy. I love you."

Dalton turned those bright blue eyes on Orrie, his face full of hope. "I love you, and I love your crazy little nephews. I thought we made a great team tonight."

Orrie kissed his hair. "We always make a great team."

Dalton grinned and slid his hand up the inside of Orrie's thigh. "I'd love to do a bit more teamwork. You know, since you came all this way." He finished that statement with a lingering kiss, the kind that begged for an answer.

Orrie ran his fingers through Dalton's hair and tugged his head back. "You did look pretty damn adorable with those littles on your lap. Competent, too. I think you'll be a phenomenal father."

"So will you."

Dalton moved to the floor in front of Orrie and ran his hands up Orrie's quads, letting his thumbs graze the sensitive spots along the way.

Orrie jumped under his touch and placed his hands over Dalton's. Orrie's tattooed hands covered Dalton's freckled ones completely, his long fingers tracing the pale blue lines under the surface. Dalton loved Orrie all the way down to the blood that gave him life.

"Orrie, I want to get married. I want it more than ever. We can pull out our calendars right now and pick a date..."

"Once more it occurs to me that I must have done something right in this fucked-up life to deserve a man like you. Whatever it was, I'm going to continue being grateful every damn day."

"I'm serious," Dalton said, feeling terrible that Orrie had been away the whole time feeling less than secure in their relationship. "We can fly to Vegas right now and do it."

Orrie snorted. "What will we do with the boys?"

"Take them with us! I don't care. Or we can go to city hall tomorrow. I don't care. Whatever will make you feel better."

Orrie's chin trembled. "I love you so much. I'm sorry I'm such a mess. I can't wait until this tour is over." He linked his fingers with Dalton's. "Happy Valentine's Day, baby."

———

IT WASN'T QUITE the Valentine's Day Orrie had imagined

they might have when he'd snuck home. There was no Claremont, no room with a view, no sparkling cider or chocolate-covered strawberries. Instead, he and Dalton made love in the bed they'd shared for over a year and a half, reconnecting after Orrie's tour schedule had caused him to feel off-balance where their future was concerned. He'd come home to pamper the man he loved and make sure they were still solid and headed for the altar. He intended to follow through with the plan.

"So, let's be clear," Dalton panted as they came up for air. "We're going to city hall when you get back from your European tour at the end of May."

"If you want," Orrie said. He flipped Dalton over onto his stomach and straddled his thighs so he could massage his back. "Or we could go to Hawaii." He took a couple of nibbles out of Dalton's backside until Dalton was quivering beneath him.

"Okay, Hawaii." Dalton moaned. "Wherever you want."

"Or the desert," Orrie said, using his thumbs to work the stress out of Dalton's neck. "Do you want a big reception afterwards?" He hit a particularly tender spot, and Dalton arched his back.

"I just want you." Dalton's face was smashed into the pillow, making his voice sound even more adorable.

"We'll have to have at least two witnesses," Orrie reminded him. He worked his way down Dalton's spine and felt his lover relax into a puddle.

"No family. I don't want any fights."

"Good point," Orrie said. "You bring Sanjay and I'll bring Joshua."

"Perfect." Dalton rolled over and wrapped himself around Orrie. "They're our best friends. That way there's no drama. Let's not tell anyone until it's done. *Then* we can deal with the drama, while we're still on a high from our wedding."

"Then there's the honeymoon," Orrie said close to Dalton's

ear. He sat back, grinning to himself as goose bumps appeared on Dalton's chest.

"I don't think I can handle talk of a honeymoon right now." Dalton bit Orrie's lower lip and sucked on it just enough to make Orrie moan. "I don't think I can form any more words."

Orrie gazed down at Dalton and saw exactly what he'd needed to see when he'd decided to come home. Love. Determination. Lust. Hope. The time away from each other had only made those feelings grow stronger.

Orrie could leave knowing that things were solid between them and the next time they were together, they'd be getting married. They'd done all the talking they needed.

"Who needs words?"

————

DALTON WOKE before his alarm the next morning. He turned it off and rolled over to watch Orrie sleep. He was so grateful that Orrie had come home. They had an incredible night and an important conversation that made them both feel more secure and content.

They'd not only decided to get married as soon as possible, but to research the necessary steps to becoming fathers. Orrie promised Dalton as soon as the ink dried on their marriage license, they'd go see an attorney about their options to adopt. The idea scared them both, as they had a lot of baggage to deal with when it came to family. They agreed they'd see a therapist together to talk about their concerns before moving forward with adoption.

It was a good plan. A solid one.

Thinking about the boys kissing their cheeks as they'd kissed each other hello, Hendrix's theory on true love, and the stern voice Orrie took on when they got feisty, made his joy at thinking about parenting grow to ridiculous levels.

He was going to be a dad. With the man he loved. They would give a child a home and create their own little family, different than the ones they'd been born into.

Dalton smiled. He would definitely be the good cop in their partnership—it was difficult not to give in to Hendrix and Clapton. What would it be like with their own little bundle of joy? Orrie would be the perfect partner to take this journey with, and Dalton was grateful he'd been open to the idea.

Dalton couldn't resist tracing lightly over the stark black tattoos on Orrie's shoulder. He slept on his stomach with one hand touching Dalton's side. Orrie always maintained contact when they slept together, whether it was a hand, a leg, or even the ball of his foot resting on Dalton's calf.

He heard the pitter-patter of little feet outside their door as the boys tried to sneak up on them. Dalton feigned sleep, waiting for them to pounce. He should warn Orrie, but then he wanted to see how Orrie would react. At least they'd both remembered to slip into their boxers before falling asleep.

The door creaked open and the giggles grew louder. Dalton cracked open one eye to see if Orrie'd heard them. Orrie watched him from underneath his dark hair. He rolled over onto his back with a big yawn and rested an arm over his eyes, smacking his lips for effect.

The boys froze for a moment, and then they whispered to each other before counting, "One...two...three!"

The two beasts pounced on Orrie and Dalton. They squealed in delight when Orrie greeted them with a loud roar. He picked up Clapton with one hand and held him over his head while pinning Hendrix to the mattress with the other so Dalton could tickle him until he begged for mercy.

"Unkie Oh-wee down down! I want to hug you."

Orrie slowly lowered Clapton to the mattress with another roar, and then wrapped the little monster in his arms. He squeezed him tight, burying his face in the little boy's curls.

"I'm so glad we found these delicious creatures to eat for breakfast." Orrie winked at Dalton.

"Oh, yes," Dalton said in the fiercest voice he could manage. "I'm so hungry I could eat both of them!"

"No unkie, no eat me pweeze!"

"Don't you know, little man, that if you disturb a sleeping giant, he'll eat you for breakfast?"

"You're not a giant," Hendrix said with an eyeroll as he moved to the end of the bed. "Daddy is taller than you. And I'm starving. My belly is so empty. See?" Hendrix held up his shirt and sucked in his tummy.

"Hmmm," Dalton said. "I see. That's terrible. I should take a closer look." Dalton pulled Hendrix to him with a serious expression, but once the little guy was in his grasp, he made obnoxiously loud raspberries on his bared torso. Orrie followed his lead, and pretty soon both boys hiccuped with laughter and went running back to their room.

Orrie and Dalton shared a satisfied smile.

"I'll take this over the Claremont any day," Dalton said as he leaned over for a kiss.

"I can't wait until this is our life every morning," Orrie said against Dalton's lips. "I love you, baby."

"I love you back."

Dalton drove them to meet Olive on the other side of the bridge at Baldie's Cafe for breakfast and to make the child exchange. Orrie's plane didn't leave until late afternoon and he wanted to see Olive and the baby. Olive was over-the-moon excited to see her brother, and Orrie immediately grabbed Janis and cuddled her the entire meal.

Dalton made eye contact with him, and Orrie's hopeful smile

was a huge improvement from his dour expression the day before.

Dalton's own expression was probably as dreamy and dopey as he felt. Olive asked them questions about the night before, but they'd agreed to keep their plans under wraps. Dalton was having a hard time keeping up with the conversation.

His phone buzzed in his pocket. Terrence.

Thanks again for coming last night.

"Terrence texted to say thank you."

Orrie stared at him with a frown, while Hendrix and Clapton pulled on his ears and used his gauges as peepholes.

"That's...interesting. Maybe he's changed?"

Can you send me a Lyft?

"Hold that thought," Dalton said. He dialed Terrence's number and stepped outside.

"I didn't end up home. Tasha wanted..."

"Tasha wanted?"

"You going to make me say it?"

Dalton couldn't hold in the snicker.

"Fine. We came out to some park. She said she wanted to look at the stars."

"Okay."

"So we looked at the stars! Then she wanted...you know, and I wanted to, and we did, and then we were cuddling, and I said I was hungry. That was it! She got pissed and she left me here! I slept on a fucking bench. Well, actually, I lay on that bench all night watching the fucking bats fly around and listening to noises. I didn't really sleep until the sun came up and it got quiet."

"She left because you said you were hungry?"

Terrence cursed. "I might have said I wanted a steak."

Dalton barked out a laugh. "What's wrong with that?"

"She works with animals, Dalton. She's vegan, right? She couldn't believe she let me do...well, *that* to her when I eat meat. I might have led her to believe I was vegan, too. Now, can you send someone or what?"

Oh, this is priceless. "Not unless you tell me where you are!"

"I don't know where I am!"

Dalton sighed. "Do you see any signs? Any...landmarks?"

"I see a bunch of fucking trees, Dalton."

"Wait. Is this the same phone I bought you last year? When yours got broken?"

"Yeah."

Dalton clicked over to the Find My iPhone app and proceeded to scroll through all of his devices and the ones he'd bought for his family members, until he found "Terrence 7th iPhone." He'd been through a few of them. Sure enough, it pulled up his location.

"Looks like you're at Garin Park in Hayward. I'll have it there in fifteen minutes."

Terrence mumbled a thank you.

"Don't thank me. Consider it long overdue payback," Dalton said and hung up. He walked back into the restaurant as Orrie was paying the bill, shaking his head and laughing out loud.

"Everything okay?"

Dalton kissed him on the cheek. "Oh yeah."

Orrie frowned again. "What the hell was that all about?"

Dalton tugged on his fingers. "I'll tell you in the car."

Orrie kissed his hair as they walked out. "I can hardly wait."

They hugged the boys and Olive, who thanked them profusely, and then wrangled the beasts into their car seats in the back of Olive's SUV.

"Patrick and I had such a great night. You guys are my heroes."

Dalton almost told her she could reciprocate, but instead, he traded a knowing look with Orrie. They said their goodbyes and climbed back into the Tesla.

"Terrence get himself in a bind?"

Dalton chuckled. "Oh yeah. Let's just say Tasha didn't appreciate hooking up with a carnivore and she left him to nature's mercy."

Orrie shook his head. "Sounds like Terrence. That guy…"

"We've got time before your flight. Shall we head back home, or did you want to go look at rings?"

Orrie's eyes glazed over with lust. "Goddamn but you are the most delicious man I have ever laid eyes, hands or tongue on."

Dalton shifted in his seat. "I can't wait to have those things on me once again."

"Let's go home." Orrie leaned over and kissed Dalton with slow, drugging sweeps of his tongue. He dropped a hand to Dalton's fly and began to tug on the buttons. "I'm still hungry."

"I'm all yours, baby."

Laughter outside the car reminded Dalton they were still in the parking lot and diners had to walk past them to go inside.

"Maybe we should get on the road before we give the Baldie's patrons a show?"

Orrie pulled back and smiled, the stress lines gone from around his eyes.

"Happy Valentine's Day, baby."

Dalton grinned. "Best ever."

"CUPID'S REVENGE" BY PRESLAYSA WILLIAMS

ROSALIND AQUINO SCRUNCHED her nose at the latest report showing the television ratings for her talk show, *Chat with Roz*. Her stomach twisted into a ball of tangled knots at the sight of those declining digits. Despite the sunshine blazing through the windows of her Manhattan office, Rosalind was feeling cloudy. If she didn't have this show, this fame, this attention, and this huge salary to go with it, she wouldn't have anything.

The muscles in her neck tensed, and she tilted her head to the right in the hopes of erasing the pain. Didn't work.

"Four straight weeks of low ratings," she whispered. "How am I gonna dig myself out of this one?"

Her cell phone buzzed, indicating a text. She picked it up and read the message from Kira, her best friend.

I landed a Valentine's date for you.

Rosalind rolled her eyes and replied to the text. *Not interested.*

Aww, come on. He's a model, Roz. Stop working so much. Have more fun.

Kira didn't understand. Every time Cupid shot an arrow

Rosalind's way, the arrow ended up poking her in the eye. And being a talk show host demanded twelve-hour days. Minimum. It'd probably demand more.

Not probably. It would definitely demand more. Her egomaniacal boss, Greg, was probably freaking out.

Rosalind's phone buzzed with another notification.

If you don't get your patootie out of the stifling television studio for this Valentine's day date, I'm gonna kidnap you from your job.

She stared at the text from Kira. "Ain't happening, girl-friend," Rosalind said to the phone. "I'm single for life." Instead of typing her response, Rosalind sent a smiling emoji and turned off her cell. She had bigger things to deal with today.

Rosalind had spent countless days and months and therapy sessions trying to find her way. She'd eventually found her way—and her life's mission—when she landed this job. She would help women to live their best lives, with or without a man. This talk show was her vehicle to live out her purpose.

She had dreams of becoming an Afro-Asian Oprah, but those dreams might not happen now. Who had time to worry about Valentine's Day dates?

Rosalind plunked her head against the desk. If she didn't get her show back on track, this was gonna be a big ol' mess, the kind of mess that would jeopardize her chances of signing a contract for another television season. The media was a brutal hamster wheel. If she wasn't at the foreground of the people's interest, then someone else could come along and steal her spot. She'd lose everything she'd spent these past three years working to find.

Her desk phone rang so loud it startled her. That phone never rang unless it was her boss. And sure enough, the caller ID read Greg Philips. Great. She wasn't ready for this call.

"Good morning." Rosalind put on her neutral newscaster voice.

"What the hell is going on with the ratings, Rosalind?"

The nerve. He always made every failure her fault, and every success his credit. "Oh, that?"

"Yes. That. We can't afford these drops. We'll lose advertising dollars and network support. Let's discuss a new strategy over lunch."

Lunch? Rosalind was planning to review script revisions with the show runner. "You could ask me respectfully, Greg, instead of making a demand."

"Respectful requests don't pay the bills. Meet me at Charlie's Grill on 53rd at noon. Bring some ideas for your Valentine's show. I have a few in mind too."

Annoyance shot through her. This man was a walking ego bomb. Being the executive producer didn't mean Rosalind had to drop everything to meet him. "I was planning to go over the script with the production team today." Now there was a little less newscaster in her tone and a lot more irritation.

"And I sign all your checks. Reschedule your meetings. See you at noon."

The phone clicked, and a dial tone buzzed in her ear. Rosalind's heart gave one huge whap against her rib cage.

Was Greg an overbearing boss? Yes.

Was she out of her mind for staying in this job? No.

Not only did this place give her a sense of purpose, her career made her feel like there was life after Kevon, the man who broke her heart three years ago. On Valentine's Day.

———

ROSALIND WAS ravenous by the time the waitress from Charlie's Grill arrived at the table with one plate piled high with french fries and another plate piled high with mozzarella sticks. Stress made her hungry. The waitress slid the plates before her, and Rosalind scooped up four fries and shoved them in her mouth. Greg wasn't here yet, which was typical. He always arrived late to meetings. It was his way of putting the staff in their place. They waited on him, not the other way around.

The entrance to the grill swung open and, in the doorway stood Greg Philips, creator of *Chat with Roz*. As he unfastened his blazer and placed it over his forearm, the drafty late January air seeped into Charlie's Grill, leaving Rosalind cold.

Greg made eye contact, and a furrow grew around his thin mouth. A deeper thread of anxiety wove through her, but Rosalind mustered up the last of her resolve and smiled.

"Hello, Greg."

He glanced at the appetizers in front of her. "Looks like you didn't wait to get started on eating."

Jerk. "TV personalities need fuel to keep going."

"They also need to stay slim." He adjusted the half-spectacles on the bumpy ridge of his nose and ran his fingers through his thinning brown hair. "A ratings drop is bad enough."

What an ass. "I never took you for the chauvinist type, Greg."

"You can take me now...oh wait. I don't need a lawsuit on my hands." He laughed sarcastically. "Seems women like to fling around lawsuits at the first hint of impropriety these days. So let's get down to business."

Her entire body tightened. This was a stepping stone on her career path. A stepping stone. Rosalind wouldn't be under his thumb forever. "Yes. Let's."

"What are your ideas for the Valentine's show?" Greg asked, his tone conciliatory, almost too conciliatory.

Over the last three years, Rosalind had received hundreds of emails from her viewers, women who'd been down and out but were inspired by her talk show. She'd reread some of those emails before this meeting to build her confidence.

At first, the emails seemed like a fluke. There was no way

Rosalind could impact America, not with the way she'd messed up her life with Kevon. But the affirming messages kept pouring in. The emails revealed Rosalind's loyal audience, her people, her purpose. "I was thinking of having a few couples appear on the show and tell their stories of how they met. Something feel-good and hopeful."

A humorless smiled crossed his lips. "No one wants feel-good and hopeful, Rosalind. This is the age of internet dragging. People always want drama and gossip. Our ratings will go up."

"I'm not a tabloid host."

"If tabloid gets the ratings up, you will be a tabloid host. This is my creation. Not yours."

A stifling and stuck feeling handcuffed her again. He was right. This was his show, but she was gonna stand up for herself. She averted her eyes to the plates of fries and mozzarella sticks.

"This is what you think? I'm going to have to sacrifice my brand image for ratings?"

"I made your brand image too, Rosalind. If we need something dramatic, we'll go dramatic. It'll give us a boost. Then you can return to your feel-good, empowering stories."

"Obviously you have something in mind," she said. "What is it?"

Greg didn't answer right away. Instead, he flipped through the menu and Rosalind felt the full reach of the distance between them: television executive versus television star. The public thought Rosalind called the shots on the talk show, but the opposite was true. Greg was in charge.

After Greg placed his order, he perused her with hooded eyes which turned her into a ball of ick. His gaze held an edge. "I want you to become a matchmaker for a single guy on this year's Valentine's episode."

No way. "Not my thing. I'll be happy to feature folks and their love stories, but I am not the person to help someone create their story. I'm all about helping people make their own decisions, not forcing my choices onto their lives." She'd done the forcing thing before, and it hadn't ended well.

"You'll be a great fit for this idea. You're the least likely person. You're always so Girl Boss." His voice sounded mocking. "If you played a matchmaker, it'd be borderline comical."

So now she was gonna be his clown? Hell no.

"Especially after what happened to you in your prior life," he added.

What did this man know about Rosalind? She made it a cardinal rule to never let her personal life go public. She had guarded everything about herself, all in the name of maintaining the friendly Black-girl-next-door image viewers loved. She'd never aired or showed her grievances publicly. Never.

Rosalind didn't dig further, however. She was already teetering with the lower ratings. No need to push it.

"My assistant searched through potential actors for the gig, but no one quite fit," Greg said. "So we decided she'd make a casting call for everyday people instead."

"Wait a second." Rosalind raised her hand and her voice shrieked. "You did what?"

"My assistant searched potential hopefuls for the upcoming episode." He shrugged. "What's the matter?"

She could barely comprehend his words. This man pretended to ask for ideas in order to...to what? To play on her emotions when he already had a plan of his own? Who did he think he was? "My production team and I have weekly meetings where we decide these matters. You never consulted us."

"Your ratings are dipping. It was time to take matters into my own hands." Greg straightened as he removed his glasses, setting them on the speckled granite table.

Rosalind couldn't believe she hadn't anticipated this latest move from Greg, a man whose veil of rigidity hadn't softened, a man who couldn't possibly empathize. She'd first applied for this gig shortly after she'd broken up with Kevon. She'd given up her TV journalism career for Kevon and moved in with him, in the hopes of eventually getting married and living the suburban housewife life.

Didn't happen.

She'd put her life on hold for the loser. Until he'd sent her Valentine's Day flowers with a sweet message in his own handwriting ... but addressed to his secret side chick. Distraught, she'd broken up with him, then applied to every potential news outlet she could find. Anything to get her career back on track.

The only person who'd taken her seriously was Greg, and she'd jumped at the opportunity. Now, she second-guessed how much Greg respected her, because the more popular she became, the more ornery Greg became.

"Here's my pick. Help this man find the perfect Valentine's match." He placed a photo in front of her.

Her skin tightened, and her legs turned to lead. Kevon. No. Hell no. Rosalind swallowed, then gulped down a glass of soda.

"How'd you find this person?" Her tone remained matter of fact.

"This *person?*" A dull shade of delight eased onto his face. "You know him. He said you did."

"Is this some kind of joke?" Her words fell off.

"Not a joke. It's television. He said he's looking for someone to help him find a special someone for Valentine's Day." Greg tugged on his ear, looked down for a moment. "After a brief interview, he was chosen for the episode."

This man was lying. "Not doing this. I'll work with anyone but him. It's too much."

"Having our ratings drop four weeks in a row is too much. This is one episode. I'm not asking you to share your personal history with this *person* on television."

"Because you know the camera will pick up on the tension."

"Exactly." He winked. "He's coming to the studio on Monday for a walk-through rehearsal. Sound good?"

Oh, now Greg wanted Rosalind's buy in. Greg expected her to do a run through *and* tape the actual show with Kevon. She'd have to see her ex. Twice. Nope.

And why was Kevon doing this? He hadn't cared about her journalism career when they were dating, and when she'd been a nobody. Did he want to hook up with her now she was successful, despite the fact he'd once convinced her to let go of her career aspirations? Nope. Nope. Not happening.

"Sound good?" Greg repeated.

She didn't answer.

"Good. I'll get a to-go plate for my lunch. Finish it up in the office. I have a ton of calls and emails to return." He got up from the table and lightly tapped her shoulder. "Thanks for being a trooper. Knew I could count on you."

After he left, Rosalind pressed the pad of her thumb against the sharp edges of her fork, pressing until the tips of her fingers whitened. No way could Rosalind see Kevon again. She exhaled and focused on the bumper-to-bumper midtown traffic outside.

Why had Rosalind assumed getting this job would get her mind off Kevon? Greg didn't care about her well-being—he wanted a successful show. For Greg, her utter and complete awkwardness and embarrassment was a nonissue.

Rosalind needed to talk to Kira. Kira would know what to do.

As Rosalind gathered her things to leave, the mozzarella sticks turned rancid in her stomach. Ugh. Her lunch frowned upon this turn of events. Rosalind tried to hold the feeling down with an invisible flimsy piece of tape, but it proved useless.

And so I must face my menace. Somehow.

———

"YOU'RE GONNA DO WHAT?" Kira closed the screened patio of her New Jersey ranch home.

"Set up Kevon with his dream date on live television."

The scent of vanilla candles and coffee provided a comforting mix of hearth and home. Rosalind had been working a lot, so hadn't had many Saturdays off. With everything Greg had thrown at her, she'd decided to spend this Saturday with her friend in Jersey.

"How hilarious!"

"The hell it ain't," Rosalind said. "I'm gonna make Kevon's life a living hell, humiliate him as much as he humiliated me."

"You should be happy you found out. In a way. He could've been cheating on you for longer, and you would've been ignorant of the entire thing."

Rosalind reached for the metal TV tray next to her Adirondack chair and poured three packets of sugar in her black coffee, then a fourth. How else would she calm her nerves? "My plan is to kill him on live television, but I wanted to check in with you first. See what your thoughts were."

"Murder is a reasonable reaction." Kira combed her dark curls away from her freckled, brown face. "And I'm here for it. But don't you want to keep your job?"

Rosalind considered all the times Greg had tried to overpower her during business meetings, and this last move was her tipping point. "I've considered it, and I say screw being America's Girl Boss. If it means I have to face the likes of Kevon to get a ratings increase, then I don't need it. I have to live out my ideals in public and in private. I can't say I'm empowering women if I'm getting bulldozed behind the camera."

"You've worked so hard to get to where you are in your career. Are you sure?" Kira asked.

"Yep."

"You've got guts, girlfriend."

The taste of bile gathered in her throat. "I wouldn't call it guts. More like necessity. I have to save face somehow. I ain't a punk."

"You shouldn't risk it, Rosalind. I say you let the world know the truth of your history with Kevon. Then make a good faith effort to help Kevon find the perfect date. It'll make you look like the bigger person, and your viewers will love you more. Your ratings will skyrocket. Greg is counting on you getting all tabloid television, but if you become the better person, you'll one-up Greg AND get your ratings hike."

"Mean sounds better."

"I know your relationship with Kevon wasn't the highlight of your life. He did some pretty crappy things to you, not just the cheating. Like when he convinced you to loan him three thousand dollars until his credit improved." Kira picked up a paper plate and lifted the lid from the bowl of fruit.

"What a money-sucking leech. And he never paid me back. I was so gullible."

"You live and learn." Kira smiled. "Being kind would be a great way to heal and move on."

Rosalind's pulse went thump, thump, thump, and her eyes smarted. "I've already moved on from Kevon. I've been moved on for the past three years. I have an entire career to show for it."

"Keep telling yourself that tale. See how far it'll get you." Kira handed her a Kleenex. "It's okay to cry."

"I'm not crying! It's seasonal allergies." Rosalind crushed the tissues in her hand and gnawed the inside of her cheek.

"It's not allergy season."

"It is for me."

Kira leaned forward, placed her warm hand over Rosalind's cold one. "You can talk to me. I'm your friend."

Why'd Kira have to be such a discerning friend? Her eyes alone could unscramble the Greek alphabet backwards. "I'm trying to process everything. I need time. I'm not ready to see him. I hate Greg for setting this whole thing up. And I'm not gonna forgive Kevon."

"Why do you think Kevon is reaching out to you?"

"He must be in desperate straits or something." Rosalind shrugged. "Well, I'm not loaning him any more money, and he ain't getting nothing remotely romantic from me."

"Good for you, girlfriend. You deserve better for your life. I'm proud of how far you've come. You got your career back on track. You're making way more money than the three thousand dollars you loaned him. And you're an inspiration to women around America. Whatever you decide with Kevon, revenge or forgiveness or whatever, I'm here for you. I'll support you all the way." Kira handed her the plate of fruit.

"Thanks, sister." A warm and winsome pulse shot through Rosalind. She'd been living in the public eye so long. Hearing her friend's kindness was almost disconcerting.

"I believe your show is on the air for a purpose, to give people a slice of laughter and joy. To help women feel they can do something good with their lives. If you think getting payback on live television will bring joy, then hey, go for it."

"Your perspective has definitely complicated this matter." She mashed a piece of cantaloupe into tiny little pieces with the rounded edge of her spoon. "This is gonna be a mess. I can't see Kevon again."

"Maybe this time, you'll set things straight...on your terms." Kira gave her a mischievous smile.

She really was a true friend. "Thank you."

"And once you've closed the door, you can move on. Sometimes falling in love is a matter of cupid time."

"Cupid time?"

"The time when love strikes its arrow, and Rosalind meets

her prince, preferably before midnight." Kira squeezed her eyes shut and smooched the cool air with one big *mwah*.

"Hasn't happened for me."

"Yet. It hasn't happened for you yet." Kira said. "Hey, if you want something, you have to believe for it. You have to prepare for it. You have to work for it." She gave her two thumbs up and smiled with the conviction of a motivational speaker.

"I don't want to fall in love."

Kira shrugged. "If you say so."

"I know so."

"Whatever makes you happy."

"I'm happy right now. Happy. Happy. Happy. And I'll be even happier once I embarrass Kevon in front of the entire country."

Kira stopped munching her fruit and studied Rosalind for a moment. "I'm a fan of grace, even when it's hard. But do you, boo. Do you."

No one gave Rosalind grace when Kevon had lied and deceived her. Everyone had told Rosalind that's what men did, and that she should move on. Rosalind moved on, but the anger never left. It transferred it into...workaholism and getting one-upped at work by her boss.

Now was the time for payback, for both Kevon and Greg. Two birds, one show.

———

PAYBACK STILL ECHOED in Rosalind's mind when she arrived at work the following Monday, ready to meet her nemesis for the walk-through. She was gonna put him through the wringer. Her first step would be a pre-interview interview on why he thought he deserved the perfect Valentine's date.

Then when the show went live later this week, she was gonna

counter all his answers, so all the hopefuls would see what a douche bag he was.

Hopefully the contestants would then opt out, leaving him without a date for Valentine's.

She stepped into the empty conference room armed in full TV personality battle gear: black suit, matching pumps, studded earrings, perfect makeup, queasy stomach. For all her tough talk with Kira the other day, Rosalind was nervous at the thought of seeing him again.

Not a good thing.

"Hey, you."

The bass-filled voice thrummed through her, and she hated it. How dare he try to be so casual with her after everything he'd done? She turned. Kevon stood off to the side near the water cooler. Those dark brown eyes sucked her into a cloud-nine vortex.

Stop looking. Stop looking. Stop looking.

She kept looking.

"I didn't think you'd show up." Kevon buttoned his perfectly pressed navy suit jacket. "Glad you did."

If he didn't think she'd show up, then why was he here? Was he so desperate to see her for whatever selfish reason he had planned?

"What kind of stunt are you trying to pull, Kevon? This is my job, not your chance to accomplish whatever your ulterior motives might be."

He sat next to her, sat so close his aftershave enveloped her. Their forearms touched. A buzz filtered through her skin, the subtlest sensation, enough for her to relish the feeling. No. Not relish. Pull away. *Pull away, Rosalind.*

"Personal space, buddy. Keep out of my personal space." She moved away.

Kevon shrugged. "I don't have any ulterior motives. I am

really looking for the perfect Valentine's date. Relationships have been slow going since we broke up."

"Hold up. We didn't break up. You dumped me by cheating on me."

"You sure?" His eyes widened a smidge. "I remember feeling bummed for weeks, but I don't remember dumping you. Then I hear about you becoming this big-time TV star and I figured you moved on."

"Reading the card with the flowers addressed to another woman was enough of a dump for me. You wrote the card to a woman named Laura. It was over for me afterward. So yeah. You dumped me."

"Ah, yes. Laura." His tone was solid, assured, with no cracks. The man had no shame.

"Laura was a woman I met at the deli a week before Valentine's Day. She was recently widowed. It was her first Valentine's Day without her husband. I sent her flowers as a friendly gesture."

Yeah, yeah, yeah. He'd told her this BS story when it happened. Kevon thought she was some desperate fool who'd believe anything he said. Liar.

"First, I didn't believe you then and I don't believe you now. Second, if it's true, then manipulating a widow's heart is gross. Third, if it's true, why did you let me go?"

He was silent.

Why did you let me go?

It was the question Rosalind wanted answered, except she was afraid of the answer. Afraid of discovering she wasn't worthy of love.

Rosalind hadn't been worthy of love when her father had walked out on them when she was in third grade. She hadn't been worthy of love when her mother had told her to settle for Kevon's antics, and she wasn't worthy of love today.

"I'm not here to have a heart-to-heart with you about what went wrong in our relationship." She put on her best professional TV presenter voice, the one she used on Greg or the intern who brought her coffee in the morning. "I'm here to set you up with someone else." In her little hell-hath-no-fury way. "So what's your idea of a perfect date?"

"A date with you."

Aw, crap. Rosalind slammed her padfolio closed. "I don't know what you and my boss talked about, but I am not one of your options for a Valentine's date. Get that through your thick skull, and let's proceed with the questions."

He gave her one of his impossible smiles. "Agreed. Let's continue with the questions."

Rosalind focused on the yellow legal pad in front of her, so she wouldn't have to stare at his eyes or his face or his lips.

"What's your ideal woman like?"

"Like you."

She stared him down and huffed. "You can't say that on television."

"We're not on television."

"You can't say that off television either. I'm the matchmaker, and I'm the woman who can't stand you."

He held up his hands. "Okay, okay. Don't have to be so touchy."

"It's not touchy, Kevon. It's the truth."

His shoulders slumped a bit, but she pushed aside any remote feelings of remorse. This man wasn't gonna mess with her head. She continued with her questions about his ideal date and his ideal woman, but a stream of thoughts attacked her, distracting her. What if he found the ideal woman as a result of this episode? What if they discovered they were compatible and ended up in a committed relationship or something? What then?

Her foot jiggled at the awful possibility.

"It'll be fine. It'll be fine. It'll be fine," she said in low rapid-fire murmurs, murmurs reminiscent of the desperate pleas she'd prayed when her father skipped out on them. Except she was never the praying type. She was more the worrying type.

"Hey, Rosalind," Kevon's words snapped her out of her musings. His lips turned up in a gentle half smile and she shifted away from him, uncomfortable.

"Oh right, yes." She cleared her throat and scanned the rest of her questions. "You answered enough of them. I'll give these to the assistant producer, so they'll be ready for taping on Thursday."

"So that's it between us?"

She paused. "That's it."

"All righty then." He didn't budge. Neither did she. In one millisecond, Kevon must've sensed her mixed feelings towards him, and mixed feelings were a trap. If she gave in, she'd be a puddle of goop. Not gonna happen. Puddles of goop were a quivering mess.

"See you Thursday, Kevon." She swiped up her legal pad and made a beeline for the studio.

She wasn't gonna fall for whatever Kevon and Greg had up their sleeves, at least not fully. Okay, so she still got a sweaty-palm feeling in Kevon's presence, but she for sure wasn't gonna do anything about it. Even if his eyes were the dreamiest on the planet.

Sigh.

Had Rosalind truly believed she'd live the rest of her life without being the least bit attracted to Kevon?

No.

Double sigh.

So what if he still managed to make her feel like she was a woman? It meant nothing. Nothing at all. Perhaps one day

Rosalind would find the man who was for real and committed to her and her alone.

But one day wouldn't be any time soon.

———

ROSALIND SURVEYED the packed studio audience from the makeup room. They were a fifty-fifty mix of men and women, not the usual majority-female audience. Man, Greg was really trying to make Rosalind turn into a tabloid television host today.

Not wanting to focus on the challenge, she refocused on the four dating contestants sitting on stage. They all seemed normal, except for trusting their love life to the national media.

The director of photography was busy adjusting the lighting while Frieda, the lead makeup artist, powdered Rosalind's nose. "You look tired today," Frieda said. "But I put on extra concealer to help you out a bit."

Rosalind gave her a smile. "Thanks."

As if reading Rosalind's mind, Freida added, "They love you out there. There's nothing extra for you to do. I promise."

Rosalind's eyes smarted. Frieda was right. There wasn't nothing extra Rosalind needed to do to get the ratings up. She needed to be herself.

"Thank you," Rosalind said to Frieda. "Means a lot."

But what would being herself look like in this situation? Was she gonna roll hard on Kevon and drag him in front of this studio audience? Or was she gonna take the high road, as Kira had suggested?

All the fluffy feelings she'd felt when she had spoken to him the other day complicated the matter. Now she didn't know what to do.

After Frieda finished with Rosalind, she walked on set and the studio audience cheered. A rush of energy zipped through her. Being in the spotlight filled a void she hadn't known existed until the fame came along, a void neither her father nor Kevon had filled. With the audience, her voice was valued. What she had to say mattered.

Rosalind made quick introductions with the four women on stage: a professional-looking woman with ebony skin, a Latina-looking person in her twenties, a blonde Jersey gal, and a gorgeous Lisa Ling lookalike. Rosalind didn't know anything about these women personally, but none of them deserved to be with Kevon. Rosalind needed to inform the entire female population to stay away today. Somehow.

When Rosalind got to Kevon, her skin pricked in a puppy-love-crush kind of way, but she nodded briefly. No handshake for him.

"Help me through this," she whispered, another of her prayer pleas. Her stomach clenched as she took her place on the yellow X in front of the camera and placed her index finger on the first of ten bullet point questions she'd asked Kevon during their meeting. She usually winged these conversations, but she'd practiced extra hard this time, trying to figure out the angle she'd take. Greg would not forgive her if she messed this up.

"Rolling!" the cameraman shouted. "And action!"

"Welcome to Chat with Roz! Today we have a special Valentine's episode where I get to help a lonely, awful ... I mean single ... man find the perfect match. Everyone, meet Kevon Jackson." She gestured to him, and the crowd clapped on cue.

Greg appeared from stage right and stepped behind the cameraman. Why was he looking for high drama? Just to spite him, she'd remain cool. "Let's proceed with our first set of questions for the eligible bachelor. Kevon, what are you looking for in the perfect Valentine's date?"

Kevon rubbed the side of his eye. "We already discussed this, Rosalind. I'm looking for you."

The crowd gasped.

Rosalind opened and closed her mouth twice before deciding what to say. Greg grinned, and she wanted to barf, but she kept her cool. "Okay, you say you want a woman like me. What qualities are you most interested in?"

"You're independent, but you also know how to obey a man when you need to." A smug smile formed on Kevon's lips. Greg chuckled.

Rosalind wanted to disappear. Kevon and Greg were making a fool of her on live television. Not happening.

"Obey?" the blonde shouted. "What do you mean obey? I don't obey men. This is the 21st century."

"You right!" the woman with ebony skin said.

The Asian woman pumped her fist. "Woman power!"

Kevon's eyes widened. "You're taking this the wrong way. What I meant to say was Rosalind knows a relationship is give and take."

"Well, you take, take, take." Rosalind said. "You took three grand from me and didn't pay it back. And you tried to take my career!"

The four women studied her with interest. Oh, Lord. She'd let loose an outburst. She'd lost control. Greg must be loving this. She didn't want to look in his direction.

"This is all coming out wrong. I love you, Rosalind," Kevon said. "Let's work things out."

Kevon's manipulative grandstanding was not only messing with her image, it was messing with her purpose for this show. If she fell for this crap, then she might as well throw out everything she'd worked so hard to achieve: her independence, her voice, her sense of self-worth. All her time in therapy would be flushed down the toilet.

"You had your chance with me, and you ruined it." Then Rosalind faced the audience. "Ladies and gentlemen, this is a classic example of male emotional centering. It's a tactic used to guilt-trip women into reverting back into unhealthy codependent relationships. Don't fall for it."

The women in the audience nodded. The men looked confused. Rosalind gave Greg a quick once-over. No way would she let him win this one.

"Excuse me," the Latina said. "Is this some kind of joke?"

"Nope," Rosalind said. "On this show, I am all about helping women live their best lives. I cannot, in clear conscience, be a matchmaker for this man when I won't date him myself."

Greg's face turned red, and the studio audience turned silent. Why was Greg's face red? Wasn't this the drama he wanted?

Kevon appeared as if he wanted to run out of the studio. Ha! "Now let's continue," Rosalind said. "Have you ever cheated on a woman?"

Kevon flicked a speck of lint from the lapel of his suit jacket. "Never."

"Liar!" Rosalind blurted, even as some small part of her cringed at how much drama she was delivering for Greg. "You are a whole entire lie. Ladies, don't listen to this man. He cheated on me three years ago on Valentine's Day, of all days! I received a bouquet of roses from Kevon but addressed to another woman."

The crowd gasped.

The blonde directed her attention at Kevon. "Is that true?"

"Yes and no," he said, nervous. "I sent the roses to a woman who was sickly. She was a friend of a friend."

"Hold up." Rosalind held up her hand. "You told me you sent it to a widow."

Kevon's eyes shifted. "A widow who was sick."

"This man is trash, ladies! Pure trash," Rosalind said. "And I need to make a public apology to all of you. I knew my boss was going to have him on the show, and I should've taken a stand then. Instead, I was quiet because I wanted to work towards ratings. But ladies, you are worth more than anyone's show ratings. So for Valentine's Day I say, forget about vying for a man. Forget about trying to land the perfect date. Forget them. Let's celebrate Valentine's on our own."

"Yeah!" One contestant stood. "I am woman, hear me be single on Valentine's Day."

The second and third contestants stood up and nodded in sync. The last one remained seated. "I was looking for a date."

There was always one who betrayed the revolution.

"If you still want to date Kevon after everything I told you, go ahead," Rosalind said. "But you can't ever say I never told you."

"That's right!" a voice called from the studio audience.

Energized by the excitement of the crowd, Rosalind felt something about to break lose inside of her. Years of waiting on no-good men to do something in her life. First her father. Then Kevon. Now Greg, who wanted to turn her life into a ratings spectacle.

Hell to the no.

"And you know what?" Rosalind pointed to Greg, who was now cringing. "That man concocted everything. He wanted to make a fool of me in front of the entire world. He set this up, and I'm not playing by his rules anymore. I quit this show. I refuse to be a puppet in another man's game. Happy Valentine's Day, folks. Ladies, let's get out of here."

The crowd cheered.

For the first time, Rosalind felt free.

"ASKING FOR A FRIEND" BY AVERIL DAYE

Go back. Cancel. Continue.

SARAH MACNEIL STARED at the options on her laptop screen for so long that a fifteen-second "please make a selection" timer in the shape of a peach appeared in the middle of the matchmaking site's page.

Fifteen, fourteen, thirteen...

Feeling the heat of panic and indecision, Sarah hit 'go back.' The timer vanished, and the previous page reappeared.

What are you looking for?

She scoffed, just as she had the first time she saw the question. *Hell if I know.* She'd checked the boxes next to "companionship" and "friendship" and ignored the more romantic choices. Sarah didn't want a lover, boyfriend, or anyone else looking for regular access to her vagina. Not now, anyway. Probably not ever.

Friends and family had tried to tell her otherwise—at the

repast, no less—not thirty minutes after she and her daughters had tearfully left her husband's casket at the cemetery.

"You should get back in the game ASAP, " her cousin had advised in the buffet line, dumping a heaping pile of macaroni and four cheeses on her plate. "Greg would want you to keep living. Those kids need a daddy and you're gonna need some Vitamin D." She'd nudged Sarah's ribs with her elbow."If you know what I mean."

"He would want you to be happy," a distant aunt of Greg's with ashy hands had told her at the dessert table.

"Greg wouldn't want you to be lonely," his mother had said.

Sarah was so sick of hearing that Greg would want her to have a love life. How could anyone possibly know that? Maybe he wouldn't have wanted her to waste her time or get hurt. Maybe he'd never even given it a second thought because he'd planned to stick around a lot longer. Fit, seemingly healthy, strong men don't expect to drop dead of a heart attack at 50.

Cancel. Continue. Need more time?

Sarah continued.

The next set of questions focused on hobbies: sports, movies, watching television, etc. Unfortunately the list didn't include staring into space and getting envious of her friends' happy Facebook posts. She had mastered that over the last three years. So Sarah clicked "reading", "writing", "watching TV shows and movies", "going to the theater" and "attending concerts". She actually hadn't done the latter in several years, way before Greg died, but she liked the idea of dressing up and seeing a live performance with someone other than her two kids. If she could do it in the days leading up to February 14th —a horrible period on the calendar she referred to as "Febzilla"—even better.

The anniversaries of Greg's death, their wedding, and Valentine's Day occurred within days of each other. Last year, to keep her mind off the terrible trifecta, she raked about ten tons of left-over autumn leaves into garden refuse bags on all three windy, chilly days. Her daughters—at the time five and eleven—watched her from the family room bay window, crying. They didn't recognize or understand her behavior. Sarah barely raked leaves on the nicest of days, let alone in the dead of winter for hours over multiple days.

"I just want my Mommy back," Grace, her youngest, said after Sarah came inside last February 14th.

Sarah didn't have the heart to tell her kids that the person they used to know died with their father. Women don't spend years pouring their all into building a life with their partners without losing an enormous sense of purpose when the loves of their lives check out. Between her weight fluctuations, disinterest in cooking and touch-and-go listlessness, Sarah didn't recognize herself, either.

Her grief therapist recommended exercise, a healthy diet, and a social life without the kids. Exercise? She walked around the block a couple of days a week and ate healthy most of the time. She still liked chocolate almond crunch ice cream way too much.

As for her social life...

"My husband was my social life," she told Dr. Hudson at her last session.

"You shouldn't have let that happen. Everyone needs friends besides their spouses."

"I had friends, I just preferred to spend time with Greg."

"Well, you can't do that anymore."

Sarah rolled her eyes. *No shit, lady!*

"Go out with some girlfriends from work," Dr. Hudson suggested.

"I work from home." Editing student essays for college

applications and scholarships helped put food on the table, but survivor benefits from Social Security paid the big bills.

"You said you had a lot of support after Greg died. Surely someone from that circle can be a movie buddy sometimes."

"They're busy." Sarah's once-sympathetic friends had stopped checking on her as soon as their procession of post-funeral casseroles ended. She had no siblings, and none of her extended family lived in the state or the region. She'd lost her parents years ago, before having kids.

"Then you're going to have to find someone who's available. You're only 45, Sarah. You have a lot of living to do. You don't have to have a lover. A companion will do."

Cue PeachDate, the site with the peach-shaped timer and a billion questions to answer. A play on Georgia's nickname, the peach state, the year-old site had received rave reviews for its spot-on matchmaking algorithm. It claimed hundreds of happy platonic and romantic pairings, but received scrutiny for its tagline, "uniting the souls of people who are destined to meet, from booty calls to BFFs."

It had made her laugh—one of the few things that could outside of her daughters' corny jokes. Sarah had taken it as a sign to register and submit her profile.

Congratulations, you're almost finished!

An animated waving banner with tiny peaches appeared, followed by - what else? - peach-colored confetti.

Now, add a PeachPic (selfie) and/or a Peachvid to your profile! Don't worry, if a potential PeachDate sends you a PeachNote, you'll get to see their theirs

too! And remember, there's absolutely no obligation to respond to anyone!

Sarah had totally forgotten about the selfie requirement. She picked up her phone and scrolled through her camera roll, already knowing she had nothing on it but photos of her and Melody during a recent field trip to the Atlanta Botanical Garden. Sarah had stopped taking vain selfies a long time ago.

She would just have to crop Melody out of the pictures and hope that the passerby who shot the photos got one of her looking peachy.

When a set of unfamiliar photos came up, Sarah inched her face closer to the screen. She recognized herself in front of a shelf of canned goods. Apparently, Grace had taken a handful of candid photos of her the night before at the supermarket instead of playing the spelling game app Sarah had downloaded for her.

Pics of Sarah squeezing avocados and reading the nutrition label on a six-pack of candy bars hardly seemed selfie material. But one photo caught her eye: she had a wide, genuine smile on her face, and she looked directly into the camera. Sarah loved how her long brown braids, cascading from her Mardi Gras-inspired head wrap of purple and gold masquerade masks, lay against her high cheekbones.

Grace must have snapped the photo after telling that joke about a cow, a pie and a milkshake. Sarah and Melody had both laughed at the gross punchline.

"We have a winner," Sarah said.

After she uploaded the photo, the site unleashed a fresh butt-load of animated confetti. The site presented her with her final options.

Go back. Submit. Cancel.

Sarah pressed submit before she changed her mind.

———

CARTER PULLED the chair back from the table and offered a warm smile to his girlfriend as she took her own sweet time sashaying over.

"I've got it from here, thanks," Maggie said. He stopped sliding her chair forward toward the table.

"That's right. Sorry."

He took his seat across from her and tapped the menu. "This place is famous for its blackened salmon," Carter said. "They have a really great sweet-and-sour shrimp dish, too."

"I hate seafood." Maggie didn't look up as she glanced over the menu.

Damnit! Another miss. He should have committed that detail from her dating profile to memory.

"We can go somewhere else," he said.

"No need. They've got plenty of other things I like." She looked up that time and gave him a thumbs-up.

Carter already knew he wanted a salad, the blackened salmon and a glass of white wine, so he slid the menu aside and folded his hands.

"How are the kids liking the tablets?"

Maggie finally perked up. "Oh, my goodness. They love them!" she exclaimed. "They can go to a lot of great math game sites that reinforce my lesson plans. I'd say about a third of my students didn't have access to a computer before now. Thanks to you, they do."

Carter beamed. "That's awesome."

"I still can't believe you did that. Neither can the other teachers."

"Do they need tablets, too?"

"Of course. But no one's expecting you to do that again. I certainly didn't even expect it."

The waiter brought them two glasses of water. He took Carter's order, but Maggie said she needed another minute.

"What are you guys famous for, besides seafood?" Carter asked.

The waiter twisted his lips and looked at the ceiling, tapping his pen to his notepad.

"Um, our cocktails, I guess?"

"I'm talking food-wise, sir."

"Carter, it's OK." Maggie turned to the waiter. "I'll have the baked ziti and a glass of Merlot, please."

"The ziti's pretty good." The waiter wrote down her order.

"But not great," Carter said.

"I mean, I guess *some* people think it's great. I personally prefer the pasta and shrimp over the ziti."

"Ashley doesn't eat seafood," Carter said.

Maggie furrowed her brow. "Who's Ashley?" She folded her hands under her chin and waited. Carter's mouth opened slightly, but no words came out. It felt as if his brain had abandoned him.

"I'll just get these out of the way," the waiter mumbled as he swiped the menus from the table. He hurried off.

"Ashley was my wife," Carter said. "You know I'm a...a..."

The "w" word caught in his throat. Six years later, he still couldn't stand to say it.

"You know my wife died," he said.

"I guess I forgot. You haven't said her name once since we've been seeing each other."

Well, not exactly. He'd moaned Ashley's name during his first night with Maggie, but she hadn't hear him. He didn't dare bring that up now, though. He sipped his water and looked away sheepishly.

"What'd she die from?"

"Complications from diabetes. I told you that, too."

"Damn. I'm really sorry." Maggie took a sip of water. "Was she a math teacher, too?"

"She was a seamstress. She worked with a lot of costume designers on movie sets."

"Still, though. She dealt with numbers. And she had to have a certain amount of creativity."

Carter nodded, sensing something bad about to go down.

The waiter returned with their wine. Carter positioned his glass under his nose and inhaled deeply, detecting the pear and lemon notes. He took a few small sips, savoring the liquid on his tongue.

Maggie slowly traced the top of her glass with her index finger.

"I think we should take a break," she said.

Still in mid-sip, Carter coughed and dribbled a small amount of wine down his thick beard.

"Why?" He dabbed his face with his napkin.

"Come on, Carter. You know why."

He sighed. "It was just a slip of the tongue. I know you're not her."

"You're with me because your website told you that you should be with a math geek who's also creative. That was your wife. I took a few pottery classes at the community center. That's where my creativity ends. But you think your logarithms found a copy of Ashley."

"Algorithms." Only his mouth moved. His body sat rigid as a rock.

"And another thing: you've got to stop trying to fix everything. My chair, my food options, the tablets - "

"You can't be serious. I was just trying to help! You wouldn't have gotten those tablets otherwise."

"How do you know? I casually mentioned on our fourth damn date that the kids could use tablets and the next day, thirty tablets are being delivered to my classroom. You just wanted to fix a problem."

"I can't win." Carter let out a bitter laugh and threw his hands up.

"I don't think it's always about winning. Sometimes you just have to let life happen and stop trying to straighten its course."

"Yeah. OK." Carter wanted to gag. He couldn't remember when he'd heard such inane trite. *Let life happen.* Easy for her to say. Hers hadn't fallen apart.

A member of the kitchen staff brought their salads. Carter stabbed his fork through a spinach leaf and cherry tomato, then dropped it.

"OK, maybe you're right," he said. "I do have a tendency to want to - I don't know - make things right. Set things up for success. Look at PeachDate. I started it so people don't have to rely on pure chance to meet someone special. PeachDate fixes that. But I guess I do go overboard in my personal life, too. That doesn't mean we have to break up."

Maggie finished her wine.

"There's more to it, Carter. You just have to figure it out."

———

HER ARMS FILLED with grocery bags, Sarah blindly unlocked the front door and pushed it open with her foot.

She still couldn't get used to doing the task alone. Since they'd both worked from home, Greg used to accompany her to the store, help her shop, load and unload the car, stealing kisses along the way. Her body still ached to feel his arms around her, his mouth on her.

Sarah's phone started to vibrate in her back pocket. She had two email notifications from the matchmaking site. Both subject lines read:

You have a PeachNote from a potential PeachDate!

Finally. A week had passed since she'd uploaded her profile and photo. Several PeachDate testimonials claimed that their love connections had happened the same day they registered. She could have checked out other profiles and made the first move, but she rather liked the old-fashioned idea of being pursued, even for companionship.

Though, anxiety, anticipation and hope trumped her jitters. She went into the family room, plopped on the couch, and opened her first message from a member named Arnie.

The incorrect grammar and lack of proper punctuation struck her first:

You come to the wrong place your pretty but this site isnt for your kind.

The room suddenly got very hot. Sarah fanned herself with her hand before reading the PeachNote again.

Only a few words stuck out this time. Wrong place. Your kind.

Sarah looked at his PeachPic. He had short hair, wore a T-shirt and had a thick neck. She couldn't really tell anything more about him because of the poor photo quality.

Sarah grabbed her purse and removed her reading glasses. Surely her bare, nearsighted eyes had skipped a word or misinterpreted the context.

Wrong place. Your kind.

Sarah began to tremble, just as she had when some random, high, tenth grade loser walked through the quad and shouted "Hey, shouldn't you people be cleaning up our shit?" to Sarah and her friends sitting in the grass after lunch, minding their own business. The same rage and hurt flowed through her veins now.

Well, forget Arnie. She wouldn't waste another sliver of energy on a bigot. But she *would* report his ass.

She opened the second message from a guy named Devon. Decent name. Another bad PeachPic. This stringy-haired person wore sunglasses, which the PeachDate instructions discouraged.

I like my black coffee with a little cream. How do you like your cream?

Sarah frowned. What in the sweet hell did that even mean? She scrolled up. Underneath Devon's thoughtful prose, he had attached a photo of his pasty, bumpy penis and hair-sprouting ball sack.

She dropped her phone to the floor and leaped from the couch, her hands covering her mouth in disbelief.

"What. The. Actual. Fu -"

"Hi Mommy!"

Grace bounded into the family room and gave Sarah a tight hug around her waist. Sarah hadn't heard the school bus's telltale squealing brakes, or the front door's creaking hinges, or her daughter's fast-paced footfalls. Arnie's ignorant message and Devon's sorry family jewels had temporarily cut off her senses.

She forced herself to recover for Grace. She bent down to her daughter's level and gave her a proper hug, holding on longer than usual.

Sarah pulled back so she could look at her daughter's beautiful brown skin and eyes. Grace had inherited most of Sarah's features, including the bright highlights in her hair, while Melody looked like Greg's mini twin, with her big hazel eyes and lopsided grin.

"Did you have a good day at school?"

"Yes! We had our Christmas party today."

"Oh, shi...shoot!" Sarah thumped her forehead. "Wasn't I supposed to send in some popcorn or something?"

"You did! Everybody loved it. And the juice."

Sarah had zero recollection of purchasing anything for that party. She thought that, after nearly three years, the widow fog would have dissipated. It had certainly gotten better, but not completely vanished.

She sat back down on the couch and Grace joined her.

"You were supposed to help pass out the food, though," Grace said in a small voice. Sarah closed her eyes and groaned. She hadn't remember that, either.

"Don't worry. Other moms helped. And dads." Grace twisted her lips and batted her eyes. Sarah stroked her cheek.

"How did that make you feel?"

"I don't know. Bad." Grace fiddled with her fingers. She hadn't broken down in a long time, but every so often she got quiet and pensive. Sarah would have given anything to take her kids' pain away.

"I'm so sorry I missed your party, honey. I think my brain is fried."

"You just need to sleep more. And you know, be happier." Grace perked up and grinned. "Can we put up some Christmas decorations? Asking for a friend."

Sarah hadn't put up a tree or lights since their world imploded. "Without your dad, it just doesn't feel like Christmas," Sarah said.

Grace patted Sarah's shoulder. "But *we're* still here, Mommy."

Tears stung Sarah's eyes. That girl's wisdom amazed her.

"You know what? You're right. We'll get the lights out tonight. I'm not sure about a tree, but we'll see." She kissed Grace's forehead. "Tell that to your 'friend.'"

"Yay!" Grace raised her arms in triumph. Several crumpled papers fell from somewhere. "Oh. I forgot about my homework."

"Right before Christmas break?" Sarah shook her head. "Let's put them under something heavy to flatten them."

"It's OK. Watch this." Grace lay the papers on the couch and ran her small palm over them several times. When she finished, the dog ears remained, but she held the papers up with pride.

"See? Good as new!" Grace smiled broadly at her mother, her two thick braids swinging like pendulums over her small shoulders.

"Very good. You want to get started at my desk while I fix you a snack?"

"Yeah, but first, I gotta pee!" Grace jumped down, shed her coat and raced to the hallway bathroom.

"Make sure you wash your hands!" Sarah called. She grabbed her phone from the floor. Moving fast, she took screenshots of the nasty messages, then brought up PeachDate's site and searched for the "report abuse" button. Done. She got as far as attaching the images when Grace returned, shaking her wet hands as proof that she'd washed them.

Sarah assembled a paper plate of fruit salad and cheese-flavored tortilla chips. She handed Grace a small glass of water.

"Thanks, Mommy."

"You're welcome, baby. Try not to spill anything on your papers."

Sarah leaned against the counter and finished her report. The site sent her an automated thank you and promised to get back to her within 24 to 48 hours.

All the talk about Christmas made Sarah wonder if anyone at

PeachDate would even see her message before the holiday, let alone launch and complete an investigation.

Sarah mouthed an F-bomb. She couldn't continue accepting messages until this mess got straightened out. Sarah went into her account and deleted her profile to stop the incoming PeachNotes. PeachDate's inquiry might not get resolved until after the first of the year. She saw her chances of vetting a companion ahead of Febzilla dwindling right before her eyes.

The dates rattled her skull.

February 7, February 10, February 14.

February 7, February 10, February 14.

She imagined herself raking leaves in freezing temperatures again, falling into the pile and getting lost forever.

She needed this companion thing to work.

Sarah went back the homepage. Maybe she could email someone about her situation and get the ball rolling sooner than later.

She had trouble finding the "contact us" button because an article covered about a third of the homepage. The headline read, "Q&A tonight with PeachDate founder Carter Sheffield at his alma mater." Sarah studied his photo. Yuck. He had such a thick, full, itchy-looking beard, she couldn't tell what he truly looked like. She liked clean-shaven men, like Greg. .

Sarah scrolled down for the details of the Q&A. A sly smile spread across her face. Who better to help her than the creator of the site?

"*Hola, mami,*" Melody sang. Sarah jumped. She hadn't heard her come in, either.

"*Calma, calma.*" Melody loved practicing and teaching Spanish to her family, even when neither Sarah nor Grace could remember most of the words. Melody hugged them, then plopped onto the couch, earbuds in.

Sarah walked up to her and gently kicked her foot. She looked up.

"I need you to watch Grace for a few hours tonight."

Melody pulled her earbuds out and cocked her head. "Do you have a date?"

Grace gasped and ran over to them, her face aglow. Well, at least Sarah knew how they felt about the prospect of her dating.

"Of course not. I'm going to a business Q&A."

"Ew." Melody scrunched her face. "Sure, I'll watch *mi hermanita*."

Grace's face fell. "What about the Christmas lights?"

"You and Mel can pull them from the garage and start untangling them. I'll hang them up tomorrow."

Melody nodded. "*Muy bien*."

"*Gracias*." Sarah had hit the jackpot for great kids. She blew a kiss to Melody and started for the stairs.

———

" DO you use your site to find dates for yourself?"

Laughter broke out among the standing-room only crowd gathered in Central Atlanta Technical College's auditorium. Carter sat in a club chair on the stage, a microphone in one hand and an index card with the question in the other.

"Why is that always the first question?" he asked. The laughter continued, rising to the vaulted ceiling. Carter loved these kinds of gatherings. Nothing beat interacting with a live crowd about the subject he loved.

"The answer is, yes. I've actually had a few PeachDates. My matches are usually women who are mathematically inclined, with an artsy streak."

"That's me!" someone in the crowd shouted.

Carter blushed and shook his head. "Some dates were

friendly get togethers for coffee or a baseball game, others were more serious, with dinner by candlelight and all that. I enjoyed them all. But as you may remember from my video welcome, I lost my wife six years ago. Dating can be complicated. I'm not looking for anything long term at the moment."

A portion of the crowd let out a collective whine.

"You just want the beard," he said.

"And a beard ride!" someone called out.

The uproarious laughter that followed didn't pipe down until the event coordinator grabbed Carter's mic and made a plea for silence.

The next several questions had to do with creating a memorable profile, taking an attractive selfie, and responding to potential PeachDates. Carter breezed through them with efficiency and confidence.

"OK, next question: How soon after reporting dick pics and racists can one expect action from PeachDate?" Carter froze for a moment before lowering the card in his lap. "P.S. Asking for a friend."

The room's energy went from party to funeral.

Carter puffed his cheeks, then blew out a rush of air.

"Let me start by stating under no uncertain terms that Peach-Date does not tolerate impropriety of any kind," he said, his voice strained. "My team vigorously enforces our community guidelines. In the few instances where members have stepped out of line, they were banned for life. We don't mess around. It's a serious issue that we fix as quickly as possible, usually within a few days." Carter scanned the crowd. "If the person who asked this question wants to talk to me directly after the Q&A, please don't hesitate to pull me aside. I need to get to the bottom of this."

———

FROM THE MIDDLE of the auditorium, Sarah watched a small crowd flank Carter near the stage stairs. The event coordinator had instructed everyone to let Carter walk through to the vestibule in the front of the hall, then form a line to ask him quick follow-up questions.

Sarah squeezed through the assembly and made her way to the line, wishing she hadn't blown off watching his welcome video. She'd had no idea that a widower had started PeachDate. Listening to him speak about his wife, Sarah felt a connection to him, even while sitting in the audience. He had walked in her shoes. He would understand her pain, and why she needed to alleviate it.

After a few minutes of not moving, several people got impatient and left the line. The coordinator started doing the "cut" signal, waving his hand back and forth in front of his throat, when questions ran too long.

The closer Sarah got to Carter, the better she could make out his features. He had a beautiful head of golden hair styled into a man bun. But his beard looked even itchier in person. She thought of the beard ride comment and winced. She couldn't imagine sitting on that scratchy thing.

And then suddenly, she could. Clear as day.

Sarah got wet, fast. She shifted her weight from side to side. She'd had dirty thoughts about models and celebrities, but not a real person, and certainly not a hipster who looked like he had a woolly mammoth glued to his face.

As if hearing her thoughts, Carter looked up and locked eyes with her. She gave him a single, polite nod, and he smiled. He had a perfect set of gleaming teeth. She could see his lips too. Fuller than she imagined, they looked extremely kissable.

Sarah fidgeted again. She had to focus. The person in front of Carter continued to talk, ignoring the event guy's hand signal to stop. Finally, the man walked away and Sarah stepped up.

She suddenly realized she hadn't rehearsed what she'd say. She'd had all that time in line to come up with something intelligent and clever. Instead, she mentally went on a beard ride.

Carter extended his hand. "Thanks for coming."

"Hi." Sarah's lips trembled and her heart raced. She glanced at the coordinator, who pointed to his watch as if to say "hurry up."

She blew out a breath.

"I'm Sarah. The friend."

Carter wrinkled his brow and tilted his head, but it only took him a second to figure out what she meant.

"Oh!" he cried. "My God, I'm so sorry that happened to you!"

"I appreciate that. I didn't come here to embarrass you. I was told the only way to ask a question was to write it down. Obviously, that's not true." Sarah glared at the coordinator, who waved her off.

Carter whispered something in the man's ear. He cupped his hands around his mouth.

"OK folks, we're going to have to end things now," the man announced. The seven people behind Sarah grumbled and cursed as they filed out of the vestibule.

"You didn't have to do that," Sarah said.

"Yes I did. This is serious." Carter asked the event guy if they could hang out in the auditorium for a while and chat.

"You've got about an hour," the guy said.

"That's more than enough time," Sarah assured Carter.

———

ONE HOUR TURNED INTO THREE.

The coordinator hung around in a back office for as long as he could. When he emerged and saw Sarah and Carter still chatting, he told them they'd absolutely have to leave when the custodial staff came through.

Sarah showed Carter the nasty PeachNotes and described how they'd made her feel: pissed. Violated. Worthless. She talked about her late husband and her two children, and explained why she'd registered on PeachDate in the first place.

"Febzilla," she said. "I've got a triple whammy coming up."

Carter listened intently, juggling outrage, empathy, sorrow and a powerful attraction - his first to an older woman, and a mother.

He'd spotted her in line before she noticed, and could hardly keep his eyes on the people in front of him. Her high cheekbones brought to mind a young Eartha Kitt, and even in the vestibule's harsh canned light, he could see the gleaming bronze, auburn and silver highlights threaded among her dark brown braids. She wore a black scarf dotted with white tiny hearts headband-style, the long ends hanging down the back of a black sweater embellished at the neckline with white faux pearls. And although her jeans had a relaxed fit, they couldn't hide her marvelous curves.

Carter took notes on his phone about her awful PeachDate experience and vowed to get to the bottom of it long before Febzilla. He promised to refund her money but keep her account open, free of charge.

"On a personal note," Carter said, "I want you to have my cell number. Feel free to call me if you need someone to talk to, anytime. The hand we've been dealt can suck."

"You're not lying," she sighed.

He asked if she had a piece of paper and a pen, but Sarah gave him her number instead, which surprised him. He worried that his cell phone offer had come across as too forward.

Carter dialed her number, hanging up after the call buzzed her phone. Sarah created a new contact, and Carter did the same.

Just then, the custodial staff came in and quickly began tidying up the discarded cups, napkins, and soda cans.

"I guess that's our cue." Sarah stood and slung the long straps of her colorful Bohemian purse across her body. She checked the time on her phone.

"Shoot! I didn't know it was so late!" She dialed a number, then brought the phone to her ear.

"Hey, Mel. I'm about to get on the train. See you soon."

Carter rose from his seat. "I can give you a ride."

Slowly, Sarah looked up from her screen. The wide-eyed expression she had when she caught him looking at her in the line returned.

"Oh, I don't mean like that," Carter clarified through a nervous chuckle. "I mean, I can take you home. You might be waiting a while for the train. Or I can call you an Uber."

Sarah checked something on her phone again, then agreed to the ride.

As soon as Carter opened the vestibule door, a sharp, cold wind slapped them both across the face. Sarah shivered violently and hugged herself, rubbing her arms. She didn't have a coat.

"Here." Carter lifted his poncho over his head and handed it to her.

"Are you sure?" Sarah's teeth chattered.

"Of course." He helped her put it on, accidentally grazing the top of her sweater in the process. .

"Sorry!" Now he'd done it. *Down boy*, he chided his excited wood. It didn't listen.

Either Sarah didn't notice the unintentional feel-up or she didn't hear Carter's apology. She adjusted the poncho and thanked him. They continued the walk to the parking garage, talking about the weather, which led to a chat about Christmas, which rolled into a conversation about how much holidays sucked after losing a spouse.

"Especially Valentine's Day!" they said in unison, laughing.

When they got to his car, Sarah gave him her address so he could put it in his phone's GPS. The talked during the entire twenty-minute ride to Sarah's side of town.

"Nice lights," Carter said as he pulled up to her house. Multi-colored lights hung in the living room bay window and in each of the upstairs windows.

Sarah brought her hands to her mouth and sucked in a breath.

"They did it," she cried. She brought her hands down and stared at the house.

"Your kids sound amazing."

"They are. They deserve a better mom." Her voice broke.

"I'm sure you're a great mom. You're doing this thing solo. I can't imagine how hard that must be. Go easy on yourself." Carter handed her a tissue from the center console. Sarah dabbed her wet eyes, then unhooked her seatbelt.

"Thank you for the ride. I mean, the lift. Fo bringing me home."

"No problem. I'll update you on the investigation as soon as I can."

Sarah exited the car and started up the walkway. Carter didn't want to see her go, and for the life of him, he couldn't figure out why. They didn't have anything in common besides losing their spouses. He'd only met her a few hours ago. Sure, she had killer looks and he'd copped an inadvertent feel. But he had absolutely no other viable reason to have such a strong attraction to her. She didn't fit his ideal match in the least.

"Whoops!" Sarah turned around and hurried back to the car. She took off his poncho. "Almost forgot."

Carter thanked her for returning it and put it on the passenger seat. He stayed until she walked inside.

He just needed a good night's sleep. Surely he'd wake up

without a Sarah boner. She needed him to catch those Peach-Note dumbasses, and nothing more.

That night, Carter dreamed of making love to Sarah under the glow of Christmas lights, his poncho crumpled in the corner.

———

ON CHRISTMAS MORNING, Sarah sat on the sofa in front of the potted evergreen on her fireplace mantle, sipping peach tea and gazing at the silver jingle bells and tiny, battery-operated lights resting on the delicate green branches.

Beside her, her phone seemed to call out conflicting messages.

Go ahead, invite him over for Christmas brunch. You've texted every day since you met, anyway.

Don't do it. He probably has a mile-long list of women he's giving holiday beard rides.

Do it, but don't make it a big deal. Act like you don't care one way or another. If he declines, don't text back.

Don't. You. Dare bring him over! What will the girls think?

Carter had initiated texting the day after they met. He told her how much he'd enjoyed their talk, and apologized for the thousandth time for the awful PeachNotes she'd received.

It had taken Sarah half a day to text back. She'd blamed it on Christmas shopping, but, in truth, she hadn't known how to respond. The last attractive man she'd texted now lay six feet under. She'd *known* Greg. They'd had their own euphemisms for sex ("flip-floppin,' 'daily grindin,' 'hip-dippin'). They'd talked and texted about everything from the kids' grades to house repairs. She didn't have that familiarity with Carter, or anyone.

She'd gotten over the hump by convincing herself that she needed to practice chatting it up with a man. After all, when she re-uploaded her PeachDate profile, she just might just get a good nibble.

She'd replied with a simple 'thank you for listening.' He'd texted back, asking about Melody and Grace. She'd told him they'd gotten the holiday decorating bug, putting up even more lights that they'd unearthed in the garage. They had even talked her into getting a little tree.

The subjects had varied as the texting continued throughout each day: work, the PeachNote investigation, missing their spouses. But Carter never crossed any lines. Sarah looked forward to hearing from him.

Still, she couldn't help but think inviting him over for Christmas brunch seemed a bit aggressive. The girls didn't know he existed. It would blindside them.

Just like that, she decided against it.

And just like that, he called.

"Hi there." Her face hurt from smiling so hard. "Merry Christmas."

"Same to you. I've got a present for you," Carter said, his morning voice deep and illegally sexy. "We found out who those bastards were, or should I say, *the* bastard. It was the same troll. He wasn't a member, but he's way too stupid to be a hacker. Obviously we've still got some research to do, but this is a great start."

Sarah breathed a sigh of relief. "That *is* a great gift! Thank you for letting me know."

"So you can go ahead and upload your profile again whenever you're ready. I definitely think you'll find a good match before Febzilla."

Out of nowhere, an unexpected melancholy overcame her. Sarah stared at the little tree in silence.

"Still there?" Carter asked.

"You should come over to celebrate," she blurted.

Now Carter fell silent. A voice in Sarah's head shouted *Abort mission! Abort mission!*

"I mean, it's cool if you don't want to, or can't," she said, doing her best to sound nonchalant.

"No, I'd be honored. I'm just wondering what stores are open, so I can bring your girls a little something."

Sarah's heart melted. "That's sweet, but trust me, they're taken care of. I got them the electronics they asked for *and* a karaoke machine."

Carter laughed. "You did mention wanting to see some live performances."

"Exactly! Come by around noon, and just bring yourself."

"Sounds good."

Sarah hung up.

That really happened. She pinched herself just to make sure. Then she grabbed the sofa pillow beside her, covered her face, and screamed into it.

———

GRACE PUMMELED Carter with questions the moment he stepped over the threshold.

"How old are you?"

"33."

"What are you wearing?"

"A poncho."

"Why?"

"It's super warm, and super special."

"Why?"

"My late wife made it for me. Wanna try it on?"

"No. How do you know Mommy?"

"Grace Elizabeth MacNeil!" Sarah scolded. "You've asked him about everything but his name."

"You told us. Carver Shuffle."

Sarah pulled on one of her braids. "Carter Sheffield, silly."

"Mom," Melody said, taking long, exaggerated strides into the foyer, "let me handle the pleasantries. Some of us are civilized." Melody extended her hand to Carter. As he shook it, she squeezed his fingers and pulled him to her, hard.

"Whoa." The girl had a mean grip.

"Melody Raven!" Sarah cried. "Let him go!"

"*Eres amigo o enemigo, Señor Sheffield?*"

Sarah pinched the bridge of her nose and shook her head.

"*Amigo, absolutamente, señorita.*"

She freed his hand.

"You may enter," she said, a cheeky grin spreading across her face. The girls ran ahead of them into the family room. Sarah stood in place, dumbfounded.

"Don't be too impressed. My parents made me take Spanish all four years in high school," he whispered. He presented her with a rectangular bag decorated with snowflakes. "For your table. The grown-up table, that is.

"Carter! I told you not to worry about it." Sarah pulled out a bottle of champagne from the bag. "But I'm glad you did. Now I can make mimosas."

"And I got some gift cards for the kids. I couldn't resist."

"You are too much! I'd wait to give them the cards, after we've cleaned up. Gift cards will get lost in there. And we have something for you, too."

Tripping over the large area rug that anchored the family room, Carter did a bad job of hiding his surprise. Thankfully, no one saw him.

Carter felt instantly cozy in the room, bathed in bright yellows and warm grays. A low fire burned in the fireplace. Crinkled wrapping paper and new clothes with tags still on them covered the wood floors. A mix of aromas wafted in from the kitchen: clove, cinnamon, garlic, onion. Beyond the family room, a harvest table decorated with greenery and silver Christmas ornaments sat in a wide dining alcove.

Sarah went to the kitchen while he took a seat on the sofa and watched Melody and Grace with their gifts. Melody unboxed a smart phone and started reading the instructions. It looked as if Grace had already set up her new tablet as she opened different apps. The karaoke machine, out of its box with the mix resting atop it, appeared to have gotten some use, too.

Sarah returned, sat beside him and handed him a package covered in newspaper.

"I just got back. I didn't have time to wrap it," she said.

Carter peeled back the layers of newspaper, revealing a tool set. He chuckled and shook his head, thinking of Maggie calling him a fix-it man.

"Lame, I know," Sarah said. "That's the only thing the store had that looked halfway useful."

"I love it, and I'll tell you why a little later. Thank you." Without giving it one iota of thought, Carter gave her a quick peck on the cheek.

Grace and Melody rushed over and started chanting, "Mistletoe! Mistletoe!"

"We don't have any," Sarah said, "and that was a kiss of appreciation between acquaintances, not a mistletoe kiss."

Acquaintances. Carter's heart sank a little. What did he expect? They'd known each other only a few days, and she'd told him a million times that she wanted a companion for Febzilla.

"Everybody ready to eat?" Sarah said, rising from the couch. The girls hollered yes.

At the dining table, each silver-rimmed white plate had a place card.

"You're sitting next to me, Carter," Sarah said. "Hope that's OK."

Carter grinned, showing way too many teeth for the situation. He looked as if he'd just won the Mega Millions jackpot.

"That would be great."

———

You have a message from a potential PeachDate!

THE ALERT, her fifth since the new year, popped up while Sarah reviewed one of the worst essays she'd ever seen. Although she needed a break, she didn't feel like opening another PeachNote.

Just to test the waters, she'd had coffee with each of the other four men who had messaged her. Unfortunately, they all fell into one of two categories: too eager or too boring.

One man, George, had the most potential at first. A widowed, retired firefighter, George had an 11-year-old son and a 20-year-old daughter. He liked to read, watch TV, and attend concerts.

As Melody would say, "*perfecto*."

But it hadn't taken long for him to show his true colors. After having coffee with her one time and speaking on the phone twice, he'd proposed spending a long weekend together "bumping uglies."

"Oh, hell no," Sarah had responded. She hadn't heard that sex euphemism in ages.

"Look, you're available, and probably horny as all get-out, and I know I am, especially after checking you out. Hot damn."

"I thought you wanted a companion."

"I'd rather get my cock stroked."

"Goodbye, George."

"I think your husband would want you to -"

Sarah had disconnected the call and blocked him. She'd told Carter about it, but hadn't taken things beyond that point. If she reported every jerk she encountered, PeachDate would only have a handful of members left.

Weary of the companion interview process, Sarah had half a mind to delete her latest peachy message and forget the whole thing.

Carter kept her and the girls entertained with weekly visits for karaoke and Scrabble. He'd started coming over so much, Sarah joked about giving him a key.

WYD?

Sarah's face lit up when she received his message. Carter sent her that text at least once every day.

Working & ignoring my PeachNotes, she replied.

What about Febzilla?

She frowned before answering. *It's going to suck no matter what.*

I promised you it wouldn't, he shot back.

Her fingers hovered over the screen for a moment before she tapped out her response.

Some promises are impossible to keep.

The somber tone of their texts made Sarah feel even more exhausted. She hoped Carter wouldn't take her attitude personally. He really did try to fix things.

A second later, her phone rang.

"Sounds like you could use a pick-me-up," Carter said.

"Coffee?"

"No. Begins with a 'c' though."

"Ugh..." Sarah feigned disgust.

"Not *that* 'c'! Geez, who do you think I am, George?"

"Heaven forbid. Now, stop playing games."

"The 'c' is for cruise. As in, cruise ship. There's a sailing from Miami during two of your Febzilla dates, the seventh through the tenth, to Key West and the Bahamas. You'd have to pull your girls out of school, of course. And this doesn't cover Valentine's Day.

We still have to come up with a plan for that. But it would be an excellent distraction."

Sarah sat up straight. She'd never gone on a cruise, although she and Greg had talked about it for years. They couldn't afford it then, and the only way to afford it now involved dipping into her savings.

"Sounds nice," she said, "but a cruise is way too rich for my blood."

"What if I paid for -"

"No!"

"I get a nice discount through a business association I'm part of."

"No. Way."

"Cruise ships have a ton of live entertainment. And lots of mimosas. I'll bet they even have chocolate almond crunch ice cream."

Sarah blew a raspberry into the phone. She still didn't want him to pay for it, but the idea of sailing away during Febzilla sounded mighty tempting.

"I insist on paying you back," she said. "It might take twenty years, but..."

"Sarah, please don't worry about it. You guys just go and have a great time."

"You're not going?"

"I thought about it, but I didn't want you to think there were strings attached. There aren't. I made a promise to you, Sarah. I intend to keep it."

Sarah had never met anyone, not even Greg, who wanted to right wrongs and solve problems as much as Carter. She could see how it would annoy his ex-girlfriend, but to a person whose universe had collapsed when her husband died, Sarah found it refreshing and admirable.

"I think you should come, too," she said.

———

SARAH FASTENED her scarf with a knot at the nape of her neck, then did a 360, her forehead collapsed in wrinkles.

"Anybody seen my pool bag?"

"Mom, hurry up! Please!" Grace begged. Melody stood behind her sister, holding her breath while nervously tapping her foot.

Sarah grinned. "Ah. There it is." She skipped across the suite and grabbed her blue straw bag.

Sarah stood in front of her daughters and put her hands on her hips.

"You guys are in an awful rush to leave me."

"You can stay at the slumber party with us," Grace suggested, "but whatever you do, we need you to take us there now, before they start the movie.

"Come on, Mom! It's the last day of the cruise!" Grace whined.

Sarah drew them in for a hug. She had never allowed them to go to a sleepover, and even this one didn't completely qualify. The Kids' Cruise Crew Club Pajama Party ended at ten. But for the first time since Greg died—outside of school and extracurricular activities—Melody and Grace would have several hours of fun in someone else's care. It felt strange, but necessary. Before Sarah left on the cruise, Dr. Hudson had made her pinky-promise to do some things without her children.

"OK, OK.," Sarah said. "I'll sit this one out. Just make sure you look out for each other, and have fun."

"We will!" the girls cheered in unison. They headed for the door.

"Are you meeting Carter after you drop us off?" Melody asked.

"Yep." Sarah closed the suite door and started the walk down the long corridor.

She and Carter planned to sip cocktails poolside, something they hadn't done the whole trip. They'd had too many other things to do. They'd taken a trolley tour of beautiful, colorful, casual Key West and braved the water slides at Atlantis in the Bahamas. On the ship, they'd attended Broadway-style productions, fitness classes and food demos. But Carter and Sarah had spent most of their time getting spa treatments while the kids had fun at the cruise club. Sarah had once read that widows and widowers craved touch. Massages and facials fit the bill without the complication of sex or emotions.

Not that sex hadn't crossed her mind a few billion times.

Carter hid a buff body underneath his poncho. Judging by his ample beard, she had imagined he'd have hair galore everywhere else. But he had only a small tuft of blond chest hair that looked silky and soft. The hair on his muscular legs looked like fine baby hair. And his bulge... *well, damn.*

After she signed the kids in for the party, Sarah took the elevator to down to the pool deck. A dance party in full swing had at least sixty people shaking their groove thangs.

"Sarah!" Carter waved his arms. He stood by the bar in black swimming trunks, a statuesque platinum blond in a pink bikini to his right and a curvy, brick house of a brunette to his left, letting it all hang out in a midriff and booty shorts.

Sarah stopped in her tracks, suddenly feeling huge, awkward and plain in her simple white one-piece.

"Come on over, come on over," Carter called, continuing to wave. Sarah schlepped toward him and his groupees.

"What is this, Carter's Angels?" Sarah asked. Her tone sounded much more envious than she cared to admit. Fortunately for her, the loud music playing over the speakers swallowed her comment and the venom behind it.

Carter placed his hand on the small of the blond's back.

"Sarah, this is Candi," he shouted.

"Of course it is," Sarah mumbled. She shook the woman's limp, French manicured hand.

Carter turned to the brunette. "And this is Tawny."

"Even better."

Tawny didn't offer her hand. She said hi, then turned to the bartender and ordered a drink.

"Well ladies, I've got to go." Carter stepped away from them. "Nice meeting you."

"Nice meeting you, too, Carty," Candi said. She winked at him and gave him a little wave.

Carter gently took Sarah's elbow and walked off in a hurry, right into the dance party. He started to shake his hips from side to side. Sarah reluctantly joined him with a two-step.

"God, they would not leave me alone!" he complained.

"Poor you."

He placed his hand behind his ear and leaned forward.

"What'd you say?"

"Poor you. Must be terrible to be hounded by beautiful women!"

Carter straightened up and frowned. "I swear you're whispering."

"Was at least one of them good with numbers and art? That's who you're supposed to be with, remember 'Carty'?"

Sarah took off, her emotions raw and confusing. What the hell? Had she turned into an irrational baby all of a sudden? She'd never once told Carter she found him attractive, or that sometimes she woke up in the middle of the night from vivid dreams of him making love to her, or that she didn't need to open PeachNote any more because she had him.

"Sarah!"

She picked up speed toward the bank of aft elevators, feeling her scarf loosen as the evening wind began to whip across the deck. Sarah touched the top of her head to keep the scarf in place, but not in time. Off it soared behind her, toward the dark aubergine sky, the full moon shining through the tiny white hearts in the fabric.

She turned around. The scarf twisted and turned to the Latin rhythms now rocking the dance party. Carter reached up and the scarf fluttered obediently into his grasp. He held it in the air like a banner, showing Sarah the way back to him.

All at once, a fire burned beneath her sandaled feet. She jumped into Carter's waiting arms and kissed him with complete abandon. She found his lips in that bushy mess of facial hair, separated them with her urgent tongue and plunged into his mouth. It didn't feel or look pretty. Sarah hadn't kissed a man like that since before Greg died. She drooled a lot and accidentally bit his lip a little too hard. But man, it felt good.

And very public. A crowd nearby broke out in hoots and cheers.

Carter broke the kiss but kept his face near hers.

"I want to make love to you, Sarah."

———

IN THE MIDDLE of his king-sized bed in his state room, Carter brought his face between Sarah's ample breasts, licking and kissing her soft skin as he tugged on the straps of her one-piece. Her whimpers and moans turned him on to no end. If he didn't slow down, he'd get a little too happy in his trunks. He forced himself to concentrate on pleasing her, tasting her, building up the anticipation for her.

Carter had had four lovers since Ashley died; two semi-serious relationships if he counted Maggie, and two one-night stands. Sarah hadn't had *any* intimacy.

Carter didn't want to take anything for granted. This moment — this time—belonged to her. God, she deserved it. Sarah deserved every good thing for the rest of her life.

He pulled the straps down her arms, lowering the front of her bathing suit. Her nipples, dark and large, soft and pert, seemed to call to him. Carter leaned in and praised them with his tongue. Sarah cried out and clasped her hands against the back of his neck as she turned her head to the ceiling.

Carter ran his tongue back and forth between her nipples, licked each breast from bottom to top, and started to inch toward her neck. With every move, she released a new, sexy sound. He dotted her neck with tiny kisses, pressing his hands on her back as he reached her jawline. He tilted her head toward him, gently. Carter wanted to kiss her lips and look her in the eyes one more time before continuing. He wanted to make sure he wasn't dreaming this as he had so many times before. She had to give him the real, final OK.

Carter nibbled her chin before facing her fully. Tears streaked her face.

Carter stopped cold.

"Keep going," she said, her voice less audible now than in the middle of the dance party.

Carter cupped her face in his hands.

"You're not ready."

"I *am* ready. I'm just...emotional." She closed her eyes. "Greg was the only one."

Carter nodded as he moved to the edge of the bed to give her space. He remembered her telling him that with pride.

He pulled a few tissues from a box on the nightstand and handed them to her. She thanked him and dabbed her eyes.

"Now this is what I call killing the mood," she said, lifting her straps back onto her shoulders.

"You have to stop being hard on yourself." The word 'hard'

reminded him that his little buddy got left in the lurch. It twitched and throbbed in protest.

Sarah scooted next to him.

"I guess this was a mistake," she said.

Carter thought about it. A mistake, no. Bad timing? Yes.

"I think we assumed that just because we lost our spouses, we were on the same journey," Carter said. "But our paths are different."

Sarah rested her head on Carter's shoulder.

"What do we do now?"

"I don't know about you, but I need some fresh air and a drink." He jumped up and started looking for his boarding card.

"You're angry."

"Absolutely not. I just have to clear my head. You should do the same."

She flopped her back onto the bed and stared at the ceiling. "I don't even know *what's* in my head anymore."

"All the more reason for a little breather."

Carter sounded far more pissed off than he intended. He wanted to apologize, but he didn't. He could only think about her beautiful breasts and her moans and how badly he wanted to make love to her and what a damn fool he must have looked like, accompanying her and the kids on this cruise, knowing he had deeper feelings for Sarah than he ever cared to admit.

He grabbed his boarding card off the floor and slipped on his sandals.

"I'll swing by your suite before eight so we can all disembark together," he said, his voice monotone this time. He opened the door and let it slam behind him.

———

CARTER WALKED around the ship for 90 minutes. He stumbled onto more parties, casino tournaments, live bands and conga lines, but he didn't hit any of the bars. He needed air more than a buzz.

When he returned to his room, Sarah had already gone. He decided not to chase after her, and fell asleep, dreaming of nothing.

In the morning, he went to her suite at 7:45 a.m. as planned. A member of the housekeeping staff handed him a note.

> *Got a very early start. We're changing our flights only. Thank you for making good on your promise.*
> *- Sarah*

––––––

FEBRUARY 10, 7:25 p.m.

"Hey, Ma. It's Sarah. I was just calling to check on you. We just got back from a fun cruise to the Bahamas and Key West. I'm sure the girls will tell you all about it when you call back. I'm sorry we weren't able to call you on the anniversary of Greg's...you know. We hardly used our phones on the cruise. Anyway, in case we miss each other, I just wanted to thank you for Greg. He meant everything to us, and I know he was a wonderful son to you and Papa. I hope you're doing well. Love you."

FEBRUARY 10, 8:15 p.m.

"Hey Papa MacNeil. Melody, Grace and I just wanted to hear your voice. I called Ma's phone a little while ago and it went to voicemail. Maybe you guys are at church or out to dinner or something. All right, well, I'm gonna go. Talk to you later."

. . .

FEBRUARY 10, 7:30 p.m.

"Hey, babe. Geez, I haven't called your number in a long time. I remember your voice, though, especially today. It's our anniversary, babe. If you were here, I'll bet you'd take me and the girls out to a great restaurant, maybe see a movie, maybe go for a drive through downtown. We don't do that anymore. That was your thing. Our thing is karaoke and learning Spanish and making new friends. Yes, me, the introvert, made a new friend. I think you'd like him. He thinks he can fix everything. I think he blames himself for not being able to save his wife, so he tries to make up for it in every other way. For a while, I believed he could. But he can't mend a broken heart. I think that's up to me, and time. Maybe it will never be fully repaired. I think it will always long for its other half. But I've got to keep it beating, and that means I have to keep moving and loving and doing right by our girls. I think that's what you'd want. I love you Greg."

FEBRUARY 11, 10:12 a.m.

"Dr. Hudson, its Sarah MacNeil. We have an appointment on the seventeenth, but I was wondering if you could see me sooner, like, today? I'm just feeling a little...I don't know. Confused, I guess. Today Greg and I would have been married fifteen years. And of course, we've got Valentine's Day right around the corner. The thing is, I found a companion like you advised, but then I lost it. He was actually more than that. He was my friend, and I think I messed everything up. Anyway, let me know your availability. Thanks."

FEBRUARY 13, 3:56 p.m.

"Carter, it's me, Sarah. I just wanted to thank you again for a great trip and for just being there for us. I know things ended pretty awkwardly, but I wanted you to know that I really enjoyed spending time with you. You listened, and you tried to make things better. You're my friend, Carter. My best friend. I'll always be grateful for that. Truth is, I think I had it all wrong. I didn't need a distraction from Febzilla. I think I needed to feel all the pain and loneliness of it. I read somewhere that, when it comes to grief, the only way to get to the other side is to go through it, you know? So that's what I'm doing. We didn't cry or reminisce at all on the cruise, so we're doing that now. We're crying and just holding each other tight, because that's part of grieving, and that's how we get to the other side. There's no going around it.

Anyway, I just got your voicemail's warning to wrap up this diatribe within ten seconds or else. So I guess that's it. Take care of yourself, Carter."

———

CARTER STARED AT HIS REFLECTION, stroking his beard with one hand and opening and closing a pair of scissors with the other.

Ashley adored his beard. She had encouraged him to grow it long and bushy, "like a wild man," in the first place. She loved that he wore the poncho she made, even in warm weather. She loved that he cooked healthy meals and tried to get her to exercise more and take her medicine regularly, even though she didn't always comply.

He'd tried to fix her, but he couldn't.

He'd tried to fix Sarah, but she didn't need it.

Carter needed to fix himself.

He brought the scissors to his beard and started to cut. With each snip, he gained a little more confidence, and looked more like the person he'd hid inside for six years: a man under construction. A widower.

"I am a widower," he said when he finished. He ran his hand over his close-cut, tamer beard.

After showering, Carter washed and dried his poncho. He put it in a plastic storage bag, and placed it in the back of his closet.

———

"CARTER'S HERE!"

Melody and Grace opened the front door and started to run to him until they saw his face. Sarah stood at the threshold, her arms folded. All three wore matching red two-piece pajama sets with hearts on them.

"What happened to your big beard?" Melody asked, stunned.

"I made it a little beard."

"And your poncho?" Grace pulled on the sleeve of his gray suit.

"I put it away. It was time."

The girls finished their hugs and invited him in. "We're about to have a Valentine's Day karaoke party! We've got cupcakes and ice cream and those little heart candies!"

"That sounds like fun. But I'd like to speak to your mom for a minute, if that's ok."

"Sure!" The girls ran back inside.

Sarah stepped outside and closed the door. After several chilly nights, the weather had warmed up to the mid 50s.

"I won't keep you long," Carter said. "I just wanted to tell you...I needed to say..." *Dammit!* He blew out a nervous breath.

"*Calma.*" Sarah reached up and caressed his cheek. His

breathing steadied to a regular pace, and he pulled the words from his heart.

"Sarah, you are strong as hell. I don't ever want you to forget that. You don't try to pretend to be somebody you're not. You don't take anybody's crap. You're beautiful and real and brilliant. And I want to be there for you and your amazing daughters, however you need me to be."

Sarah threw her arms around his shoulders and kissed his cheek as he held her close, his hands circling her waist.

"I'm so sorry I left you in my state room all alone," he said. "I should have been more sensitive." He pulled away so he could look in her eyes. "I was gentle one second, pissed the next. I feel like I confused you."

Sarah sniffed and wiped a tear away. "I'm not confused. I know I'm in love with you."

Carter broke into a goofy, boyish smile.

"I knew it!" he said, pumping his fist in the air and laughing. She gave him a playful punch on the shoulder.

"I love you, too, Sarah." Carter kissed her lips softly, sweetly. The kiss lasted the length of the pop song the girls were crooning inside. He never wanted it to end.

"All this is new to me, Carter. I don't need you to fix anything anymore. I just need to take it slow."

He kissed her forehead. "I know. And I'll wait."

She put her hand in his. "You've already done so much. Valentine's Day doesn't suck, and we're about to see a live show. I just have one question." She began to giggle.

"How long will it take you to grow your beard back?"

"CHASING THE NIGHT" BY DEB LEE

ANNE

"Help! Please, I need help!"

The clinic door slammed hard against the adjacent window, nearly shattering it as the familiar rugged face burst through the doorway along with a gust of ice and sleet.

Anne Riley lunged to her feet, her stomach sinking through the floor. *This* was her worst fear and it was happening. A large gash on his forehead dripped blood but none of that mattered when she saw that he cradled a limp, blood-soaked, ninety-pound German shepherd.

She covered her mouth, tears springing to her eyes. "James! Oh, my God, is he d—dead?"

"Well, he's not skipping around playing fetch is he?"

Anne bristled at his harsh tone, frantically scattering her hands over the mess of papers on the desk for the vet hospital's number. People brought animals here all the time thinking the clinic could help. They kept the number to the veterinarian with the other specialists' numbers. "I'm not equipped for animals. I can't help him here."

The cop's eyes cut to hers. "He's been shot. Where the hell am I supposed to take him?" It was less of a question and more of a direct statement. The nearest vet was forty-five minutes away and Anne knew by the amount of blood pooling at James's feet that, if the dog wasn't already dead, that trek would do it.

Anne snagged the phone. "I'll call EMS then. They'll transport a K-9 to the vet hospital in Ellington. This is just a clinic. I have limited recourses for animals."

James wasn't wearing his typical K-9 BDUs, but that didn't mean he wasn't working. Her eyes shifted to the poor creature draped over his arms, and her throat swelled. Her legs wanted to move but she felt anchored to the ground.

"EMS will never get here in time. And if I thought he'd make it, I'd have driven a hundred miles an hour to get him there. But there's a storm blowing in and he doesn't have that kind of time. Please, Anne, help us."

Anne's legs finally came unglued and she rushed around the counter, side-eyeing the *People* magazine still open to the celebrity crossword puzzle she'd just been working on, trying to stay awake. How could life change so drastically in a moment? A few seconds ago she'd been waiting for her shift to end, and now...

She swallowed a sob.

Tonight would have been difficult enough. At the stroke of midnight—exactly ninety minutes from now—her divorce would be final. The night had been quiet until then, probably due to the weather—so quiet Anne had sent her only back-up home. Not so much as a runny-nosed kid had walked through the door all day. Now, here she was. Alone.

Except for the man standing before her, desperation in the lines of his ruggedly-handsome face, holding a ball of fur she had known since he was twelve weeks old: her soon-to-be ex-husband, James, and Chase, the police dog they had raised together.

JAMES

James couldn't feel his feet anymore and he couldn't care less about the throbbing pain shooting through his head. He didn't give a shit that his fingers were numb or that his pulse raced heart-attack fast. All he cared about was that his wife—at least for a couple more hours—was being an infuriatingly stubborn gate-keeper between his dog's chance at survival and no chance at all. Now was not the time for pleasantries.

"James, I'm sorry. I . . . I don't know what to do. Let me call the attending. Maybe he knows."

James lumbered closer so the only thing separating him from her was Chase. He towered a foot above her and even he knew how intimidating he must look with blood pouring down the side of his head and dripping from the wounded dog in his arms.

He didn't care. Screw being gentle. He needed her to act.

"There's no time. Do something—anything. Now!"

Anne frowned. "I don't know the first thing about canine first-aid."

"But you know first-aid. You're a doctor."

She lifted the dog's eyelids and shined a light into his right eye, then the left. "But I'm not a vet. Completely different training."

"Try," James demanded.

He didn't deserve her help. But this wasn't about him. This was about Chase.

Keeping her eyes fixed on his, Anne palpated the dog. Even though he kept a firm hold over the hole, James could feel the blood mercilessly seeping through his fingers. "He's alive but I don't know how much I can help. He needs a vet."

"He needs *you*."

James leveled his stare at the woman he'd loved for so many

years. She couldn't possibly understand how much he needed her right now. The past year had been awful. Emotional. The hardest year of his life.

They didn't have children; they had Chase. But he got the dog in the settlement because Chase was his partner.

Anne shook her head. "What if I screw up?"

"Try," he whispered.

Determination clicked into her eyes. Maybe no one else knew that look, but he did. He wanted to weep with relief.

"Of course. I'll try. Bring him in here."

She whipped around and charged forward, leading James into a back room. She shoved through the double doors, flicking on a light, bright as the sun, and pointing to the stainless steel table. "Lay him here."

James obeyed, gently setting Chase down. He took a step back, shaking to his core. He crossed his arms over his chest to steady his trembling hands, his forearms soaked with blood.

"The gash on your head. It's bleeding pretty bad," Anne said to James, not looking at him.

"I'm fine." He stared at Chase. He was nowhere close to *fine*.

"Go wash up and tape a Kotex on your forehead. I can't believe you can still see with all that blood. I'll stitch you up after I stabilize him."

"A Kotex? Like a tampon?"

"No, a pad. We use them for immediate blood absorption."

"I am not sticking a tampon on my head."

She glared at him. "Don't argue."

James wiped his head, smearing blood on the sleeve of his hunter green flannel shirt. "I'm not leaving him." His tone left no room for negotiation.

"Listen," Anne began, peering up at him, her eyes as hard as his, reminding him he was talking to his wife. One of the things that he loved about her was her ability to read right through his bullshit.

"I'm breaking between thirty and three hundred laws right now, not to mention the billion health and safety code violations. My license is on the line and I'm not about to go through all that to save Chase just to lose you to some sort of hemorrhage. You're covered in grime. Get out of here with those infection-spreading hands," she ordered. "When you're clean with a Kotex stuck on your face, come back." Her eyes narrowed even more. "Or else I will stitch a lightning bolt on that pretty forehead of yours that even Harry Potter will be proud of."

James grimaced. Blood dripped into his eyes, clouding his vision. He probably looked like something out of a Tarantino movie. He raised his hands, backing off.

"Fine," he said, biting his lip on the "*f*".

"*Fine*," she repeated his insinuating enunciation.

Just like when we were married.

"Go to the sink and wash under hot water for thirty seconds. Use that soap and scrub hard. Kotex are on the shelf. I promise we'll be here when you get back."

James didn't have the time to argue. His dog—*their dog*, really —didn't have the time. He sprinted to the large stainless steel sink and kicked the water pedal on. The freaking cold water stung his skin and he bit out an expletive. "This water is freezing!"

"Other pedal, genius."

James narrowed his eyes and swapped pedals. Hot water burst through the pipes. At first the hot water hurt like hell against his thawing hands. But after a moment, it felt good.

He squeezed his eyes against the guilt. Why had he taken his dog for a hike and some training in this inclement weather? What he deserved was a good ass whopping. But how could he have anticipated the front coming in so fast and hard? And that Chase would have risked his life to save him? The weather app's winter advisory said the storm wouldn't roll in until well-after midnight. A rogue tear mixed with the blood that burned his cheek.

James blinked, scrubbing the bar of soap against his bare fore-arms until his skin was raw. He splashed water on his face, grinding his teeth when the water hit his wound, a blinding shock of pain shooting through him.

"You done yet?"

James shook the water from his arms and snagged a towel from the rack, first drying his hands and then wiping his face as best he could. He spotted the box of Kotex on a nearby shelf and tore it open, grimacing as he fastened it against his head using surgical tape.

Wonderful. A man wearing a Kotex.

He hustled back to Chase's side, laying hands over his dog's head, not sure whether praying or begging was in order. He'd done all the bargaining during the run to the clinic, and had nothing left to offer.

Except, "I promise I'll make it right by you." And, "I'll get you the biggest Valentine's Day steak money can buy. A Ruth's Chris steak."

"Would have been nice if you'd done that for me once in a while," Anne muttered.

"What?"

"Nothing. Take off your gun."

James raised his eyebrows. They both knew he never took it off except to sleep and have sex, and even then, it was right by his head in the nightstand. Always within arm's reach. Just in case.

"Why?"

"Because you're making me nervous. It's clunky, and I need you to hop up on this table and press this gauze to the wound while I give him some oxygen."

James didn't argue. He knew it wouldn't get in the way, but

she'd always hated it being an ever-present factor in their relationship.

His goal was to appease her right now, and he was in her
arena. He removed it from its holster and set his gun on the
counter—still within arm's reach—before hopping onto the table
and straddling Chase.

"What do I do?"

She grabbed fresh gauze and guided his hand to replace hers
over the wound. The feel of her touch sent a lightening bolt
through him. He bristled for a second, unprepared for that reaction, but before he could hide his emotion, Anne caught it.

"You okay? Can you handle this?"

"Yes," he said flatly, letting her believe the reaction had been
because of Chase.

"Good. Because if blood still makes you queasy, I'm not going
to tell you what I'm about to do."

"Just do what you have to do. Save my dog!"

Anne's eyes cut to his. "Our dog." She pressed an oxygen bag
over Chase's nose and wrapped her hand around his mouth.

"Our dog," he repeated with a murmur. "Can he breathe
like that?"

"It's oxygen," she muttered.

"I realize that, but over his nose?"

"It's fine. Stop questioning me." She wrapped Chase's mouth
shut with a rubber band and kept the bag in place. "Always questioning my methods," she murmured.

"I heard that," James said.

"Well, you're five inches from my face. I'd be concerned if
you didn't hear me." She slipped her stethoscope from her neck
and pressed it against Chase's chest. "He's got a weak but steady
heartbeat. The bullet didn't go through. I need to find it."

"That's not good."

He hadn't considered that it hadn't been a clean shot. What if the bullet had ricocheted around inside?

"Ah, shit, he's going to die, isn't he?"

Anne placed her hand over James's, raising her eyes to meet his. A reassuring smile curved at the corners of her lips, and for the first time in ages, he caught a glimpse of the face he'd fallen so hard for.

"We're not out of the woods yet, but the fact we have a heart-beat is good. Had the bullet struck a major artery, he would be dead by now. I need to start an IV and get this bleeding under control. Here." She grabbed his fingers. "Press your hand here."

For the second time in three minutes, touching his wife sent a wave of emotion that he'd set on dormant since August 12th—the night he'd read her texts messages from that doctor and learned she had been lying about being out with friends. She had been with the doctor—Joe-something—the night he decided to file for divorce instead of fight for her.

———

ANNE

Anne ran through an acronym she'd come up with in med school. A.C.T.S. *Assess, control, treat, survive.* Or maybe that was a book of the Bible. Either way, it was a simple method for handling any situation. Because it spoke to every situation. Especially emergencies involving soon-to-be ex-husbands.

Step one, assess the scene and remove the emotion. At this moment, she couldn't think of Chase as *her* dog. He was a patient. Step two, control the bleeding. If she didn't, her patient would die. She glanced at James's now-steady hands holding the gauze in place, then at the determined look on his face.

Damn, he looked good. When did he grow that beard? Her heart sped up and she shook the thought.

Focus, Anne.

Step three, treat the patient's life-threatening ailments first. A freaking gunshot wound. How did this even happen? How did James let their boy get shot?

Finally, at all costs, help the patient survive and she would do that because she *had* to.

"Be right back," she announced. "Don't move."

With James's hands covering the wound, Anne bolted out of the room and raided the emergency supply closet. She snagged an IV bag, a small needle and her tray of tools. When she returned, she picked up Chase's paw and eased the needle into a vein.

"What are you doing?" James interrupted her concentration.

"Shock. Steroids. Fluids. It's a cocktail to keep him alive and sedated for now," she answered calmly, not looking up.

"Can you do that?"

Anne tapped the threaded line and raised a brow at her husband.

"I mean, is that helpful?"

"I don't know. I missed my vet rotation in school." James's eyes yielded a pained expression and Anne realized he had even less of a clue than she did. In medical school, she'd practiced on animals as part of her training so she wasn't completely unfamiliar with the species. It just wasn't her expertise.

Nope, not in the least.

James was her patient, too....and her ex-husband. She glanced up at the clock. He *would* be in T-minus-one hour.

Clearing her throat and changing her bed side manner, she clarified, "He needs fluids. We are not set up for anything more intense than that. If you walked in here with a man who had a GSW, I'd have done my best to slow the bleeding while calling in a helicopter or ambulance to transfer him to Mercy Grace."

James nodded and seemed to settle. "Right. Okay. Sorry."

"Don't be. I just need to concentrate."

Okay, Anne, she thought. *Treat the wound. Save the patient.*

As she tapped the IV, one question loomed in the back of her mind: how had Chase been shot? James was dressed in civilian clothing, not his uniform. He also hadn't explained the large gash on his head. What the hell had happened out there and why wasn't his boss informed? Chase was their dog, but he was also police property, and this required notifying James's sergeant. If James *had* called, Anne expected the waiting room would be teeming with Oakwood County officers.

James must have sensed her mental unease because, just like a cop, he got right to the point. "What?"

She glanced up. "What do you mean?"

"I know that look. What's wrong?"

"Just . . . did you call your sergeant?" she asked as if the question were part of an every day conversation.

"No, not yet."

"Do you think you should?"

"I will. I'm currently holding the gauze, however."

Anne nodded. But why hadn't he earlier? Everything happened so quickly that maybe he hadn't had time. Or...Anne gulped, fearing the worst.

What if James accidentally shot Chase?

She eyed his shirt. "Were you working undercover?"

"We were training. On a hike."

"In this weather?" she asked, incredulous. Her cheeks warmed under James's scrutinizing gaze. "I mean, it's just so cold and a front has moved in. The news said it could be the worst storm of the season."

He raised a brow. "Chase has to be ready to work in all weather conditions."

Anne bit back any further questions, not wanting to know the answers. The fact that he was working in this harsh weather, hadn't contacted his sergeant, and wasn't working with a partner gave her pause. If there was an accident due to carelessness that could cost both their lives, she didn't want to know.

———

JAMES

James watched Anne work like a freaking magician. In a span of a few minutes, she'd swapped out the gauze, barely shifting his hands to do so, zipped out of the room and then reappeared, pulling a tray with a whole mess of tools on a rolling table. She started the IV and then swapped out the gauze again. M.D. followed her name on her lab coat, and, damn, if she didn't look sexy in it. As far as he was concerned, she could be Bear Grylls using a roll of floss and dinner knife to do the job. She was certainly as brilliant as him, but way more gorgeous.

In her quiet way, she was doing her job by asking all the required questions, but he didn't like her treating *him* like just any patient. No, he probably shouldn't have been out tonight but, in his defense, Chase was a wimp in the snow and tonight's weather had provided a great opportunity to train. He'd been fully prepared to bring Chase in before the weather turned bad, but then, all hell broke loose.

Anne finished shaving a clean spot around the wound and looked up. "Okay, he's prepped."

James nodded. "What does that mean?"

She trekked to the sink and washed her hands. Then she gloved up and very calmly said, "I don't know if you want to be in here for this. It may not be pretty."

The words sent a chill up his back. "I'm not leaving," he said with finality in his voice.

"I didn't think so. Why don't you stand by his head and comfort him? What I'm about to do is going to hurt. Without an available x-ray, I need to try and feel for the bullet. I sedated him, but keep him calm if he wakes up."

James felt hot. "You mean feel, as in, put your finger in the hole."

"Probably two fingers."

James swallowed dryly. "Oh, God."

Anne ignored his sudden queasiness. She filled her lungs and honed in on the injury, slowly inserting her fingers. "Based on the wound's location, the obvious clot, and the anatomy similar to a human, my best guess is that it's lodged in his abdomen. I need to get it out. It'll greatly increase his chances of survival until we can get him to the vet hospital."

James slowly bobbed his head up and down, deciding he didn't care if she had to open him up completely, he'd stay here for his partner and stay calm. He swallowed all the doubt and fear that had steadily washed over him since the moment he'd heard the deafening pop and his dog yelp. He hopped off the table, ambling around to Chase's head. He laid both hands on Chase's head, scratching the coarse fur behind his ears. This was his partner—his friend—the only true companion he still had left. He'd walk through fire for him.

"Do you know if it was a handgun or a—" Anne's lowered lashes appeared to fixate on his weapon on the counter. "Or something else?"

"I don't know. Probably a . . ." *Wait, shit, that's her real question.* "Are you insinuating *I* shot my dog?"

"*Our* dog, James. You might have retained him in mediation, but he's our dog."

He glared at her. "Fine, *our* dog." Why were they even arguing about this right now? "You think I shot him?"

"All I know is you came into my clinic carrying our dog with a bullet hole in his side. That's it. I didn't ask those questions, I just got to work."

James clenched his jaw. She was right. She didn't ask questions, at least not *that* question. Of course, she had every right to know what happened. She was the one putting everything on the line, not him. He owed her an explanation.

Chase had saved him. That's all he knew. "It was a mountain lion."

Anne's eyes shot to his, then immediately back to her task. "What?"

"We were deep in the woods. I had Chase running tactical maneuvers when I saw it about ten yards from me."

Anne stiffened, her brows furrowed, searching his face. "Did you try to scare it?"

James shook his head and continued, keeping his eyes trained on Chase. "It's not typical for them to come out like that, but sure enough it was there, haunches raised, fangs exposed. I reached for my revolver, but Chase was faster. He came out of nowhere and chased the threat away. I called him back, but that's when I heard the pop followed by the yelp."

She sucked in a breath. "Oh, James."

"Yeah, I saw Chase slow down, and he just sort of laid down, his big brown eyes looking at me. And then they closed."

"Jesus, James. Who shot him? Did you call 911?"

James eyes narrowed. "I'm almost positive it was some kids messing around. I saw small boot tracks earlier. I figured kids were shooting at rabbits. But since we were the ones who wandered into the open-fire zone without the proper hi-vis vests, it was my fault. The bullet ricocheted off a log before lodging into Chase. And no, I didn't call 911 because there's no cell signal up there. I ran him to my truck and set him right next to me, holding my jacket against his wound.

"At that point I reached for my cell to call for help." He squeezed his eyes shut, seeing what happened next as vividly as if he were reliving the moment. He swallowed but kept going. "I must have dropped it in the snow. That's when I hit a patch of black ice. Ran me right into a ditch. When I came to, blood was in my eyes and my head felt like a knife went through it, and Chase was completely out."

Anne's brows knit together. She pressed her lips into a line, holding back a sob. "Thank God you're okay."

That wasn't the response he expected. He didn't know what to say. She was acting like she cared. She held his gaze for a few long seconds, then broke away, a bit of a flush on her cheeks, her hands working diligently.

Chase flinched and James startled. "Is he awake?"

"No, involuntary movement from my fingers probing."

Anne closed her eyes and leaned into Chance's body, her eyes flickering and lips silently moving as she felt her way around his insides. The thought reignited his queasy stomach. Not because what she was doing was gruesome, he'd seen his share of gnarly scenes, scenes he'd never share with Anne, but because her hands were in *Chase*. What she did or didn't find there would play a large role in the dog's chances.

"I should have named him Chance."

"What?" Anne's eyes opened before closing again.

"Chance. He took a chance on me today. Lunging after that cat the way he did. He takes a chance every day he leaves the house and hops in the back of my truck. His chance of survival today depends on a chance you can find that bullet."

A ghost of a smile rippled across her face and her eyes met his. "You named him Chase because he chased everything. He chased his litter mates, his food, his toys, his trainer, but mostly, he chased you. We couldn't even have a proper one-year anniversary because he chased you all the way into our bed, and wouldn't leave you as long as I had you pinned under me."

James laughed. "Well, that'll teach you to seduce me."

Anne rolled her eyes. "I was your wife. Naked. In our bed. Hardly a threat."

Anne grimaced and James wondered what she was thinking. Was it about him or their dog?

He pushed away all thoughts of Anne's fingers in Chase and said, "Three months ago, he took down a guy running through a deer blind, waving a machete, and naked as a blue jay. The guy was about seventy pounds overweight, potbellied as a pig, and greased up in some sort of oil so he couldn't be taken down."

Anne raised her eyebrows. "Crazy?"

He shook his head. "Staging a protest against the inhumane and unethical treatment of animals."

"So, crazy." Anne smirked, sparking something in him. "What happened?"

"No time to wait for back up because there was a kid about twenty yards from where he was waving the knife. I couldn't shoot and he was too far away to taze him, so I let Chase loose." James chuckled remembering the look of horror on the loon's face as Chase charged him. "Chase took him down and had his jowls locked on his knife-wielding arm like *Jaws*. The original movie.

"Then what?"

"The man squealed, and I arrested him."

"That's awesome."

"It was."

"You know what else is awesome?"

James looked up. "What?"

"This." Anne held up the bullet. It was smashed so flat it looked like a razor blade.

"You found it! Definitely a 22-millimeter."

"Clean too. It was right in his intestines. Plenty of cushioning there. I can't promise there isn't any internal damage, but this looks good. But he's off duty for a while, okay?"

Tears burned his eyes and he wanted to crush her to him. Instead, he clutched his fist to his sides. "Thank you."

"I assume when I write the report, I'll be given lenience considering the circumstances."

James blinked. "Report?" How could she be worried about her job at a time like this? Didn't she always think about her job first?

Anne looked around and raised her brows. James hadn't noticed until just now, but the room looked like the aftermath of a war zone. Bloody gauze, discarded towels and tools. Not to mention the trail of blood that led from the lobby to the surgery room, which wasn't a surgery room at all. The stainless steel table was actually the break room table. There was a vending machine in the corner. A fridge hummed against the back wall. Even brightly colored flower wallpaper bordered the top of the walls. But James had been too preoccupied to notice any of this. She'd brought Chase into their employee break room? *Where people eat!*

"Why did you bring him in *here*?"

"Because this is a clinic and our exam rooms have tiny beds that are meant for checking throats and looking in ears or performing the occasional Pap smear."

James did not need the visual, which reminded him that he still had a Kotex on his face. "Gross."

"If it's medically necessary, we do it. But what we don't do is remove bullets."

"What's going to happen here?" James asked, finally grasping the full weight of what she did for him.

Anne set her hands on her hips. "For starters, I'll call someone in to dispose of this table."

James snickered. "Well, That's a start."

"Then I'll probably have to call in a HAZMAT cleaning service to handle the deep cleaning.

"Really?"

"No, just some bleach and a ton of disinfectant will be fine."

James grinned, taking her in from head to toe. "I'd start with a change of clothes."

Under her lab coat, her silky, floral shirt and tan slacks were covered in blood. She looked like something straight out of a horror film.

She glanced down and shrugged. "Nature of the job. I was married to you, I've seen worse."

"You're still my wife."

Anne shook her head and glanced at the wall clock, a somber look in her eyes. "An hour doesn't count."

He took a step toward her, hoping he read her right when they signed on the dotted line. Hoping *she* knew, like *he* knew, that neither of them wanted this.

"I don't know what I would've done without you. My wife."

It was the truth. Even when midnight struck, they would still be married. Call it shitty timing, but since the call he'd received last week from his lawyer, he'd been grateful for the opportunity to reconcile. An opportunity he had hoped to share with her over a Valentine's Day surprise.

"And," she said with forced lightheartedness in her tone, "by the looks of the blood soaking through your Kotex, you still need me."

ANNE

One thing was certain. Anne was covered in dog. Dog hair, dog fluids, dog blood.

She squeezed her eyes shut at the thought of loosing that gorgeous black German Shepherd. Dogs like him always seemed to be phased out. The Belgian Malinois were quickly becoming a

K-9 favorite for their fierce noses when tracking both drugs and criminals. They also ranked higher in the agility department because they were smaller. But, one thing she knew being married to a K-9 cop: departments always came back to the German Shepherd. It would always be her dog breed of choice. And here was her baby, the pup she watched grow and train over the past four years. The puppy who hated to be picked up but always wanted to tuck his long, cold nose under her butt after being out all day. This was the smart canine who'd find a marble and drop it into a shoe and then chew the shoe apart to get that marble. He would eat his food and then grab his food bowl and throw it at her, demanding more. All these little nuances that proved how smart and neurotic he was. And now here he was, lying helpless on her break-room table, bleeding out.

Anne pressed her hand against James head. "How are you feeling?"

"It doesn't hurt much."

"Let's get you taken care of."

James flinched against her touch. "Why don't you take a moment to get cleaned up?"

"May as well stitch you up first."

He took her hands in his and, though she wanted to fight against his hold, she couldn't help feeling safe. "You're shaking. Give yourself a few minutes to regroup. That was really intense. I'll be okay. Get yourself taken care of."

As much as she hated to agree, he was right. A few moments to pull herself together wouldn't hurt. "Okay."

She glanced toward Chase. He slept, his breaths coming in quick, short pants, but with the wound sewn tight, her best guess was that the worst was over.

"I might have a change of clothes in my locker, I'll be right back," she told James. "Go ahead and wait in exam room number one."

"Sure." He retrieved his gun from the counter and sauntered down the hall, where he disappeared into the first room on the right.

It didn't matter how many times she watched him walk away, she couldn't ever *not* watch. Divorce or not,everything about James was perfect. She sighed. Except his jealousy.

Anne stripped her coat off, wadding it up as she walked into the cramped co-ed locker room. It was barely twice the size of their office bathrooms, with one shower stall, six lockers, and a gurney against the back wall. She had probably logged an average of two nights a week on that thing. Small towns have small ways and, with a total of seven staff working at the clinic, it wasn't unheard-of for someone to catch a nap.

Anne tossed her lab coat into the basket, then started on her blouse buttons. Then the tremors started.

"Dammit," she muttered to herself. The tears welled up and wouldn't stop. She couldn't contain her sobs long enough to get a hold of herself, and, no matter how hard she bit her tongue, she couldn't gain control over herself.

She dropped to her knees and her hair fell over her face. She'd allow a minute to compose herself. Her dog had nearly died. Her divorce to a man she still very much loved would be final within an hour. Her career would be in jeopardy for what she'd just done in her goddamn break room. It was all too much for one night.

A hand on her shoulder shook her from her thoughts. She pressed her fingertips to her eyes, and swiped at her tears.

"Annie." Like it or not, his sure, steady voice sent calm through her. "Come here."

James sat on the gurney and pulled her into his arms. He pressed her head into his shoulder and smoothed down her hair.

"I'm fine," she said, sniffling back the tears. They didn't stop, and now that mucousy thing tears did to women made her look like a mess. She dabbed her face with a clean spot on her shirt, fighting a losing battle.

"Sure you're fine. And I didn't just spend the last twenty minutes with a feminine product on my head."

Anne burst out a laugh, then choked on the phlegm. She looked up at her husband's face. It was Kotex Free. "You took it off?"

One more hour. He's only your husband for one more hour.

"As much as I enjoyed it, yes. It was time to change my pad."

Anne laughed again. "Stop it." She swatted his arm. "You can't say 'pad'. Only woman can use that word."

He squeezed her one more time, before releasing her. "Buying feminine products for you earned me that right. But seriously, one way or another, it's going to be okay."

The way she melted into his body reopened a thousand gaping wounds she'd sewn shut after he'd left. She'd suture those wounds again later. For now, she wanted this moment.

Anne blew out a puff of air. No, she wasn't okay. But, yes, she was absolutely grateful that he was here, even if it was under the worst circumstances. "I'm better. I just needed a minute. It's a little...much, I guess."

"Understandable." His hand grazed hers.

Anne stood. She couldn't keep letting her heart break. She glanced toward the door, hoping he'd get the hint. "Let me get cleaned up and I'll stitch you."

He stood up, leaning entirely too close. "I think it's clotting well enough."

Anne held up an authoritative finger. "Don't even think about trying to get out of it. You need a stitch." She grinned, her skin way too warm this close to his. "But no Harry Potter. I promise."

His half-smile slanted up. "Thank you."

"Zorro is way more you."

He cocked a brow. "Funny."

"You need a change of clothes, too," Anne said, yanking a navy-blue nurse's smock off of a hanger from her locker.

"Don't worry about me, I got this." He shrugged out of his flannel top where his white undershirt flipped up, exposing his ripped abs beneath.

A guilty shiver of want crept through her and drool may have pooled at the corner of her lips.

Nope. Not going there.

She turned her head to face the bleak metal nothingness of her locker.

"The blood will dry on my pants. The rest I'll wash off while you take a shower."

Before Anne could argue that she could just wash the blood from her hands, arms, body, face, she side-eyed James. She surmised that she'd also have to rinse the salty layer of nervous perspiration coating her armpits where her untimely sweat glands had jumped into hyper drive in response to having her untouchable husband's ripped muscles in such close proximity.

Okay, maybe a shower wouldn't hurt.

James reached out and flipped on the water. A genuine smile, one she'd fought the past half hour—actually, the past six months —crept across her lips. Actually having James here gave her a small sliver of happiness on this otherwise awful day. She hated what tonight was. Valentine's Day Eve on top of Divorce Eve.

Worst Valentine's Day ever.

She scratched the thought from her mind, not allowing another bout of phlegm to make another cameo. "Thank you," she managed.

"I'll, uh, I'll see you back in the exam room."

Anne nodded.

Fifteen minutes later, feeling a million times better thanks to a great smelling body wash on a soft loofah and the feel of smooth, shaved legs, Anne slipped into her scrubs and slid on a pair of hospital-grade socks. She towel dried her hair and sprayed something pretty to offset any chance of lingering dog smell.

Anne tossed her soiled clothes in a plastic bag and chucked them in her locker. Before stepping out of the room, Anne paused and took a deep, steadying breath. "He's just a patient."

When Anne checked exam room one, it was empty. Of course. She grabbed the stitch kit and pushed through the break room door. James had pulled up a chair and sat directly in front of their dog. Anne bit her lip, taking in the James she once knew. He more than filled out his t-shirt, his rustled hair stuck up in every direction giving him a boyish charm, and no matter how strong he was, when it came to something as delicate as life or death for his animal—his partner—his best friend, James was reduced to child-like innocence. To pleading and crying. Just like she was the night he walked out on their marriage.

He rested his chin on his arm, a hand tracing Chase's nose.

"How is he?" Anne whispered, leaning against the door.

James sat up. "You tell me. You're the doctor."

Anne smiled. "About that stitch."

James went a little green. Anne flopped her tool kit on the table next to him. She grabbed the disinfectant and the cleaning pad. "Ready? This may hurt a little."

He didn't flinch away from this threat, but instead, looked up at her, seemingly putting all his faith in her hands. The trusting look in his deep-set eyes made her want him even more.

She swallowed down the want and cleaned the wound, trying to simultaneously wipe away the pain.

Irreconcilable Differences. That's the box he checked.

Irreconcilable, because he was sure she'd cheated on him.

Thirty minutes and they would both start a new chapter.

"Was it Zorro? Or, considering the holiday, did you want Cupid's arrow stitched on here?"

JAMES

Man, she smelled good. What sort of sexy lotion did she apply after her shower? He stared at the wall, failing to not visualize her wet and naked.

When he'd heard her crying in the back, his heart broke. What did he expect, bringing Chase here without warning? He'd had the drive, the crash, and the run to process what was happening, but she'd had no warning. Not that he could have with his phone gone. He'd crashed through the door, knowing exactly what he'd looked like, thanks to the reflection on the door window, and asked her to risk her job, save their dog, and not acknowledge what today was. How could she not to break down?

When her sobs had echoed through the hallway and seeped into his room, he'd had to go to her. Only an ass would ignore that. He'd forgotten how beautiful and vibrant she looked, especially when she was vulnerable.

He only wished he could take back time and not accuse her of something as heinous as cheating. His only proof was a few misleading texts from a doctor, long hours at the clinic alone with that doctor when she said she was out with friends, and a personal insecurity that probably stemmed from his own cheating dad. Except, unlike his mom, he didn't stay and try.

"Hold your chin up," Anne instructed.

"Sorry," he said, fixing his gaze on her deep brown eyes. They had a hint of gold flecks in them.

"This might sting a little. I'm going to give you a shot of Lidocaine."

"I can handle it."

Anne sat back on her heels. "Oh really? Ever had a needle stuck directly in a wound?"

James shrugged. "Can't be worse than pepper spray to the eyes like I had at the academy."

"I beg to differ, but we'll see." Anne leaned forward. "Ready? Should I count down from three?"

James squeezed his eyes tight. "Just do it. But make it quick. Ahh, don't pinch the skin, just do it."

"Done."

"What?"

"Yeah, old maid's trick. Get you thinking it's about to happen, and do it while your body releases cortisol to absorb the impending stress."

James blinked. "I'm sorry, English please."

"I tricked you. It's done. Give it two minutes and you'll be numb."

James raised his brow. Well, he tried to raise them. The medicine seeped through his skin, ceasing that ability. "Well played, Dr. Riley."

Anne cracked a half laugh. "Yeah, I guess I'll have to change my lab coat when I go back to my maiden name."

"Oh." That stung. "You're changing your name?"

"I'm not going to be a Riley any more. We don't have kids. There's no reason to hold on to something that's not mine."

James dropped his eyes to her left hand. Her rings were also removed. Something he didn't realize she'd done. But he couldn't blame her. He hadn't worn his ring since the day he filed. "I gave you that name. It's yours for as long as you want."

Anne breathed out. He saw her dry swallow and thought he felt her tense at the same time. "Hold still. I'm almost finished."

"Annie?"

She shifted uncomfortably. After years of reading body language, he knew the ambivalen look of discomfort well. Her hands stilled. "Annie, you okay?"

She glanced at him, then concentrated on the stitches. "You don't have to do that, you know."

"Do what?"

"Call me Annie. Be extra nice. All that. I'd stitch you up even if you were being a jerk. Sort of a Good Samaritan thing. Comes with the health care service."

"I'm not . . . not being extra nice."

Anne's eyes briefly bounced to his. "You are and I'm telling you that you don't have to. You don't have to let me keep you name. You don't have to act like fifteen minutes from now won't mean something different."

James didn't respond. What could he say? She was right. He'd initiated things. Cost her the price of filling out the paperwork herself since she never retained a lawyer, though they had a pretty straightforward mediation. No fighting for property. He moved out. She'd kept the jeep. He'd kept the dog. It was all very amicable. At least at first. Okay, maybe cold was a better term, but she was willing to let him go. She hadn't become bitter until he'd maintained full custody of their dog. But Chase was *his* partner, more than her companion. Due to the circumstances, the mediator ha suggested that Anne have visitation, something James always found a reason to reschedule.

The regret had started as soon as he'd had her served, but pride had kept him on this path. Wasn't this how cops lived? A two-wife minimum?

Was it really too late to win her back? Especially when he'd told her that the divorce was nullified do to a freaking mishap. Or maybe it was a miracle. "I'm sorry. About everything," he said. "Annie?"

"I'm done. Three stitches. No room for a Nike swoosh, sorry. I did add a Scooby Doo Band-Aid in honor of Captain Chase here," she said with a tentative smile. She closed her kit and wiped an eye on her way out the door.

It wasn't too late. He'd make sure of it.

James pet his dog and whispered in his ear. "Time to get mommy back, don't you think?"

———

ANNE

What the heck was James doing? She refused to let him drag her through the trenches again. Because, quite honestly, she didn't have it in her to go through it.

Anne tossed the sewing kit on her desk and pressed the back of her hand to her mouth, silencing the raw emotions. He was just another patient. That was it. Nothing more.

Annie straightened. She could do this. The first order on the agenda was to call the attending. Maybe if she alerted him to everything before he walked in here and saw the disaster, he wouldn't report her to the medical board. Or maybe considering the circumstances, he'd tell her how he'd have done the same thing. She couldn't be sure. And having James here did nothing but fog her brain.

She picked up the handset on the desk and pressed it to her ear. Nothing. Dead. She clicked the reset button several times, and, just like in the movies, nothing happened. She slammed the handset back down.

"Hungry?" James's voice filled the room, permeating through her and piercing her heart.

Anne clenched her jaw and slowly turned around. Barely stifling a giggle when she spotted what he deemed food. She motioned toward the cartons. "What is that?"

He shrugged. "Sustenance."

On top of a medical tray, James carried two packaged mystery meat sandwiches, a fruit roll up, a Hershey bar, two individual sized cartons of Milk of Magnesia (uh, did he not know what those were?), a bottle of sparkling grape juice, and a pair of beakers, which lay on their side. Anne bit the inside of her lip, trying to keep a straight face. "Looks like you raided our employee fridge."

"And the vending machine."

"Yes, and the vending machine. Hey, did you know the phones were dead?" she asked, trying to distract from how cute clueless looked on him.

"Doesn't surprise me, considering the storm."

"Oh, right."

"Care to join me for dinner?"

Anne sighed. "James, I don't know if that's such a good idea."

"Why, don't you get a lunch break?"

"I do. That's my fruit roll up on the tray."

"I know. It's your favorite. Hard to miss a six-year-old's favorite snack in a grown-up's refrigerator."

"Well, I didn't ask you to go digging."

"Come on. Humor me."

Anne pressed her lips together and closed her eyes. She knew what he was up to, and no matter how many times she played this scenario in her mind—hopeful he would come home—every night the silent prayer went unanswered. He'd *clearly* made his position known. So, why was he attempting to rehash an old, burnt-out flame now? It was too late. In less than ten minutes, everything would be final. She'd reconciled with it, as much as she ever could.

When she opened her eyes, James stood before her, the tray stashed on the desk. He gently took her hands. She narrowed her eyes, snapping them away. "What are you doing?" Her voice cracked, betraying her. So was her fluttering heart.

He didn't back off. He was close enough that she could smell a hint of his cologne. *Oh, how I love his smell.*

He smiled down at her. "Just talking to you."

If only she'd just added that lightening bolt. Harry Potter was way less intimidating than her six-foot-three husband. She'd use that nifty cloak of invisibility. Being invisible would be helpful right about now.

"I mean, what are you *doing*"? Her voice waned on her attempt to be authoritative, which, with her heart misfiring, was like trying to talk with a mouth full of marshmallows. She left the accusation hanging between them.

His unfair advantage—that breathtaking smile—was like a sucker punch to her heart. It rendered her powerless.

Anne heard herself swallow. Which meant, so did James. Which also meant he knew he had her heart. *White flag waved. I give.*

The lights flickered, and Anne flinched. She wasn't worried about the power going out, because the generator would kick in, but the very real storm surrounding her felt more like a threat with James this close, looking at her like that, and them so, so alone.

"You scared?" James asked, his breath somehow sweeter with every word.

"It's really coming down."

"Better to be inside here, where it's warm and dry than out there, weathering the storm."

"I'm not so sure about that."

James smiled, accentuating his ridged jaw line. "So, shall I ask again? Care to eat?"

Anne considered the sandwiches. Her stomach must have accepted the invitation without her permission because it rumbled at his request. Embarrassed, she grabbed at her midsection with both hands.

He raised a brow at her stomach. "Seems like I have my answer."

"I'll eat my fruit roll up first."

"Deal."

———

JAMES

James grabbed the tray of food and led Anne back into the break room, which he'd dubbed as *Carrie's* locker room in his mind. Blood was still splattered on the floor. He used some Clorox wipes, a few towels, and a can of Febreze for a quick clean —he didn't want to be away from Chase any longer than necessary.

Speaking of which, Chase's breathing remained steady. The gauze Anne had wrapped around his midsection to bind the stitches for when they moved him to the vet had only a trace of blood. As far as he could tell, his partner was doing okay. Probably just resting now. But when he woke up, James wanted to be the first person he saw.

"You cleaned up," Anne declared with an overly-surprised tone.

"A little. I didn't want you to be grossed out while eating."

She leered at him. "Trust me, I've seen worse."

"In any case, it's been a long time since we've eaten as a family. You shouldn't have to eat in The Overlook Hotel."

Anne's cheeks seemed to warm at the mention of family. "Good point."

"Milk?" he offered when she peeled open the sandwich's plastic wrap.

"Nope."

James lifted a shoulder. "Suit yourself." He cracked open the bottle but she slapped it out of his had, busting into hysterics.

"I so wanted to let you, but I'm sorry, I just can't."

"What?"

She laughed so hard, she snorted.

James shook his head, clueless. "What's so funny?"

Anne's hyperventilating forced her to do some labored breathing exercises. "I just can't. I can't. I'm dead."

"Clearly." James set the carton of milk down and fanned her face. "Delusional."

"No." She sucked in a shaking breath, pointing at the milk, tears in her eyes. "That's Milk of Magnesia. Unless you want to clean your colon in the next thirty minutes, I suggest you give that *milk* a hard pass."

James held up the carton. He winced at the clear direction scripted on the back. "What the...why is this in your break room fridge?"

"Because," she panted, trying to catch her breath, "because it doubles as our medical overstock."

"Good to know."

James chucked the two cartons in the trash before unscrewing the lid of the sparkling grape juice—also found in the fridge—and double checked for medical anomaly uses. Then he handed Anne a beaker.

Her laughing faded. "What's this for?"

A sudden unease washed over him. "It's the closest I could find to a champagne glass."

Anne took the beaker. "Okay. I'll play. What are we celebrating?"

James paused. He allowed this moment to fill his mind with everything his eyes could take in. From the top of her sandy-blonde hair tied in a damp, messy bun, to her chocolate-colored eyes, which some would say were set too far apart, to her full lips. She never needed lip gloss. They maintained a pink tint that seemed to shine at all times. Her skin flushed under his stare. He smiled, remembering that same flush when they first time he laid eyes on her.

"Remember how we met?" He poured the juice, and it

bubbled to the top of the beaker, even when it was only halfway full.

"I do."

"Remember what I said?"

"You said a lot of things. You were under heavy anesthesia following the surgery."

James took her free hand and placed it on the right side of his abdomen, right where he still had the surgical scar. When her hand touched him, her breath caught again.

"My appendix burst. You were there when I woke up."

Anne rubbed the spot where the silver-colored scar remained.

"And now you have a matching set," she said, jutting her chin to his forehead.

"But do you remember what I said?" he asked, pouring himself an equal share of the juice.

"That there were six inches between where my hands saved your life to where they now held your heart."

"Exactly."

A tear dripped from Anne's eye. His chest ached.

"What's your point, James?" Anne asked, almost a plea.

"I mean, you still have that hold. From my gut to my heart to my head."

She squeezed her eyes. "You filed."

"I was wrong."

Her eyes opened, meeting his. "Yes, you were. But that can't change things now. Look," she nodded at the clock on the wall. It's after midnight. The divorce is final. You're a free man."

"No, that's not true."

"But it is. You can't un-sign that line. Or un-say the accusations you made. Or un-hurt the pain you caused."

James scrubbed a hand over his mouth. "In part, yes. I'll

spend a lifetime proving to you how wrong I was and how very sorry I am. But the other part . . . I can."

"What do you mean?"

God, he needed his cell phone for this. The screen shot his lawyer sent him was all the proof he needed. But this stupid night ruined all his carefully-laid plans to woo her back. He'd have to improvise.

"I got a call last week from my lawyer. She sent me something."

"A bill? Because I already paid for my share."

James sighed. "No, not a bill. May I finish?"

Anne smirked. "Didn't mean to interrupt. Especially over these fancy beakers of grape juice. I'm sorry. Please continue."

"She sent me a screen shot of something regarding our divorce."

Anne's eyes grew big. "What do you mean? I didn't get anything regarding it."

"I know. I did some freelance work for her on a few security details and asked her for a favor."

Anne shook her head. "I don't understand."

"Your social security number was entered wrong."

"What do you mean? I typed it in."

James shook his head. "Incorrectly. So the divorce can't be final until that's taken care of. She was going to call you, but I asked her to let me tell you, that I was wrong about the divorce, and to give me a week to fix it with you. I wanted the chance to talk to you. To tell you how I feel. To tell you how sorry I was— how sorry I *am*."

He caught her gaze and held it, making sure she heard every word. "I'm sorry I didn't believe you about the text messages. I thought you were seeing your Dr. Allen and that's why you lied about working late hours."

Anne dropped her head to the side. "I just didn't like you

getting upset about my hours. That's why I lied. But I shouldn't have. Joe was just doing what I asked. Not mentioning work when he asked if I was still coming."

"No, that was my fault. I'm sorry I let my insecurities dictate how my heart beats for you. I love you."

Anne guffawed. "Tonight completely distorted your thoughts."

"No. I was planning to come in tomorrow, well, today now. But I planned to beg you to let me try again. I trained Chase to walk in with flowers and a well-timed whine. I even bought him a tux. That stupid tux took two hours of alternations. But he got shot and everything changed. Everything except how I truly feel."

Anne's eyes widened again.

"Please don't say no."

"James," she whispered, looking past him.

"Give me another chance."

She stiffened and her mouth dropped. "No. James—"

"I'll do anything . . ."

Anne gripped James' chin and forced his head to turn. "Look!"

Before James could fully turn, he heard the most beautiful sound he could imagine. Chase whined and blinked rapidly before trying to lift his head. James dropped the beaker, and in one swift motion had Chase's head in his hands, pressing his face into his partner's neck. "Hey, buddy! Welcome back."

ANNE

Anne's heart swelled. Chase's whimper was the most amazing sound she had every heard. She slowly stood and approached Chase. "How you doing, big guy?"

At the sound of her voice, Chase's tail started thumping against the table. He whined a howl as German shepherds do and lapped her face as if it was a T-bone marinated in beef gravy.

"Well, I missed you too."

Chase started to squirm, and Anne laid her hand over his body. "Shhh, buddy. Hold still, boy. You don't want to over do it."

His whining intensified, but not typical of pain, rather joy. He was greeting his people.

Anne grabbed a pin light from the tray and bumped James out of the way, checking Chase's pupils, mouth, and wound. "Good boy."

James' stroked his fur and Chase watched him, his tail thumping again. "I know, buddy. Let Anne look you over."

Anne nodded, smiling so hard her cheeks hurt. "I think he's going to be alright."

Chase's head knocked Anne's arm out of his way, throwing her off balance. Her foot slipped on a wet spot, and she slipped. Before she could hit the floor, James grabbed her and pulled her close, their noses nearly touching. Her heart competed for a new world record for beats per minute.

"Thank you."

James's smolder said it all. He wanted her. For as many reservations as she had about starting over, she couldn't resist the desire that thundered through her. Before she lost the nerve, she stood on her tiptoes and smashed her lips against his.

James crushed her to him, then, in one sudden movement, scooped her up under her rear. She wrapped her legs around his waist and devoured his mouth. He met her need with heat of his own.

Anne finally broke the kiss, searching his eyes. She loved what she found there. Desire. Love.

"So, we're still married?"

"We are."

"And it's officially Valentine's Day?"

"Ten after."

Anne's eyes flickered to the door. "Care to turn the worst Valentine's Day into the most intense?"

James swallowed. "Definitely."

"You think Chase will be okay for a few minutes?"

A coy smile draped across his face. "If I tell him to stay. Why do you ask?"

"Because there's a gurney in our locker room that I'm pretty sure hasn't been, uh, *slept* on in a very long time."

James went brows up. "Are you suggesting I take advantage of you, wife?"

"Technically, husband, you're in my place of employment so, if anything, I'd be taking advantage of you."

James cocked his lips to the side, eyeing her cautiously.

"Unless you don't want to—"

"Chase, halt," James ordered in his commanding voice as he effortlessly plucked Anne's legs from around his waist and flipped her over his shoulder in a very sexy fireman hold. "I'll be back in a minute."

"A minute?" Anne balked.

"Trust me, he'll wait for me as long as I ask. And as soon as I get you out of those scrubs, I'll be sure to give you an incredibly exhilarating minute. It is Valentine's Day and all. Cupid demands exhilarating."

"DEFINITION OF LOVE" BY CERI GRENELLE

STUPID AWESOME LOVE SERIES #0.5

ROSIE

"Cold. Cold. Cold. It's cold. Fuck-fuckety fuck it's cold."

Damn, that's almost catchy. I could make a Christmas carol out of it. Except it's no longer Christmas. Father Time has given way to a baby New Year. It's shiny and cooing and reminding all New Yorkers that their year must start in icy, slushy, thirty-degree misery.

It's now 1980. January has come and gone like the hangover after my sister Nancy's drunken New Year's Eve party. We get a buffer month to reflect back on the good times of 1979, and then February happens, and it's time to get on with living our lives.

You'd think after the hectic holiday season, we'd get a break from the gatherings and marketed ploys by card companies and department stores.

But no. Come February, the cheery red of the holiday season is replaced with a red so thick and fluffy it can only mean one thing.

Valentine's Day.

That special time of year when, once you finally get over not having a date to all the holiday and new year's parties, couples come out of hibernation like clockwork. They rub it in your face that you are single as fuck and no one will ever tolerate your love of work, meaning it's impossible to maintain a relationship.

I hate Valentine's day.

"Can you move faster?" I yell at the folks at the head of the line, ignoring the people who holler back at me. I just gotta pick up a token for the subway and get to the Definition of Love fair before registration starts. The machines are broken, and only one person is working the booth. Of course.

I may hate Valentine's Day, but this year I'm gonna make it my bitch.

The city of New York had a genius thought, for once, and decided to capitalize on the idea of Valentine's Day. Set up a festival in the park, get the people to spend their money, bring some revenue into the city and, by extension, to me. I like drawing couples, and I have a ton of that mushy stuff to sell to folks in love, their brains filled with bubbles and love and a bunch of crap they honestly might as well be high on.

It's a brilliant idea that I'm sort of surprised our useless local government thought up, especially with the way the city's financials have been going. Crime has never been higher, the city never more unsafe. I'm shocked that Manhattan hasn't started to cannibalize itself, or at least crumble from the edges with all its boroughs out for blood.

"Will you fucking move it?" I yell, hearing a train approaching and just knowing it's probably mine with the way this day has been going.

First, my car runs out of gas, and no wonder it does as I've been avoiding filling up with the exorbitant gas price of one dollar and twenty-two cents per gallon. They're robbing us blind. Then Lisa, my other older sister, told me she couldn't drive me because her tires are frozen to the ground. Then my third older sister, Barbara, said she couldn't help me carry my art to the fair because it turns out she's pregnant again. Then I couldn't get a taxi. I walked three blocks with all my crap, and now I'm waiting on this damn line while some out-of-towners try to make sense of the subway system.

Sometimes I hate this city.

"Let's go," a young man in front of me yells, as frustrated as I am.

He turns back to me to share the misery, and I glare at him, beleaguered by four bags of artwork, a few easels and extra supplies for charcoal drawings. He does not get to say he's as miserable as I am.

"Fuuuuuck," I moan on a shiver.

Oh, and it's freezing. I'm underground and wearing a wool coat, but I may as well be standing on top of the Empire State Building naked.

The couple starts to ask the clerk a new line of questioning, and I've just about had it. I've probably missed four trains at this point.

"That's it." I push past the four people in front of me—bags, easels and all—ignore the annoyed cries of those in front of me, and sidle up to the old couple at the head of the line. They glance at me askance and then start speaking rapid Italian.

Mama Mia. This I can handle.

I use what Italian I know from school and my Mama and Aunties and Uncles and everyone who resettled here after World War I. It's enough.

I ask the couple where they need to go, then give them instructions on how to get there. I even offer to walk them to the platform, though the clock over the token booth says early registration for the festival is about to start.

But Mama would never let me live it down if she ever found out I didn't help these people.

I rush them over to the A to Far Rockaway—why anyone would want to go there I'll never know—wave them off as the lady insists on kissing both my cheeks, then just make my first train. I've gotta transfer to the LL at Halsey-ENY Bwy. According to the schedule, there should be a train pulling up just as this one arrives. A jaunt down a short tunnel—my many bags and sweaty face making me look crazed, and warding off any would-be muggers—and then I'm off to Union Square.

I can do it.

I can make it. I can get to early registration on time and make sure I have my own stall where I can spread out and showcase my art and finally get my name out there. This is my big shot to actually make some money off of what I love doing. My days of waitressing at Uncle Frank's diner are almost over.

The train pulls up to the stop where I need to transfer, and it's a minute early. Yes, I can make it. I can make it.

I dash off, take the exit that will lead me to the LL connection. The frames and supplies in my bags jangle and twist around me, attempt to hold me back like the roots of a great beast, keeping me from achieving my goals.

Fuck you, beast. This Valentine's Festival is mine.

I turn a corner, and I can see the train pulling up to the platform. I put on the speed. My short legs pound the stone walkway. I ignore the odd looks and catcalls from fellow commuters grumbling at me for getting in their way. None of it matters now, the doors are so close I can almost taste them.

Twenty feet. Fifteen.

Ten—

Out of the corner of my eye, a guitar comes flying at me, knocking into my bags and shoving me out of the way. I slip on a plastic bag left on the ground and fall hard to the dirty floor. My bags scatter. My easels hit stone with a sickening crack. I look up to see my art spread across the floor, and beyond that, the doors to the subway car closing with a static chime.

I can't make out his face because of the graffiti covering the glass, but the last thing I see before the doors shut is an acoustic guitar with a blackbird etched into the wood.

"Asshole!" I yell as the train departs my station, taking with it the last chance I have of getting my own stall at the fair. The instructions were pretty clear that if you didn't arrive for early registration, the chances of getting your own space were slim.

With a sigh, I gather my art back into the bags and try not to bite my lip off in anger at the site of my broken easel. I can't afford another one. I trudge over to a bench and sit down, knowing it will probably be another twenty minutes until the next train comes.

Forty minutes later and I'm still waiting.

If I ever see that guitarist again, I'm going to make him wish he was never born.

———

DIEGO

"I don't need a lot of space."

"You sure?" The lady at the registration desk asks. "You want to share a stall with someone? You could have your own space."

"It might be nice," I explain. "This is a holiday for celebrating love, no? Why be alone?"

The older woman stares at me for a second before shrugging. "Whatever you say."

She stamps my entry sheet then hands me a map with directions to the stall. I give her a nod then exit the maze where the registration has been set up for the city workers organizing the fair. I brace myself for the cold. It's times like these I miss Colombia. Sure, the mountainous regions could get chilly, especially with the high elevation, but I would not actively seek out this frigid weather.

Then why, oh why did I choose to move to New York City?

The music, I think as I grip my guitar and find stall number sixty-nine. This city has a veritable undertone of music and art and life. Passion runs through the very veins of this city, and the last time I visited my cousins and snuck into a Jimi Hendrix concert, I promised myself I'd come to stay forever.

Of course, it was summer then, and I hadn't known what terrors the winter could bring.

Or how hard it would be to achieve my goals here.

The movies made it look so simple.

Arrive. Be talented. A manager conveniently walking by on the street would then sign me.

I suppose there is a reason they call it movie magic.

I amble past the artisans setting up their stalls, admiring their wares. Spotting blown glass expanded into the shape of hearts, I stop and chat for a second, complimenting the man on his skill. At the next covered tent, a baker sells cupcakes and donuts shaped into hearts. They look delicious. I ask if she'll give me a muffin if I play her a song. Another woman comes around from the back of the tent, carting a crate of croissants. She looks me up and down then offers me a muffin if I'll go away, putting her arm around the other woman.

I can see where I'm not wanted, but I graciously accept the muffin and bid them a happy Valentine's Day.

Not that it's the holiday yet. That's on Thursday, at the end of the festival. Four days of selling goods and services in honor of dear St. Valentine and the spirit of love.

Americans turn everything into profit. What's next? Selling Christmas trees as early as their Thanksgiving holiday? No, they'd never go that far.

Passing the many heart-shaped and themed items on sale, I'm

grateful to be offering something different. Anyone can make something heart-shaped, but it's experience that stays in the memory forever. That's what I'm selling. Memories. Experiences. Life.

Music is life.

My tent is toward the back, an undesirable spot, but I refuse to look down on the opportunity to get my sound out in the world. I sit down in the provided chair and start to play some love songs, warming up.

After a while, a striking woman clatters over to the opposite side of the booth. She sets four heavy looking bags on the table as the easel and backpack she was also holding smashes to the floor. Her hair is covering most of her face, but I can make out sensuous, thoughtful lips painted in red on surprisingly golden skin despite it being the dead of winter. Brown hair is wavy and wild around her face. She's wearing a wool coat and gloves to battle the cold, and tight —very tight—jeans on an ass any man would have a hard time not watching. She's petite, she's lovely, and I think she might hate music because she's staring at my guitar as if it were the source of all evil.

She looks up at me and practically growls, "You."

"Hello. I'm Diego Rodriguez. I suppose we're stall mates."

"No. No no. We are not anything-mates. I am going to spread my stuff across this stall, and you are going to find somewhere else."

"I'm sorry, I do not understand." I look down at the paper listing my stall number. "This is stall sixty-nine, no?" I show her the paper. "I am supposed to be here."

"Fuck—stall sixty-nine, damn it." Her glare might melt the icecaps. "Get out of my tent."

"This is not your tent. It is our tent. If you wanted your own tent, you should have arrived earlier, that is when there was a greater abundance of—why are you pointing a paintbrush at me?"

She advances on me, the hard end of a paintbrush aimed my way as if it were a switchblade.

"I'm thinking of how best to jab this through your eye."

"I know New Yorkers can be hostile and slightly territorial, but this is beyond anything I am used to. What borough are you from?"

"Brooklyn."

"That explains it."

"Want to know the reason for my hostility?"

Her menacing narrowed eyes make me think twice about my curiosity.

"Actually, I am good not knowing—"

"If it weren't for you, I wouldn't have been late and could have had my own stall which I sorely needed."

"You cannot blame me because I am simply here."

"No, but I can blame you for knocking into me as you ran for the LL train."

"I didn't—"

"You did, you were swinging your guitar as if it were a battle ax and you whacked it into my bags, sending my stuff all over the gross station floor, and I missed the train because I had to clean it up. That was you. Your fault."

She turns away from me, thankfully having decided not to stab me with a blunt piece of wood. At least for the moment.

"I apologize, I did not realize that happened. I was focused on making the train so I could arrive on time—"

Another glare, and this time she's actually baring her teeth. If it weren't for the fury in her gaze, she might be cute. Scratch that —even angry she's cute, especially with the small gap between her front teeth, but I'm not idiot enough to point it out to a woman on the rampage.

"Let me make it up to you. I can help unpack your things."

"The only way you can help is by being completely silent and pretending you're invisible for the next four days."

I clutch the fretboard on my guitar and try not to be too contrary when I say, "It will be complicated to play music and be silent at the same time."

She doesn't answer me, but there is an extraordinary amount of mumbling and cursing from her side of the tent. I follow my father's wise advice when my brother and I would ask about why he never argued with Mamá when she was angry.

Be silent. She can't get angrier at you for something you haven't said.

She sets the broken easel to the side, along with the backpack and starts to unpack sketches, canvas paintings, and drawings from the many bags, laying them on the provided table. I try not to be nosy, but I can't help but watch her. She's...something else.

The wind has picked up slightly, and though we're shielded from the worst of it by the closed sides of the tent, her dark hair still flutters around her face like coy wisps in the wind. Her boots crunch against the cracked pavement, catching my attention. Knee-high brown leather boots with thick heels accentuate her delicate calves and legs. She's projecting a "don't mess with me" vibe, but it comes together to create an amalgamation of ferocity.

I'm attracted to a woman who believes me to be the cause of all her ills and probably hates me.

This might not be good for business.

———

ROSIE

Mother cock-sucking piss pot. Of course. Of course, I'd be in the same tiny space as this dipshit. Not only did the world seem to crumble around me in twenty-four hours, but God has singled me out today and decided: *hey, I need a little bit of comic relief.*

Let's see what Rosie Caputo is up to. Life not miserable enough? Well, Rosie, have I got a shit day planned for you.

Not shit *day*. Shit *week*. Because since we're not allowed to switch tents once they're assigned, I have to remain in this tiny space with the guitar-wielding bozo for four days.

I stop arranging the paintings on the narrow table space for a moment and look up, beseeching God and asking him, ever so politely, why he's such a dick.

"You okay?" The bozo asks after a minute.

"No."

"Is there something wrong with the tent roof?"

"No."

"Then..." I hear him take a step toward me. "Why are you looking at the roof?"

"I'm not. I'm looking at God."

"Oh. Right." A pause. "So, God is on the roof?"

I sigh, use what will power I have not to stab him in the eye with my art tools and go back to unpacking.

After a while, he sits on his chair and starts to play.

I'm about to yell at him again, tell him he doesn't need to play yet since we've got no customers. And then I start to listen.

The music is lilting. Light and sinuous, as if each note were married to the next. He transitions from major to minor chords with ease, and when I glance over, trying to be as stealthy about it as possible, I find him strumming a steady beat with his eyes closed.

His leather jacket hugs his upper body, and his light jeans are snug enough to highlight the taut muscles in his legs as he props one foot up on the bar beneath the chair seat. A knitted hat covers his hair, and his leather gloves have the fingers cut out, making it easier to play. I noticed earlier he's not much taller than me, nor is he beefy like the guys my sisters tend to go for. He's lean, and though it's cold as hell out, his copper skin sort of glows with warmth and peace as he strums the tune, hitting the guitar's hollow base for a solid beat every now and again.

His square jaw tenses on specific notes, his emotions mixing up with whatever he's putting out into the world. He's got stubble and a mustache that gives him a better-looking version of Burt Reynolds's vibe. His accent makes it clear he's not from New York, maybe not even this country, but there's one thing that's transparent above any other superficial observation I can make while pretending I'm not stalkily staring at him: he loves music. It's evident in every breath and gesture.

I want to hate what he plays on principle. I want to continue resenting him for the rest of the week—something I am truly capable of with the way my family's been taught to hold grudges —but I don't think I can ever hate this music. The sweet cadence and almost hypnotic rhythm. The depth and length he's able to stretch the notes into. It's magical.

Not that I care. I hate him, and we're sworn enemies for the rest of the week.

"You're definitely in the right place because couples will eat this shit up," says a man with a pot belly and a clipboard, passing by and checking something off his list. "I'm Richard, I'm with the city. I'm supposed to tell you the rules and give you complimentary marketing advice for participating in the festival."

Oh boy, this should be good.

"No heavy drinking. No drugs. No dealing drugs. No buying drugs. No littering. No setting litter on fire. The city is not responsible for your stuff going missing or you gettin' mugged. No switching tents for any reason. We're putting a map of what goods are where at the front, and that map is not changing. Capisce?"

"Yes, sir," Diego says, so chipper you wouldn't think it's as cold as my mother's icebox out here.

"Yeah," I mutter, crossing my arms. Hating life.

"Don't look so glum, sweetheart," Richard, who I now hate, instructs. "You can make some serious money here this week." He glances over my art. "Though you might want to add some hearts to these. Hey, that's a great idea actually. If you've got some extra paper or canvas, paint some hearts. It's the hearts that sell the best. Couples love that stuff."

I smile and try not to bite his ear off. "Thanks. I'll get on that right now."

"And keep smiling like that, except less scary. You don't want the customers to think it's Halloween."

"Thanks." *Don't punch him.*

"You're welcome. We're opening up in ten."

Before Richard leaves, Diego stands, his guitar in one hand.

"And what about my marketing advice?"

Richard pauses, taking in Diego with an appreciative eye. "You're perfect just the way you are, friend," he says with a wink. "But you need a sign. People are gonna think you're sitting here for no reason playing free music. Sell yourself. Hype yourself."

"A sign. Yes. Thank you." Diego sits back down, one leg bouncing nervously.

"Uh," Diego begins, then mutters to himself in Spanish.

How convenient for Diego that he's got an artist next to him with tons of extra paper. And how unfortunate for him that because of his carelessness this morning, those papers are now gross and creased from being tossed onto the nasty subway floor.

"Ma'am."

"Don't call me that."

"Miss."

"I'm not a Miss either."

"What should I call you? We're going to be together for a few days."

"Yes, it's the tragedy of my life."

"*Señorita*, I am very sorry I bumped into you this morning—"

"Knocked me over with your guitar so you could selfishly shove me out of the way and beat me to the festival."

"How could I know you were going to the festival?"

"So, you're not discerning when it comes to the women you knock over? Good to know. Tomorrow I'm bringing a baseball bat for protection."

"This is ridiculous. We can't live in this tent together and fight for a week."

"Oh buddy, clearly you've never heard of the Caputos from Bensonhurst. We're known for how long we can hold a grudge. When my sister was in second grade a boy sneezed on her homework, ten years later they were crossing the stage at graduation together, and she turns back and sneezes on his newly minted diploma. On purpose. It was a snotsplosion."

"That is...disgusting."

"My cousin Frank once had some guy cut him off on his way to work. Do you think he went to work that day?"

"I'm guessing no?"

"He didn't go to work for a whole week. Instead, he stalked the guy, learned his driving route and then decided to purposefully go out of his way every day for a year so he could cut the guy off."

"And where is your cousin Frank now?"

"Prison."

Diego nods then crosses himself before sending a prayer to God.

His eyes find mine, and they're a dark mahogany. Rich and shining with what I think might be mirth. Or fear. I can never tell after talking about my family.

Maybe I should tell him more stories, and he won't come back tomorrow.

He shuffles where he stands and pulls the knit hat off, rubbing his hands through wavy black hair that frames his face.

It's not too long, but longish in that glam rock early days Freddie Mercury way.

Diego is handsome, shockingly so.

But he's gonna have to do more than be pretty to get back into my good graces.

———

DIEGO

"Can I have a piece of paper and a pencil to write my name on?"

That's right, blurt it out like a crazy person.

"Huh?" She asks, flipping her hair away from her face as a gust of wind tumbles into the tent. "You said that in Spanish. I think I understood one word."

"Do you speak Spanish?" I ask in Spanish.

"*No, ma io parlo italiano.*"

"*Italiano?*" I ask. The word is the same in Italian and Spanish.

"*Sì.*"

"We might be able to figure out a common language."

She smiles briefly, almost grudgingly, then crosses her arms, her gloved hands tucked into the creases of her inner elbows.

"What do you want?"

"I would appreciate if I can have a piece of paper and a pencil to write my name."

"All you're gonna write is your name?"

"You think I should write more?"

"I don't know, prices for whatever it is you're selling? What are you selling?"

"Music of love."

"You're gonna stand and play music?"

"Yes."

"There are bums on the street who do that for free. What's your gimmick?"

"I will...I hadn't thought that far."

She frowns then pulls a piece of paper out. "I'll make your sign. How much per song?"

"Two dollars."

"That's a hefty amount of change for a song. You better be good."

"You were listening before, what did you think?"

"It was...passable."

"What does that mean?"

"It means you didn't suck."

She sits behind her chair and starts to draw, and it's like watching the sun rise over a cold wintery morning in Central Park. She switches between reds and purples. At one point her tongue peeks out from between her lips and her brow furrows in concentration. The creases are endearing and her focus admirable.

She's doing this for me, someone whose eyes she wanted to gouge out with a paintbrush earlier. Perhaps she does not carry the Caputo grudge gene.

Would it be a crime if I allowed myself to become captivated by *Señorita* Caputo?

Shit, I don't even know her first name.

As she draws I walk over to her side of the tent to look at her art. She glances up at me, warningly. I raise my hands in innocence and continue my perusal.

Her work is...as captivating as she is. Except it shows a side more playful than what she's allowed me to see. There are couples holding hands, blurred around the edges and painted in deep blues and reds so striking they could be heart's blood. Others show children running with dogs, the parents trailing behind with their hands interlinked. There are no faces, only the outlines, and colors. All the pieces are signed by Rosie Caputo.

Her art shows the meaning of love, how the very definition embodies that love has no boundaries. It can be the love for a pet, for a parent, for a husband or wife or child. For a sibling, as she illustrates in one sketch. A little boy cradles a small child as his parents look on from a hospital bed. These images are life.

"Here you go," she says with a cheerful smile, handing me the paper face-down.

I take it, eager to see what an artist of such talent has made for me.

"Thank you, it means a lot to me."

"You're welcome!" She glances past me, and sighs. "Oh, look. Customers."

I flip the sign.

Diego Rodriguez
Asshole Guitarist Extraordinaire

"Really?" I ask her, not even knowing if I should be pissed or if I should laugh.

I choose pissed.

She shrugs, as innocent as the day she was born. "I warned you about Caputo grudges, and you accepted my help anyway."

"Would you give me paper and pen to write it myself?"

"No."

"You're setting me up to fail."

"You should think about the consequences of your actions before knocking into people."

"I didn't—" I cut myself off and turn away before I start yelling, my anger boiling. I will not let this ruin today for me. I will go to the bakers and ask for some cardboard to write on and I'll hang that.

I glance at Rosie. She's got her arms crossed and is staring straight ahead, no doubt still angry at me.

"I was careless this morning, and that I regret. Especially if I hurt you. But I would not have done that on purpose. Never. You could have let it go, but instead, you chose to be cruel."

Her frown dips further, and she swallows deeply.

But she doesn't look at me or apologize or offer to draw something new. She sits in silence, living with her choice.

If that's what the next few days have in store, then so be it.

———

FIVE HOURS later

I can't live like this for another day. How am I supposed to make any money with a grumbly pissed off woman stewing in the back of our tent? Whenever someone comes over to ask me to play, she scoffs loudly, as if the idea of a love song is so abhorrent. When a man asks for pricing on one of her paintings, she points to the sign without a word.

She doesn't make a cent all day. It's almost impressive.

She sits and grinds her teeth and shivers as the day moves from cold to frigid. If someone so much as mentions love near our tent or pays me to play something sappy and sweet she groans in her chair and shifts restlessly.

I swear, she's trying to purposefully make sure that we're both miserable and that neither of us makes any money.

This can't go on.

When the day is over, and I step away from the tent to use the restroom before heading home for the night, I notice she's got her pencils out again and is scribbling away at something furiously. I'll talk to her when I get back, maybe offer to take her out for a drink. Make peace between us. That's the only way this week will get better, and I really need it to get better. I can't have my days being harder than they already are.

No, I'll make amends. Somehow.

When I get back to the tent, she's gone. Of course, she's packed up as quickly as possible to escape me.

Something catches my eye, flapping in the wind on my chair, held down by a rock. I pick it up cautiously, not knowing what to expect.

It's a new sign, elegantly drawn with stylized hearts. On it is my name and the price for my songs, with one heartwarming difference.

Diego Rodriguez
Player of Love Songs

I guess those Caputo grudges don't last as long as advertised. Tomorrow is going to be a good day.

———

ROSIE

He's there when I arrive, and so are two Styrofoam cups of something steaming hot paired with muffins in the shape of hearts and as big as my head. He's sitting on his chair, now pulled up to my table, waiting for me. He's wearing pretty much the same thing he was yesterday, except now he's wisely put on a red scarf. The color makes his skin glow, even more, today, and his warm smile does something fluttery and weird to my stomach.

"¡Buenos días!" he says, not as chipper as yesterday, but kindly.

"Buongiorno."

We stare at each other for a second, not knowing who should talk first or what to say.

"Thank—" he starts, but I can't accept it.

"Don't. Don't thank me. You were right, I was a bitch."

"I never said that."

"I was having a shit day, and you bumped me, and I took it out on you and then I didn't make any money all day because I was so mad at myself for writing that sign but wouldn't admit that's why I was mad. It was awful. I was awful. I'm sorry."

He slides the cup over to me, his smile kind. "We are allowed to have bad days."

"What is this?"

"Coffee. I hope it's okay, I made it how I take it."

"And how's that?"

"Light and sweet."

I take a long drink, and the sugar and earthy taste of the coffee warms my soul.

"It's perfect."

"*Salud.*" He taps my cup with his and after we sip for a moment, he offers to help me unpack.

I accept.

"Do you have a big family?" he asks, pointing to an image with a lot of figures.

"Three sisters, a million cousins. How about you?"

"One brother."

"Is your family here?"

"No, they're back in Colombia."

"What brought you to the city?"

"Music. I love all music, and this city is brimming with clubs and potential places to create music. I want to be a part of that."

"You want to be a professional musician?"

"No, I want to be a part of the process. I love to play, but I've got no fantasies of being a rock star. My mamá thinks I have a better chance at being President than I do of being a rock star."

"Why didn't they move with you?"

"I asked them to come with me, but my parents are stubborn, and my brother didn't wish to leave them without care in Cartagena."

Hearing horror stories in the news of what's happening in Colombia, I try to think of a polite way to ask if his family is in danger. I don't want to assume everywhere in Colombia is rife with crime, but that's all anyone in the states hears.

His laugh brings me out of my thoughts.

"What?"

"When you're concentrating your tongue sticks out on the side of your mouth. It is charming."

Was that flirting? That wasn't flirting.

"You're a smooth talker, huh?"

"It's hard not to be, with a lovely talented woman."

Okay, that could definitely be flirting.

"Don't let Richard hear you flirting with me, he might get jealous."

"Poor Richard will have to find someone else. My flirtation is for the artist Caputo."

Okay, he's flirting. Fuck. What do I do? Do I flirt back? No, that will only encourage him. Maybe I should just ignore it and walk away awkwardly until he gets the hint that I don't want to be flirted with.

"I'm sorry, did I make you uncomfortable?"

Or he could be considerate and ask my thoughts and opinions.

"No. I just—I'm not looking for anything right now."

"Looking for anything? Did you lose something?"

I shove him playfully. "You know what I mean. Your English is perfect; don't pretend to misunderstand."

"Tell me what you mean then."

"I'm not interested in being in a relationship right now."

"Oh good, I hoped after I smiled at you that you wouldn't think I was about to get down on one knee and propose."

"Is sarcasm a common occurrence in Colombia?"

"No, mi amor, that is all New York."

We finish setting up, he hangs his new sign with a bright smile, nodding and showing me the care he's taken in making sure none of my art is pierced by the hook he sets it on. I can't help but smile as he struts back to his chair, looking proud and professional. He's sweet and kind and when he looks at me my skin goes hot, and I start to bite my lip so hard it hurts.

I'm smitten with a charismatic, handsome, guitar player, who seems to maybe be attracted to me. Oh right, and my resolution for the year was to swear off relationships and focus on my art and my career.

This might be the worst Valentine's ever.

"I have an idea," Diego says as the fair opens for the second day. "Let's combine forces. Anyone who wants a song will get a discount on your art. And anyone who buys your art will get a discount on a song. Sound good?" He snaps his finger and stands abruptly, his face open with excitement.

"What?" I laugh, wrapped up in his enthusiasm.

"You could take requests. Have you ever drawn on demand?"

"What do you mean?"

"If someone asks to have their portrait done in the style of your drawings, can you do it on demand? I can play them a song while they sit, and we can sell it as a package. What do you think?"

I have to admit, it's an excellent idea.

"I love it."

"Yes, wonderful. I'll go get more chairs. Can you draw up some signs?"

"Sure."

He spontaneously kisses me on my cheek, and the warmth of

his soft lips lingers as he sprints away, flying on the wind of his idea. I take my gloves off and touch the spot. There's a bit of wetness, and the thought of his tongue or any part of his body on my skin makes my heart beat faster, and the space between my legs turn warm and frustrated.

And I thought it was a good idea to be celibate this year?

Yup, the worst Valentine's ever.

DIEGO

The day is a complete opposite of yesterday. Rosie and I are actually speaking. In fact, we're working together in perfect harmony to make beautiful music and art. The customers are practically lining up to get their pictures drawn while I play music. At one point Rosie adds a note to one of the signs, stating I'll take requests. When I ask what happens when I don't know a song, she merely smiles coyly at me and says, "Surely someone as passionate about music as you won't be stopped."

It's a challenge I can do nothing but rise to. And I do. By the end of the day, I have played every love song written since Beethoven. Twice. *Dios ayúdame*, if someone asks me to play *How Deep is Your Love* one more time I may throw my guitar into the East River.

"I thought you were gonna choke on your smile when she asked you to play that song again," Rosie says on a laugh, enjoying the hot chocolate she bought for both of us as an end-of-day reward.

"I might choke on that song. Is it okay to ban requests?"

"Not if you want to make any money, honey."

"Damn your capitalist society. I love it and hate it all at once."

"This was a good day," she says, sighing happily.

I want to imagine she's thinking about the fantastic time

we've spent together, but she's probably thinking about all the money we made. I, unfortunately, couldn't care less about the money at this point. Instead, I can't stop thinking of the way she moves when she walks around the table to chat with a customer, how her wool coat doesn't hide the sway of her hips or how those tight jeans frame her delightful ass. I had to step away a minute this afternoon after staring at it a bit too long and feeling my cock go hard.

She's not looking for a relationship. She doesn't need one, as funny and bright as she is. Why would she want to complicate a good thing, especially with a man like me? She was probably being polite earlier, and didn't want to point out that she's interested in someone so different from her.

I chastise myself for the thought. That's not who she is. Is it so hard to think that a woman as beautiful as Rosie simply doesn't need a man? No. Is it hard to convince myself that she doesn't want me as much as I want her? Yes. Because I'm an ass, and clearly, all women must love me and fall at my feet because that is what they were put on this earth for.

"Whoa, now you look like you want to punch somebody."

"Sí. Myself."

"Why? You did great today. Your songs were so tirelessly romantic I thought some of the men and women would leave their other halves for you."

"I may have been given a few phone numbers."

She laughs, but the sound is loud and awkward. "Really? No kidding! Wow. That just shows you what a bunch of baloney this holiday is. Am I right?"

"Do you really hate Valentine's Day?"

"It's a corporate ploy to get people to buy shit. It's not about the so-called definition of love." She gestures to the large banner at the front entrance of the festival. "Heart-shaped baked goods and red scarves don't mean love. They don't show your boyfriend or girlfriend that you care about them."

"No, but the time spent with that person shows it. The small things, the willingness to take your time and pause your busy schedule to be with that person...that shows them. Time. Effort. Care. That is the definition. It is not one thing."

"It's a load of hooey, that's what it is."

"Love?"

"Yes."

"That is even more cynical than I'm used to from you."

"Well, you hardly know me. And just because we work well together doesn't mean I've forgiven you for knocking me over."

"Not that again."

"I will forever hold that incident against you."

"Well, I suppose I will just have to find a way to make it up to you."

"And how would you do that?"

"Dinner? Drink? Coffee? Tea? Movie? Dancing?" Her eyes light up on that last suggestion. We have a winner. "Ah, you like to dance. I know a wonderful, slightly not-so-legal place that has the best music for dancing. Come with me."

"Diego..."

Without giving her a moment to overthink, I bring her hands to my shoulders then lightly hold her waist. I make sure not to place my hands too low or high, not wanting her to think I'm trying to take advantage.

We spin around the concrete in front of our stall, the deserted park our dance floor, with the other sellers too wrapped up in their own business to notice the magic happening in front of their noses. Rosie laughs as we twirl, and when I show her the basics to a salsa, she picks it up instantly.

"You and me in a dark club with music so loud you can feel it in your feet. It rises through the floor up into your shoes and your legs. It gives you and your partner wings so the world disappears, and you can only see each other. That is where I'd like to take you. Come with me, Rosie."

"I gotta admit, that sounds fun."

The wind picks up, blows a strand of hair into her face. I push it away, tuck it behind her ear. I don't move my hand when I'm through. Her skin is soft despite the harsh wind of winter. Her lips are parted as they look up at me, the full temptation of her mouth too inviting to ignore.

Her hands slide down to rest on my chest as our dancing slows. Heat bandies between us, let off by one and absorbed by the other. And in this moment, surrounded by the light of a setting sun and the heart-shaped kitschy paraphernalia of the nearby tradesmen and women, it's hard not to believe in the magic of Valentine's Day. It's hard not to pull her close when her lids lower intimately and her head tilts toward mine. It's hard not to meet her lips as she goes up on tip-toe, gripping my jacket. And it's hard not to kiss her with every inch of passion and need I feel for this lovely, stubborn, brilliant woman who doesn't understand the definition of love.

I will show her. No, I'll share it with her. Because even though I'm sure there is a reason for her to be so cynical when it comes to love, it doesn't mean she doesn't have space in her heart to discover it again.

Wind gushes past us, a cold bucket of frozen water over our fused bodies. A clatter and crash echoes behind us and I end the kiss, holding her close to see what it is.

"It's a garbage can," I say, looking down at her, eager to see how she's feeling after a kiss so heated I'm feeling slightly tight in my pants.

The expression on her face is anything but comforting. In fact, it looks like she just ate an arepa covered with stale and moldy cheese. In fact, she looks like she is about to hurl.

Good. I'm glad I've still got it with the ladies.

"I have to go." She steps back quickly, and as much as I hate to stop touching her, I release her instantly.

"Of course. Yes."

"That—that was. Um...I need to pack my things." She doesn't look me in the eye. The suave and fiery woman I've known the past couple days is gone, leaving behind a stuttering stranger who is tripping over her own feet and attempting to fit a foot-long frame into a purse that maybe when stretched to its limits would only hold a six-inch image.

When she continues to mutter and nearly throws a piece of art away, I can't let it go on anymore.

I've found the ever searched for Italian-American's kryptonite. A scorching kiss from a Colombian musician.

I take the frame from out of her hands, and she looks up at me in shock, as if she forgot I was even there.

"Can I help you? It will go faster if we work together. And it's getting icy out."

She sighs, seemingly at herself, then nods with a grateful smile that warms me from the inside out.

I help her pack up, and the silence between us is louder than the pounding of my heart when we were kissing. When the stall is clean, and our hot chocolate cups thrown away, we walk out of the park together.

"Can I take you home?" I ask when we reach the street, not wanting my time with her to end. "Are you far into Brooklyn?"

"No. I've got my car. I was able to get gas after the fair yesterday. Where are you living?"

"Queens. Jackson Heights."

"Right. Do you need a ride?"

"No. It's out of your way, and I need to head to my cousin's restaurant."

"You work there?"

"I am a proud dishwasher."

Her hand lands on my arm. "Nothing wrong with honest work."

I smile down at her, regretful that I ruined what harmony we found today.

"Goodnight, Rosie."

With a nod, I watch as she walks across the street and loads her car. There's a parking ticket on her windshield, but she glances at it, shrugs, then crumples it up and tosses it in the street.

I might be in love.

With a woman who apparently wants nothing to do with me, my dancing, or my kisses.

ROSIE

A cacophonic sound of laughter, loud accented voices, and Italian phrases rise over the crowd of the fair. It can only mean one thing.

"Oh, shit."

"What?" Diego asks, looking up from the lunch we're sharing.

"They're here."

"Who's here?"

"They promised not to come, the lying bitches."

"Who?"

I reach over and grip Diego's wrist, wanting to apologize and run away with him all at once.

Yesterday had been a dream. A good, beautiful and ticking-time-bomb dream. The kind you indulged in for a minute or two then faced reality. Or at least, the reality I have constructed for myself with rules and limits.

No dating. Focus on the work. On the art.

I got to the fair this morning, expecting and hoping to live in that dream some more. But clearly, my weird-as-fuck reaction to his kiss scared him off. I couldn't help it. He kissed my socks off. I forgot the English language. Hell, I forgot the Italian language. I forgot what language even was. The only words I could speak were gibberish as I thought of the best way to jump his bones without him thinking I was some sort of hussy.

He'd been kind and sweet after my fumbling, and I let myself have the night to get over being a dumbstruck fool and then be the modern woman I am and ask the guy out for some dancing.

Then I arrive this morning, and the heat is gone. All that is left between us is polite distance and chatting. He doesn't want me anymore.

As if that's not humiliating enough. Now I have to face them.

"I'm sorry, but I told them all about you last night, and the kiss, but they promised they wouldn't come here and stick their ugly noses where they're not wanted. I'm sorry."

"You talked about me?" He asks, his gaze assessing.

"Yeah, I was like a school girl after a first kiss, I couldn't shut my trap."

"So, you liked it?" He asks, standing and taking a step toward me, eager and open in a way he hasn't been all morning.

"Of course I liked it, couldn't you tell?" I stand, meeting him in front of my display table. "I could barely form a coherent sentence."

His fingerless gloved hand cups my cheek, stroking me with a callused thumb. It's better than any heating unit I could ask for in this cold-as-hell park.

"I thought you were trying to find a way to let me down."

"What?" I hold his hand against me, not wanting to let go. "No. No. It was good. Really good."

"Rosie, would you like to—"

"Oh. My. God. Rosie. You didn't tell us what a hunk he is."

"You've been holding out on us, girl."

"I can't believe you've finally found a man after a five-year dry spell. Really, buddy, you might want to check if things are still working down there before you invest yourself."

I close my eyes and take a deep breath. Ma would not be happy if I killed her other daughters.

"Diego, I'd like you to meet my sisters. Lisa, Nancy, and Barbara."

"Pleasure to meet you." Nancy, the eldest and most stringent of the four Caputo sisters extends her hand. Her brunette hair is fluffed out to Farrah Fawcett perfection, and if her leather jacket were any tighter, it would be molded to her skin.

Diego, because he has to go the extra mile, doesn't shake her hand, but kisses the leather gloves over her knuckles.

"Ooh, so charming," Lisa squeals, sidling up to him. She's the only blonde in the family because she insists on putting peroxide in her hair. "Are all Colombian men so debonair?"

"Lisa, get off." Barbara pulls her away as she winks at me. I mouth a big thank you to my big sister.

In fact, they're all my big sisters, but Barbara has always been the most sensible and level-headed out of the lot.

"You gonna make a woman of our sister?" Barbara asks. "It's about time she settled down."

Except when she's a sarcastic asshole. What the hell?

"Barbara!" I yell-whisper at her. "Will you all lay off him?"

"What?" Nancy asks, stepping into the stall. "We got a right to see who's sweeping our sister off her feet."

"I swept you off your feet, huh?" Diego asks with a gleaming smile I'm about to smack off.

"Don't get too cocky. It was an okay kiss."

"Oh, really?" Lisa asks, her eyes twinkling with the light of the devil. "I thought it was so good you were ready to drop your panties for him then and there. Single digit temperatures be damned."

"I did not say that."

"Yes, you did."

"Don't listen to them," I growl at Diego.

"Actually, I would like to listen to more of what your delightful sisters have to say. Especially if it involves your panties."

"Hey!" Barbara points her menacing finger at him, the one that makes her kids quiver in fear. "Only we get to talk about our sister's panties."

A man in a trench coat and thick scarf steps up to the tent, he looks around with all the subtlety of a rhino before asking in a low, scraggly voice, "Did I hear you're giving out panties at this booth?"

Before Diego can even take a step forward to defend my honor, my sisters form ranks. Nancy shoves the creep out of the tent and Barbara and Lisa give him their best Brooklyn mother rants. The man is soon escorted from the park.

Diego watches the whole thing in fascination. "Your family is amazing."

"Amazingly obnoxious."

He elbows me playfully, his head tilted my way. "They love you. They protect you."

"I know," I say on a groan that can also be considered a sigh that only a person burdened by an annoying family can make. "They just...they want me to have their lives."

"What does that look like?"

"Husband. Kids. Baking cupcakes for birthdays. Baseball games."

"That's not what you want?"

"That's not all I want. I want my work. I want my art."

"You think it isn't possible to have both?"

"I know it isn't."

"Says who?"

"Life. The world."

"Again, with the cynicism."

"It's in my blood."

Customers pop into the tent and we get back to work. The day flies by, especially with all the tantalizing flirting happening since the panty incident. During a slow moment, Diego steals paper and some pencils and draws a rough stick-figure couple kissing with hearts above their heads. It's so awful, I can't help but laugh. He crumples the paper up and throws it at me, his bright smile the shiniest light in the park.

"Hey, Diego, c'mere." Nancy waves him over toward a bench they've parked themselves at, watching us like hawks throughout the day as they drink coffee and chow down on pastries and hot dogs. A combination only my sisters can love.

"Be right back," he says, squeezing my gloved hand before running off, kindly providing me with a delicious few of his tight ass. Oh, my Lord, it is fine. He's like a compact gift bundled in leather, musical talents, and just enough scruff to get my body sizzling. I'm surprised there isn't steam coming out of our tent from all the hormones and heat getting tossed around.

But even if I give in—even if we spend some time together past the festival, and we start something—it can't last. I won't get knotted up into a marriage like my sisters. I won't give up my dreams to have a family and kids. It's not a crime to not want to have kids...even though I really want to have kids and I'm just telling myself that because I love my art.

"Rosie, get your ass over here."

Diego and I switch places as Nancy beckons, the queen in a castle wherever she goes. As we pass, Diego's hand finds mine, and his fingers manage to locate a bare stretch of skin above my glove. The caress sends a different kind of chill across my body.

Thank God I've got heavy layers on, because if it were

warmer weather, my nipples would be pointing themselves sky high.

"What?" I ask my sisters as they sit in judgment of me and my predicament.

"What?" Nancy demands. "How about, 'What is wrong with you?' That man is fine, and he likes you. Why aren't you asking him to get hitched?"

"We just met."

"Doesn't matter," she continues. "We've been watching you two."

"Yeah, I noticed because you'd whistle at him every time he bent over. Don't you miscreants have anything better to do with your time? Like, be with your children?"

"They're in school," Lisa points out. "And their fathers are at work."

"You could be at work too if you didn't marry the first men you dated."

"Hey," Barbara says, directing her finger at me. "Enough of that. We could still be at work if we wanted, but we chose our own paths. We wanted to be full-time moms. There ain't nothing shameful about that."

"I know, and I'm not trying to make you feel bad. I love your kids and husbands."

Lisa snorts. "At least one of us does."

I ignore her sarcasm. "But that's not what I want right now. I'm in a good place with my art. A couple of gallery owners have even stopped by and asked to see more of my work. But I can't be spending my time with some man and not focusing on my work if I'm really gonna make this a career."

"Honey," Nancy says, standing. "We're real proud of everything you're doing. But you gotta see, you're the only one putting these limits on yourself. These aren't the world's rules anymore. They come from a place of fear."

I bristle at the insinuation. "I'm not afraid of anything."

"We know, girl," Nancy says, hugging me close. "You're fearless as fuck, except when it comes to trusting someone to love you for who you are. And if anyone can do that, I kinda think it's gonna be him. See you later."

Lisa lowers her voice, "If you're smart, we won't see you until tomorrow."

"Hey," Barbara smacks Lisa's arm. "Don't encourage her." Barbara turns to me on a low voice. "Use rubbers."

"I hate you all. Please leave."

"Love you," they chime together as they walk out of the park.

"Love you too," I call back.

"Hey."

I turn, and he's there, bags full of my stuff in his hands, the tent fully packed up.

"Hey." Apparently, I am again incapable of speech and all he's done this time is say a one syllable word. In that sexy accent of his. With the stubble and the mustache and the leather and guitar strung over his back and, fuck, stop looking at him, stop looking at him.

He laughs, but it isn't unkind. I laugh too. This whole experience has been ridiculous.

"I meant to say hey, then I started to say hello."

"I understand. You speak my language."

He bends his head, and I do nothing to stop the descent of his kiss. His lips are smooth and warm, and the tease of his tongue beckons just beyond my reach. We linger for a moment, relishing the taste and sensation a simple kiss can stir in a body.

"Kisses are weird," I say as we part.

"Huh?"

"I mean, we're just mashing our faces together and rubbing them around and lapping at one another with tongues."

"Oh, we can use tongues? Because I was holding back."

"Yeah, I'm cool with tongue."

"Great."

He drops my bags—gently—then pulls me against him, fusing our bodies together as tightly as we were the night before. Only this time, there's no hesitation, no wondering what's okay and what isn't okay. He goes for what he wants, and clearly, what he wants is to hold and touch and kiss me without reservation. And damn. It is good.

"Come dancing with me," he says on a breathless gasp as we separate.

There's no question in my mind of what I want. At least for this moment. For tonight.

"Yes."

———

DIEGO

We pack her car up and head to Jackson Heights. Queens isn't the prettiest of boroughs, not that I'd call New York City pretty at all, especially when compared to the gleaming shores of Cartagena, but it is a city full of life and sound made by man alone. The whispering of tree leaves is replaced with the clicking of heels on the pavement. The water lapping at the shore is now an elevated train rushing past my window. Some would say I've gotten the short end of the stick, moving to Queens, but I'm glad New York is now my home.

And with a lovely woman on my arm, I wouldn't have it any other way.

We head to Romeo's restaurant. He serves traditional Colombian fare mixed with some modern options like chicken wings and pizza. It's eclectic, to say the least, but the food—at least the Colombian food—is a taste of home.

I take her below the restaurant, to where the music is loud

and thumping, like I promised. The room is small, and the music comes from a boom box rigged to connect to more massive stereos. None of it's legal, but it's fun as hell.

We shed our winter clothes, the heat from the dancing bodies more than enough to keep us warm, and for the first time I see Rosie without the layers of scarves, gloves, and coats.

"You are beautiful," I tell her, marveling at the curves of her hips, the sexy shape of her ass as it moves beneath jeans with the word Sassoon stitched over a butt pocket.

Her body is divine, and I can't wait to see her wearing nothing except my body draped over hers. But it's her gapped tooth smile that hooks me beneath my stomach and makes me fall.

We dance, first to fast-moving Latin rhythms, then to slower, sadder songs. She trips over the steps at first but quickly catches on as I teach her. We go for an hour before the man at the stereo switches it up and plays *Somebody to Love* by Queen.

She looks up at me, her eyes bright and her cheeks feverish from the hot and sweaty little room. "This is my favorite song. I love Queen."

"It is an interesting choice for somebody who doesn't believe in love."

She shrugs, resting her head on my shoulder. "I can't deny good music when I hear it."

"What of my music?"

That stirs her, her eyes full of mischief as they find mine.

"I love your music. When I first heard you play, I wanted to hate you and your music, but those fast fingers of yours won me over pretty quickly."

"But not me." She rubs my shoulder as our bodies refuse to separate.

"I'm still undecided about you."

I kiss her, wanting to take any indecision away.

"I love your art," I say as we separate. "And I would never do anything to keep you from making it. *Comprendes?*"

Instead of answering, she kisses me again, her hands skimming my ass and slipping into the back pockets of my jeans. It takes all my manly will power not to jump.

"Is there somewhere we can go?" she asks.

Knowing this could be it, could be the only time we're together with the last day of the festival tomorrow—Valentine's Day—I take her up to my tiny, one room apartment. There's nothing more than a mattress on the floor, a dresser with some clothes, a record player in the corner, and about ten boxes of records.

"Look at all this music," she says, amazed by the collection and not caring about the sad state of the room. "I've never heard of most of these artists."

"It's a lot of underground stuff, people who aren't given the time of day by record labels because they don't fit the mold of what's in. But I swear, I'm going to help musicians like these make music. One day."

"That's a beautiful dream."

"So is yours, and it doesn't have to be just one thing."

"Diego—"

"Let me show you."

We end up on the mattress, and I am more than glad I listened to my mamá's voice in my head and made my bed that morning.

We touch and kiss and go slow, my hands asking for permission before taking on a will of their own, palming her full breasts and gripping her hair. Then, they slowly slide down to the hot space between her legs. And, through it all, I talk—paint a picture for her to see and trust.

"During the day, we will find our jobs. You at a gallery, me at a music studio." I unhook the button on her jeans and lower the zipper. "When we come home, we'll cook and chat about our day." I tease the lace edges of her panties, wiggling my eyebrows as she giggles at the inferred memory of the panty peddler. "We'll keep some time to work on our projects, share our thoughts and struggles." I dip my fingers beneath the cotton, keeping my eyes on hers to know she's with me every step of the way. "Whenever I have a block, I will come to you. You will do the same. We will talk and share ideas." My fingers find the wet center of her sweet pussy, and she moans.

"Keep talking, don't stop," she pants, gripping my shoulders.

"This is really turning you on?"

"If you stop talking I will clock you."

Never disobey a hot and bothered woman.

I push my fingers inside, slowly gliding and driving past the clenching walls of her channel. She's stunning. Her head thrown back, her hands searching my body, roaming and stroking me until she finds the hard bulge of my erection.

"Oh, shit," I mumble as she unzips me.

"Didn't I tell you not to stop talking?"

"It's hard to speak when you're gripping my cock like a vice—yes, just like that."

"Keep going, or I stop."

"So, so cruel." Though, it's a much more pleasurable cruelty than the one we discussed after first meeting. So I give her what she wants.

I weave a tapestry. The two of us living together, making art and music, sharing our lives and our passions. I describe a particularly sexy night where our desire for one another can't be contained, and I take her right in her studio, bent over a table full of paints that splashes down her front. She laughs a little at the idea, but when my fingers find her clit and begin to rub, the laughter is stolen away.

"It's a perfect life," she groans against my lips, sliding her hand up and down my cock in sync to the rhythm of my fingers thrusting inside her pussy, taking me to the edge. "I want that life."

"And there can be more. So much more if you take a chance on me—"

"Ah, I'm coming," she cries. "Right there."

"Yes. Yes, me too. *Dios*."

It's a perfect moment, the hard grip of orgasm tunneling through my groin and stomach, leaving me speechless for a long time afterward. We doze, our scents and bodies mingling to create one seamless mass of passion and dazed love. This is the definition of love for me. Sharing a gasping breath and caring for one another, falling asleep in each other's arms.

In the morning, we dress, and she doesn't complain when we have to wait for the shared bathroom down the hall. We grab breakfast-to-go at the restaurant—some arepas and fruit—then drive to the fair. She's quiet, not telling me whether today will be it, or whether she's changed her mind. I should have said something last night, should have made it clearer I want to be with her. That I've fallen in love with her.

A few minutes before the opening, she asks if I can go buy us some coffee.

I want to tell her a million things, but my grasp on English evades me as she looks at me sweetly and openly. I nod, thinking there might only be one thing I can do to convince her of what she means to me.

ROSIE

I'm in love. It's clear as the sign I've hastily drawn to replace the one I made earlier in the week. Being in bed with Diego, dancing with him, waking with him this morning, has made it abundantly clear how much he's come to mean to me. It's scary as hell, and my hands shake as I sketch, using all the colors in my palette. It's the last day of the fair—Valentine's Day—and crowds of couples are lining the sidewalk, waiting to come in.

But none of that matters. Only this moment. This piece of paper and the words I write.

It's possible to have a career, to have a goal and dreams and still find time for love and family. I never saw it as clearly as I do now because I needed the right partner to help me see. One who won't demand that I sacrifice myself for the sake of our domestic life.

He'd never ask that of me because it would be akin to asking him to set down his guitar and go find a so-called real job.

With these lines of work, we'll never be rich. We'll probably struggle more than not. But I don't care. As long as Diego is with me, shit, I can conquer the damn world. And I plan to.

Familiar notes find their way to my ears. A soulful, rock anthem I know well, one we danced to just last night, plucked and strummed on a simple yet perfect acoustic guitar. I think it will forever be the best sound in the world.

He's there, playing and singing my favorite song, and when he comes to the guitar break, starts to speak. And damn, it makes me kind of mad because he's stealing my moment.

"Rosie, I know you have a particular idea of what your life will be. So did I. Until I met you. Your paintings show me the true beauty of who you are, and your determination and spirit thrill me and inspire me—"

"Wait. No!" I stand, waving my hands at him.

"No?" He asks, confused. His hands faltering on the strings.

"No! Shuddup. This isn't fair."

"What? I am confused."

"You can't come over here, playing my favorite song in some grand romantic gesture."

"I can't? Do you want me to go?"

"No! I was going to make the grand romantic gesture. You totally stole my thunder."

"Oh!" His previously defeated expression lights up in comprehension and butterflies take flight in my belly. "I'm sorry, please dazzle me with your gesture."

"Well, now it's ruined. It's nowhere near romantic as yours."

"Please, *mi amor*, I want your gesture."

He steps back, waiting patiently while I huff at him.

"Here." I thrust the paper into his hands then cross my arms, tapping my foot as I wait for him to be suitably awed.

He reads the sign silently. For a long a time. Like, a really long time. Did I spell something wrong? Is it illegible? Is it not what he wants? It's only three lines.

After a while, my confidence dips.

"Um, I—"

"Please!" He holds up his hand, stopping me. "I am trying not to be unmanly and cry with joy."

Relief pours through me—so intense and ecstatic that I nearly crumple to the ground.

"Why would you think that's unmanly?"

"I've noticed you Americans are averse to men showing any kind of emotion. Be a man, and all the shit."

"Honey, I'm Italian. We're as passionate as a people can get."

"Oh good," he says wrapping me up in his arms, his eyes glistening. "Because I am going to cry when I tell you that I love you. And I want to make a life with you."

"I love you. I love you."

We kiss, and the folks in the surrounding booths and tents clap for us, join in on the love we've found. If someone had told me last week, I'd fall in love over a few days, leading up to Valentine's Day no less, I probably would have laughed in their face. But now it seems easy, like the most obvious thing in the world.

The fair starts and we sort of have to stop kissing. But it's okay, because we work our combined magic to bring in customers and gift them with a piece of our love whether it be through music or art.

But the real magic truly starts when we hang the new sign.

Diego Rodriguez and Roseanne Caputo
Musician and Artist
The Definition of Love is Us

"HEARTBREAK & HIGH GEAR" BY DAPHNE MASQUE

RIPPED out of her sleep by the horrid clang of the doorbell, Grace sat straight up and her stomach lurched. Groaning, she shook her head and wiped her face with her hands. Damn.

Grace normally didn't take naps—didn't have time. Between kids, jobs, and worrying about money, she couldn't afford the luxury of an afternoon snooze. Today however, she had the extremely exciting task of folding laundry even though she desperately needed to close her eyes for just one smidge-of-a second. It must have happened somewhere between sorting socks and folding tee-shirts that her exhaustion won the battle. She had unexpectedly drifted off into glorious oblivion before being rudely interrupted by some idiot at the door.

"Damn," she said, and staggered around the house for a moment. The doorbell rang again, louder, it seemed, this time. The stinging sound rattled through her brain, momentarily rendering her stupid. If the kids were home, they would have raced, at a break neck pace, to answer the door first. They had uncanny synchronicity and would have hit the door at the same time. Next, the obligatory argument about who got to pull the door open would have ensued.

But the kids, by the generosity of their neighbor, Charlotte, were spending the day and evening out of the house. Grace had two jobs, and three days a week there was barely an hour-and-a-half between the two. Charlotte offered to take the kids on Mondays, Wednesdays and Thursdays, which left Grace about forty minutes to grab a snack for dinner and clean up before starting her evening work at a local Craft Barn. That was her life these days. There was no getting around the responsibilities she struggled to carry. Spending forty hours a week as an office manager and three nights a week at Craft Barn, followed by one weekend shift, left her little time for anything else.

The doorbell blasted again. "Coming," she called out so loudly that she startled herself.

"Shit," she grumbled under her breath. "What the hell do you want anyway?"

Every Sunday, she and the kids had their discovery fun day. They would find something free for them to do in town, discover something new, and have fun, the priority being fun and laughter —lots and lots of laughter. It was simple and uncomplicated. She longed for Sundays.

The deafening ring of the door bell sounded again. It sliced through her brain, leaving little patience. As she stumbled toward the front door she could feel pieces of laundry, dishtowels and underwear sliding off one piece at-a-time, falling off of her shoulders and leaving a trail across the carpet.

Before she could get the door completely open, a young male voice barked, "Are you Grace Anderson?"

"Um, yeah." She tried to focus on both the voice and the unfamiliar face.

"This is for you. It's from the attorneys of Blacken & Theibald for Robert Anderson," he said as quickly as possible.

Then, he shoved the envelope toward her. Reacting instinctively, she took hold of it.

"Thanks and uh, happy Valentine's Day," he said cringing. He turned and walked off. Her stomach flopped. She watched him until he disappeared on the horizon. Assaulted by nausea, she swallowed the anger. She'd just been served.

Insult stacked upon insult, building a wall of despair. Today of all days. Resisting the urge to scream hollow threats at the young man, she looked at the official letter in her hand. She wasn't sure which stung worse: the document and what it meant, or the reminder today was Valentine's Day.

Having successfully pushed V-Day out of her mind until this moment, she was crushed by the memory. After striking it off the calendar and having resolved not to let the whole of notion of "happy ever afters" creep back into her thinking, she was once again reminded.

What new tricks will Dr. Jekyll and Mr. Hyde be demanding today? Wasn't it enough that he left for a younger woman, took the house, both cars, the all the available money?

She'd already been fooled by the promise of happy ever afters and, thank you very much, she'd rather not do it again. Pulling the sock off her shoulder, she moved toward the sofa, sat quietly, and, with a hardened heart, she stared at the envelope.

Sighing. Debating. Sighing again.

Can't get worse than this.

She had two jobs, two kids, rent that was too high, a car that was running on empty and patience that had become threadbare. Holding her breath, she opened it. Even the crinkle of the envelope made her skin crawl. She really thought she was done with attorneys and the never-ending cost of the worst battle of her life.

The words looked like little ants crawling all over the page like some horror story.

Focus Grace, focus.

"This custody agreement..." She faltered. "...is made and entered into by and between Robert Anderson, the father..."

She cringed seeing her own name listed in bold print. Taking another deep breath she continued.

"...in consideration of the circumstances and mutual covenants..."

Mutual?

"You bastard, there is nothing mutual about this garbage!" she shouted to no one.

She started to pace the living room.

"He has no right to do this." Almost shouting, she spat, "Wasn't it enough to move our entire life savings to Caribbean accounts? Or forget the kids birthdays, holidays, and school plays every year?"

Knowing that her ex-husband was still out there hacking away at the divorce was more frustrating than she could manage. She took in one more deep breath and turned back to reading the subpoena aloud.

"The father shall have sole and exclusive custody of the children and all final decision-making authority related to significant matters impacting the welfare of the children, including but not limited to, matters of education, religion and health care."

She stopped reading, and sucked in air, having forgotten to breathe. Grace stood for a moment in shock. He didn't want to change his visitation rights—he wanted to move the kids to who-knows-where.

Slightly shaking, she set the letter on the coffee table amidst the unfolded laundry. Lizzy and Jake were her reason for living—hidden treasures in her stormy life. Grace couldn't, in a million years, let him or that ditzy-dirty blonde raise her kids. But she had no answers, no money, and, least of all, no attorney this time to fight the battle. Something had to change.

But time didn't stop for heartaches. Her evening shift at work was nearing, and she really couldn't lose this part time job, especially now. Bringing herself back to life, she changed clothes, freshened up, made a cup of hot instant coffee and grabbed a breakfast bar for dinner.

———

PULLING into the parking lot at work, she noticed a small classic Jaguar XJ6 sitting in the parking lot. The headlights were blazing into the distance and nobody was sitting in the driver's seat.

Huh.

Curiosity got the better of her and she leaned close to peer inside the car, as a child would lean close to watch a baker icing a cake.

"What kind of a doof would leave on their headlights with a car like this? Must have too much money for his own good." She fought back vicious thoughts of her ex-husband.

Taking in a deep breath, she headed for the front door of the store. Years before, she'd resolved not to bring her personal life to work and she wasn't going to change her attitude now.

Bright lights nearly blinded her as she entered the store. Red and pink hearts hung from the ceiling like Christmas bulbs, bouquets of red and white roses were strategically set about the store, yet another reminder of her loveless life. Hell.

Pushing on and passing through the store to put away her purse, she spied a man standing at the ribbon racks wearing a tuxedo and looking way to dressed-up for the Craft Barn.

She heard her name being called from behind the register.

"Hey Grace, am I happy to see you. I need a little relief, if you get my meaning," Rainbow called out.

"Or what's going to happen?" Grace said passing the counter.

"I can't be responsible for my actions, if you don't hurry," Rainbow pleaded.

Grace smiled."Be there in a second Rainbow," she called back and kept walking.

A moment later, Grace was tying her smock behind her back as she walked toward the register. She nodded her head toward the man in the tuxedo.

"What's up with the formal attire?"

"Yeah," Rainbow giggled, "Halloween is long past so it's not a costume party. I think he's probably one of those secret shoppers corporate was telling us about. He's here to watch us and report back to the suits about our behavior. You know, watching to see if we're skimming from the till, that kind of thing. You better be on your best tonight. I'll be back in a minute," she said walking away from the booth with a wink.

"You're a conspiracy theorist at heart, Rainbow," Grace said quickly.

"So, tell me something I don't know. He could have a date or something. It is Valentines, my most reviled holiday of the year." Rainbow smiled.

"Seriously? Reviled?"

Rainbow shrugged. "Well, we should love people and tell them we love them, not just on a commercially-generated holiday. It's just a sales pitch wrapped in roses and chocolate, designed to raise expectations, and to hawk clichéd romance movies."

"Thanks for the diatribe. I'll be sure to call you when I'm feeling bad about love," Grace said, laughing as she watched Rainbow leave the store.

Grace stood at the register, rearranging the boxes of sugar hearts and sweetheart decorations so she couldn't see them.

Every so often, she eyed the dapper shopper and wondered whether it was his car in the parking lot. *Must be*, she figured. New car, new person in the store, and he didn't fit the profile of the average middle-aged, slightly-bulging, woman who regularly shopped there. Maybe he *had been* sent by corporate.

Not my problem, she finally told herself and began ringing up a sale for a customer.

"He's awfully handsome," the pretty silver-haired customer mentioned as if it were a secret.

"What?" Grace asked, shocked back into the moment. She hadn't realized she'd become mesmerized by the nameless Romeo. "Oh, I just...he's not a regular here, I didn't mean to stare," she said.

"Well, dear," said the shopper, "if I were twenty years younger, I would do my best to make sure he came here as often as possible. Doesn't it make you curious what he's after? I'm going home to my cat. I hope you have more exciting plans than I do," the shopper said and walked out the door with her purchase in hand.

Grace sighed. The truth about her real life flooded back into her thoughts as soon as the shopper mentioned exciting plans. Feeling a little ruffled by the reality check, Grace started looking for someone to relieve her. It was a night she'd rather walk around and clean up the store and avoid customers. She had nothing to talk about and would probably blow up if someone said the wrong thing.

Just then, Rainbow returned, smelling slightly of cigarette smoke and snapping her gum. Her violet lipstick had been freshly applied, and her multicolored hair looked recently brushed and spun up in a clip.

"I'll give you a dollar if you go tell him the lights are on in his car. What do you say?" Rainbow gambled and tied on her smock.

"It is his car?"

"Yeah, he came in about five minutes before you did, and he never noticed his lights were on," Rainbow offered.

"Idiot. Thanks but, no I'm not interested in dealing with him tonight," Grace said, walking away from the conversation.

"Hey, are you okay, Gracie? You seem a little down."

The simple, kind question unleashed a tidal wave of humiliation inside Grace. She fought back the tears. She really didn't want people at work to know her personal struggles and she'd fooled herself into thinking that others didn't notice.

"Just been a long day," she lied. Grace would rather lick the kitchen sink than talk with customers.

"Okay then, I'll bet you five dollars. Will you take the bet for five dollars?" Rainbow asked with a crooked smile.

Grace started laughing. "Why don't you tell him and keep your five dollars?"

Rainbow called Grace back to the register by signaling with the crook of her finger. Grace reluctantly agreed and returned.

"Listen sister, he's more your type. I would totally lose my reputation as a snide political reporter for the Gazette if I was caught dead talking with someone like that off the record."

Grace leaned in over the counter staring Rainbow in the eye. "You're not a reporter, you work at a craft store."

Rainbow smiled, "A girl can have her dreams, can't she? Go tell him about his lights. Come on, it's Valentines Day. It's about time you had a good flirt. I have a good feeling about this. Ten dollars?"

Grace's shoulders drooped. "Okay, I'll tell him about the lights, but I'm not flirting. I never got the flirting gene and I'm not even going to try."

Grace walked through the pink and silver balloon hearts filled with helium that were lining the aisles. How she managed to pass the balloons without popping them was a mystery to her. Milling through the web of customers—women with half-baked craft projects, unfinished blouses that need just the right button, and others on the prowl for their next project—was typical. It was a normal night at the Craft Barn.

He was standing in front of a gigantic hot pink heart that was trimmed in white lace. In his tuxedo, and with his slightly-silvered hair, he could have been posing for a cheesy romance novel cover. If it were a better day, Grace might have liked the image. But today, she had to shake off her own sarcasm. He was at the cutting station talking with Janie, a chirpy, large breasted youth who didn't know much about much. But he seemed very intrigued, or perhaps confused. Grace couldn't tell which by the expression on his face.

"Sir?" Grace half mumbled into the air. He continued to focus on Janie.

"Excuse me, Janie? I need to tell your customer something," she said with a tinge more force this time.

Both Janie and the shopper slowly turned and looked at her.

"Sir, I think you've left the lights on in your car," she said. Feeling a moment of relief, she started to turn and then he spoke, drawing her back into the exchange.

"Damn it, I keep forgetting that old cars have a manual switch for the headlights." Then he started furiously patting his pockets. After finding his keys and pulling them out of his pocket, he held them out to Grace. "Would you mind?" he asked turning back to the project and his conversation with Janie.

Absentmindedly, Grace held out her hand and he dropped the keys smack-dab in the middle of her palm. Grace swallowed. A familiar, hollow feeling gathered in the pit of her stomach.

Customers and employees alike were stupefied by the exchange. To avoid further embarrassment, Grace headed for the door and quickly passed through into the night. It was happening again: low self-esteem, like quicksand, was dragging her below the surface. Emotionally, she wasn't standing on firm ground and another entitled bastard had just shamed her in public—a total stranger. She saw the looks in the other peoples eyes, part awkwardness, part judgement. It was all a little too much today.

The chill of the evening air soothed her over heated cheeks. She stood beside his car now, his beautiful Jaguar—sleek, sophisticated, and painfully romantic. Staring down at the keys in her hand, it felt like she was somehow trespassing, breaking and entering. A devilish grin passed across her mouth.

What would he do?

She thought again: respect, consideration, codes of ethical conduct, all the things she said to her children regularly.

Take the high road.

She sighed and touched the glistening handle of the car door. An unexpected sensuous chill ran up her spine. As she slid the key in the lock, it gently popped open, as sweetly as a startled breath. Her own heart started to *thump, thump, thump* in her breast. Grace was rapidly growing a taste for engaging in prohibited behavior and was ready to satisfy her desire.

Cracking the car door open, the hearty scent of leather and cologne wafted out of the car, wooing her to enter. She eased her body into the soft-black leather seat. Long-stemmed roses sat amiably on the passenger side. She could smell their sweet scent.

Her hips rested harmoniously in the seat and her heart continued to pound. Her arms glided toward the burl-wood steering wheel and her imagination flew into high gear. She was immediately transported into indescribable freedom, unbound by responsibility and the burden of money, children, and laundry— no cares about her struggles, the rent she couldn't pay, the dates she didn't have.

The further she settled into the luxury of the car, the more she was drawn toward emotional freedom. Big-eyed, big gulp, enormous horizon, kind of freedom. Nothing would ever be the same again.

Without thinking, Grace shut the car door. Tucking comfortably behind the steering wheel, she ran her hands across the smooth surface. Control. Deftly sliding the key into the ignition, Grace felt a dizzying sway. Enticed by the myriad possibilities, she started the car, listened to the purr of the engine and pulled slowly out of the parking lot, grinning.

Cruising down main street, she started to breathe a little deeper. Perhaps it was the cologne—maybe the leather, the soft roses, or maybe she was just reaping a moment's peace in someone else's world. It didn't matter. Nothing mattered except independence—head-spinning independence. At that moment, she wasn't strapped to any responsibilities. She was untethered, almost whirling out of control.

Suddenly, she heard an electronic version of *Nights in White Satin* by the Moody Blues blast out of nowhere. A light flashed from underneath the roses. Her moment of bliss had been invaded by the outside world: the phone. Reality seeped slowly back into her thoughts. Resistant to the sound of the song, it eventually stopped. She rationalized not answering. It wasn't her phone anyway.

It rang again, seemingly louder this time. She pulled the car over and peeked under the flowers. *Grace Anderson* popped up in digital writing on the caller-ID.

"Thanks Rainbow," she mumbled under her breath, realizing that Rainbow must have given the owner of the car her phone. Now she knew that he was aware of her absence.

Hovering her hand over the phone, she took a moment to review her options.

Ignore it? Answer it? Drive back to the store? Keep driving until the car runs out of gas.

Slightly giggling, she swiped her finger across the glass.

"Who the hell do you think you are? That's my car, and it's worth a fortune. Bring it back to the store this very second or I'm calling the police," he demanded.

She felt pushed-against the wall again.

"Oh, okay, go ahead," she said feeling sparks of ideas chasing through her head. "But wait a second, you gave me the keys. Explain that to the police."

She briskly tapped the phone and disconnected the call.

Staring for a moment at the phone, she was hard-pressed to know where her courage had come from.

Wow, who knew?

She smiled and took a deep breath. She leaned a little into the leather seat, allowing herself to bask in her audacious behavior.

Looking at her surroundings, she realized she had parked at her alma mater—the high school where her adult life had begun.

She flipped on the radio. Janis Ian was playing.

> *I learned the truth at seventeen,*
> *that love was meant for beauty queens*
> *and high school girls with clear skinned smile*
> *who married young and then retired.*

She promptly switched it off. She was haunted by things hadn't understood back then.

Did I really retire after marriage? Is that when I lost myself?

Looking out of the car window, she saw some teenagers sulking in the bushes, hiding from their parents, no-doubt—having a quick cigarette in the shadow of the night. She shook her head, remembering the number of times she had snuck out her bedroom window and stolen away to meet with Robert. Would she be out someday searching for her own children once they reached the teen years?

Maybe, if they still even live with me.

In the distance she saw the old cafeteria-slash-multipurpose room. Memories flooded through her. They first met at the auditions for the senior play, *Guys and Dolls*. It was kismet, right there, amongst the unfinished lunches and half-drunk coke cans, cold french fries, and abandon notebooks. She had worked so hard in high school: drama, voice lessons, dance lessons, and scene study. It had finally been her time to play the lead role in the senior musical, a dream which she'd relished every day of her life. It had been her time. He hadn't been a part of her drama classes. He'd swept in from the football field and charmed the director into giving him the lead role of Nathan Detroit, the charming gangster. Grace had been given the role of Puritanical Sarah Brown.

Robert had been great, hands down the best person for the role: charming, confident, with just enough fire to make him interesting. Besides, he'd had a penchant for gangsters and little had she known that he would turn out to be one.

Everyone had been impressed when he'd swanned into the audition and winked at the girls, faked maturity with the director, and sung well enough to make the vocal coach happy.

Grace had barely believed her good luck: the most popular guy in school would be playing opposite her in the play. She would have to kiss him, on stage. Unbelievable.

When they'd sung together, reaching the perfect crescendo, both of their hearts had swelled to a perfect pitch. It had been a match made in heaven. In her heart, she'd believed that it would never end—had believed that their kaleidoscope of love, lust, passion, and dreams would carry them to the brightest stars and beyond. It had all meant so much to her.

They'd married just two years out of high school. At the time she had asked for a long engagement. In retrospect, she wondered why. Perhaps she'd had some intuition about their future. In any case, she'd been compliant to his wishes and had eventually capitulated.

After all, everybody had known that he was going places

and she'd wanted to go with him. He had gotten a job with his father's firm and they'd been set. It would have been too much —for both of them to chase their dreams at the same time. She'd willingly shifted her priorities, made way for his ideas, his desires, and his dreams to grow. After all, she'd rationalized, he'd been making the money. He'd had the right to ask for more.

Grace had pacified herself with the idea that her time would come—that she wouldn't wait forever. It would certainly come to the point where Robert would make room for her dreams.

She'd wanted to go to college and return to their town as a high school teacher. She'd wanted to give back to her own community. But school was expensive and they'd lacked the funds to send her. But her day would come—she'd known it would. She'd had a mountain of faith. Tonight, she wished they would have waited long enough to realize marriage was a bad idea.

She stepped out of the car and stared though the wire mesh past the football field and toward the old cafeteria.

"Is this where I lost myself? Is this where it all started? I was so fiery, jubilant, and determined that my life would stand for something important. That I was born for a reason and that I would fulfill my destiny. What happened to me, where did I go?" she said to the night sky.

She slipped back into the drivers seat and started the car again. Her shoulders slumped a little this time.

Pulling out onto the street, the phone rang again. She looked at her name and focused this time on *Anderson*. She picked it up at the third ring.

"Hi, look we need to talk," he said.

"No, I don't need to talk with you," she said, and got ready to hang up again.

"Wait, I'm not going to threaten you either. Or scream or

anything like that. In fact, we both need to stay calm and talk like adults. How does that sound?" he said.

She thought for a moment.

"Sounds condescending," she said and abruptly hung up the phone.

Immediately, she flipped on the radio to drown out any negative thoughts. She listened to a talk radio interview.

"Now let me get this right, most relationships fail because people don't know what they want or they don't really know who they are getting involved with?" the DJ said, moving the conversation forward.

"That's right, and then when the inevitable happens everyone runs around with their hair on fire, blaming each other. My suggestion is, of course, to get to know the person your dating. Take some time, have fun—" said the caller.

Disgruntled, Grace snapped off the radio. "I hate pop-psychology."

Continuing to drive through town, she wound up at the downtown mall; the old one had been replaced by a newer, younger version, when nobody expected it.

At the back of the mall there was Leonard's Furniture store. They'd had the swankiest furniture in town when she was a newlywed. She and Robert had had the world by the tail. They had entertained clients within a year of him working at his father's firm. They'd needed the best-of-the-best furniture and Leonard's had had it. They'd been determined to climb the social ladder and it had been important that Robert have the furniture he thought best.

At the time, she'd agreed. After all, he'd been making the money. He'd have known best how to spend it.

The phone rang again. She stared at her name in neon again. This time, she stared at her first name. *Grace.* She tapped the phone on the third ring. There was silence on the other side.

Grace sat, staring at the run-down, dilapidated old building that used to be Leonard's Furniture Store. The treasured building had fallen into disrepair when nobody was looking. Just like her life.

"Where have you gone?" he asked, carefully.

She sighed.

"I've been asking myself that same question, over and over, where have I gone? And for the life of me, I can't find the answer," she said.

"We're not talking about the same thing are we?" he asked.

"No, I don't think so," she said without making any effort to define what she meant. "Memories can be sneaky teachers," she whispered into the phone while staring at the ruins.

"Tell me about it," he said.

Fury bubbled up in her again. He didn't care about her. He just wanted his car back in mint condition.

"Don't patronize me..."

"Wait, wait," he said interrupting her, "please don't hang up again. I'm trying here, I'm really trying. I don't know you. But you've got my car. I can't call the police. Your right. I gave you my keys. I was an ass to do it like that, but I was trying to figure out what that girl was saying. It just seemed like the most logical thing to do. That's not normally the way I am," he said and stopped talking, and took a big breath.

"So, you couldn't understand what Janie was saying?"

"No, I was confused and then I gave you my keys and you took so long to come back in the building. Hell, what am I saying, you still haven't come back in the building."

"Did you ever get the help you needed?"

"Do you care?" he asked.

She turned back on the engine of the car and pulled away from the curb.

"No I don't, sorry. It's just habit to ask."

There was a long silence while she puttered through the town.

"Is it always your habit to be habitual?" he asked.

She thought about the question.

"Yes, I think it is. But I don't habitually borrow cars," she said.

She didn't hear anything for a minute then shrugged and kept driving. She could hear his breathing—even, deep, and strangely intimate.

"If you don't habitually steal cars then why are you doing it tonight? If you don't mind my asking?" he said, his voice a little deeper than it was before—more personal, more real.

Instinctively she wound through town, no particular destination in mind. Just driving.

"I'm on a quest. Just so happens, it was your car that inspired me," she said.

"A quest? What do you hope to find?" He sounded genuinely inquisitive.

"Myself," she said pulling up to the first apartment where they had lived in nuptial bliss, just after the wedding.

It looks smaller now, a little cheap.

When they'd first rented the apartment, it had been such a luxury, and right around the corner from where her parents had lived. It had recently been built and everyone in town was talking about it.

Of course, rent had been on the high end of the market, but they'd wanted to live in style. Why, she wondered now, was she bemoaning her fate and blaming Robert? Perhaps she hadn't known what was important in a marriage at eighteen. Had the talk show been right?

She heard the man clear his throat on the other end of the phone.

"Is it far, where you left yourself?"

"Are you teasing me? Because if you are. . . "

"I'm not, I know the consequences. I'm serious. Where did you leave yourself? Do you know?" he asked.

"What's your name?" she said just realizing she was sharing some familiarity with a man, over the phone, smelling his cologne and enjoying his company and didn't know his name.

"Logan, Logan Wong. And yes, my parents did name me after a character in a movie. I wish they hadn't but they did," he said.

Interesting reveal.

"Well, Mr. Logan Wong, named after a character in a movie, I've never owned a new car."

Silence rested between them.

"Not that I own your car, but I've never been so fortunate to sit in a car like this," she said with a sigh.

"You and your husband never bought a new car together?"

"Ex-husband, thanks for asking. And all the cars we owned were his. Literally, he said that to me, many times, just to make sure I understood."

"That sounds like he drew battle lines."

Instantly, her thoughts were pulled back to memories of Robert and even her father. A mosh of memories collided in her mind's eye. Her ex-husband and her father, swimming together in her thoughts, both of them making demands, controlling others, putting their needs before the rest.

"Yes, you could say it that way—battle lines—and you'd be right," she said.

"Did they get what they wanted?"

"Always. Otherwise there was hell to pay," she said staring up at her old apartment. "I wanted to teach," she coyly added. She heard him chuckle, just a little. She didn't feel ridiculed but more like he really heard her.

"I get a little misty when people talk about teaching," he said. "My mother was a teacher. Not my father—he worked in an office and quite honestly, I'm not sure what Dad did for a living. I've found, through the course of my life, teachers are great people. Sorry if I sound sentimental, but my mother passed several years ago. If I had a nickel for every time she was right about something, I would be wealthy man," he said.

"You own this car, you must do well," she said almost wanting to know more about him and thinking better of it. She has the kids to think about now and getting too interested in another man was not part of the game plan.

"So what cologne do you wear? It's familiar and yet not so familiar?" she said and realized too late that was not the best subject to change the conversation to.

"What I mean is. . . "

"I know what you meant," he interrupted.

Then she heard a long slight moan.

"It's not an expensive cologne, it's Grey Flannel, by Geoffrey Beene. I've worn it for years. You hate it?"

She laughed, "No I don't hate it. Why would you jump to that conclusion?"

"I don't know. Have you found yourself yet?"

"Sorry, I'll be back...no wait. This journey isn't about you. I can't capitulate again, never again. I've destroyed my life and probably my kids' too, because...oh it's a long story. You don't have to keep talking to me, you know. You can wait," she said.

"I am waiting, and listening. Look, let's step back a second. Journeys are about discovery, right?" he said.

She snickered. "Are you a therapist or something?"

"Not even close. But we're not talking about me. Look, to be perfectly honest..."

"What's up with being perfectly honest? Isn't honest just honest. Why do you think there are levels of perfection around honesty?"

"Still, that's more about me than I'm willing to discuss. This is about you."

"I don't like being the focus of this conversation," she said.

"No, you're not going to change the conversation now. It's all about you. And, by the way, where are you?"

"I'm sitting outside my first apartment. It's difficult to look at. I feel so much shame and I don't know why. It's like I'm stuck in some strange emotional place. It's holding me back in a time that I'm not living anymore. I don't know where I am," she said.

"Are you in a safe location?"

"I meant psychologically," she said

"I understood. I mean physically, do you feel safe?"

"Yeah, why?"

"Lock the doors and close your eyes, let's just explore a minute. Okay, can you trust me?"

"Ah, I don't. . ."

"Just for a couple of minutes. If you don't like anything I say, hang up on me. I'll get the message," he said.

To Grace, it sounded as if he were smiling, not laughing or ridiculing her, but smiling.

"Okay, but what happens if . . . "

"Grace," he said, so soothing, so calming. She was a little taken back.

"How did you know my name?" she said sitting bolt upright in the seat.

"Your work friends know your name. They shared," he said.

"Oh, that's right. Thanks Logan," she said.

"Okay I'll shut my eyes but if you try to manipulate, connive or . . . "

"Got it," he cut off her thought, "you don't have to worry. I'm really not that kind of a man."

She could lie, say she'd closed her eyes and then didn't.

Geez, what have I gotten myself into. Who's the fool here?

Him, asking me to trust a total flipping stranger? What has my life devolved into? I had dreams, goals, plans, big plans to change the world. Now, I'm losing my kids, I'm totally broke, I've stolen some idiots car in a feeble effort to save myself. Next thing to go is my sanity. Closing my eyes in the dark while being locked in a stolen car. How do I know he's not some kind of pervert? I don't know if I should laugh with embarrassment or cry with shame. Oh what the Hell, what have I got to lose? My dignity? I lost that years ago.

She took a deep breath. "Okay, so you're not some kind of strange..."

"Deviant? Sexual predator?"

"I wasn't going to say that, exactly, but now that you mention it, are you?" she asked as innocently as possible. "Cause I'm not really into that kind of thing."

All she heard was a slight, impatient groan.

"You are, aren't you?" she said, really not sure of herself.

She heard another deeper groan and half-laugh.

"You're right; let's think this through," he said and chuckled. "I came to your craft store tonight, a place I've been stalking for months, looking for my target employee. The one who might steal my car so I can, what, practice my sexual prowess over the phone? What do you think is my next move?"

"Since you put it like that..." She didn't know where to take the conversation.

"Look, you're in some kind of midlife crisis, right?" he asked.

There was a long pause.

"Right?" he asked, a little more demanding this time.

"Yes, a crisis. Mid-life is a little much. What have you got in mind for me, Logan?" she asked.

"I was just going to offer you a little visualization. It's a trick I use to help me through difficult times. If you don't want to do it, that's fine, but I will need my car back. I have to deliver flowers to my mother. It's her birthday."

She took in a gasp of air.

"Your mother? Are you teasing me? Or just trying to get the car back and you're using sentimental means to do it?" she asked, and afterwards felt entirely foolish for having made the accusation.

"Close your eyes. I've got a little time," he said.

"Okay, here goes," she said, shutting her eyes and relaxing her neck and shoulders into the head rest.

She took a deep breath and let his velvet voice brush against her ears. It was a throbbing rush like she had never known before.

"Imagine your fear, your biggest fear. What does it look like?" he asked.

There was silence.

"That's a big question. One thing first," she said, but her eyes were closed. "Why did you think cologne needed to be expensive to be enjoyed?"

"This is a stalling tactic if I've ever heard one. But I don't know. I guess it's an insecurity of mine. Or, I've always thought, women like expensive things, and wouldn't cologne fit in the same category? Does that answer your question?" he asked.

"Alright, thanks. But, for the record, cologne doesn't have to be expensive to impress," she said starting to enjoy her eyes being closed.

"Now, I'm serious, what does your biggest fear look like? It's a real thing. Is it hairy, got one tooth, a loud roar, the voices in your head telling you your insignificant, unimportant, incapable?" His voice was so gentle, soothing, and compassionate that Grace felt safe in the hands of this man.

"Wait, wait this tickles. Your voice tickles a little," she said with a slight giggle.

"Really?" he said, "'cause your voice feels good to me, and I love that little laugh."

"I don't know." Her voice felt feeble, timid.

"Don't know what?" he asked.

"My biggest fear."

"Oh, we're back to business then. Right, I disagree. Most people know what they fear. Some run towards it, some run away from it, and nobody likes to admit it, but they know what they fear," he said.

She could feel the honesty in his voice, and the sting of tears rolling down her cheeks told her she knew her own fear as well.

"You can't fight something you don't know. Come on, we're not boxing ghosts here—we're looking at real life...gut wrenching, got-to-get-over-the-hurdle-in-order-to-get-to-the-finish-line   kind of work. You know what I mean?"

"Are you a therapist?" she asked again.

She felt his breathing ripple all the way down her spine.

"No, but I see a therapist, or at least I used too," he offered.

She sighed. Sucking in another gulp of air, she started to talk. Her shoulders softened.

"My second biggest fear is that I will have to admit my first biggest fear," she said holding her breath.

"I didn't ask about your second biggest fear, only the first one. My therapist used to say that our fears will guide our lives until we grapple with them, and win. What other options do you have right now?" he said and fell silent.

She imagined his lips, so close to her ear she yearned to have him with her, beside her, arms around her. His voice was seeping into the sad and lonely part of her life and washing it away without ever even trying.

"Okay, my biggest fear is that I will never be deeply loved. Never. And my divorce put the nail in the coffin on that thought," she said holding back her shame as best she could.

"Oh. Sorry. That's painful. But now, we have to reframe that thought. We do. You can." he said.

She felt his masculine, deep voice touch her soul, filling her body with low-grade passion. Her anger was softening. It felt like a gift: the idea that she could give herself permission to stop being afraid of her life and face the challenge.

"My future looks awfully dim right now, and I really, really don't know how to reframe the bullshit that was just thrown at me," she said.

"Let's work on one thing at a time. I'll tell you what I believe and then you can tell me what you believe and we can talk out the difference, okay?" he said.

"I believe we are all born important to this world. Sometimes, we get lost among other people's opinions and swallowed into their lives without meaning to," he said and then left room for Grace to talk.

"You do, you really do, believe that we are all born important?"

"Yes, and well, all I can say is that you deserve love, Grace. We all deserve to be loved. I can't promise you'll get it. But I also notice that people receive as much as they give. I know that sounds trite and yes, I heard that from my mother, but it's true. People get as much as they give. So you can't shut down, and steal cars, and avoid life and reach the goal of having love in your life," he said.

"You sound a lot like a talk show I heard not long ago," she said with a sigh.

"One last thing: if you don't fight for what you deserve then your children will learn not to fight for what they deserve. You know that's true, don't you?" he said.

She slowly opened her eyes, looked at the old apartment, the disrepair of the building. Picking up the roses, she drank in a deep breath of their delicate scent.

"You're right. I have a situation in front of me that I have to fight. With your indulgence, I have one more thing to do, and then I'll be back at the store. Okay?" she said and immediately hung up the phone.

This was it. She was at the moment of take-off.

"Come on, Goddess of the Divine, take me home. Please," she said turning on the engine of the car.

Slow and steady, she pulled away from the curb and started driving toward her future.

"He thinks he can waltz off with the children because I've allowed him to take everything else from me without a struggle. I've gone along, I've capitulated. I've given him everything. My submission is his permission. No more buddy, no more," she said and held firm to the steering wheel.

Grace was headed toward the old dam, the long road that leads to the edge of town. But mostly, to where she could think, and drive, and find her courage again.

Her head was spinning.

Money buys space, distance which breeds disinterest, indifference and a disconnection from everyday life. Will he even be able to deal with our kids, all the activities, the clothes, meals, endless energy, fulfilling their constant need for attention?

Soon she'd hit sixty five miles an hour, then seventy, then seventy five. She managed the car with confidence and style. The headlights were glaring into the distance. Tonight, for the first time, Grace would travel past the edge of town, climb her mountain, and move into her future. She was keeping pace with the wind now: eighty....eighty-five miles an hour. It was the fastest she'd ever driven in her life. She moved through town, empowered, having given herself permission to engage fully in her own life.

"I will not let my mind swerve from my commitment to my children," she said, roaring into the night sky, going ninety miles an hour.

She slowed, cautiously, and pulled out onto the edge of a cliff.

The hidden place where, legend has it, that if you need help from a power greater than yourself, then you go and offer the Goddess your sorrows and she will heal your heart. She pulled the car to the side and stopped the engine.

Opening the door slowly, she pondered what she would offer as her sorrows. Without thinking, Grace started to walk around and pick up little sticks, twigs, dry leaves and bits of bark. She gathered the small pile and stared at it for a while. She could feel her confidence rise like heat from the fire in her belly. Breaking free from the confines of traditional expectations, she threw her arms open to the night.

The denial of a lifetime was lifted—like the sunshine on heavy morning fog, it was all fading away. Clarity broke through to her senses. Grace knew she had drowned her energetic spirit by trying so hard to please others.

Rearranging the makeshift campfire, she puzzled through her own attitude. The opinions of others eventually sucked her into a demoralizing spiral heading straight into the hell-mouth of complacency. The bits of kindling had become quite a small mountain of fuel. She needed more.

Gathering continued and, with each new thought, she started dropping heaps of sticks and twigs onto the mound. "That's for my letting go of my dreams," she said dropping more leaves.

"Goddess, this twig represents my silent self, the one who lets others make decisions," she said. And on she went, dropping sticks, twigs, bark into the fire, and with each gesture she offered more of her inadequacies, self-recrimination, helplessness, fear. She continued until she had no more to offer. Reaching the deepest turning point, her offerings came to one final gesture: she opened her arms to the sky.

"Please let my loving truth surface. Let my creativity emerge. Let my true self rise to protect my children, and to have love in my life."

Sitting in silence now, she lit the smallest twig and reached in to light more and more until finally she understood that she was laying her funeral pyre and respectfully putting to death her misgivings. She leaned into the grieving and self-forgiveness and unleashed her lamentations of a life misspent. Bit by bit, her tearful wail became the song to honor her future and embrace all the fullness that life can offer. She stayed, warming herself by the fire until the last ember had extinguished. Breathing in the cool air she stood.

She slipped once again into the driver's seat, turned on the engine and slowly drove back to work. The radio was playing another fortuitous song, Billie Holiday's rendition of *God Bless the Child*. Listening carefully, she understood the lyrics in ways she had never known before. She parked her chariot right in front of the door. The store was getting ready to close.

Walking in the front door she was greeted by Rainbow.

"I hope it was worth it, girl. I think it was. See you on Saturday." And, with that, Rainbow walked out of the store.

Logan came swiftly to the front of the store once he heard the voices.

"Thank God, you're back," he said, almost out of breath.

"I am back, I really am. And your car is fine. Thanks for everything. It's a lovely ride. Here's your keys," she said tossing them toward Logan.

She started toward the back of the store. He reached out and touched her on the arm. She turned to face him.

"I wonder if maybe you might go to dinner with me? I enjoyed our conversation, as strange as it was," he said.

She looked deep into his eyes, clarifying whether he was serious or not. She decided he meant what he said.

"I'm not really in a good place to go to dinner. I've got some serious work to do before I can date anyone," she said.

He pulled out a business card and handed it to her. "If you ever change your mind, I would enjoy hearing from you," he said.

She pulled the card from his hand and took a moment to read it.

Logan Wong, Inc.
Law offices of Logan Wong
Specializing in Family Law

She smiled and shook her hair out of her eyes.

"Okay Mr. Wong, I'll let you take me to dinner on a couple of conditions," she said.

He nodded in agreement.

"First, you handle the custody suit against my ex-husband, pro-bono. Second, you win. Third, I pick the restaurant," she said smiling.

PART 2
THE AUTHORS

L.G. O'CONNOR

AUTHOR OF "PERFECT ODDS"

L.G. O'Connor writes smart, sexy, and soulful romantic fiction. She is the author of the multi-award winning second chance romance trilogy, *Caught Up in Love*, which features the romantic lives of three women in the same New Jersey family as they deal with love, loss, and family secrets. L.G. is also the author of the angel paranormal romance series, *The Angelorum Twelve Chronicles*, about a modern day investment banker and her friends who find themselves embroiled in the final battle between a cadre of angels and Lucifer's Dark Ones. Her upcoming series, a romantic suspense, takes place in Pennsylvania's Amish Country. To learn more about her books, get some freebies, and stay in touch, check out her website, https://www.lgoconnor.com/

To get more Liv & Bach and Lucky in Love, Inc. books when they release, sign up for LG's newsletter.

f facebook.com/lgoconnor1

O instagram.com/lg_oconnor

BB bookbub.com/authors/l-g-o-connor

🐦 twitter.com/lgoconnor1

MARIE BOOTH

AUTHOR OF "LOVE YA, BABY"

Marie Booth is an award-winning author of spicy contemporary romance and hot paranormal romance and makes her home in the San Francisco area. A musical theatre geek with two perfect daughters, Marie also writes sweeter paranormal romance as Gayle Parness and can usually be heard reading her latest manuscript out loud to a very tolerant big-boned black cat named Stealth.

Love Ya, Baby is from Marie's *The Gate Series* world. Damien and Victor, Rachel's two bosses, are the heroes of the first two books, *Stroke* and *Simmer*. Book 3, Split, will be out this spring and Rachel Abercrombie Winchester and her hubby, Marley will be recurring characters in the series.

If you want to know more about her books, sign up for Marie's and Gayle's newsletters at www.mariebooth.com and www.gayleparness.com

f facebook.com/marieboothbooks

🐦 twitter.com/marieboothbooks

📷 instagram.com/marieboothauthor

BB bookbub.com/authors/marie-booth

EVA MOORE

AUTHOR OF "LOVE IT OR LEAVE IT"

Eva Moore writes sexy contemporary romances in between soccer practices and glasses of rosé. She lives in Silicon Valley, after moving around the world and back, with her college sweetheart, her three gorgeous girls, and a Shih Tzu who thinks he is a cat. She can be found most nights hiding in her closet-office, scribbling away, and loves to hear from the outside world. Please visit her at www.4evamoore.com.

If you'd like to know about future releases and giveaways, you can join her newsletter here:http://bit.ly/evamoorenews

f facebook.com/4evamooreauthor

🐦 twitter.com/AuthorEvaMoore

📷 instagram.com/authorevamoore

BB bookbub.com/authors/eva-moore

KILBY BLADES

AUTHOR OF "RIGHT HAND MAN"

KILBY BLADES IS A FRESH NEW VOICE in smart contemporary romance. Critics laud her "feminist fiction", noting empowered heroines and multi-dimensional heroes. Her debut novel, "Snapdragon", was a ten-time finalist and a five-time winner for honors including the HOLT Medallion, the Publisher's Weekly BookLife Prize, and the Foreword Indie Award. She has been nodded for a total of twenty honors for her complete library, including a win for Best Debut Author in the 2018 RSJ's Emma Awards.

When she's not writing, Kilby goes to movie matinees alone, where she eats Chocolate Pocky and buttered popcorn and usually smuggles in not-a-little-bit of red wine. She procrastinates from the difficult process of writing by oversharing on Facebook and giving away cool stuff to her newsletter subscribers. Kilby is a mother, a social-justice fighter, and above all else, a glutton for a good story.

facebook.com/kilbybladesauthor

twitter.com/kilbyblades

instagram.com/kilbyblades

bookbub.com/authors/kilby-blades

ERIN ST. CHARLES

AUTHOR OF "A WOLF AT THE WEDDING"

Erin grew up watching Star Trek and reading Barbara Cartland novels (don't hate), wishing she could create something that brings her love of science fiction together with her love of romance. Still a romantic nerd at heart, she writes sensual, diverse stories that blend fantasy, adventure, and love.

Look for the rest of Bubba and Vanessa's story, coming Summer of 2019! Join Erin's newsletter for updates for this and other Gods and Concubines universe stories.

https://erinstcharles.com/newsletter/

f facebook.com/erin.st.charles.1

🐦 twitter.com/erinwritesbwwm

📷 instagram.com/authorerinst.charles

BB bookbub.com/authors/erin-st-charles

R.L. MERRILL

AUTHOR OF "VALENTINE'S DAY FROM HELL"

ONCE UPON A TIME a teacher, tattoo collector, mom, and rock 'n' roll kinda gal opened up a doc and starting purging her demons. Several self-published books and a debut gay romance with Dreamspinner Press later, R.L. Merrill is still striving to find that perfect balance between real-life and happily ever after. She writes stories set in the places she loves most and she loves connecting with other authors online at the RT Booklovers Convention and RWA chapter meetings.

A sucker for underdogs, Ro has adopted cats, dogs, rats, snakes, fish and a chameleon named Godzilla. Her love of horror is evident the moment you walk in her door and find yourself surrounded by decorative skulls and quirky artwork from around the world. You can find her lurking on social media where she loves connecting with readers, educating America's youth, being a mom taxi to two busy kids, in the tattoo chair trying desperately to get that back piece finished, or headbanging at a rock show near her home in the San Francisco Bay Area. www.rlmerrillauthor.com

 facebook.com/rlmerrillauthor

twitter.com/rlmerrillauthor

instagram.com/rlmerrillauthor

 bookbub.com/authors/r-l-merrill

PRESLAYSA WILLIAMS

AUTHOR OF "CUPID'S REVENGE"

Preslaysa Williams is an award-winning author who writes contemporary romance and women's fiction with an Afro-Filipina twist. Proud of her African-American and Filipino heritage, she loves sharing her culture with her readers. She is currently earning her MFA in Writing Popular Fiction at Seton Hill University, and she has an undergraduate degree in Spanish Language & Literature from Columbia University.

Preslaysa is also a professional actress, a planner nerd, an avid bookworm, and a homeschool mom who often wears mismatched socks. To follow along with her busy life, visit her at www.preslaysa.com where you can sign up for her newsletter community.

facebook.com/preslaysa

twitter.com/preslaysawrites

instagram.com/preslaysa

bookbub.com/authors/preslaysa-williams

AVERIL DAYE

AUTHOR OF "ASKING FOR A FRIEND"

Averil Daye's first novel, *Insignia* was a 2018 Emma Award final-ist. Although she has a journalism background, her true love is writing fiction. She lives in Atlanta with her three amazing children, two hyper dogs, and a moody cat.

 twitter.com/alasswithapen

 instagram.com/averil_writes

DEB LEE

AUTHOR OF "CHASING THE NIGHT"

Deb Lee found her voice writing what others wish they could say. She channels it in the form of contemporary romance, with plenty of emotional baggage to give her readers all the feels. Deb has the perfect husband and four spritely children, who test her sanity daily. She's also an avid swimmer, which ironically enough, happens to be the one place her children can't find her.

Deb lives in Northern California with her family and enough animals to make people really start to question her sanity. Find her on her ever-changing-until-she-eventually-gets-it-right website at www.debbilee.com. Also find her on Facebook and Instagram at WriterDebLee. And please share stories about your crazy kids. She yearns to normalize her daily dose of children-induced insanity.

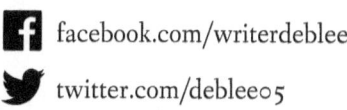

facebook.com/writerdeblee

twitter.com/debleeo5

CERI GRENELLE

AUTHOR OF "DEFINITION OF LOVE"

Ceri is the author of quirky and sexy contemporary romance novels. She has a major weakness for sappy cuddle moments, hot and steamy sex scenes, and a penchant for writing snappy and sarcastic dialogue. She loves romance that isn't afraid to be awkward and uncouth and thrives on flawed characters with big hearts. You can find her haunting the Twitter machine or posting pictures of her ridiculous cats on Instagram.

facebook.com/CeriGAuthor

twitter.com/cerigauthor

instagram.com/cerigrenelle

bookbub.com/authors/ceri-grenelle

DAPHNE MASQUE

AUTHOR OF "HEARTBREAK & HIGH GEAR"

Daphne Masque is brimming with stories about romance in the theatre. The longest relationship of her life has been with theatre. Either as a performer, director, educator and writer she's never far from working on a production where she's continually honing her craft and challenging her own skills. The second longest relationship of her life has been love and romance. Writing has taken up the last fifteen hears of her life, with plays, short stories and now Romance Novels. The novels have grown out of the desire to share her experience with people who love both romance and theatre. Having sat in thousands of rehearsals, hundreds of play readings, dozens of costume fittings and an incalculable number of hours set building she feels ready to bring you a wide breadth of stories with some factual accuracy. Please join Daphne in her sometimes wacky, often fascinating, naturally heartfelt, journey into backstage romance.

facebook.com/DaphneMasque

twitter.com/daphnemasque

ALSO IN THE "WORST DAY EVER" ANTHOLOGY SERIES

Worst Holiday Ever: A Family Drama Romance Anthology

To hear about future "Worst Day Ever" releases, visit
http://www.kilbyblades.com/subscribe

www.ingramcontent.com/pod-product-compliance
Lightning Source LLC
Chambersburg PA
CBHW051207120726
47905CB00004B/1013